PENGUIN BOOKS

Dead to Me

Lesley Pearse was told as a child that she had too much imagination for her own good. When she grew up she worked her way through a number of jobs, including nanny, bunny girl, dressmaker and full-time mother before, at the age of forty-nine, she became a published writer. Since then Lesley has become an internationally bestselling author, with over seven million copies of her books sold worldwide. Lesley lives in Devon and has three daughters and three grandchildren.

Find out more about Lesley and keep up to date
with what she's been doing:

Follow her on Twitter @LesleyPearse
Sign up for her newsletter at www.lesleypearse.com

KT-559-454

Dead to Me

LESLEY PEARSE

PENGUIN BOOKS

PENGUIN BOOKS

UK | USA | Canada | Ireland | Australia
India | New Zealand | South Africa

Penguin Books is part of the Penguin Random House group of companies
whose addresses can be found at global.penguinrandomhouse.com.

First published by Michael Joseph 2016
Published in Penguin Books 2017
001

Copyright © Lesley Pearse, 2016

The moral right of the author has been asserted

Set in 12.42/14.97 pt Garamond MT Std
Typeset by Jouve (UK), Milton Keynes
Printed in Gr eat Britain by Clays Ltd, St Ives plc

A CIP catalogue record for this book is available from the British Library

ISBN: 978–1–405–92104–6

To Chris, Ed and Captain Lever, for being such fun and making me feel so welcome in Torquay.

Also Ian and BJ at The Salon in Wellswood, for restoring my hair, making me laugh and caring.

Chapter One

'Will you look at that!' Ruby exclaimed, directing her remark to the girl standing near her. She too was staring, mouth agape at the sight of a man being dragged from the Hampstead swimming pond.

'Is he dead?' the second girl asked with a tremor in her voice.

'I reckon so. They ain't even tryin' to bring him round.'

It was early April, just after Easter, and although a sunny day, it was cold. Apart from the two girls there were only a few other people watching – in the main, adult dog walkers.

The girls watched in silence as the two burly policemen continued to haul the sodden body up on to the path beside the pond, and then on to a stretcher manned by two ambulance men.

There were three swimming ponds on the heath: one mixed bathing, and the other two for single sex only. All three were surrounded by thick bushes and trees, and fenced in. The ladies' pond was almost impossible to see into as the foliage was so dense. But the drowned man had chosen the mixed pond, and as a section of hedging had been cut back to enable a fence repair, the girls could see very clearly.

Ruby felt an odd little stab of emotion as she saw the ambulance man cover the drowned man's face. It was the first dead person she'd ever seen, and although she was some thirty yards away and had not known the man, it still felt like a loss.

'I wonder who he is?' the second girl asked. 'And if he's got a wife and children? S'pose we'll have to wait till it's in the newspapers to find out,' she added sadly.

Ruby sensed that this girl felt as she did, and so she turned to look at her properly. She guessed she was a bit younger than her, perhaps twelve or thirteen, her long blonde hair held back off her face by a blue velvet band. She had a posh voice and her clothes were expensive; Ruby was usually invisible to such girls.

'They'll only write about 'im if 'e was rich or important, no one cares why poor people die,' she said with authority. 'D'you live round 'ere? I ain't seen you afore.'

'I live the other side of Hampstead Village, down near Swiss Cottage,' the blonde said. 'I don't normally come up on the heath on my own; Mother thinks murderers prowl up here.'

Ruby liked the way she said that, like she was scoffing at her mother's opinion. 'Do murderers prowl looking for people to kill?' she asked, grinning because she liked the image. 'Don't they usually kill someone they know? Anyway, what's yer name and 'ow old are you?' she asked.

'Verity Wood, and I'm thirteen. How about you?'

'Ruby Taylor, and I'm fourteen. I live in Kentish Town and it ain't nice like round here, 'spect your ma would 'ave a fit if she knew you was talking to the likes of me!'

'I don't much care what she thinks.' Verity tossed her

head and her shiny hair flicked back over the shoulder of her coat. 'Where do you think they'll take that man's body? Will the police find out where he comes from?'

Ruby liked that this posh girl didn't seem to feel it was beneath her to speak to what most people would call a 'ragamuffin'. She was also thrilled that her opinion was being asked.

'They'll take 'im down the morgue, that's the place they cut up dead people to see why they died. If 'e's got stuff in 'is pockets that says who 'e is and where 'e lives, the police go round there to tell 'is family, and make one of 'em go and identify 'im.'

'Fancy you knowing such things,' Verity exclaimed.

Ruby shrugged. 'Mrs Briggs what lives downstairs to me and my ma, she had the police call to say 'er old man was found dead in Camden Town with his 'ead smashed in. My ma went with 'er to identify him. They was both sick cos 'e looked so bad. But when the doctor cut 'im open they found 'e never died from the wound on his 'ead, he'd had a bleedin' 'eart attack and fallen over and smashed his bonce on the kerb.'

'Gosh,' Verity said reverently, looking admiringly at Ruby. 'What a lot you know!'

They fell silent as the ambulance drove away with the drowned man, and watched as four policemen spread out to examine the ground around the pond.

'They'll be looking for sommat to tell 'em whether the man fell or waded in all alone. But if they find other foot-prints or sommat, they may think someone pushed him in, or even killed 'im first and dumped his body in the water,' Ruby said knowledgeably. 'I reckon 'e was killed and they dumped 'im in there last night, after the pond closed.'

Ruby was very interested in detective work. Coming from rough, slummy Kentish Town she was used to seeing policemen searching for evidence after a crime. She'd often been questioned about whether she'd seen this or that person, and just as often she questioned the young constables about the incidents they were investigating. She'd learned from the moment she could talk that she should never 'grass' on anyone, and she wouldn't – but there was no law, written or unwritten, against gathering information for her own satisfaction.

The girls watched for a little longer, but seeing nothing further of interest they began to walk away, towards Whitestone Pond and Hampstead Village.

'You got any bruvvers or sisters?' Ruby asked, keen to hold this posh girl's interest for as long as she could.

'No, I wish I had, it can be very lonely being the only one,' Verity replied.

Ruby didn't really understand what lonely meant. Living in one room with her mother, with all the other six rooms in the house holding entire families, there was always noise and people. That was why she'd walked up to the heath today, to have quiet and solitude.

'I likes being alone,' she said with a shrug. 'Well, at least I likes quiet – don't get it where I live – but I likes being with you. You ain't rowdy, and you're real pretty.'

'Well, thank you,' Verity said and turned to face Ruby. The girl had curly red hair which, although it needed a good comb, was a lovely colour, and her green eyes enhanced it. 'You are pretty too, I like your hair, and I like being with you because you know so much. The girls from school are all so dull and prissy, all they can do is giggle and talk about frocks.'

'I can't talk about frocks cos I've only got this one,' Ruby said. It was a rough brown cotton one that fitted where it touched and was very grubby. Over the top she wore a boy's tweed jacket. Her mother had found it on the way home from the pub one night and would have worn it herself but it was too small. 'But I'm glad you like my 'air, most people call it carrots.'

'It isn't a carrot red, it's more copper and very lovely,' Verity said. 'Though I think you should try combing it now and again.'

Ruby didn't really know how to respond to that. Verity obviously came from the kind of home Ruby had only ever glimpsed at the pictures. A place where brushes and combs sat on a dressing table, where a hot bath could be run any time, and someone picked up her dirty clothes and washed and ironed them for her.

Ruby knew Verity wouldn't have any idea what it was like to live in one small room with a mother who was always in a drunken stupor when she was home, or where washing yourself and your clothes meant hauling a bucket of water up to their room, or choosing to do it down at the communal tap out the back. When Ruby washed her dress she had to watch over it while it dried, wearing only her petticoat with a sack around her shoulders, in case someone even worse off stole it. Even the comb was always going missing.

'If I had a comb, I would,' Ruby said, not taking offence at what Verity had said. She noted the girl's thick navy-blue coat with a brown fur collar and cuffs, and would do anything to have such a coat. She could see too that Verity's dress which peeked out from under the coat was pink wool. She even had thick stockings to keep her legs warm. 'I'd also like a nice warm coat like yours, and a dinner every day, but as my gran used to say, "If wishes were 'orses, beggars would ride."'

Verity's face fell and she looked embarrassed. 'I've been rude, haven't I? I didn't think. I'm sorry.'

'Nuffin to be sorry for,' Ruby said airily. 'Your sort don't know nuffin about the poor. I bet you don't normally go beyond your own street? You should, though, London is an amazing place.'

Verity's blue eyes sparked with interest and she looked questioningly at Ruby. 'Would you show it to me?' she asked.

Ruby shrugged. She was in fact thrilled that a girl like Verity would even walk across the heath beside her, let alone wish to spend more time with her. 'If you want,' she said, as nonchalantly as she was able. 'My school's on 'oliday this week, is yours? We could do sommat tomorrow?'

'Yes, yes!' Verity danced from one foot to the other, smiling broadly. 'That would be wonderful.'

Ruby laughed, such enthusiasm making her forget she was hungry and cold. 'You'll need a bit of money for the underground or the bus, and if you want to eat anything. I ain't got any.' She didn't want to sound like she was begging, but she had to make her situation quite clear.

'That's fine, I've got some money,' Verity beamed. 'Would you like to get something to eat and drink now, and we could talk about where we'll go tomorrow?'

Ruby stiffened. She very much wanted to eat and drink, but she didn't think she'd be welcome in the kind of places Verity was probably used to visiting. 'I'd like that, but –' She broke off, unable to bring herself to say that.

Verity frowned. Then, as if she suddenly understood, she grinned. 'I think I know just the right place. So come on,' she said, and held out her hand to take Ruby's.

The girls ran down Heath Street, hand in hand, laughing because people were looking at them. When they got to the underground station Verity led Ruby down towards Belsize Park and, around five hundred yards further on, turned left into a narrow alley. There were several small shops there – a cobbler's, a haberdasher's and a hat shop – all of which were a bit scruffy, and once past these there was a pie shop. A wonderful smell was coming from it and Ruby's stomach contracted painfully with hunger.

'A maid we had for a while took me in here once,' Verity said. 'She said they make the best pies in London. I couldn't say if that was true as our housekeeper makes lovely ones, but I thought the one from here was really tasty.'

Ruby could see it wasn't an ordinary pie and mash shop because it didn't have one of those big counters to keep the pies hot, and she thought they must sell their pies on to other shops and restaurants. But it did have two small tables for anyone who wanted to eat a pie here.

'If you think it's alright for me to go in, then I'd love one,' Ruby said, finding it hard to form the words because she was salivating so much. 'I'm starving,' she added.

That was no exaggeration as she'd had nothing at all to eat for two days. Her sole reason for coming to Hampstead today had been to steal whatever she could find.

7

She'd discovered that people here had daily deliveries of bread, milk and other groceries and if they were out the delivery man would often leave them in a porch. But she'd been sidetracked by the activity at the pond as she walked across the heath and had temporarily forgotten her hunger and her purpose in being there.

Verity asked for two meat pies and two cups of tea and within minutes their order arrived at their table.

'Oh, Gawd!' Ruby exclaimed as her nose was assailed by the aroma of steak and kidney beneath the golden pastry. 'I'm so bleedin' 'ungry, I'm gonna show you up gulping that down.'

'Our housekeeper takes it as a compliment if I bolt down food she's cooked, and I expect they will here too.' That was in fact a lie. Miss Parsons would not be impressed by anyone bolting their food, no matter how delicious. She had a big thing about good manners. But Verity wanted Ruby to feel comfortable.

Ruby sensed the lie, but decided it was kindly meant, because she doubted that the woman who had brought the pies to their table would take any pleasure in seeing her eat. It was likely she was out the back right now wondering how to separate a little rich girl with a kind heart from a guttersnipe who was probably planning to rob her. But right now Ruby wasn't concerned with what anyone thought of her, she just wanted to fill her belly.

Ignoring the knife and fork, she lifted the hot pie up to her mouth and took a bite. It was without a doubt the best pie she'd ever tasted, rich and succulent, the meat almost melting in her mouth. As for the pastry, that was flaky and as light as a butterfly's wing. She closed her eyes, the better to savour the taste and the delicious aroma.

The pie was gone in a flash and she opened her eyes to see Verity toying with hers using a knife and fork. 'That were great,' she said breathlessly, licking her fingers and wiping her mouth on her sleeve.

All at once she became aware just how uncouth she must seem to Verity. She had stuffed the pie into her mouth with dirty hands, and even if Ruby had never watched rich people eat, she knew it wasn't done like that. She was flooded with shame and tempted to run out of the pie shop and back to Kentish Town.

But Ruby was too grateful for the food to want to hurt Verity's feelings still more.

'I'm sorry,' she said, her eyes cast down. 'I ate that like a pig, didn't I? I was just so 'ungry I couldn't 'elp myself. I showed you up, and you eating so daintily.'

Verity just smiled, a real smile that made her blue eyes sparkle. 'You couldn't help it, not if you were really hungry. Eat the rest of mine, I've had sufficient. But don't eat it so fast or you'll get indigestion, that's what Miss Parsons always says.' She pushed her plate, with more than half of her pie remaining, over to Ruby.

Ruby needed no further encouragement, but this time she picked up the knife and fork and tried to copy the way Verity ate.

Outside the pie shop, some ten minutes later, Verity caught hold of Ruby's arm. 'Are you often hungry?' she asked. 'Doesn't your father go to work?'

'I ain't never seen my father,' Ruby said gruffly. ''E were

gone afore I was born. And bein' 'ungry is usual. I come up 'ere today to nick stuff to eat. That's usual too.'

Shock widened Verity's eyes. 'That's dreadful,' she said. 'I mean dreadful that you have to, not that you were dreadful. I wish I could take you home with me and make everything right for you, but I can't.'

'Of course you can't,' Ruby laughed. 'Talking to me and buying me a pie was more than enough. If your folks saw you with me, they'd have fifty fits.'

'But we can be friends, can't we?' Verity asked. 'I like you.'

A warm feeling washed over Ruby, and it wasn't just because she'd eaten and had a cup of tea. 'And I like you too,' she said. 'But if we're gonna be pals, you'll have to teach me some manners.'

'I can do that, and you have to teach me about London,' Verity said. 'Starting tomorrow.'

Verity let herself in the basement door at her home in Daleham Gardens very quietly, hoping she could sidle up the stairs to her bedroom unseen. But luck wasn't on her side, and she ran straight into Miss Parsons the housekeeper coming out of the laundry room.

'Where have you been, child?' she asked in her usual sharp tone.

Verity's heart sank, the housekeeper always reported any misdemeanours. 'I just went for a walk up to the village. I'm sorry, was Mother looking for me?'

Miss Parsons was a small, bony, middle-aged woman who had come to work for the Woods when they first bought this house. Verity had been about three then. That she came from Cambridge was the limit of Verity's knowledge about her background; she never divulged anything about herself.

Even her mother found the woman chilly. Verity had overheard her talking to a friend about Miss Parsons. She'd said she thought most housekeepers working for a family for so long would become almost like an aunt or a cousin, especially towards a child they'd watched grow up. She was quick to add that Miss Parsons ran the house superbly, and she couldn't manage without her, but she just wished she wasn't so stern and had the ability to chat in a friendly manner.

Verity had ventured up to her room in the attic a few times, when she knew the woman was out for the afternoon, in an effort to discover something more about her. But she was always disappointed. The room was as neat and tidy as the housekeeper was, the white counterpane smoothed as if she'd taken the flat iron to it, her navy-blue uniform dress hung on a hanger behind the door, her stout, highly polished black lace-up shoes tucked beneath the dressing table. Beside her narrow iron bed were a few library books and an alarm clock. Verity hadn't been rude enough to look in drawers or open the wardrobe, but she had hoped to see a few photographs or something which might suggest the woman had family and friends.

'Yes, she was looking for you. She wanted you to accompany her to Selfridges. She wasn't best pleased, Verity,' Miss Parsons said, pursing her lips in disapproval.

Verity knew she would get a lecture later, and it wasn't fair because whenever her mother went to Selfridges she only wanted to look at dresses or try on hats, and her role was to just stand there and be admiring. There was no point in even trying to get Miss Parsons on her side, she always seemed to relish Verity being in trouble.

'I'll go and read in my room,' she said, and walked quickly up the backstairs to the entrance hall.

Meeting Ruby had made a huge impact on Verity. It wasn't just that she was from a completely different way of life, however fascinating that was, but it felt as if she'd been intended to meet the girl for some specific reason as yet unknown to her.

That was why she paused in the hall; she was trying to see her home as Ruby might see it. She thought her new friend would be awed by the large semi-detached, three-storey house with a basement. Even from the front gate it looked rather grand, with the manicured front garden, the stone lions on each side of the wide stone steps, and the impressive front door at the top of them.

Once inside, the entrance hall was spacious, the floor tiled black and white like a chequerboard. A glass door opened on to the front veranda, with her father's study next to it. Then, at the back of the house, overlooking the garden, were the drawing and dining rooms. The staircase was wide with polished wood banisters and a beautiful stained-glass window at the turn of the stairs, halfway up.

At Christmas time her father always had a big tree delivered for the hall, and her mother made garlands of holly and red ribbon to decorate the banisters. All the presents, including those for people who joined them for Christmas Day lunch, would be arranged around the tree. Until last Christmas Verity had thought it a completely magical time, and that she was lucky to have such a wonderful home.

But on Christmas Night something had happened that spoiled that belief for ever. Verity had tried to blot it from her mind, but she couldn't, and she lived in fear of it happening again. Once she wouldn't have dreamed of going out alone, but now outdoors – even alone – seemed a great deal safer, even if she did incur her mother's wrath by going out without permission.

She moved on then, turning to run up the stairs to her bedroom. Like the rest of the house, it was beautiful – a large room overlooking the back garden, and decorated in soft peach and cream. She had a wardrobe full of clothes, a huge doll's house complete with a whole family of dolls living in it. She had hundreds of books, jigsaw puzzles, games, dolls and other toys, all sitting neatly on shelves, yet she hardly touched them now. Something dark and bad had entered this room at Christmas and she could still feel its presence, even in bright sunshine.

Yet it wasn't so obvious today, after meeting Ruby. She knew her parents would be horrified if they knew she'd been fraternizing with what they would call 'a guttersnipe', but Verity had really liked her and, regardless of their opinions, she fully intended to see Ruby again tomorrow.

Cynthia Wood sipped her pre-dinner gin and tonic and looked out on to the garden reflectively, wondering what to do about Verity. It was dusk now, Miss Parsons would be ready to serve dinner soon, and if Cynthia was going to punish her daughter by making her stay in her room without any dinner, then she had to act now.

She really couldn't be bothered with this sort of confrontation, but she knew Miss Parsons was likely to tell

Archie what had taken place when he returned home from his business trip. He would be angry if she hadn't taken a firm line, both with her and Verity.

Archie always seemed to be angry these days, and she seemed to spend a huge amount of time trying to appease him. Once upon a time, she would have sneered at any woman who did that, but the truth was she had become scared of him. Nowadays when he flew into a rage it was like viewing a really dangerous twin brother who was normally locked away.

Cynthia got up from her armchair by the window and looked at herself in the overmantel mirror. She had been a very pretty child – tiny, blonde and blue-eyed – but now, as a woman of forty-two, she could see her features were too sharp and birdlike to be thought of as pretty, and her once pink and white complexion was a little muddy, with many fine lines around her eyes. Other women envied her slender shape, and her dress sense, but in truth she would rather be envied for being fun, or for her intelligence, than for a shape that owed everything to being too nervous to eat much. Besides, anyone could learn good dress sense if they studied fashion magazines and browsed through Selfridges as often as she did.

Sighing deeply, Cynthia left the drawing room just as Miss Parsons was coming up the stairs from the basement.

'I'm going up to tell Verity she'll get no dinner tonight and must stay in her room,' Cynthia told her housekeeper. 'I think I'll have my dinner on a tray in the drawing room, as my husband won't be coming home tonight.'

'Very good, Mrs Wood,' said Miss Parsons. 'I'm glad to

see you being firm with her. Girls of her age do tend to be wilful and disregard parental advice.'

Cynthia was tempted to remind the woman she was a housekeeper, nothing more, and to keep her opinions about how to deal with wayward girls to herself, but she didn't. If Miss Parsons was to leave, or to tell Archie what she'd said, neither outcome would be a happy one. Cynthia needed a housekeeper. Without one, she'd never be able to hold her head up on her bridge nights, as everyone who was anyone in Hampstead or Swiss Cottage had one. As for Archie, he would almost certainly slap her around because he loved Miss Parsons' cooking and claimed his wife couldn't boil an egg without burning it.

Without knocking, Cynthia went straight into Verity's bedroom and found her lying on her stomach on the bed, reading a book.

'No dinner for you tonight,' she said sharply. 'Perhaps being hungry will make you sorry you chose to ignore the fact I'd said we were going out together this afternoon.'

'I'm sorry, Mother,' Verity said, sitting up on her bed. 'I was just walking and forgot the time. I didn't mean to upset you.'

'You know your father doesn't like you wandering around alone,' Cynthia said, irritably. 'There are all kinds of dangers out there for young girls. We just want to keep you safe. Now promise me you won't do it again?'

'I can't promise that, Mother,' Verity retorted. 'Situations just crop up sometimes and change things. But I will promise that in future if you've asked me to go somewhere with you, I will be there.'

Cynthia was quite aware that her daughter hadn't given her the kind of pledge that she'd wanted, but it was enough for now.

'Make sure you do,' she said, and backed out of the room.

Verity smiled with relief as the door closed. It was clear her father wasn't coming home tonight, as her mother hadn't changed for dinner.

Verity couldn't care less about missing dinner. She had no appetite, and she had some biscuits in a tin if she felt hungry later.

She'd got off lightly.

Chapter Two

Verity felt quite relaxed as she left the house the next morning. Mother hadn't told her they were going anywhere today, in fact over breakfast she'd been talking about sorting out her summer clothes in readiness for when the warm weather arrived. Verity had offered to post some letters on the way to the library. Of course there would be trouble when she eventually came home, but Verity had already argued with herself that she wasn't breaking a promise – and anyway, Ruby might be bored with her company within an hour or two so she'd be back by lunchtime.

She had chosen her clothes with care, wanting to make the difference between herself and Ruby less obvious. Last year's navy-blue coat was well worn and too short, ear-marked by her mother to send to the next church jumble sale, and the dress beneath it a dull, dark green one which she'd never liked. A navy beret pulled down over her ears completed the picture of a very ordinary girl, and though Miss Parsons had looked a little surprised at her appearance, she'd made no comment.

Verity had only been waiting by Hampstead underground station for a minute or two when Ruby came haring up the road.

'I thought you wouldn't come,' she yelled breathlessly while still fifty yards away. 'But I came just in case you did.'

'Why didn't you think I'd come?' Verity asked once her new friend was beside her.

'Posh bints like you don't normally even speak to me,' Ruby said.

Verity wondered what 'bints' meant but she was so pleased to see the delight on Ruby's face she didn't ask. 'I try to keep promises,' she said. 'I was in trouble yesterday for not being home in time to go out with Mother; I didn't get any dinner.'

'You're lucky your ma cares where you go. I could stay away for a week and mine wouldn't even notice I was missing.'

'Why wouldn't she?'

'Cos she's always drunk,' Ruby said with a resigned shrug.

Verity had only seen two drunk people in her whole life. One was Uncle Charles two Christmases ago, and the other was their neighbour's maid. The maid had staggered in through the basement door late one afternoon, mistaking their house for the one where she worked. Verity had been helping Miss Parsons fold up laundry at the time, and she thought the maid was ill, she hadn't known strong drink made a person wobble about and slur their speech.

Miss Parsons had forcibly ejected the woman while berating her on the evils of drink and what drunkenness could lead a young woman to. Verity had watched and listened open-mouthed, and it had made a lasting impression on her.

As the two girls began to walk down the road towards Chalk Farm, Verity asked what her father thought about her mother's drinking.

Ruby laughed. 'I told you yesterday I ain't got a dad. Maybe that's what's wrong with me ma. She told me once that 'e was her sweetheart till she told 'im 'e'd got 'er up the spout, and then 'e scarpered.'

'Up the spout?' Verity queried.

'In the family way,' Ruby said.

Verity realized that meant having a baby, but she didn't know babies could come without a couple being married. Until last Christmas she wouldn't have had the least idea of how they got a baby either – or even wondered about it – but because of what had happened to her, she was now fairly sure it was something like that which made babies.

'You seem to know about so much compared with me,' Verity said, deciding that she was never going to learn anything new unless she admitted her ignorance.

'I bet you knows loads of stuff what I don't,' Ruby said with a little grin. 'All about other countries, the kings and queens of England, and what makes a "lady".'

'I suppose I do,' Verity agreed. She had never been able to understand what point there was in being able to recite the list of kings and queens, long turgid poems, or knowing about the mountains in Africa or the longest river in the world. But knowing about how babies came or what the police did when they found a body could be very useful. 'Most of the stuff I've learned at school seems pointless to me, but maybe there are bits that would be good for you.'

'I'd like to talk nice like you,' Ruby said wistfully. 'And to look clean and neat the way you do. Reckon you could make me ladylike?'

Verity looked hard at her new friend for a moment. She

was wearing the same boy's tweed jacket and dirty dress as the day before, but she had made a real effort to look better. Her red hair was combed, she'd even tied it back with a strip of cloth, and her face looked well scrubbed. She wasn't what anyone would call pretty, but there was something very arresting about her. Maybe it was her green eyes that sparkled with mischief, the few freckles across her small nose, or the way her plump mouth turned up at the corners, as if she was smiling constantly. It was certainly a good face.

Verity knew that a properly fitting jacket, dress and shoes would transform Ruby. She could easily smuggle these things out of the house for her, but she was reluctant to offer them in case she embarrassed her.

'I'd love to help.' She reached forward and took Ruby's hand. 'If you'd allow it, I'd bring you some clothes and some ribbons for your hair next time we meet, but I'm afraid that might make you feel bad.'

To her surprise Ruby laughed. 'It wouldn't make me feel bad, but if I went 'ome with new togs, ma would 'ave 'em down uncle's soon as look at you.'

'Why take them to your uncle's?' Verity asked.

Ruby shook her head, as if amused at the question. ''E ain't my uncle, it's what we call the pawnshop. Don't suppose you know about that neither. We get money there by taking in things of value. We pay more to get 'em out again.'

'You take clothes into such a place?' Verity was horrified.

'People like me ma that needs a drink do,' Ruby said. 'I'll show you one today, if you like.'

*

An hour or two later, Verity had learned about a great many more new things, including pie and eel shops, music halls, and potato and hop picking in Kent. Jellied eels sounded disgusting, but she would like to go to a music hall, and Ruby had made potato and hop picking sound like fun. She'd also peered through a very dusty window of a pawnshop and seen men's suits, polished boots, a trumpet and assorted jewellery amongst mountains of clothing, bedding and books inside.

Some of the more conventional sights Ruby had shown her – Trafalgar Square, Buckingham Palace, and the statue of Eros in Piccadilly – she'd seen many times before. Also, some of the theatres Ruby pointed out, speaking excitedly about the actors and actresses who had performed there, were ones where Verity had seen plays or shows with her parents. But she got a different perspective by hearing Ruby's thoughts on them.

'I loves to stand outside theatres and watch the toffs arriving,' she said outside the Haymarket Theatre. 'I ain't never bin in a car or a cab. Fancy being rich enough to go everywhere in one! Or being rich enough to 'ave a fur coat, or a diamond necklace! Just the price of a ticket for up in the gods would buy me food for a week.'

For Verity it was commonplace to go about town in either her father's car or in a cab. Her mother had both diamonds and a fur coat, and it certainly had never occurred to her that a theatre ticket cost as much as a week's food for some people. Suddenly she felt ashamed that she had so much and Ruby so little. It wasn't fair at all.

At home she had dresses she'd only worn two or three times before they were too small for her, and each mealtime there was so much food left uneaten. Granted that sometimes this was made into a meal for the following day, but mostly it went straight in the dustbin.

But as shocking as the inequality between her and Ruby was, it was nothing compared to discovering what Ruby's mother did for a living.

They were sitting on a bench in St James's Park, looking at the ducks on the pond, when Ruby said she often went through her mother's pockets when she was asleep to get money to pay the rent and buy food. She said if she didn't do this, it would only be spent on drink.

'So how does she earn the money?' Verity asked.

'Selling herself, of course,' Ruby replied.

'But how? What way?' Verity asked in bewilderment.

'She lets men fuck her.'

Verity was so shocked she could only gape at her new friend. She'd been told that word at school just a few weeks ago; the girl who told her said, though it was mostly used as a very bad swear word, it also meant the sex act.

'You mustn't say that word, it's a really bad one,' Verity protested.

'Round where I live folk use it all the time,' Ruby said defiantly. 'Besides, it's what ma does. And it ain't no good you looking like that at me, all big eyes and stuff, cos you don't know how 'ard it is to get respectable work when you've got a kid in tow. When I was born it was either that or the work'ouse. I'd 'ave bin taken off her and she didn't want that. She did what she did cos of me, and I know she only drinks to forget what she's become.'

As shocked as Verity was, she was also touched by Ruby's understanding of her mother's predicament and her loyalty to her. There was no bitterness at all, and it made Verity realize that she had no business to complain about her own home life.

To be told something like that was quite enough of a shock for one day, but then Ruby took her to Soho, and showed her where prostitutes lived.

'There ain't much to see during the day,' Ruby explained as they walked through narrow streets and alleyways. It was a grubby, mixed sort of area, with very old buildings and some very seedy-looking shops, but there were proper businesses there too – printers, garment manufacturers, bookshops and haberdashers – and the streets were teeming with normal working people. 'But come seven in the evening, it's all change. There's pros on street corners and in doorways looking for business, their pimps and other villains arrive to do their mischief, and there's nobs too what come for the restaurants and nightclubs.'

'Really?' Verity was astounded to think that rich people would want to go slumming.

Ruby chuckled. 'Folks is always surprised by that! They say some of the best food in London is served round 'ere. I wouldn't know that for certain, seeing as I ain't got two farthings to rub together, but they say there's good music in the nightclubs an' all.'

'Gosh!' Verity said, feeling like she knew nothing about anything. 'I've learned so much today.'

'Time you taught me sommat, then,' Ruby laughed. ''Ow's about you take me in a caff and teach me 'ow to eat like a lady? It don't 'ave to be a fancy place, I don't want to show you up.'

*

Verity chose a place that was marginally smarter than a working man's cafe. It had red and white checked table-cloths and a menu with standard dishes.

Ruby picked up the menu almost as soon as they'd sat down at a corner table. Verity noticed she was running a finger along the words and her lips were moving as though she was trying to sound them out.

'The light is awful here. Shall I tell you what the choices are?' she offered, wanting to spare her friend the indignity of admitting she couldn't read very well. 'There's sausage and mash, liver and bacon, steak and kidney pie, shepherd's pie.'

'Shepherd's pie,' Ruby exclaimed. 'I love that.'

Verity smiled. 'First thing,' she began, 'keep your voice low, we don't want everyone in here looking round at us. I'll order for us.'

Verity duly ordered shepherd's pie for both of them, and a glass of water each.

'I likes tea,' Ruby said, once the waitress had gone. She had looked very hard at Ruby as if tempted to ask her to leave.

'Yes, I'm sure you do, but it's more correct to have tea or coffee after the meal,' Verity said quietly. 'Now when the food arrives, don't attack it like you haven't eaten for a month. And hold your knife and fork correctly, like this.' She picked hers up to give a demonstration. 'You mustn't turn your fork up the other way to shovel the food in; you push it on to the back of your fork with the knife.'

She wanted to laugh at Ruby's baffled expression. She guessed that Ruby would normally use a spoon, unless the meal required a knife to cut it up. 'Just do what I do,' she suggested. 'Now put your napkin on your lap in readiness.'

Ruby did very well with her meal; she struggled a bit with the knife and fork, and had to be reminded not to chew with her mouth open, but she didn't bolt it down or use her fingers. In no time at all her plate was clean. 'Put your knife and fork together neatly,' Verity instructed. 'Even if you can't eat it all, that's a signal to the waiter that you've finished.'

'What a palaver!' Ruby said. 'But it were lovely.'

'Was lovely,' Verity corrected her. 'But we'll save speech correction for another day.'

They had treacle tart and custard, and a cup of tea to follow. Verity had to stop Ruby when she was just going to pour some tea into the saucer with the intention of cooling it down and pouring it back into her cup.

'That is not done,' she said firmly. 'Just wait until it's cooler.'

But once outside the cafe, Verity praised her friend. 'You did very well, you learn quickly. But I'd better go home now, or I'll be in big trouble.'

'I ain't never 'ad a pal like you afore,' Ruby said, looking a little embarrassed.

'Nor me,' Verity replied, and she felt a prickling of tears at the back of her eyes. 'But I don't know when I can see you again; once my father comes home it can be difficult to get out.'

Ruby frowned. 'I'll come to 'Ampstead tomorrow about 'alf two. If you can't get there then, send a note to me at the Red Lion at Camden Town. I wash up glasses there most nights, and they'll give it to me. But if you want to meet, make it a couple of days ahead cos I might not get the note straight off.'

Ruby led Verity to the bus stop to get her to Swiss Cottage.

As the bus drew up Verity pressed a shilling into Ruby's hand. 'For your fare home,' she said. 'And thank you for a wonderful day.'

Verity went upstairs on the bus and looked back at Ruby. She was just standing in the middle of the pavement, seemingly unaware of the people going past on either side of her. She looked terribly sad and alone. It occurred to Verity that she felt the same. She wasn't alone, of course; she had family, an aunt and good neighbours. If she compared her life with Ruby's, she lived in paradise.

Yet it didn't feel that way.

She was so very lonely.

Chapter Three

'So you got away?' Ruby said when Verity met her the following afternoon and they began to walk up to the heath.

'Yes, but something a bit strange is going on at home. Mother didn't even ask why I'd been so long at the library yesterday, or why I didn't come back for lunch. It was like she wasn't even aware of me.'

'Sure she wasn't drinking? That's how my ma is all the time.'

Verity smiled. 'No, she doesn't ever drink more than a couple of sherries, and then only just before dinner. I think she must have got some upsetting news while I was out. She told me to have my lunch with Miss Parsons in the kitchen and she went to her room. I asked Miss Parsons if she was ill, but she said Mother had things on her mind. What can that mean?'

'I dunno, maybe it's sommat to do with your father?'

'What, though? He's found another lady? He's dropped dead? What?'

Ruby shrugged. 'Would you like it to be one of those?'

Verity immediately felt ashamed of herself. 'No, of course not. But the only thing which would make her act like this is if there was something wrong with him.'

They didn't speak again until they were up on the heath and had sat down on a bench by Whitestone Pond.

'You don't like your pa, do you?' Ruby said suddenly.

'What makes you say that?'

Ruby shrugged. 'I dunno exactly. Just a feeling.'

Verity didn't respond. She very much wanted to admit how horrible her father could be, the way he belittled her, scoffed at anything she said, and shouted at her for nothing. But most of all she wanted to talk about what had happened at Christmas. She felt Ruby would offer some advice about it. But she couldn't bring herself to, and so she just sat in silence watching some small boys sailing a boat on the pond.

'I've got to do something near 'ere,' Ruby said after a few minutes. 'You can stay 'ere and wait for me, I won't be long.'

'What is it?'

'Best you know nuffin,' Ruby said, getting to her feet. 'If I'm running when I come back, pretend you don't know me. Just walk on down Heath Street and if I can, I'll join you.'

She walked swiftly away before Verity could ask her anything else, and disappeared behind Queen Mary's Maternity Home.

Verity remembered that when they first met, Ruby had said she came up to Hampstead to steal food and milk left on doorsteps, so maybe that was what she was doing. Yet by three in the afternoon surely anything left earlier would have been taken in? But she had to be planning to do something bad or she wouldn't anticipate being chased.

Verity waited, and waited. Half an hour passed, then another, and she was just getting to her feet to go home when Ruby came haring round the corner with a tall, dark man in hot pursuit. Verity could see that he was gaining on her friend and at any moment he was going to grab her.

Despite having been told to go if Ruby was being chased, Verity couldn't. Instead she walked towards them, with a vague idea forming of somehow getting in between them.

Ruby made a little 'get away' gesture with her hands, but Verity took no notice and walked right into her friend's path. She didn't dare call out for fear of alerting the man to the fact that she knew Ruby, but she hoped her friend would guess what she was trying to do.

She was less than five yards from Ruby, and the man was stretching out to catch her shoulders when Verity made her move. She stepped sideways to let Ruby pass, then quickly regained her old path so that the man would bump into her.

Verity wasn't able to see if her ruse had been a success because the force of the man's body crashing into her knocked her over. As she fell she must have clutched at him, because he fell too.

'I'm so sorry, sir,' she said breathlessly, still on the floor and not daring to look round to see if Ruby had got away. 'I didn't see you.'

The tall man disengaged himself from her, got to his feet and glowered down at her. 'I know perfectly well you are in it together,' he panted out. Glancing over his shoulder at some people watching, he yelled for someone to get the police.

'Whatever do you mean?' she said with all the indignation she could muster. She sat up and dusted off her clothes. 'In what together? I have no idea what you are blaming me for. All I did was avoid that girl who was running down here, and somehow I banged into you. I couldn't help it. And you've hurt me, I'm not sure I can even get up.'

She could hear a murmur from the bystanders, which she hoped was sympathy, but to her dismay she saw a policeman coming. Her heart began to hammer with fright but she forced herself to get up slowly, making a big display of being hurt.

The police officer was just a few yards away now, and the dark man made a gesture for him to grab Verity. 'She is in league with the girl who stole a valuable carriage clock from my house,' he bellowed for the whole world to hear. 'Officer, arrest her, please! And send some of your men to catch her accomplice. She has red hair.'

'That girl has already been caught,' the policeman said. 'She's back there in Heath Street, held by the officer I was with. We saw her drop the clock, and I came on up here to see what people were looking at.'

Before Verity could gather her wits the policeman had caught hold of her arm, and he said he was taking her to the police station.

Verity was suddenly really scared. Everything had happened so quickly, and to find herself being led away by a policeman, as if she was a common criminal, was too shocking for words.

As she was being taken into the police station she saw Ruby fleetingly, but Ruby didn't acknowledge her in any way, not a smile, nod or wink. Verity felt that was her way of trying to make out they didn't know one another so the police didn't think they were in it together.

The only thing she was asked was her name. Then she was put into a tiny box-like room, with just two chairs and a metal table. It smelled of cigarettes and stale sweat. The policeman left, and she heard him locking the door behind him. Then there was nothing. No one came in, she could hear nothing outside the door; it was as if she'd been forgotten.

Fear engulfed her and she began to cry. All she had done was try to stop the tall man catching her friend. Surely that wasn't a crime? Or was it?

She had no idea what the time was, but it had to be after five o'clock by now. If she wasn't home soon, Mother would be angry. What if the police went to her home?

But they hadn't asked her where she lived, only her name. She prayed silently that Ruby would tell the truth and say she acted alone, and perhaps make out she didn't know Verity at all.

Finally, just as she felt she'd go out of her mind in that room, the door opened and an older man in a dark suit came in. He was perhaps fifty, stout, with a narrow moustache and thin, greying hair. He introduced himself as Detective Inspector Charmers.

'How old are you, Verity?' he asked.

'Thirteen, sir,' she responded.

'Old enough to know the difference between right and wrong?'

'Well, yes,' she said. 'And this is wrong keeping me here all this time. I haven't done anything, and my mother will be frantic.'

'You may not have taken part in the actual robbery, but you are an accomplice.'

'How can I be? I didn't know that girl, I just walked into her.'

'But you do know her,' Charmers smirked. 'We have a

witness who saw you sitting together and talking on a bench at Whitestone Pond sometime earlier.'

Verity knew she'd been caught out. If he hadn't said where she'd been seen with Ruby, she might have thought it was a bluff. But to say the bench at the pond proved he really did have a witness.

'You see?' he grinned. 'You can't get out of that one, Miss Wood, you were spotted. And do you want to know why anyone would remember?'

Verity shrugged.

'Because you were total opposites. Our witness wondered what a well-dressed girl like you could be doing with such a guttersnipe.'

'Yes, I was there, but I don't know that girl. We just got into conversation,' Verity lied. 'I don't know anything about her, we only talked for a few minutes and she said she had to go. Next thing I saw her running with that man after her. So I tried to help her! For all I knew he might have been trying to attack her. I didn't know she'd done something bad.'

Charmers looked at her long and hard, and she wilted under his stare.

'You've been a silly goose,' he said eventually. 'I can guess why a nicely brought up girl like you would be curious about someone from a different way of life. But believe me, a girl like Ruby Taylor would only drag you down to her level. Now it's time to take you home.'

Verity's stomach lurched. She knew there was no point in refusing to say where she lived. The police were clever, they would find out eventually, and it would only make her look more guilty. But she was so scared of what her parents were going to say. She couldn't hope this would be brushed away.

'Can't I go home alone?' she begged. 'My mother will have fifty fits, and it's cruel to upset her just over me talking to that girl.'

Charmers reached out and took her arm, drawing her to her feet. 'If I let this go, I would be failing your parents,' he said. 'They need to know what their daughter gets up to when she is away from home.'

Another policeman drove Charmers and Verity to Daleham Gardens. She sensed Charmers had already spoken to her mother on the telephone, because the new man didn't even ask her address. That would make it worse for her, as her mother would have had time to consider what Verity might have been up to.

Miss Parsons opened the front door, her face as frosty as usual. 'Mr and Mrs Wood will see you in the drawing room,' she said curtly. So she clearly knew what was going on.

Verity's heart plummeted on hearing her father was home. But as she and Charmers walked into the drawing room she knew it was going to be even worse than she had feared.

Archie Wood was a very intimidating man. He was tall – well over six foot – and well built. He rarely laughed, smiled or looked as if he had any interest in her at all. With dark, slicked-back hair, a swarthy complexion and a dark moustache which he oiled and tweaked out, she often thought he had the look of a Hollywood villain.

Over meals he would speak to her, ask her about school and such things, but it always sounded to her as if it was just polite behaviour, not real interest. His eyes were very dark, and there never seemed to be any light or expression in them – the same as the dead fish on the marble slab at the fishmonger's. He had never picked her up and cuddled her when she was little; she couldn't remember ever sitting on his lap, or even being given a piggy-back ride. That was what had made him coming into her bedroom at Christmas so alarming; he said he wanted to kiss her goodnight, but he'd never done such a thing before. As it turned out, it certainly wasn't a kiss that he wanted. She couldn't bear to dwell on what he had made her do to him.

And now, as she saw his angry expression, she quaked. He looked like he despised her.

'Just tell me, what could be the attraction of fraternizing with riff-raff?' he asked.

'I wasn't fraternizing with her,' Verity said. 'She just said something about a boy sailing his boat on the pond and I replied. I didn't know her, it was just a little chat with a girl who was about the same age as me. Was I supposed to ignore her, to get up and walk away like I'm too grand to speak to ordinary people?'

His hand shot out and slapped her face hard. 'Don't take that attitude with me,' he snarled. 'I know you went out to meet her and that you have been with her before. Don't lie to me.'

Verity put her hand on her cheek; it was burning from his slap. And in that second, rage welled up inside her at the injustice.

'I lie because you and Mother don't allow me to go out

and meet friends. I can never invite them here either. Shall I tell the policeman what you did to me at Christmas?' The second that last angry retort had left her lips she regretted it, because she saw her mother's eyes widen in alarm.

Charmers looked curious.

She didn't want to tell anyone really, it was far too disgusting. But at the same time she wanted to hurt her father, as he had so often hurt her. She didn't dare look at her father to see his reaction.

'I think Verity understands now that it wasn't wise to involve herself with a street urchin,' Charmers said quickly. He sounded as if he was just trying to smooth things out so he could leave. 'There is no evidence to support her being this girl's accomplice. All Verity is guilty of is being a bit gullible and headstrong. I'm sure the time she spent at the police station will make her more careful about who she speaks to in future.'

With that, he backed towards the door and left hastily without even a goodbye.

For a second there was complete silence in the room. Her father stood by the fireplace, one hand on the mantelpiece, and glowered at her. Mother was perched on the arm of the settee; she had her hand up to her throat, as if she was struggling to breathe.

'I cannot believe my daughter was involved in something like this and had to be questioned by the police,' her father eventually barked at her. 'Get to your room now and I will come and deal with you in a minute.'

That order terrified her. At best it would be a severe beating, the worst was a repeat of what he had made her do to him at Christmas. She rushed out into the hall and was just on the first stair when she heard her mother speak.

'How convenient this is for you, Archie. I suppose you think it will distract me from what you've done.'

Verity paused to listen further.

'I'm not best pleased that my daughter chooses to mix with ragamuffins,' her mother continued. 'But compared with her father embezzling funds, that is nothing.'

Verity didn't know what 'embezzling' meant, but it sounded bad.

'Don't take that high-and-mighty tone with me,' her father snapped back. 'You've been happily living off the proceeds for years.'

'I believed every penny that came into this house had been earned,' her mother's voice rose to a shriek of indignation. 'If you were struggling and had told me, I would have made reductions in the household expenditure, I would even have agreed to move to a smaller house. This has been the worst day of my life. Mr Gladstone told me they are taking legal action against you and that you will go to prison. Where is that going to leave me?'

'That's right, as always, only thinking of yourself,' he retorted. 'Don't spare a thought for where I'll be.'

'And what did Verity mean when she said something happened at Christmas?'

'That girl is as stupid and hysterical as you,' he said. 'It was nothing. She was trying to distract you and that policeman. I must go and deal with her now, I'll speak to you later.'

Verity moved swiftly up the stairs then; he would beat her even harder if he caught her eavesdropping.

*

Her father came barging into her room seconds later. His face was flushed and his eyes blazing. Verity shook with terror, she'd never seen him as angry as this before.

'You touch me and I'll go to the police,' she warned him, hoping attack was the best form of defence.

'Do you think they give a damn about a stupid girl like you?' he snarled. 'You more than deserve a good hiding, trying to make trouble for me.'

He pulled at the leather belt slotted into loops on his trousers. When he'd got it all out, he wound it tightly around his fist, leaving the end with the buckle free to beat her with.

'Bend over the bed,' he ordered her.

Verity was frozen with fear and so he grabbed her by the neck and forced her down on to the bed. Still holding her there, he hit her with the belt once. That hardly hurt at all, as he hadn't been able to swing his arm, but he soon rectified that by standing up straight and raining blows down on her back and buttocks.

Normally when he beat her it was four or five strokes at the most, and not that hard – but even so, it stung like mad – but this was frenzied, almost as if she was responsible for all his misfortunes. The pain was red hot and searing. Despite wearing a dress, petticoat, knickers and a liberty bodice, it felt like the belt was biting into her bare flesh.

She could hear him ranting at her as he hit her, but over her screaming she couldn't hear what he was saying. She thought fleetingly that no one could be beaten this hard and survive, and then she stopped screaming and prayed that she would pass out with the next blow.

Maybe her prayers were answered because, through what felt like a thick fog, she heard her mother's voice, ordering him to stop. Then Miss Parsons' voice joined in, and suddenly the blows stopped.

But not the pain.

That was like a fiery blanket on her back, bottom and legs.

Chapter Four

'Oh, Verity, what has he done to you?'

Verity heard her mother's horrified question through what seemed to be a thick red mist. But she was in too much pain to open her eyes or reply.

'I'll get clean linen, she's had an accident.' Miss Parsons' voice came from close by her.

Verity realized then that it was the housekeeper's hands that were gently examining her – not her mother's – and unusually for Miss Parsons, her voice was soft and concerned. 'I can't believe a father would inflict such injuries on his child!' she said. 'I'll get water, a cloth and some soothing cream to try and make her more comfortable.'

'If he wasn't about to be arrested for embezzlement, I'd call the police to him now,' her mother said, her voice tight with anger. 'Has he got up and slunk away yet?'

Verity heard the sound of the door opening. 'No. He's still out there on the landing, where I dragged him to.' Miss Parsons sounded angry now. 'He's trying to get up, though, so I didn't kill him. More's the pity!'

Much later that evening, Verity learned that her beating had ended abruptly because Miss Parsons ran upstairs armed with a golf club and hit her employer over the head with it, knocking him unconscious. Then she took his feet and dragged him out of Verity's bedroom on to the landing. That in itself was astounding; she had never imagined

Miss Parsons could attack or defend anyone. But clearly this woman, who had always seemed so chilly and uncaring, did have tender feelings for Verity. From the first examination of her back till several hours later, when she gave Verity a herbal sedative to help her sleep, she was unbelievably kind and concerned.

Those hours were filled with searing agony. It was hardly surprising Verity had lost control of her bladder; her clothes were torn to ribbons with the force of the beating and her whole body, from her shoulders down to her knees, was lacerated and bloody. She could only lie on her stomach – there was no question of being able to turn over, or sit up.

Miss Parsons did all of the nursing, bathing the wounds and applying some healing cream. As she worked, Verity's mother merely sat on a chair and went on and on incessantly about her husband's crime.

'I wish I was dead,' she exclaimed at one point. 'The shame of it! I can't even begin to imagine what our neighbours and friends will say about it. It seems he not only robbed the company but many small investors too. I wouldn't blame them if they came here to lynch him. I'll have to move away,' she said repeatedly. 'They'll take this house and all our fine furniture anyway. I'll have nothing.'

Verity did try to rally herself to reach out a hand towards her mother.

'You'll have me,' she croaked out. 'We can make a new life together.'

But her mother didn't take her hand or even acknowledge what she'd said.

*

It transpired that her father left the house that night, running away from what he'd done. Verity wasn't aware of it until the next morning when she heard a commotion downstairs. It was the police looking for him. Not the local officers she'd seen in Hampstead police station but special detectives who dealt with serious crime. She heard her mother insisting to them that she had no idea where her husband had gone, or even what time he'd left the house the previous night, because she'd shut herself away in her bedroom.

'They are going to search the house, and they may come in here,' Miss Parsons said to Verity as she put more cream on her wounds and covered them with dressings.

She had helped her out of bed to walk gingerly to the lavatory that morning, brushed her hair and washed her face, and Verity had drunk tea and eaten a bowl of porridge, standing up. But the act of walking hurt, and sitting down was impossible, so Verity had got back into bed to lie on her stomach.

'They are working their way through the downstairs rooms now, but don't be afraid if they come in here, they are just doing their job, looking for evidence.'

'What will happen to us?' Verity asked her.

For the first time Verity ever remembered, Miss Parsons showed some emotion. Her eyes filled with tears as she took Verity's hand between hers.

'I think you two will go to stay with your Aunt Hazel,' she said. 'I shall have to find another job.'

By late afternoon Verity was feeling very sorry for herself. She hurt all over, her mother hadn't seen fit to come and reassure her about anything, and until an hour ago the police had been rampaging around the house like a herd of elephants. When two constables came into her room, she told them her father had beaten her the night before, but they made no comment, merely shook their heads and left her room after a brief search. Clearly embezzlement was a far greater crime than hurting a young girl.

She didn't care where her father had gone, she hoped the police would lock him up for the rest of his life, but the prospect of living at Aunt Hazel's was just terrible.

Aunt Hazel was six years older than her mother. She had never married and had stayed in the family home in Lewisham to look after their widowed mother. Grandmother had been a fierce, spiteful woman who was famous for not having a good word to say about anyone. She had died a year ago and Aunt Hazel had inherited the house. She also appeared to have inherited her mother's nature, as she too was mean-spirited and cold.

Verity recalled at the funeral there being angry words between the sisters about the legacy. Mother thought the property should have been left to both of them. But Aunt Hazel got angry and said Cynthia had a husband to take care of her and lived in some style, whereas she had never had the opportunity to marry because she'd been forced to deal with their cantankerous and incontinent mother for years. She said she deserved the house – and anyway, it was hardly palatial.

Verity hadn't been to her grandmother's house very often – only twice in the last three years – and it had always given her the creeps. The dark, cold and smelly Victorian terraced house was small with only a tiny back garden. It was also in a very working-class part of London. She'd noticed on previous visits that boys played football in the street and old people sat on their doorsteps. It didn't bear thinking about what a huge step down it would be to live there. And she doubted Aunt Hazel would welcome them, as the sisters had never been close. In fact it was difficult to believe they were related. Aunt Hazel was quite common, and made curtains for a living. Cynthia looked, dressed and sounded like she'd been brought up in Hampstead.

What would happen about school now? At present she went to a private girls' school in Belsize Park; obviously, she wouldn't be able to continue there. Even if the money could be found, the journey from Lewisham would be impossible.

She wished she could talk to Ruby about all this, but in all likelihood she was on her way to wherever judges sent fourteen-year-olds caught in the act of burglary. Did they go to prison like grown-ups? Or was there some other place for girls like her?

Father's crime was in all the newspapers on the second day. Verity wasn't told but Miss Parsons had a copy under her arm and she'd caught a glimpse of a photograph of her father and part of the headline. It said: 'Twenty Thousand Pounds Embezzled'. She overheard Miss Parsons say to her mother that he couldn't run for ever and the police wouldn't give up until they'd found him.

Lying in her bed, still terribly sore and unable to sit up, Verity pondered over that huge sum of money. Had it all gone? What had her father spent it on? To a girl who had never held more than a pound note in her hand it seemed inconceivable that so much money could ever be spent.

She wondered too what the difference was between theft and embezzlement, and why her father hadn't run away the moment he knew he was found out? Why did he come back to the house, if he knew his wife had been told what he'd done? He couldn't have expected her to be sympathetic, surely? Or did he have some of the money tucked away here and needed to get it? Stranger still that he delayed his departure to beat his daughter! Was that pure spite, because she'd hinted that he'd done something bad to her at Christmas? Or just that he was so angry at being caught that he had to take it out on someone?

Whatever was in his mind, whatever he'd come back here for, Verity felt very glad that Miss Parsons had hit him. She hoped the police would catch him quickly, she wouldn't even care if they shot him. Though she didn't think English policemen ever had guns.

She worried too about Ruby. Where would she have been sent by the police? Would she think Verity didn't care about her, as she hadn't come looking for her? Or might she have seen the newspaper and realized her father was a swindler?

In the seemingly endless days that followed, Verity's injuries slowly healed. The first time she ventured hesitantly down the stairs and out into the garden, she was unable to imagine herself ever getting back to normal. But the sight of spring flowers opening up in the garden, the sun a little warmer, was always a hint that better times were coming, and it cheered her. The following day, she sat in a chair to read for a couple of hours. And on the day after, she dressed herself, even if it was only in a loose smock dress that wouldn't rub anywhere. Each day from then on, she hurt a little less and when she finally was healed enough to have a bath, she knew she really was on the mend.

During this time the police called again and again; it seemed they didn't believe Archie Wood wouldn't try to see his wife and daughter.

'Do you really believe I would give him the time of day after what he's done?' Verity's mother exclaimed indignantly to a policeman one day. 'I'm waiting now to hear when I've got to give up my home and furniture. Our daughter is still recovering from a beating he gave her, and I've got nothing to live on. My neighbours give me pitying looks and all my friends have deserted me.'

Verity didn't actually think her mother had any real friends, just ladies she played bridge with. Not one of them had telephoned or called round to offer sympathy or help.

But perhaps they knew they wouldn't be welcomed or appreciated, because each time Verity had tried to comfort her mother she was so prickly and nasty she wished she hadn't tried. But hearing her mother say she had nothing to live on – and aware that Miss Parsons was feeding them out of the contents of the store cupboard, rather than going shopping for fresh food – Verity felt she had to try again.

Catching her mother in the drawing room listlessly picking out a tune on the piano, she decided this was the moment.

'If you think someone is going to come and take your

things away, why don't you pawn some of the smaller valuable bits, like your jewellery and the silver, before they get here?'

'Pawn!' her mother exclaimed, her eyes wide with surprise. 'I don't know what you mean.'

Verity hadn't known the word until Ruby told her, but she was astounded her mother didn't know. She had thought adults knew everything.

'Pawnshops are places you take valuables and they give you money for them,' she said. 'They have three brass balls above the shop sign to let you know that's what they do. Mostly people just use them to borrow a bit until they can pay it back, but I think they buy stuff too.'

'I can't imagine how you'd know such a thing,' her mother sniffed disapprovingly. 'Where are these places, for goodness' sake?'

'Mostly where poorer people live, I don't think there's one in Hampstead. But I have seen one in the Finchley Road. That's far enough away from here that we wouldn't be spotted going in there by anyone we know.'

'I couldn't go into such a place,' her mother replied, clutching nervously at her throat. 'But maybe you and Miss Parsons could go.'

Verity felt very adult in finding a solution to their immediate problems. 'Maybe we should just take a few small trinkets first,' she suggested. 'But we ought to find a hiding place for all the other precious things, so they don't get taken away with the house. Then we could sell them as and when you need money.'

For the first time Verity ever remembered, her mother looked at her in real admiration. 'I hadn't realized you'd grown up so much,' she said. 'Thank you, Verity, for the suggestion, I think I'll start making a list and try to think of somewhere to store things.'

'It would have to be away from here,' Verity reminded her. 'Maybe at Aunt Hazel's?'

Verity went with Miss Parsons to the pawnshop the next day. They took a diamond brooch, a pearl necklace and her father's gold cufflinks and tie pin. Mother had said she hoped for at least thirty pounds. But they must accept whatever they were offered, as there was no money to pay the milkman, baker or butcher.

'Don't be surprised at anything I say to the man,' Miss Parsons said as they hurried up the Finchley Road. 'At times like this you have to use all the wiles you possess, and you must look stricken with grief so he feels sorry for us.'

Verity saw a completely different side of the house-keeper once they were in the dusty pawnbroker's. She wasn't starchy at all; in fact she was so sweet and charming to the owner, a man called Cohen, that Verity barely recognized her. She held a lace-trimmed handkerchief in her hand and kept dabbing her eyes as she told the man her widower brother had just died leaving her with all the bills to pay and his child to take care of.

'I knew he had become a little disorganized since he lost his wife,' she said with a catch in her voice that sounded like she was going to break down. 'But I didn't realize that he'd squandered so much money and that he didn't have any savings or insurance. I feel so humiliated, having to sell jewellery he gave me, but this child has to be taken care of.'

Mr Cohen was bearded, thin and small with a slight

hunch to his back. Verity guessed him to be about sixty and she thought he looked poor, as his jacket was shiny with age and his shirt collar was none too clean. But he was kind to Miss Parsons.

'That is very sad for you, my dear,' he said. 'But don't judge your brother too harshly. Losing a loved one can make even the most steady of people behave out of character. I see it all the time in here. Grown men breaking down like small children, and women beside themselves with grief and unable to make any decisions. But these are good pearls and the brooch is a fine piece, so he was clearly a man of good taste. I expect he intended to sort out his affairs and would be distressed to think of you and his daughter struggling after his death. Perhaps it would be better for you to pawn these items so you can reclaim them when your circumstances improve?'

'I wish I could do that,' Miss Parsons said. 'But I can see no possibility of any improvement in my position in the near future. I may be able to do a little dressmaking or domestic work, but with a child to take care of I cannot even go into service.'

She actually managed to squeeze out a few tears, and Verity was impressed by her acting skills.

Yet however sympathetic Mr Cohen was, he drove a hard bargain, offering twenty-five pounds at first. Miss Parsons let out a strangled sob that sounded utterly convincing to Verity, and said she needed sixty pounds.

Verity listened to the pawnbroker insisting he couldn't go above thirty, Miss Parsons coming down to fifty, and after much fierce haggling, they finally agreed on forty pounds.

*

'You were very brave and clever,' Verity said once they were out of the shop and further down the Finchley Road.

Miss Parsons chuckled. 'To tell the truth, Verity, I rather enjoyed it. Believe me, that brooch and those pearls must have been much more valuable than we realized to get so much, so we certainly haven't robbed him. Now you may have to do this for your mother in future, so remember to aim high. You can always come down but never, ever accept the first offer.'

That evening Verity helped her mother and Miss Parsons to pack a small trunk with items that could be sold. They were mostly small items: a pocket watch, jewellery, a silver snuff box, tankards and photograph frames. But there was also the large silver pheasant, a tureen and some serving dishes, along with a complete set of cutlery.

'Archie's mother gave us this as a wedding present,' her mother said as she lifted the lid of the box and took out one knife from its velvet-covered nest. 'She bought it in Bond Street, and she never tired of pointing out that it cost a king's ransom. I just hope it brings in enough to make up for her wretched son's appalling behaviour.'

'I think it will bring you in a pretty penny,' Miss Parsons said, coming over to look at the cutlery. She picked up a serving spoon and examined the hallmark. 'My advice is to take it back to the shop it came from. This sort of cutlery never goes out of fashion; I bet they'll be glad to resell it.'

'But it weighs so much,' Verity's mother said, half lifting it. 'We can't walk around carrying it.'

Verity wished her mother would stop finding a problem with everything. If it wasn't the weight of the cutlery it was the chore of packing things, or being convinced her sister would refuse to take them in. Miss Parsons had snapped at her the previous day and said if she didn't fancy going to her sister's she could always rent a place for herself and Verity, and then get a job to be independent.

'Me work?' Her mother had looked horrified. 'What are you saying?'

'I have to work,' Miss Parsons pointed out. 'I'm quite sure Verity will have to when she is older too. So why not you?'

'But I wasn't brought up that way,' her employer protested.

'Do you have a private income?' Miss Parsons asked.

'You know I don't.'

'Then how do you plan to support yourself? I doubt your sister – who, if I'm not much mistaken, does work – will be prepared to keep you both for nothing. Funny Hazel wasn't brought up the same way as you!'

There were many pointed, sarcastic remarks from Miss Parsons in the days that followed, making Verity realize that her mother had kept her distance from her sister for all these years purely because she was a terrible snob and wanted to pretend she came out of the top drawer. But Verity was frightened about how her mother would cope once the housekeeper left. She hadn't cooked, cleaned or washed any clothes for years. Her days were spent in West End stores or having afternoon tea with her bridge cronies. The packed trunk was standing in the hall, awaiting Aunt Hazel's agreement that they could send it over to her, and then follow themselves when necessary. But how was Cynthia Wood going to survive in Lewisham?

Verity expressed her fears to Miss Parsons. 'You've

always run everything, even decided what we would eat,' she said. 'How will Mother manage?'

'I believe your Aunt Hazel will shake her out of that,' the older woman said with a smile. 'It'll be hard for you, caught in the crossfire, but try not to become their servant – or to despair, because as soon as you are fourteen you can leave school.'

It soothed Verity's anxiety a little to find Miss Parsons did really care about her; it seemed astounding that for all these years Verity hadn't known that.

'But what sort of a job will I get?' she asked. 'I've never had to think about working.'

'Well, my advice would be to go into service, at least at first, because that way you can leave home but have the security of being in someone else's home. Being trained as a maid would be easy for you, you've grown up seeing how it is done. That will stand you in good stead for all kinds of employment later on.'

Verity had a feeling that the older woman was speaking from personal experience. If she had left her family home at fourteen because of some disaster or bad feeling, it could explain why she never spoke about her past.

All that day and evening, Verity thought on what Miss Parsons had said. It was true she'd never considered that she might *have* to work, though she had sometimes imagined herself as a nurse, an actress or a secretary at different times. Mother and her teachers at school had always implied further education was a waste as she would just marry and have children. Verity actually liked the idea of working; she'd often thought that daughters who stayed at home until they married must be terribly bored all day. But she didn't fancy the idea of being a maid, not even if it got her away from home.

Maids worked very long hours, they were at the mercy of their mistress and other more senior staff, and she certainly wouldn't like to empty chamber pots for aristocratic people too lazy to walk down a corridor to a lavatory. She knew maids did have to do this, because Lily Armstrong, a girl at school who lived in a huge house in Belsize Park and had both upstairs and downstairs maids, had told her. But although Verity knew what she didn't want to do, she didn't know what she could do, or even what the choices were. Anyway, that was almost immaterial, as whatever she wanted to do – be it nursing, teaching or almost everything else – they wouldn't take her on at fourteen.

Verity felt scared. Her life so far had been utterly predictable and secure. Dull, maybe, but with good food, nice surroundings and lovely clothes, she certainly couldn't complain. Suddenly all that was gone.

Chapter Five

It was exactly six weeks from the day the police came to the house looking for Verity's father, when a letter came from the solicitors. It informed her mother that, as a result of her husband embezzling company funds, her home was going to be taken. She was advised she must leave the house in Daleham Gardens within seven days or suffer the indignity of bailiffs removing her from the property. Predictably Cynthia became hysterical.

Verity read the letter and found it was worded in a sympathetic, fair manner, explaining her mother could take clothes, bedding and essential equipment for the preparation of food with her, but she was to leave everything else in place. The solicitor pointed out that while she might feel this was unfair, as she had committed no crime, the law did not allow the wife or family of a criminal to benefit from a crime.

'How can he have done this to me?' Cynthia wailed. 'I may as well put my head in the gas oven and die, for there is nothing left for me in this world.'

'But you knew it was going to happen, Mrs Wood,' Miss Parsons said, rather sharply. She didn't hold with hysterics. 'And they could easily have humiliated you by sending bailiffs round here and ejecting you on to the street before you had a chance to sort out what you need. At least this way you can leave in a dignified manner.'

'But my wedding presents, my beautiful bureaux and the Persian carpets,' Cynthia hissed at the housekeeper, her eyes blazing. 'You don't know what it is to own such things, so how can you know how I feel?'

'In my opinion the most valuable thing in this entire house is Verity,' Miss Parsons retorted. 'You still have her, despite the deplorable way Mr Wood treated her. Be thankful for that, can't you?'

It was a revelation to Verity to hear such a thing said of her. And indeed to find Miss Parsons brave enough to challenge her mistress.

But her mother didn't ever appreciate any kind of criticism, and especially not from someone she considered to be beneath her.

'Don't you dare speak to me in that manner!' she raged.

'And I won't tolerate you speaking to me like that either,' Miss Parsons snapped back instantly. 'I haven't been paid since your husband disappeared, if you remember. I could have left then too, but I stayed because I felt you needed me.'

Verity held her breath, willing her mother to apologize to the housekeeper, because if she walked out now they wouldn't be able to cope.

There was complete silence for what seemed like minutes, the two older women staring at one another. Then finally, her mother spoke.

'I'm sorry. I'm all at sixes and sevens just now. I am relieved you didn't go.'

Verity exhaled gratefully.

By the second post a letter came from Aunt Hazel. Mother chose not to share her aunt's feelings with Verity, all she said was that they could go to Lewisham and therefore she intended to get a man to deliver the trunk of treasures there immediately.

Verity felt she'd had more than enough of her mother for one day, and had been stuck indoors for far too long. So without asking permission she picked up a cardigan and slipped out, intending to go to Camden Town to see if she could find someone who would tell her where Ruby was.

She found the Red Lion very quickly, but as she knew nothing about public houses she hadn't realized they closed in the afternoon.

Reluctant to go home empty-handed, she walked down an alley nearby and, as she hoped, she found herself at the backyard of the public house. A plump woman with straggly brown hair was putting bottles in wooden crates.

'You want sommat?' she called out when she saw Verity lurking by the gate.

'Yes, I was wondering if you knew a girl called Ruby Taylor? She told me she collected glasses here. We are friends.'

'Yes, she did help here,' the woman said, straightening up from filling the crates and coming over to Verity. 'But she's not here now.'

'Oh dear,' Verity sighed. 'Has she gone to prison?'

To her surprise the woman laughed.

'They don't send young girls to prison, ducks, not these days. But she 'as bin sent away, and it's the best thing that could've 'appened to 'er.'

'Oh no, poor Ruby! But what do you mean it was the best thing?'

The older woman leaned back against the wall and reached into her apron pocket for some cigarettes. She lit one and inhaled deeply before replying.

'Wiv 'er ma she never stood a chance,' she said. 'But a couple of years in the country wiv good people will do her a power of good. You ain't the girl she met up with in 'Ampstead?'

'Yes, I am,' Verity agreed, delighted that Ruby had told someone about her, as it implied she meant something to her. 'I really liked her too. I wanted her advice on what I should do; we've got some problems at home.'

The older woman smiled, revealing very badly stained teeth. 'I don't think Ruby would 'ave much good advice for a posh girl like you. But come on inside, I'll make us a cup of tea and maybe I can help you. I'm Maggie Tyrell by the way. And you?'

'Verity Wood.' Verity shot out her hand to shake the woman's. 'I'm delighted to meet you, Mrs Tyrell.'

'Just Maggie will do fine,' she said with a smile. 'Ruby was right about you, you are a toff.'

It was very dark inside the public house and Verity, who had never been in one before, almost gagged on the smell, which she realized must be beer and cigarettes. The back door brought them into a kind of vestibule behind the bar, and beyond that she could see lots of small tables and chairs. The walls were covered in advertising mirrors; they looked very old, as the mirror glass was speckled and tarnished.

But Maggie led her through to a small room along a narrow corridor. It was an office with piles of papers on a desk and clutter covering almost every surface. Maggie removed a box filled with jars of pickled eggs from a chair and told Verity to sit down.

'I put the kettle on earlier, so it must be nearly boiling now,' she said. 'I 'ope you don't mind being in 'ere, but upstairs is even worse. I never get time to give it a tidy-up.'

As Maggie disappeared back up the passage, Verity looked around at the piles of paper, boxes, tins, toilet rolls and even a large hank of rope lying on the floor and wondered why they didn't sort it all out. Her own home was so orderly, she found mess like this disturbing.

'Nice cuppa tea,' Maggie said as she came back with two earthenware mugs like Miss Parsons gave the gardener his tea in. 'Now you wanted to know about our Ruby?'

Verity took the tea; it was very strong and had a few tea leaves floating on the surface, she didn't think she'd be able to drink it. 'Yes. I haven't been well since the day it all happened, so I couldn't come before.'

'Well, it seems a copper down the nick felt sorry for 'er, on account of 'er ma. 'E got some welfare lady to the court, and what wiv me speakin' up fer her and that copper, the welfare lady come up wiv the plan to send Ruby down to Devon.'

'To what in Devon?' Verity was still imagining a prison.

'Well, it sounds like it's sommat like a children's 'ome. Only Ruby wrote to me when she got there and said she's the only kid just now, cos the lady of the 'ouse is too old to cope with little 'uns. It's by the sea, and she sounded 'appy.'

'I could do with being sent somewhere like that myself,' Verity blurted out without thinking.

'You! You've got the life of Riley, ain't yer?'

'Maybe I did have, but that's about to change,' Verity said hesitantly.

Maggie looked at her long and hard. 'Something bad 'appened?' she asked. 'You can tell me, if you want. It won't go beyond these four walls.'

Verity had been brought up never to talk about family matters to anyone, but this rather slovenly woman had a kind face, and she'd obviously cared about Ruby – and besides, Verity had an overwhelming desire to unburden herself. So she told her about her father, about the house and that she and her mother had to go and live with her Aunt Hazel.

'Well, well, well,' Maggie said thoughtfully. 'That is a pretty kettle of fish. I'm sorry for you, ducks, you are as nice as Ruby said you were. But it might be okay at your aunt's.'

Verity shook her head. 'She's mean, her house is nasty and she's always been horrid to Mother because she was jealous of her. I'll have to go to a new school, they'll laugh at me because I'm posh, and I'm going to hate Lewisham.'

'Well, yer aunt won't be jealous of yer ma no longer, and maybe the kids at school will like you, same as Ruby did, because you might be posh but you don't show off. Lewisham is no worse than 'ere, you might even find things to like about it. You gotta look on the bright side.'

'That isn't easy to do,' Verity said glumly. 'I feel like I'm being sent out to a wilderness all alone.'

'I bet that's what Ruby thought too when she got sent away,' Maggie half smiled. 'She's only allowed to send and get letters from folk they approve of. I'm one, but when I 'eard from her she sounded real chirpy. So when I write back I'll tell 'er you called round. I won't be able to tell 'er about yer pa or nothing like that, but I can say you'll be movin' 'ouse. If you let me have the address once you're settled, she'll know that means she can find you later on, or try and get permission to write to you.'

'You are very kind,' Verity said. 'I'm so glad Ruby had you in her corner.'

Maggie smiled. 'She's a good kid at 'eart, she only nicked stuff to live, not out of wickedness.'

Verity thought on Maggie's words as she went home. She wondered if her father had stolen from need or just wickedness. Somehow she felt it was the latter.

'Do you like fish, Ruby?' Wilby asked as she unpacked some groceries that had just been delivered. 'If you don't, I can always make something else for you. I have ham or sausages.'

Ruby was sitting at the kitchen table having what Wilby called 'elevenses'. This was milk and a fruit bun.

She wasn't sure how to answer the question. It felt to her that she'd been picked up and dropped in a heavenly place where warmth, food and kind words were the order of the day. Yet put one foot wrong and she might be whisked back to the real world. This lovely lady was really called Mrs Wilberforce but she said Ruby was to call her Wilby, as it was less of a mouthful.

'I like fish,' Ruby said, deciding that was the best choice because it must have been bought already. 'But then there ain't any food I don't like.'

'What a joy it is to have a child with me who isn't fussy,' Mrs Wilberforce replied, beaming at Ruby. 'After lunch I think we'll walk into Torquay, so you learn to find your way around without me. Would you like that?'

'Yes, please,' Ruby said. She wanted to say more, about how lucky she felt to have been brought here instead of being sent to some form of institution. How much she liked this house, Wilby and the new clothes she'd been given. But every time she opened her mouth to speak she was aware of how badly she spoke, just as she was aware that she needed to learn good manners and how posh folk lived.

Yet when she had first met Wilby at the court, she'd been sure this tall, smartly dressed woman with the posh voice was going to make her into her slave. Why else would anyone take a thieving slum kid into their home?

The judge had said that he'd listened to what Maggie Tyrell, the landlady of the Red Lion, had said about Ruby, and also the arresting police officer who knew a great deal about Ruby's home life. He'd also noted her mother wasn't present at the court.

He went on to say that he felt Ruby would benefit greatly by being put into the care of Mrs Wilberforce at her home in Devon, and he hoped that she would behave herself there and appreciate that she'd only been given this chance because good people had spoken up for her. He stressed that if she was to get herself into trouble again, he would not be so lenient next time.

When Wilby pushed the front seat of the car forward and got Ruby to climb into the back, she saw this as a way of preventing her escaping. Even giving her some sandwiches and an apple to eat felt like buying her trust. But it turned out to be a very long drive, and Ruby grew tired of remaining alert for a chance to escape, so she curled up on the seat, her head on a cushion left there, and fell asleep. The last thing she remembered thinking was that she'd run for it as soon as they got to this woman's home.

It was dark when she woke, and Wilby said they were nearly there. Ruby needed to pee, and it crossed her mind she could use that as an excuse to get out of the car and run for it. But she couldn't see a single house, and she didn't much fancy roaming around fields in the dark without any idea of which direction to go in, and without any money.

Finally they came into a town, which Wilby said was Torquay. 'My house is in Babbacombe just a few miles further on,' she said. 'Tomorrow you'll see the sea.'

Ruby was sure she was expected to be excited by that. But even though she was, she had no intention of showing it.

She said nothing when they went into the house either, even though it was almost as grand as some of the houses in Hampstead.

Wilby told her that she'd had many children staying with her over the years. She said she was getting a bit too old to run around after little ones, so now she only had children over the age of ten.

'It can be difficult at your age to fit in at a new school,' she went on to say. 'So I'm going to teach you myself, at least for the time being. Now let me show you your room.'

The bedroom with two beds and lovely polished furniture was twice the size of the one room Ruby had lived in with her mother in Kentish Town. She so much wanted to sit at the dressing table and admire herself in the triple mirror, but to do so would show some enthusiasm for both Wilby and this house. So she said nothing.

It was the bath that made her say plenty. The only bath she'd ever been in was a small tin one and she'd had to stand up in it to wash. She didn't use that very often either, because it took at least a shilling in the gas meter to heat the water. Her mother went to the public baths every week, but she had never taken Ruby with her.

But confronted with a huge white bath filled with water, she was really scared, not just of the water but of taking her clothes off in front of Wilby. And it was clear the woman intended to be there, because she said she'd wash her hair for her.

'I'm not getting in there, you want to drown me,' she bellowed at Wilby. 'I'll be at your bleedin' mercy in there, and I ain't the sort to let anyone push me around.'

'What a very silly thing to say,' Wilby said with a smile. 'Why would I want to drown you when I took the trouble to drive up to London to meet you?'

'I dunno, but it seems like you want me as some kind of skivvy,' Ruby shot back at her.

'The police officer who told me about you and suggested I came to the court is a very old friend. Through him I've had quite a few children to stay with me, mostly when they've been neglected by their parents. I do this because I wasn't lucky enough to have any children of my own, and it gives me pleasure to see children blossom with good food, fresh air and affection. That's what I'm offering you, Ruby. I don't need a skivvy, I'm hoping you and I will be happy together for a very long time. But children who live in my house have to have baths and their hair washed.'

'I'm not a bleedin' child. I'm old enough to go to work,' Ruby retorted.

'You have been made to think like an adult to get by,' Wilby said. 'I don't think you ever got to have a real childhood, but it's not too late to do some of the things you missed out on. Let's start with the bath?'

Ruby felt something kind of ping inside her; it was a realization that this woman was a good one, and living here might not be so bad. Suddenly she was crying like a baby and when Wilby put her arms around her to comfort her, she blurted out that she was afraid to take her clothes off.

'Well, I'll turn my back while you take them off,' Wilby suggested. 'Not that you've got anything I haven't seen a hundred times before. And I do have to wash your hair. But how about being really brave and peeling off and hopping into the bath? You'll find it's lovely.'

Wilby was right, of course, just as she was about everything.

It was lovely for Ruby to soak in warm water, to feel really clean and have her hair washed. Later Wilby gave her a pretty flannel nightdress and some slippers, and let her go back downstairs for her hair to dry by the fire.

'You've got beautiful hair,' Wilby said, winding a curl around her finger. 'It's your crowning glory, so you must take good care of it. In a day or two I'll take you to a hairdresser who will trim it up into a good shape and make it easier for you to manage.'

When it was time for bed, Ruby went up to her new bedroom and sat at the dressing table. She hardly recognized the girl looking back at her in the mirror, because she was pretty, with pink and white skin, hair the colour of new pennies, shining like Christmas tinsel. It felt so good to be really clean and smelling of lavender soap. She felt that the old Ruby – the dirty, thieving one – had gone down the plughole with the bath water, and this girl here in the mirror was a brand-new Ruby.

She wondered what Verity would make of her new appearance, and if she'd ever get to see her again.

Verity sat on the bed in the tiny box room at Aunt Hazel's and the tears which had been threatening all day finally fell.

The bed was hard and lumpy, she had nothing but a nail on the back of the door to hang her clothes, there were damp patches on the walls, and the ancient wallpaper was peeling off in places.

All her books, toys and doll collection had been left back in Daleham Gardens. It might be true she was too old for dolls and toys, and she'd read all the books, but without any of the props of her childhood she felt orphaned. Downstairs her mother was bickering with Aunt Hazel, because there was no wardrobe in the spare room to hang up all her clothes.

'Best thing you can do is sell them,' Aunt Hazel shouted. She had been grumpy from the moment she saw the cab driver hauling the heavy trunk to the front door. 'You certainly won't be going anywhere to wear them now.'

For once Verity felt sympathy for her mother. She might be vain, selfish and empty-headed, but surely her sister could understand that she was distraught at leaving her home? So why cast even more gloom over how her life would be from now on?

But that was Aunt Hazel all over, and Verity knew she was never going to like living under her roof one bit. Everything about 7 Weardale Road shrieked neglect and poverty – from the broken pane of glass in the front door, covered with a piece of board, to the musty smell and the lint-thin carpet runner going up the stairs. The house was probably at its worst today, because it was raining. As they'd got to the front door, water showered over them from a hole in the guttering. Back in Daleham Gardens the front gardens overlooking the street were bright with spring flowers, windows sparkled and brass ornaments on front doors were polished daily. The house there was full of light, it smelled of polish and baking, whereas this house was dark and sullen, and it didn't even have an indoor lavatory or bathroom.

Saying goodbye to Miss Parsons was awful too. She might have been harsh and cold, but she was a great cook and she'd kept their home beautifully. In the last weeks after Archie Wood had gone, she had unexpectedly proved herself to have a really kind heart too, showing sincere concern for both her mistress and Verity.

'You'll have to think for yourself now, Verity, because your mother relies on other people to do things for her,' she'd said yesterday, just before leaving to take up a position as housekeeper for a priest in Highgate. 'Work hard at your new school, get your school certificate, then maybe you can have a good career. I know you are a clever, resourceful girl, and you'll be in my thoughts and prayers.'

Verity hugged her, and for once the housekeeper didn't

stiffen but hugged Verity back. 'Keep my address by you and write now and then to tell me how you are getting on,' she murmured into Verity's hair. 'Forgive me for not telling you before how much I enjoyed watching you grow up. But I always thought it wasn't my place to say such things.'

It seemed tragic to Verity that in all the years this woman had run the house for the family, her famously starchy demeanour was what she believed was expected of her. If she had revealed her true nature years ago, maybe life would have been different for all of them.

Almost as soon as Miss Parsons left with her one small suitcase, mother had become hysterical. 'What am I going to do?' she wailed. 'I can't do this alone.'

Verity had to point out to her that Miss Parsons had already packed for them and had posted a set of keys to the solicitor. She'd cleaned the house from top to bottom and booked the cab to come and get them. There wasn't anything further for her mother to do.

Yet it was plain to Verity that this was exactly what the housekeeper had meant about her mother expecting someone to do everything for her. And it looked as if that someone would have to be Verity, as Aunt Hazel wasn't the kind to wait on anyone.

She had been trying to think of the move as an adventure for the last few days. She might, after all, make new and exciting friends; Aunt Hazel might turn out to be a lot nicer than she expected; and her new school might be better than her old one. But however optimistic she tried to be, the only real glimmer of light Verity could see was that the wide-open spaces of Blackheath and Greenwich Park were only a short walk from Weardale Road.

Lewisham did have some fine shops. One was Chiesmans, the department store where she'd once been taken to see Santa Claus. Aunt Hazel worked there, making soft furnishings. But then they wouldn't have any money to spend in such a smart shop.

Yet however hard Verity tried to think positive thoughts as the taxi crossed the Thames into South London and her mother burst into tears yet again, Verity felt she'd lost everything she held dear.

Sitting dejectedly in the tiny bedroom, her memories of the journey to Aunt Hazel's house were harshly interrupted.

'What are you snivelling for?'

Verity looked up at the question. Aunt Hazel was standing in the bedroom doorway, her hands on her hips, and wearing an extremely disdainful expression. Like her younger sister she had sharp features, but Verity doubted she'd ever been pretty like Cynthia. Her eyes were small and a faded blue, and she had many wrinkles around her mouth – probably from constantly pursing her lips in disapproval. Her light brown hair had long since turned iron grey, and she wore it in a tight little bun at the nape of her neck. In a plain navy-blue, long-sleeved dress without a bit of lace, a brooch or a necklace to lift it, she looked closer to sixty than her real age of forty-eight.

'I just feel sad and lonely,' Verity said, not knowing any other way to express her feelings.

'You'll be off to school next week, so you won't be lonely for long,' Hazel said with a sniff. 'You should be grateful I took you in, heaven only knows where you'd be without me.'

'We are grateful. You've been very kind, offering us a place to stay,' Verity said. 'It's just such a shock to have to leave our home.'

'I'm glad to see you have good manners,' Hazel said. 'Now buck up and come on down and help me get the tea.'

Verity had always known that Aunt Hazel worked in Chiesmans, but her mother obviously thought it was something to be ashamed of because when, over a supper of bread and cheese, Hazel mentioned putting in a good word for her sister with the personnel officer at Chiesmans, Cynthia bristled.

'Me work in a shop!' Cynthia exclaimed in absolute horror, as if her sister had suggested sending her down a coal mine.

'You have to earn a wage,' Hazel said with a shrug. 'I can't afford to keep you for nothing. And Chiesmans is, after all, a prestigious store, the gown department is the finest outside of Regent Street. You are knowledgeable about fashion, so put it to good use.'

'Would they take me on for a Saturday?' Verity asked. She was impressed that Hazel made curtains, and for such a smart shop, though she wondered why she hadn't made any nice ones for her own house.

'I could ask,' Hazel said.

'You plan to make us a family of shop girls?' her mother asked, eyes wide with horror.

'Now look here, Cynny,' Hazel said, using her sister's pet name for the first time. 'I know from a young girl you've always tried to pretend you came from some grand family, your ideas have always been well above your station. But this is reality now, lodging with your sister in a small terraced house in Lewisham. You have no home of your own, no money, and when Archie is found he'll be sent to prison. And you have a child to support. You cannot afford to be a snob any more.'

Cynthia's reply to this was a strangled sob. Hazel looked warningly at Verity, as if daring her to defend her mother.

But Verity had no intention of doing so; she knew Aunt Hazel was right.

Chapter Six

School was as bad as Verity had feared. It was in Leahurst Road, just a short walk from Aunt Hazel's, past Hither Green Station. Leahurst was a long, bleak road with no trees to soften the terraced houses.

Lee Manor School was right at the end of the road, consisting of three buildings originally designed for junior boys in one, girls in another and the third building for girls aged eleven to fourteen. But the boys' building was now mixed juniors, and the girls' building housed the infants.

Miss Ranger was Verity's teacher. She made Verity stand in front of the class and tell the rest of the girls about herself.

Verity said very little, just her name, age and that she used to live in Hampstead but now she and her mother had come to live with her aunt in Weardale Road.

There were around sixteen girls in the class and Verity sensed by their closed expressions that they had taken against her on sight. At the first morning break, when they went out into the playground, a tall dark-haired girl who she was later to learn was Madeline Grant came up to her with a sneer on her face. 'Speaking posh won't cut no ice with us,' she said. 'And where's yer dad? Is he dead or has he run out on you?'

Verity didn't know how to answer. It was tempting to

say he was dead, but she was afraid this girl might already know the truth about him, and even if she didn't she was likely to find out before long.

'He ran out on us,' she said, which was essentially true. 'But I'm hoping both Mother and I will make new friends here.'

'Oh, do you, now?' Madeline sneered. 'I suppose you think smart clothes and a posh voice opens doors everywhere?'

'Not at all,' Verity replied. 'I just hope that people will be willing to get to know me and like me, whatever I look and sound like.'

They had an audience now, and a quick glance around made Verity feel as if she was being circled by a pack of wolves. There were mean girls at her last school who treated new girls this way, but she hadn't really expected it to happen here. But worse still, she had no idea how to deal with it.

'You cocky cow,' Madeline exclaimed. 'You think you're "it", don't you?'

'I'm sorry if I have offended you in some way, it certainly wasn't intentional.'

A teacher rang a bell to go in then, but Verity knew it wasn't going to blow over. She was dreading dinner time, as no doubt it would start again.

It did start again at dinner time, with prods in the ribs, nasty remarks flung at her, and one girl even tried to trip her up as they were filing back into school. But it didn't stop with that day.

Every day there was something more, and she rarely ever

71

knew who was responsible. She found her coat sleeves tied in a knot, her coat pockets filled with rice, a mouldy sandwich in her desk, ink poured over her essay book. And when she went to put on her apron for Domestic Science, she found it was sopping wet. Then there were all the taunts and name calling – not just from Madeline, but other girls too.

Verity just took it, day after day, assuming that if she didn't react they would get bored and stop it. But she dreaded going to school, and feared break times even more. She had nightmares in which the girls were encircling her with knives in their hands, their eyes blazing with a terrifying light.

It didn't help that when she got home, her mother would launch into her grievance for that day: that the cat from next door was doing his business in their garden, that the bread was stale, that she couldn't possibly go to the public baths for a bath. And how did Hazel expect her to wash her clothes when all the water had to be heated? She never attempted to get the evening meal ready, even though Hazel wrote down each morning what they were having. So Verity had to do it, while her mother carried on with her catalogue of woes. Cleaning, washing up, it was all left for Verity or Hazel, her mother didn't even make her own bed.

Two, then three weeks passed, the weather was getting warmer all the time and the days longer, but this brought new grouses for her mother: that the milk had turned sour on the doorstep, that there were flies in the kitchen, that the windows didn't open and the River Quaggy, which ran nearby, smelled horrible.

But if Verity's home life was miserable, school was even worse.

Day after day the other girls found new ways to torment her, tripping her up in netball, hiding her gym shoes, pulling a few pages out of her English or Maths book. And once, while in the lavatory out in the playground, someone got into the next cubicle, reached over the dividing wall and pulled the chain, and the vigorous flush soaked her underclothes and her gymslip.

On the Friday afternoon, at the end of her third week at Lee Manor, Verity leapt to her feet the moment the home-time bell went, glad she'd have respite over the weekend from a stuffy classroom, bullying and insults.

Stopping only to grab her blazer from her peg, she was just leaving the cloakroom when she felt something wet on her back. Assuming it was merely water, she ignored it. But as she went to put her blazer on, she flicked her plaits forward over her shoulder and found they'd been dipped in ink.

A glance in the washbasin mirror showed her she had black ink all down the back of her white blouse and her gymslip; as she had moved her plaits, it was now all down her front too.

Madeline's desk was right behind Verity's, so she knew it was Madeline who had dipped them in the inkwell. It was the last straw, and this time she knew she must act or be bullied for evermore.

She waited by the school door, just hidden from view, too angry to be scared. She could hear Madeline inside crowing with delight at what she'd done. 'I hope her blonde hair will turn green with it,' she sniggered. 'I just wish I'd dripped it on top of her head.'

As Madeline came through the door, Verity pounced on her. She didn't care if she got hurt, she just wanted to give this horrible girl a taste of her own medicine. She caught Madeline by her shoulder and spun her round so she was facing her, then punched her straight in the nose with her fist. The girl's nose seemed to explode, blood spurting out in all directions.

'Not so funny now, is it?' Verity screamed at her. 'With luck your nose is broken, and you'll be ugly as well as nasty.'

Having expected Madeline to respond with extreme violence, it was a real surprise to see the girl just holding her nose and crying. But just in case this was a tactic intended to disarm, Verity didn't back away but punched her in the stomach for good measure. 'You've tormented me from my first day here and I'd done nothing to you,' she ranted. 'So how do you like being hurt and humiliated? Not nice, is it?'

The punch in the stomach had Madeline doubling up in pain and Verity noticed to her shock that none of her acolytes, the girls who had helped bully her, were stepping in to help their leader.

'Where are your chums now?' Verity asked as, one by one, the girls were stepping away. 'Did you get them in your power by bullying them too? Go on back into class and snivel to Miss Ranger. Doesn't look like you'll get any sympathy out here.'

Verity walked away then, fully expecting someone to come after her, but no one did. When she looked back, Madeline was still hunched over by the school door, and all the other girls were grouped together talking, well away from her.

For the first time in weeks Verity had something to smile about.

*

Verity went back to school on Monday in trepidation. However well she had dealt with Madeline on Friday, she knew that over the weekend the girl could have talked her chums round to supporting her. She could also have gone to Miss Ranger and claimed she was the victim of an unprovoked attack.

But as she walked through the school gate into the play-ground, Susan Wallace came straight up to her. Verity had noticed this one girl more than anyone else in the class because she was clever, top of the class, also rather beauti-ful with shiny black hair and lovely dark almond-shaped eyes, giving her a rather glamorous air.

'You were very brave on Friday,' she said. 'So brave I felt ashamed I hadn't stepped in to help you before.'

Verity had observed that although Susan seemed to get on with her classmates she wasn't particularly pally with anyone.

'It wasn't brave, I just lost my temper,' Verity said. 'I expect she'll get me back in some way.'

'I don't think so,' Susan smiled. 'Like most bullies she's a coward; now she knows you can fight back, she'll be scared. When I first met her she used to call me names all the time – mostly Chinky or Ping Pong, on account of my eyes. I slammed her desk lid down on her head one day. And then sat on it for a few minutes. She screamed like a banshee, but it did the trick, she never called me names after that. She always picks on someone who has something different – with me my eyes, and you, the way you speak. Two girls have left school because of her.'

Verity was amused by how Susan had dealt with Mad-eline, and she was touched this girl was trying to make things better for her. 'I've got no intention of leaving, not till I'm fourteen,' she said.

Susan put her arm through Verity's as they walked across the playground. 'What are you going to do when you leave school?' she asked.

'I'm waiting for some divine revelation from on high,' Verity replied.

Susan giggled. 'You're cleverer than most of the girls here,' she said. 'I noticed how good you were at Mental Arithmetic, impressive.'

'At my old school we had tests twice a week, our teacher would fire out the sums and God help anyone who was slow in answering. But I like all Maths, it's challenging. I liked Science too, but we don't have that here.'

'Do girls need that?' Susan asked.

'I don't see why girls only get to do subjects that are good for wives and mothers,' Verity said. 'Look what happened during the war! Women had to take over all the jobs men used to do, and they did them well. So many men didn't come back that we still need more engineers, scientists and doctors. There isn't any real reason why a girl couldn't be as good as a man at most jobs. If she had the right training –'

The bell ringing for class ended the conversation abruptly.

Verity was relieved to see Madeline wasn't at school that day. She wasn't hauled out of class to see the headmistress, as she'd half expected, and all the other girls in the class were pleasant to her. Verity was asked to read out an essay she'd written about her four favourite books. Miss Ranger said she'd written with such passion it would make the whole class want to read them.

76

Everyone clapped when she'd finished, and suddenly Lee Manor School didn't look so bad and even moving to this area didn't seem so tragic. She hadn't ever got any praise at Oak Lodge School back in Belsize Park – and even if she had, she doubted the girls there would have smiled at her as if she was some kind of heroine, the way they were doing here.

Madeline was away from school for three days and when she finally came back, sticking plaster across her nose, Verity was delighted to see she looked nervous. But Verity was in a forgiving mood, so she went up to her and asked how she was.

'I'm fine,' Madeline said, keeping her eyes down as if half expecting another punch.

'I'm glad to hear that, and I hope your nose isn't too sore,' Verity said. 'Now shall we put this behind us and pretend we've just met for the first time?'

'Okay,' Madeline said in a small voice.

Verity held out her hand. 'Hello, I'm Verity Wood, and I'm pleased to meet you. What's your name?'

Madeline took the hand and shook it weakly. 'Madeline Grant, and welcome to Lee Manor,' she said.

Verity smiled. 'Thank you, Madeline. I trust there is no bullying here at this school? I can't abide it.'

School became a kind of refuge from home life. Since hitting Madeline she'd found the other girls were eager to befriend her, and though she found most of them to be empty-headed and rather dull, it was comforting to be sought out. All the other girls, Susan included, had South London accents and so now and again someone teased her about the way she spoke. Verity didn't mind being teased, but she did try to modify her way of speaking so she didn't stand out so much.

Susan had become a true friend; she had a sharp mind, a wonderful sense of humour and an interesting family. Going home with her, Verity found that beyond the end of Leahurst Road, going towards Lee, there were rather beautiful tree-lined streets with big houses and lovely gardens. Susan lived in one of these roads, Handen Road, by the Church of the Good Shepherd. Her father was an accountant and her mother painted. She also had two brothers and a younger sister.

Not far from Susan's home there was also a majestic library in what had once been the manor house. The gardens of the house, complete with a large duck pond and the River Quaggy running through them, were now a pretty park called Manor House Gardens.

Going to the library gave Verity the perfect excuse on Saturday afternoons to meet Susan. They would both quickly find a book and then, if it wasn't raining, they'd go into the park. There always seemed so much to talk about that a couple of hours flew by, and it made Sunday spent with Mother and Aunt Hazel more bearable.

Verity loved hearing about Susan's home life. It sounded warm, chaotic and full of laughter.

'Father often says, "Accountants are supposed to have pristine well-organized homes, obedient docile children and a pretty wife who dances attendance on her husband." It makes us all laugh, including him,' Susan giggled. 'Mother is usually smeared with paint, she's a terrible cook and housekeeper. Ben is always playing the piano very loudly, he has ambitions to play in a big swing band. John collects creatures – caterpillars, grass snakes, mice and anything else he can find. He wants to be a vet. Then Cissie, that's short for Cecelia, she wants to be a ballerina. She's not very good at ballet, just as I wasn't. But unlike me, she thinks she is.'

Verity hadn't been invited there yet. And in a way she hoped she never would be, because she might be expected to reciprocate, and taking anyone home to Weardale Road would be so very embarrassing. She dealt with the very real possibility she might have to invite her friend one day by exaggerating her mother and her aunt's deficiencies with humour.

'Mother sits around all day sighing and talking about all she's lost, the chandeliers, the velvet curtains, our housekeeper, Georgian silver. Aunt Hazel shrieks at her to shut up and tells her to get down to the butcher's and get a bit of scrag end for our tea.'

Verity had been deliberately vague about the reasons why they came to live with Aunt Hazel. She had said her father skipped off, leaving them in financial difficulties, but not that he was on the run for embezzlement. She had already made her mind up that, if this should come out, she'd pretend she hadn't known. Police had called at Aunt Hazel's twice since they had moved there, but so far they hadn't caught Archie. The last time they came, the police said they believed he had left the country, and Mother said she thought he'd only come back to Daleham Gardens the night his crime was discovered in order to get his passport.

Late one evening Verity was in bed but she'd left the

door open, because it was a hot night, and she heard her aunt and her mother talking about the missing money.

'I don't think he was the kind to hoard cash,' Cynthia said. 'He'd be too frightened of me finding it. So he must have been putting it into another bank account, perhaps in a false name, because it certainly wasn't in our household account.'

'I told you as soon as you met him he was tricky, but you scoffed at that,' Aunt Hazel said, and Verity could imagine her aunt crossing her arms across her chest and doing the sucking lemons thing she did with her mouth in disapproval. 'But then you were a tricky customer yourself, always looking for the main chance. You two deserved one another.'

'How can you say such a thing about me? It isn't true,' Cynthia bleated.

'Come off it, Cynny, you were scheming at the age of five, making out you were practically royalty. Anyway, I reckon Archie had been planning for a long time to take this money and run out on you,' she went on, her voice sharp with malice. 'I bet he had some fast floozy in tow too.'

Cynthia burst into tears at that and Hazel went on to tell her she'd got to pull herself together, get a job and rebuild her life.

Verity thought her aunt talked a lot of sense, even if she was mean and grumpy. She said if Cynthia was bringing in a wage they could get decorators in to smarten the house up, and a new carpet on the stairs. She pointed out that she hadn't had any housekeeping money from her for two weeks now, so Cynthia had better sell something if she wanted to stay.

In October Verity would be fourteen, and her aunt had said Chiesmans would give her a trial day with a view to taking her on. They had made an appointment for Cynthia to be interviewed too but she hadn't turned up for it, claiming she was ill. Verity could sense her aunt's utter frustration; she'd pointed out that when winter came, her sister had better not think she was going to sit by a blazing fire all day, as she wouldn't allow it to be lit until she got home from work.

Verity didn't understand her mother at all. If she wanted to get on her sister's good side, all she needed to do was show her appreciation at being taken in by making Hazel more comfortable. Cooking, cleaning and doing the washing was all that was needed, and surely Mother was bored stiff doing nothing all day.

Hazel had screamed out the other day that Cynthia was a parasite – and it was true, she was. Verity had located a pawnshop in Lewisham and suggested it was time to go and sell something else to give Hazel some money, but so far her mother had refused. She still squeezed past the big trunk of her clothes in the bedroom, as if believing that any day someone would rescue her from this shabby little house and put her back in the surroundings where she felt she belonged.

Verity had told Susan a little of the situation, though in a comic manner, with her spoiled mother and mean-spirited aunt squabbling all the time. But it was hard to make jokes about it when the reality of it was so bleak. Verity was quite sure Susan didn't go home from school to clear the unwashed breakfast things still in the sink, to prepare the dinner for her family and to clean the house. But Verity felt she had to, for fear Hazel would throw them out.

Hazel got nastier and nastier about keeping them for nothing – to the point when, finally, she bought just one chop for herself for Sunday dinner and nothing for her sister or Verity.

'I am not feeding you for nothing any more,' she spat at her sister. 'What makes you think you have the right to live off me? Have you no pride? And what sort of message is this giving Verity? Is she going to grow up thinking the world owes her a living too?'

The smell of Aunt Hazel's pork chop cooking made Verity's stomach contract with hunger, but all there was left in the cupboard was one tin of sardines. She spread them on four slices of toast to share with her mother, and as they ate them Verity insisted that they sell something.

'We can take the silver pheasant and the Bond Street cutlery up to Blackheath to a shop I've seen,' she said. 'It isn't a pawnshop, but they buy silver – it says in the window. I think we'll get a better price there. We can go when I get home from school.'

'I can't possibly go,' her mother said stubbornly. 'You will have to do it.'

Verity tried pleading that she was too scared to go alone. When that didn't work, she refused to go.

'Then we won't eat,' her mother replied, without even looking at her. 'Miss Parsons told you what to do. I can't see why you are being such a baby about it.'

'Why can't you behave like a grown-up?' Verity retorted. 'You are supposed to look after me, not the other way round.'

But her mother didn't relent. She just sat there at the kitchen table staring into space, oblivious to her daughter crying, or the fact that there was nothing left in the house to eat.

That evening Verity went up to her room and lay on her bed, beyond crying now but wishing she had someone she could confide in. She thought about Ruby a great deal and wondered if Maggie Tyrell had written to her and passed on Verity's new address. Maybe she should go back to Maggie and ask? She thought she ought to write to Miss Parsons too. But with nothing cheerful to tell her, was there any point?

The next morning, as Verity was leaving the house for school, Aunt Hazel thrust a package at her. 'Take this sandwich for your lunch. I kept a few bits in my room,' she said by way of explaining where it had come from. 'I know you don't want to take the things to sell. But I'll get some time off work, if you like, and come with you.'

Verity was astounded that her aunt understood how she felt, and that she'd made her a sandwich. She had already decided she had to go to the shop alone anyway. But it was good to know she had an ally; that made her feel much braver.

'No, you don't need to take time off. I can do it,' she said.

'You are a good girl,' Aunt Hazel said. 'I wish I could say you are a credit to your mother. But however you managed to turn out so well, it had nothing to do with her. You can put the things in that wheeled shopping basket of mine, they are far too heavy to carry all the way to Blackheath.'

*

83

When Verity got home from school the house was silent, her mother was fast asleep on her bed. It was tempting to wake her up and try to plead for her to come to the jewellery shop, but she knew she wouldn't be able to persuade her. As she stood there looking down on her sleeping mother, she observed how Cynthia had stopped making an effort with her appearance.

Her hair resembled an untidy bird's nest, hastily put up without taking any care. She had a food stain on the front of her sleeveless striped cotton dress and her bare legs looked mottled, like hairy sausages. Even without getting close she smelled of stale sweat, and yet this was a woman who had once been very particular.

To see her like this was more alarming than her refusal to help sell some goods, or her not trying to get a job, as it suggested she'd given up all together. Verity wished there was something she could do or say that might give her mother the will to start again.

But getting some money was the priority for now, so Verity dug out the wheeled shopping basket from under the stairs and loaded the silver pheasant and the cutlery set into it. She stuffed a couple of towels down around them so they wouldn't rattle and couldn't be seen.

As she walked up Lee Park to Blackheath, the hill seemed extra steep and it was so hot she felt sick. She knew it was mostly nerves, not just from the heat but because she'd passed men hanging around in groups on Lee High Road, and she was afraid they might suspect she had something valuable with her and come after her. Back in Hampstead she hadn't really been aware of the Depression, which was mentioned on the news so often, but here in Lewisham it was very obvious with so many men out of work. She guessed their wives and families often went hungry.

She had gone to bed hungry last night for the first time ever, and it was horrible. It had made her think of Ruby and how hungry she'd been the day she bought her the pie. She could understand now why Ruby had to steal – in fact, if she was really hungry and didn't have these things to sell, she would too.

She paused for breath at the top of Lee Park. It was so hot the road was shimmering like a mirage, and she was perspiring. She mopped her face with her handkerchief and told herself if she could get the eighty pounds Aunt Hazel had suggested for the silver, she would buy an ice cream to eat on the way back.

Rosen's, the jewellery shop, was halfway up Tranquil Vale, and her heart was pounding with fright as she approached it.

She took a deep breath outside, mentally pulled herself up straight and opened the shop door. A bell tinkled and a small, bald man in gold-rimmed spectacles smiled at her.

'Good day, miss,' he said. 'What can I do for you?'

Verity closed the door behind her, and took another deep breath before replying. 'Would you like to look at this silver and give me a good price for it?' she blurted out.

She lifted the silver pheasant out first and put it on his counter, then the wooden box of cutlery. 'My father died suddenly a few months ago,' she said. 'I'm afraid he left me and Mother in a real pickle financially. We've had to move to a rented flat here and Mother isn't very well. I think it's the shock affecting her.'

'How sad,' the gentleman said. 'But how fortunate for your mother that she has such a sensible, brave daughter. Did she say how much she was hoping to get for these goods?'

'A hundred and thirty pounds,' Verity said, remembering what Miss Parsons had said about asking for more. 'The cutlery was a wedding present and it came from a store in Bond Street.'

'So I see,' he said, taking a knife from the box and looking at it closely. He picked up several different pieces and checked them over. Then he picked up the pheasant and, turning it upside down, examined the hallmark.

'How old is the pheasant?' he asked.

'I don't know exactly, but it belonged to my great-grandparents. They were rather grand and lived in Shropshire. Father said he used to love visiting them because they had so many treasures like that. He would hate us selling it, but we have no choice.'

The pheasant's origins were true, but she made up the bit about her father loving to visit his grandparents purely because it sounded nice. In fact her father had said they were old skinflints, and he hated going there.

'I can't give you that much, my dear,' Mr Rosen said. 'We are in the middle of a depression, as I'm sure you know, and people are not buying silver. The most I could give you is seventy-five.'

Verity looked right at the man and let her eyes fill with tears. 'Please make it ninety,' she pleaded. 'We still have to pay for father's headstone.'

Mr Rosen shook his head. 'I cannot, my dear. It might be months, even years, before I can sell these things. But I feel for you, so I'll go to eighty.'

'Eighty-five, or I'll have to try somewhere else,' she said, picking up the pheasant as if to put it back in the basket.

There was a lengthy pause, and Verity held her breath. 'Fair enough, eighty-five,' he agreed. 'You drive a hard bargain.'

After he'd counted out the notes for her, Verity asked him to put them in an envelope. She dropped the envelope down the front of her gymslip, and tightened the sash around her waist so it couldn't fall out.

'Is that safe?' Mr Rosen asked, frowning at her.

'Safe as houses,' she said, patting it. She wanted to smile, to sing and see him smile too, but she reminded herself she was supposed to be upset about her father's death. 'Thank you, sir. You've been very kind.'

It was only as she walked back down Tranquil Vale pulling the empty wheeled basket behind her, her other hand over the package in her gymslip, that she remembered about the ice cream. She couldn't take any money out now – not without attracting unwanted attention – and anyway, any shopkeeper would be reluctant to change a five-pound note for just a penny ice cream.

But it didn't matter so much now. Aunt Hazel would be happy, and maybe even her mother might raise a smile or two.

Chapter Seven

Archie opened the window of the hotel in Rouen where he'd been staying for the past week. With a length of rope tied around the handle of his suitcase, he carefully lowered it down behind a bush in the garden. He would leave the hotel within the hour, as if just popping out on business, but then double back to collect his case and avoid paying his substantial bill.

He had caught a ferry from Dover to Calais early in the morning the day after he'd run from Daleham Gardens. With a sizable lump on his head inflicted by that witch Miss Parsons, he was feeling none too clever, but he knew if he stayed in England he'd soon be caught.

Since then he'd been doing what he was best at, gambling and finding gullible women to support him until his mythical ship came in. He liked French women – they were better dressed and sexier than English women – and as his French wasn't very good, he had the perfect excuse for not telling them anything much about himself.

Archie was off now to see Françoise Albin, a rich widow in her early fifties. He'd met her in the Church of Saint-Maclou where she had been arranging flowers. He often dropped into churches, because he'd found them to be a veritable hive of lonely and grieving women. He only had to kneel for a while, pretending to be deep in prayer, then light a candle, pausing as if thinking about the person the candle was for, and before long a woman would approach him. To be fair to them, they usually offered genuine sympathy, but it was so easy to turn that into something more useful to him. He told different stories each time: sometimes a wife who had died after a long illness, a child who had met a tragic death, or a sibling snatched from him too soon.

So many of these lonely women had been wishing for love and passion, and who was he to deprive them of that? He could fake love and romance, as long as they gave him what he wanted: food and shelter. And passion was no problem, he could always manage that. He usually sensed when he needed to end it and move on, but by then he'd almost always discovered where the women kept their cash or valuable jewellery, and he took that with him.

The pretty dark-haired receptionist smiled at him as he left the hotel. They knew him here as David White, a businessman from the north of England, and Françoise knew him as Peter Lane. That was the only drawback to his new life in France, constantly changing his name. Fortunately, the French police didn't appear to liaise with their colleagues in other towns. Or maybe it was that his victims were too embarrassed to admit how foolish and gullible they'd been.

After Archie had rescued his suitcase, he made his way to Rouen Station, but as he walked, his thoughts turned to Cynthia. He wished he'd left her years ago; her constant social climbing, her pretence at being out of the top drawer, had been so wearing. But to give her some credit, she was the only woman who had succeeded in duping him. Not only making him believe she had illustrious relatives, but also passing off that brat Verity as his.

He wondered if Cynthia still had enough of her old spirit to convince some other man that she could enhance his life? Somehow he doubted it. He felt it was far more likely she'd had to slink back to Lewisham and persuade that old maid of a sister to take her in. She would be savage about that.

'Wilby!' Ruby said one afternoon after coming in from a walk. 'I really love it here.'

Wilby was busy making some soup for supper. But on hearing such an unexpected statement from Ruby, she abandoned the vegetables she was cutting up and went to the girl to embrace her.

'You've just made my day,' she said, kissing Ruby's cheek. 'But what, pray, brought on such a profound thought?'

Ruby stepped back from Wilby and grinned. 'I just went down the cliff walk to Oddicombe Beach, the sea was so shiny and clean; I had a paddle and I suddenly realized how happy I was. I think it's the happiest I've ever been. I don't ever want to go back to London, and I'm sorry I was nasty to you at first.'

'I'll tell you a secret,' Wilby said, patting her nose for secrecy. 'I don't ever want you to go away. I want you to continue with your lessons so your reading and sums come up to scratch, then find a good job. In the fullness of time I hope you'll meet a nice young man and get married. Maybe one day I'll even be holding your baby in my arms.'

'That sounds lovely,' Ruby smiled. 'You've done a good job with me. I bet my friend Verity would be amazed to see me now. She's posh, like you. But I don't know how to get in touch with her, so I don't expect I'll ever see her again.'

'That is a shame,' Wilby said. 'But you never know, Verity might be missing you too and she'll think of some way of finding you.'

Aunt Hazel and Verity were sitting together on a dilapidated bench in the tiny back garden having a cup of tea, because it was cooler than in the house. Despite the lack of care, the garden looked quite pretty, with masses of tall white daisies blocking out the weeds, and a pink rambling rose had scrambled along the broken fence.

Hazel normally worked on a Saturday, but she'd been given this one off as things were quiet in the soft-furnishing department.

'I'm worried about Mother,' Verity suddenly blurted out.

It was five days since she'd sold the silver in Blackheath and although her mother had brightened a little that night, and suggested they all had fish and chips from the shop in Lee High Road, by the next day she had sunk back into her previous apathy. Today, like most days, she hadn't even got out of bed, and it was nearly noon.

She'd given Verity a whole pound for selling the silver, and if it wasn't for the anxiety about her mother she would have been in Lewisham right now to see what she could buy with it. She had thought of a length of dress fabric from the market, or new shoes, but she didn't feel able to be so frivolous – not when her mother was seemingly unaware of anything going on around her.

'I have to admit I'm worried too,' Hazel nodded. 'She ought to have come out of it by now, but she won't go to the doctor and get a tonic, all she does is lie on her bed.'

'She doesn't seem to care about anything,' Verity said. 'I don't think she'd eat, if we didn't put it in front of her.'

Aunt Hazel put her hand over Verity's, an unexpectedly warm gesture of affection. 'You mustn't worry yourself, she's big enough and ugly enough to sort herself out. If she doesn't, she'll end up in the asylum. I told her that last night.'

'Oh, Auntie!' Verity said reprovingly. 'Telling her something like that won't help.'

Hazel shrugged. 'She always was selfish. Demanding this and that from our parents, thinking she was special. They should've slapped her down, the way they did to me when I stepped out of line, but they let her get away with it. Always on about how pretty she was. As if that was any credit to her! You get the looks you're given, it's just the luck of the draw.'

Verity suspected that, although her aunt was being harsh towards her sister, she actually cared more than she let on. 'Should we talk to the doctor and get him to come and visit her?'

Hazel pondered that for a moment or two. 'Yes, I think that might be a good plan. We could go together on Monday evening. I'll go straight from work, and you could meet me there at five thirty.'

'I bet you wish you'd never agreed to take us in,' Verity said glumly.

'Sometimes,' Hazel agreed. 'But I haven't got any issues with you, dear. I know I'm a grumpy old spinster, and this house isn't what you are used to, but you've made the best of it. I like that about you.'

That praise from her aunt meant a lot to Verity.

*

Verity went off to meet Susan that afternoon feeling happier. There were only two more weeks' holiday left before she went back to school, and as she walked up Lee High Road towards the library she was thinking of her fourteenth birthday in October. She could officially leave school then, although her teacher had said it would be folly to leave before she did her school certificate. Miss Ranger said she could arrange for her to do it in November or December.

She was happy to stay on until the new year. She thought it likely she could work on Saturdays at Chiesmans up till Christmas, and if they liked her they might offer her a permanent job. But she'd rather do some kind of office work, really – at least with that there was a chance of advancement eventually.

Susan was waiting at the door of the library. 'Don't let's go in today,' she said. 'It's too nice to be indoors.'

Verity didn't argue. She wanted to talk, and they couldn't do that in the library.

The park was very busy with cricket games, little children on tricycles or pushing doll's prams, and lots of families picnicking on the grass. The girls went down by the duck pond and found a bench to sit on.

'I was thinking how close we are getting to leaving school and going to work,' Verity said. 'I'm not sure whether to be excited or scared.'

'Well, I'll have a year of secretarial college first, bored out of my mind,' Susan said, taking a bag of sherbet lemons from her pocket and offering Verity one. 'What are you going to do?'

'I don't really know,' Verity said as she took a sweet,

wincing at the sharp taste. 'You can't train for things like nursing until you are at least seventeen. My aunt wants me to work in Chiesmans like her, but I'm not mad about the idea.'

'Chiesmans is nice,' Susan said thoughtfully. 'I'd sooner be there than go to college. I don't want to learn typing and shorthand to be a secretary; if you work in a shop, you get to talk to people. I bet the time flies when the shop is busy. Imagine just typing letters all day! How boring will that be?'

'It sounds very sophisticated to me,' Verity said with a giggle.

'Well, if you like the idea, you could try to get an office junior position,' Susan suggested. 'That way you don't have to work on Saturdays, and you could even learn to type at night school.'

'The world is our oyster, really,' Verity said. 'Who knows? We might get snapped up by a couple of rich and handsome bachelors before we've even learned to type our names. Then we'd live the life of Riley, whoever he is!' She burst into laughter and Susan joined in.

'My parents would go mad if I even considered marrying before I was twenty-one,' Susan managed to get out through her laughter. 'They believe girls should have proper careers and not think a man is going to sweep them off to a life of idleness.'

'From what I see of married life around where I live, marriage isn't idleness but slavery,' Verity said. 'I heard someone being slapped around the other night, the woman was screaming.'

'Oh gosh, how awful! The way my folks are with one

another makes me think marriage will be wonderful,' Susan said. 'But then they were nearly thirty when they tied the knot. Mum said it takes that long to find out who and what you really want.'

Verity nodded. That made real sense to her. What could be worse than waking up one day to find she'd married someone like her father?

They chatted for some little time, and Susan confided that she'd just started menstruating.

'What about you?' she asked.

Verity shook her head, embarrassed to be asked. She was already worried that she hadn't, and that her breasts hadn't started to grow, as Susan's had.

'Mum said it's a good thing, because it means I'm becoming a woman,' Susan said. 'But if the tummy ache you get is a regular thing, I'd rather be a man.'

There was so much Verity wanted to ask, but she couldn't bring herself to. For some strange reason she changed the subject entirely, and told her friend about Ruby.

If Susan thought it was odd, she didn't say so. 'Ruby sounds like fun, but I expect my parents would have a fit if I wanted to be friends with someone like her,' she said.

'So would mine, but I don't care what Mum thinks, she lies around all day feeling sorry for herself, letting Aunt Hazel keep her. Ruby only got into trouble because her mum was useless, and she had to get the food and pay the rent.'

Almost as soon as she'd spoken about her mother, Verity wished she hadn't. But she knew by the look on Susan's face she wasn't going to be fobbed off.

'I knew there was something troubling you,' Susan said, her tone gentle and sympathetic. 'Tell me, Verity, a trouble shared and all that. I won't breathe a word to anyone else, if that's what you are worried about.'

Verity needed to confide in someone, and she trusted Susan to keep it to herself. So, taking a deep breath, she told her the whole story, only omitting what her father had done to her.

'The police haven't found him yet,' she finished up, tears rolling down her cheeks. 'I think he must have left the country, but it was awful having to leave our lovely home. Aunt Hazel's house is pretty grim, but it was generous of her to take us in and keep us. Mum's gone really doolally now, and I despair.'

Susan put her arm around her friend. 'You poor thing,' she said. 'I sensed there was something bad, you often look like you've got the worries of the world on your shoulders. I thought it was a bit funny, you making friends with Ruby. Was that something to do with it?'

'Not really, I didn't know what Dad had done then. But I wasn't allowed to go out with girls from school, so I guess I was lonely.'

Susan didn't speak again for a little while, as if she was thinking it over. 'You don't sound like you care too much about your dad,' she suddenly blurted out. 'I know it's none of my business, but was he mean to you? Only just before the end of term, when we were playing leapfrog, your school blouse got all rucked up and I saw some marks on your back.'

Verity felt a little sick, she had never wanted to tell anyone about that. 'Yes, he was, but please forget you ever saw anything. I hate him, I don't want to talk about him ever again.'

Susan put her hand over Verity's. 'I'm sorry for prying. You've been through enough without me poking my nose in. But sometimes it's good to confide in someone, or so my mother is always saying. Nothing bad has ever happened to me, so I wouldn't know.'

'I hope it never does, because you're so nice.' Verity squeezed her friend's hand. 'Aunt Hazel and I are going to talk to the doctor on Monday about my mother. I'm hoping he can give her something to bring her out of this place she's slipping into. If he can't, she might end up in –' She broke off, unable to say the word.

Susan said nothing, just looked sadly at Verity for a moment. Then she got up. 'Let's go to the tea house and buy an ice cream?' she said.

Verity felt a surge of gratitude to her friend for moving things on; their conversation had been getting very gloomy, and she hadn't known how to get out of it.

'Do you think I should try to get in touch with Ruby?' she asked Susan a bit later. They had got their ice creams and had gone down by the tennis courts to watch two boys Susan knew playing. 'Or is it better to leave well alone?'

'I think you should write to her,' Susan replied. 'She'll be thrilled to get a letter. And you never know, it might help her stay on the straight and narrow. You can be honest with her too, she's not going to judge you, or talk about you to other people.'

That evening Verity wrote to Ruby and put the letter inside another one addressed to Maggie Tyrell at the Red Lion, explaining she was now settled at her aunt's house and asking her to send the enclosed letter on to Ruby.

Without knowing if Ruby's mail might be censored by someone, she couldn't tell her friend all that had happened, only that she and her mother had moved to her aunt's house in Lewisham. She said a little about her new school – enough so that Ruby would know they'd come down in the world – and she said her mother hadn't taken the move well. But her letter wasn't supposed to be about her, she wanted to know how Ruby was faring, if she still went to school, if she'd made some new friends, and if she had any plans for her future when she came back to London.

Reading it through one last time before sealing the envelope, she felt she'd hit just the right tone. She sounded respectable and educated, so a censor wouldn't think she could be a bad influence, but she also sounded like she really cared about Ruby and would always be her friend.

She was just putting the stamps on the envelopes she'd bought that afternoon, and wondering if she could walk down the road to post the letter and get some fresh air before going to bed, when she suddenly heard Aunt Hazel exploding with rage.

'You've bloody well pissed on the chair,' she yelled at the top of her voice. 'Not satisfied with lying in bed half the day, now you can't be bothered to get up and go to the lav!'

Verity was horrified. She couldn't believe her once so fastidious mother could do such a thing, and it seemed to be proof she really was losing her mind. She ran down the stairs to find her mother standing in the parlour with a vacant expression on her face, the skirt of her pale blue dress dripping on the floor. The chair in question was a dark green velvet button-backed one which had been passed down from their grandmother.

'I'll clean the chair.' Verity grabbed it and took it out to the garden. Rushing back, she took her mother's hands and led her into the scullery to strip off her wet dress and underclothes.

'As if I haven't got enough to put up with already, without her pissing on chairs,' Hazel ranted from the hall.

Verity couldn't blame her aunt for being so angry – she would be too in her shoes – but it looked as if Cynthia wasn't even aware of what she'd done. If this was the start of a new problem, how on earth would they cope with it?

'Surely you knew you needed the lavatory?' Verity asked. She put some water into a bowl and ordered her mother to wash herself. Without waiting for an answer she ran upstairs and got her mother's nightdress for her to put on.

'It just happened. I couldn't help it,' her mother bleated as Verity came back downstairs.

Verity sighed, removing her mother's brassiere and slipping the nightdress over her head. 'Mother, you aren't feeble-minded. You've got to snap out of this, as Aunt Hazel is getting very cross. She'll throw us out, if you do something like this again.'

'Hazel always was a bully.'

'She isn't being a bully. You've ruined her favourite chair and made the rug stink. It's disgusting. I'm going to take you to the lavatory every two hours now. And I'll slap you, if you do it again.'

'You can't hit me, I'm your mother!' Her incredulous tone reminded Verity of how her mother had been before everything began to unravel.

'Well, start behaving like my mother, then,' Verity retorted. 'You've been a spoiled, sulky child ever since we got here. That's why I'm treating you like one.'

Her mother's face crumpled and tears ran down her cheeks. 'You don't understand how bad it is for me,' she whined. 'I've never lived this way before, and I can't bear it.'

Hazel appeared in the scullery doorway, and it was obvious she'd heard everything that had been said. Her face was purple, tinged with anger. 'Never lived this way!' she shouted. 'You lived in this house until you married. It's no different now to how it was then. Don't come all that high-and-mighty stuff with me. You only married Archie because you were up the spout, and you thought he had money. No wonder he had to resort to swindling to try and keep you happy.'

'You don't have a clue about men, because you've never had one,' Cynthia threw back at her. 'You were always jealous of me, because I made things happen for myself. If you hadn't been so gormless, maybe you could've attracted a man.'

Hazel sprang forward, as if she intended to strike her sister. Verity stepped in front of her and prevented it. 'No more, Auntie,' she begged. 'Mum's not herself.'

'Not herself indeed,' Hazel shot back. 'You don't know her like I do. She thinks the whole world should revolve around her, never a thought for anyone else. She doesn't give a jot about you, Verity, she didn't even want a child in the first place.'

That was enough for Verity. She pushed past her aunt and mother to get outside. Suddenly she didn't care if they fought and hurt one another, she'd had enough.

It was dark now, the inky sky studded with stars when she looked up. It was still very warm, and she could smell honeysuckle from the garden next door. On such a beautiful summer's night people ought to be happy, not saying vicious things about one another.

Was it because her parents had to get married that there was always that bad feeling at home? It struck her as odd that, whether it was true or not, her mother had rallied enough to rile Hazel by bringing up the past. She couldn't be as loopy as she seemed, if she could do that. Was she doing this for effect? But why would she? What did she stand to gain?

Verity didn't know what to think, or even who she should sympathize with. What she really wanted was an adult to look after her, to make it alright. But even as she went back into the scullery to fill a bucket with water and find a scrubbing brush, the sisters were still shouting at each other – they'd just moved back into the parlour to do it.

From an early age Verity had realized her mother wasn't a sweet and loving soul, like mothers were supposed to be. She complained about everything, she was joyless, a social climber and a spendthrift. But Verity had always believed her mother and father loved each other, even if they were brusque with one another most of the time. It certainly had never occurred to her that she hadn't been wanted.

Carrying the bucket of water outside, she began to scrub at the chair seat. It seemed that everything she once believed in – that her parents loved each other, that they were good, honest people and would protect her from all things bad – was entirely wrong. Father had done bad things to her, and beaten her so harshly she thought she was going to die. Mother hadn't lifted a finger to prevent this, all she cared about was her own comfort.

Verity knew it must have been a terrible shock to her mother to find out about her husband swindling his company, and to lose her home. But surely any other woman would find enough pride and dignity to at least attempt to find a new life for herself and her daughter?

All at once Verity sensed that her mother had known exactly what she was doing when she peed on the chair. She wanted both her sister and daughter to believe she was becoming unhinged; because that way they'd look after her, and she wouldn't need to take any responsibility for anything.

How low was that?

Chapter Eight

On Monday Verity left home at midday, after giving her mother a sandwich and a cup of tea, because she could feel herself growing more and more angry with her. As so often in recent weeks, she had left her mother lying on her bed. Unwashed and still in her nightclothes, she smelled nasty because of the hot weather and lack of breeze.

Verity planned to go up across Blackheath to Greenwich Park, coming back to Lee Park in Blackheath Village for five thirty to meet Aunt Hazel at the doctor's surgery.

It was lovely in Greenwich Park, despite the long period of hot, dry weather which had turned the grass brown. She sat under a tree in the flower garden and read J. B. Priestley's *Angel Pavement* for a couple of hours, then made her way back across the heath to the doctor's.

Aunt Hazel met Verity outside the surgery.

'Gosh, it's hot and sticky!' she said, mopping her streaming face. 'Enough to fry your brain! There's talk of a storm tonight, and I hope it's true. The drains stink, everyone's getting bad-tempered, and it's too muggy at night to sleep.'

It was pleasantly cool in the waiting room at the surgery.

There was only a young woman with a small boy, and an elderly gentleman ahead of them. Aunt Hazel whispered that they wouldn't have to wait long.

Verity hadn't been to the doctor's before and she was

surprised to find his house was a big, grand one. The waiting room could do with redecoration, and the chairs were all scuffed and old, but through the window Verity could see a splendid garden with a manicured lawn and flower beds that were a riot of colour. It reminded her of the garden back in Daleham Gardens, where old Mr Angus used to come in every week to cut the grass and do the weeding. She wondered in passing whether her mother had ever thanked him for all his good work over the years, or even explained why she couldn't keep him on. Somehow, she doubted it. She resolved that she would write to Miss Parsons tonight; she wouldn't like the housekeeper to think she was as selfish and uncaring as her mother.

'It's always good to look at the magazines in here,' her aunt whispered. She was leafing through a copy of *Vogue*. 'I know it's for people who live in a different world to me, but I like a peek into it.'

Verity smiled. Aunt Hazel often surprised her. On the face of it she was just another working-class woman with no aspirations or expectations, but perhaps behind that crusty, old lady facade there was a younger, more vibrant woman trying to get out.

Dr Menzies listened to Aunt Hazel very attentively as she explained how her sister was behaving. Hazel didn't hold back on anything, allowing her bitterness and anger towards her self-centred sister to show. Yet she did add that she liked having her niece in the house and how helpful she was. The doctor then turned to Verity and asked her how her mother had been before they'd come to Lewisham.

'She was always beautifully turned out,' Verity said.

'Our home had to be immaculate at all times. Although she left our housekeeper to do the cooking and house-work, she did involve herself in how the house was run, planning menus, dinner parties and having her bridge afternoons. She played the piano, she liked to go to the theatre, she never just sat about. She only started being vague and weak when we were told we had to leave the house.'

'I see,' he said, running one hand over his bald head. He was about sixty, Verity thought, but with a nice plump face, a neat beard and twinkly blue eyes. 'You say she has made no effort to find work, or do anything around the house? She spends most of her time lying in bed, and takes no interest in anything?'

'Yes, that's right,' Hazel said. 'I can't afford to keep her for ever – and I don't want to, either. Now she's become incontinent, that's the last straw.'

He looked at Verity. 'You are very young to have such a worry thrust upon you.' His tone was so kindly and sym-pathetic that Verity's eyes began to prickle with tears. 'I will come tomorrow afternoon to see your mother, before my evening surgery. Try not to fret too much, many people become very withdrawn after a bad shock, but they usually recover in time.'

'Time and my patience are running out,' Hazel said sharply. 'I'm only one step away from throwing her out on the street.'

Verity said nothing as they walked down Lee Park, her aunt's last words to the doctor ringing in her ears. Would she really throw them out?

As they reached Lee High Road, her aunt said she was going to call in on a customer in Belmont Park. She was making curtains for her and wanted to check the measurements. 'I can't believe the window is over ten foot high,' she said. 'They sent Mr Edwards to measure, and I suspect he'd had a few drinks on the way there. But if the curtains turn out to be far too long, it will be me who gets the blame.'

'What are we having for tea?' Verity asked. 'I'll start it.'

'Peel some spuds, then. And we'll have a tin of corned beef,' Hazel said. 'I really hope it pours down tonight, I'm sick of this hot weather turning the milk sour and making everything go off.'

Verity almost said that they'd had a refrigerator at Daleham Gardens, but she stopped herself just in time. Her aunt didn't need further reminders that her sister had once had everything.

As Verity crossed Lee High Road she glanced at her aunt making her way towards Belmont Park and saw the weariness in her walk. She worked very long hours in a hot, stuffy workroom, and until Verity and her mother had descended on her, work was all her life consisted of. They may have added another dimension to her life, but instead of bringing light, some laughter or help, their presence must be like a lead weight, pressing her down still further.

'If mother was different, we could enhance her life,' Verity murmured to herself. 'I will try harder to make her change.'

The front door was no longer standing open to catch the breeze, as it had been for days now since the heatwave began. Verity had to put her hand into the letter box and pull out the key tied to a string on the back of the door.

As she opened the door she smelled gas. Not just a faint smell, but so thick and strong it caught in her throat.

'Mother!' she called out, running in and pushing open the closed kitchen door, in her heart already knowing what she was going to find.

Cynthia was there, lying on the floor in front of the open gas stove, her head and shoulders on the little footstool from the parlour.

Holding her hand over her nose and mouth, Verity turned off the gas and opened the kitchen door and window. Then she turned back to her mother. She didn't need to touch her to know she was dead. But all the same, she put her hands under her armpits and pulled her out into the back garden.

Once out there she stood for a moment looking down at her, too shocked to even cry or scream for help. Her mother just looked as if she was asleep – not deadly pale or anything telltale – and it was hard to believe she would never wake up again. She had dressed herself in a pink dress with a sweetheart neckline and short sleeves, even adding her pearl necklace and earrings, and had washed and arranged her hair.

Verity knew that the police, when they got here, would assume Cynthia had dressed up and arranged her hair because she wanted to die looking glamorous. But Verity knew better; her vain, selfish and stupid mother had not intended to die. She had staged this, assuming her daughter would come home at five as she always did. In fact, when she'd taken her mother a sandwich and cup of tea at lunchtime, she'd asked if she was going to the library as usual. Verity had nodded – she couldn't very well admit she and Hazel were meeting up at the doctor's surgery to discuss her mother. If she had said she'd be home later than usual, her mother would have asked why.

It was in fact the first time since they'd moved here that her mother had asked where she was going. That alone proved what she intended to do. She certainly couldn't have lost her mind – not if she could wash and dress herself, and think about what time she must turn the gas on to make her suicide attempt credible.

'You cruel, selfish woman,' Verity said, as tears cascaded down her face. 'I can never forgive you for this.'

Even if she lived to a hundred Verity knew she would never forget the sheer awfulness of that night. Within just a few minutes of finding her mother, just as she was running down the road to telephone the police from the phone box, the heavens opened. The rain lashed down, soaking her to the skin in seconds, and then the thunder and lightning started. Yet the thunderstorm, however scary and unexpected, was nothing compared to what came next.

Aunt Hazel arrived home, along with the police, and she was so shocked when she heard of her sister's death that she passed out. For a few moments Verity thought she'd lost her aunt too, but thankfully it was just shock, and after a cup of tea and a sit-down, she recovered. The next day she told Verity she'd felt a sharp pain in her chest and she thought she was having a heart attack.

But that night there were endless questions from the police, and their manner was entirely unsympathetic. This was made worse by the neighbours who stood out in the pouring rain, desperate not to miss anything. Yet over and above the shock, grief and guilt Verity felt because she hadn't been home that afternoon with her mother, there was also seething anger. She couldn't comprehend how any woman could be so utterly selfish that she'd put her daughter and sister through such a terrible ordeal.

Later that evening Aunt Hazel was a tower of strength. She put her arms around Verity and assured her they would come through this together. She even told Verity she loved her, and that she would always have a home with her.

But that first night as Verity lay sleepless, listening to the rain hammering down outside, she hated her mother with every fibre of her body. She knew that once the local newspaper heard about this, they would have a field day, possibly connecting the family with Archie Wood and resurrecting what he had done and how he'd brought his wife to this tragic end.

Everyone at school, the neighbours, even the ladies at the library would hear about it. How could she ever hold her head up again?

The next morning Aunt Hazel blurted out that she absolutely knew her sister had staged the gassing for sympathy, never expecting to die.

'She thought you'd be home by five as you always were, and you can bet your life she turned that gas on just minutes before five o'clock. She was the same all her life, always trying to get attention with whatever means she could. Well, this time it caught up with her. She's gone now, and good riddance – so much for crying wolf.'

Verity knew her aunt wasn't really glad her sister had died, she'd heard and seen her crying, and could see the sorrow etched into her face. She suspected Hazel felt guilty that she hadn't asked the doctor to pay a home visit weeks ago, and then maybe it would never have come to this.

But whether Hazel was grieving or glad, at least Verity could now admit she too knew her mother had staged her suicide. Why else would she have put on her best pink dress and her pearls? That wasn't the act of someone totally out of their mind with hopelessness.

It also meant Verity could talk freely about guilt and anger and all the other emotions that came in waves, threatening to overwhelm her.

She rather admired Hazel's unconventional way of dealing with her grief; she spat out words like 'sensationalist', 'traitor' and 'halfwit' as she stripped her sister's bed and packed her clothes away. She banged things around, even kicking furniture at times. Fury appeared to make her feel better.

Verity wished she could feel anger like her aunt's; it would be good to rant about what a terrible, uncaring mother she'd had. But what she felt was a deep sadness, a big lump of it inside her that made it hard to eat, sleep or share her feelings with anyone.

She wrote a letter to Susan telling her what had happened, thinking she'd be worried when she wasn't at the library. She hoped her friend would call round, as it would be a relief to talk to someone.

Hazel had a few days off work to enable her to arrange the funeral, though there wasn't anything much to arrange. She had no desire to invite neighbours to the service – Cynthia had never spoken to any of them – and those people she'd known as a young girl were almost all dead now or very old. She didn't have any real friends, only old bridge partners who certainly wouldn't come all the way to South London.

Hazel said it was best that no one came anyway – after all, suicide was a sin. She also didn't want to alert any of the reporters who had banged on her door in the past few days, trying to get more information on the still-missing felon Archie Wood.

The vicar at the local church where her parents were buried would only allow Cynthia to be buried in the unhallowed ground at the edge of the churchyard, so Hazel took the view the interment should be done as speedily and privately as possible. She added that the wisest thing for her and Verity would be to draw a veil over it all, and try to forget.

The funeral was to take place on the fourth day after Cynthia's death. In the days preceding it, Verity and Hazel spent most of the time sitting in the kitchen, drinking tea and talking. It wasn't all about Cynthia, either; Hazel spoke about their mother, and said how she too used to play games to get sympathy.

'Whenever I said I was going to leave, she always became ill,' Hazel said. 'Such an actress! She could vomit, starve herself and writhe in pain. But it was all put on, and I got wise to it eventually. She was not a nice woman, Verity, she had no real heart. So I suppose it isn't surprising that both Cynthia and I could be so calculating.'

'You aren't calculating,' Verity assured her. 'You do come across at first as chilly, but you were kind and generous to take Mum and me in. But tell me about Grandfather. What was he like?'

'Quiet, gentle, hardworking. He was a train driver, you know,' Hazel sighed. 'He deserved better than Mother, she bullied him, nothing he did was ever good enough. He used to spend all his spare time out in the garden, he made it beautiful, but she even ridiculed him for that and said he wasn't a real man. I asked him once why he didn't leave, but he just smiled and said it was his duty to stay. He passed away just before he was sixty, with a heart attack. Mother turned to bullying me after that.'

Verity had never been to a funeral before, and so she had no idea what they were normally like.

Hazel told her that it wasn't usual to be put so hastily into the ground with the minimum of prayers and no hymns, or to have no other mourners. 'So you must try to forget it,' her aunt urged her again.

When the day came, Verity made a posy of brightly coloured dahlias which she threw in on top of the coffin. It was only then that she shed a few tears, and only because she could hardly believe that anyone could have such a stark, unmourned end.

The day after the funeral Verity took some of her mother's best dresses and costumes to a shop in Lewisham that bought good quality second-hand clothes.

Maybe to an outsider this would appear callous, but Verity and Hazel had talked it over and decided they needed to take positive action to free themselves of their anger and resentment. Apart from anything else, they had to pay for Cynthia's funeral and find money to buy Verity new shoes and to keep her for the coming weeks.

Verity got twelve pounds for the clothes – more than they had expected – and Aunt Hazel decided they would keep the remainder of Cynthia's clothes to alter for themselves.

Finally, Susan replied to Verity's letter, but it was starchy and brief. She offered her condolences, but the line 'my parents feel that it isn't appropriate for us to spend so much time together now' meant that in fact she didn't want to be friends with someone whose mother had taken her own life.

Verity was very hurt, but she kept it to herself. Hazel might say she was in favour of drawing a veil over recent events, and forgetting her sister's selfishness, but Verity knew in reality she was sad and grieving. She would be deeply disturbed if she knew her niece was being made to suffer for her mother's actions.

Chapter Nine

It was Sunday evening, and Verity was supposed to be starting school in the morning. Tomorrow would be two weeks since her mother's death.

'You don't have to go back to school, if you don't want to,' Aunt Hazel said, putting her hand on Verity's shoulder. 'No one will expect you to when you have only just buried your mother.'

'I don't know what I want,' Verity admitted. 'It's all been so horrible, and I feel so mixed up.'

Aunt and niece were sitting in the parlour companionably. It had been raining all day, and since lunch Verity had been reading a book while Hazel had been taking in one of Cynthia's dresses.

When the sun came out, Verity suggested they went for a late evening walk.

'I suppose we could,' Hazel said. 'Though I'm so comfy I don't know that I want to move.'

Verity smiled. Her aunt had become a whole lot easier to live with since the funeral. She wasn't so sharp, and she seemed much more relaxed.

'You may have to move,' she said, pointing towards the window. Mrs Dean, their neighbour, was waddling across the street towards their door. 'Shall I head her off? Tell her you're lying down or something?'

'She's the last thing I need,' Hazel groaned.

Mrs Dean was one of the worst gossips in the street, in the hot weather she sat out on her garden wall nearly all day, watching people and encouraging them to stop and chat. People joked that if you told her a secret, the whole of Lewisham would know it within the hour. She had tried to befriend Hazel immediately after Cynthia's death, with the sole intention of digging up a bit of dirt.

'No, I'll deal with her.' Hazel got to her feet as the doorbell rang. 'You stay here; she knows you are a soft touch.'

Verity didn't move from her chair – like her aunt, she was sick of people calling. They often came with a gift of food, but it was just to gain information, not real kindness or sympathy. Verity was astounded at how adept her aunt could be at offering thanks very politely, even with surprising warmth, and yet not telling the caller anything at all. But getting rid of Mrs Dean would be especially difficult; it was often said she had the hide of a rhinoceros and was never deterred by insults, threats or a door slammed in her face.

A minute or two passed and Verity heard the front door close. Aunt Hazel came back into the room, a letter in her hand.

'That was quick work,' Verity said. 'How did you do it?'

Hazel half smiled. 'I told her the vicar was here. She can't have been at her usual perch in the window or she'd have known it wasn't true. It seems the postman made a mistake and put this through her door. She claimed she'd only just found it, half hidden by the doormat, but I expect she steamed it open. It's for you, dear!'

As soon as Verity saw the Devon postmark she knew it was from Ruby. The unformed childish writing confirmed it.

'It's from my friend Ruby,' she said, knowing her aunt must be curious. 'I wrote to her that night mother had the accident on the chair, and I posted it the next day. She won't know mother is dead.'

'Maybe that's just as well, and her letter might cheer you up,' Hazel said. 'I'll go and get the tea ready and leave you in peace to read it.'

Verity felt a little pang of something akin to love for her aunt, because she wasn't demanding to know who this friend was – or even to read the letter – the way her mother would have done.

She opened the envelope hastily, her excitement rising rapidly.

Dear Verity,

There's a shock! I thought you would forget me. You wrote kind of funny – I suppose you think someone would read it, but they don't. Anyways, sorry you had to move and leave the nice house. Is your aunt kind? Are the girls at your new school nice to you?

I got lucky coming here. You must have thought it was a prison place but it ain't. A lady spoke up for me in court, she said I never had a chance with my ma and I needed to go to a decent home. Well blow me down if they didn't bring me down here by the sea to stay with Mrs Wilberforce. She lets me call her Wilby, time was she used to have eight or nine kids staying, but she lost her old man and she's getting too old for real young ones. I really like her and living here, I get good food and kindness. My reading and writing is much better now and she's making me speak posh too and have manners. I told Wilby all about you and she said you can come to stay any time you like. I'll put the telephone number at the end, so you can ring me. It ain't hard to get here, the train goes from Paddington. I would love it if you came.

Big love,
Ruby

All at once the flood of tears that had been suppressed for so long came, great gulping sobs that eased the horrible lump she'd had inside her. The letter was badly spelled, with no real punctuation, but there was affection in every word, and Ruby didn't even know that things were so bad for her.

Hazel came in, stopping in surprise to see her niece so distraught.

'Whatever is it?' she asked. 'Is it something nasty in that letter?'

Somehow, through the sobs, Verity was able to tell her aunt about Ruby and how she'd got to know her. Hazel looked horrified at the bit about the stolen clock, but she took the letter and read it.

'Sounds like she's fallen on her feet,' she said. 'She is clearly very pleased to hear from you. Even if she's no great shakes as a letter writer.'

'I'm so pleased to get her letter,' Verity said and tried to dry her eyes. 'I don't know why I'm crying.'

'I do,' Hazel said. 'You've bottled it all up – not just your mum, but everything – for a long time. Ruby is like a key, she's unlocked your emotions for you.'

'Mother would have gone mad if she'd known about Ruby,' Verity said.

'Well, your mother was a snob as well as a fool,' Hazel

said. 'When we were kids, we were often barefoot, we didn't even have a better dress for Sundays like most around here. I thought I was dead lucky when I got taken on as an apprentice to make curtains and that. It's a proper trade. But your mother was always above herself. She said she'd kill herself, rather than sew or be a shop girl.'

'Did she really marry my father because she thought he had money and was well connected?'

'I know so. She met him up West. She used to hang around with Iris Petherall back then, a snooty Blackheath girl, her folks had money. They took the two girls with them one night to the theatre and afterwards went for supper somewhere a bit smart. I don't remember where, but there was a band and dancing, and Archie was there. He'd been in France during the war and no doubt he made himself out to be a bit of a hero. Of course he was handsome, and posh too. Funny thing was, Cynthia didn't talk much about him the next day, only that his parents had a big house in Shropshire. I got the feeling she'd set her cap at him, and I was right. They got married a few weeks later.'

Verity gasped. 'Really! That fast?'

Hazel winced. 'I can guess how she persuaded him, but it wouldn't be proper to tell you that, any more than to tell you why I always knew he was a cad and a bounder. Anyway, back to this letter from your friend. Why don't you go down to the telephone box and ring her now? It'll do you a power of good to speak to someone of your own age.'

Hazel put down her sewing after Verity had gone out to the telephone box. She was worried about her niece, because she knew she would be talked about at school, maybe even ostracized because of her mother, people were like that.

She wished she could speak out and tell Verity how adult, kind and sensible she was, and that she'd grown terribly fond of her, but she found it impossible to say such things. How Verity had turned out so well she couldn't imagine, as she'd had little or no parental guidance, with her mother far too wrapped up in herself to think of her child, and her father more interested in gambling and pretending to be something he wasn't. Yet however well-adjusted Verity appeared to be, she was vulnerable now; her age, her father's disappearance, the house being taken away and then her mother gassing herself, all this was far too much for a young girl to cope with.

'I wish I knew what to do or say,' she sighed. She had had ideas about selling the remainder of Cynthia's treasures and getting the house tidied up a bit so Verity felt more comfortable here. But maybe she should keep that money in case her niece needed something else – money for a training course or something?

Verity was gone about twenty minutes, and when she came back she was flushed with excitement. 'It was so good to speak to Ruby. She sounds really happy, but she was sad for me that Mother died. She said Mrs Wilberforce said I could go and stay there with them for a while, if I wanted – even tomorrow – instead of going back to school. I'd love to see the sea.'

'You've never seen the sea?' Hazel was shocked.

'No. Every summer Mother used to say we'd go to Brighton, but we never did. The only holidays we ever had were with Grandmother Wood in Shropshire. It was a lovely old house and a beautiful garden, with a river running through it, but there were no other children to play with and Grandmother could be very nasty.'

Hazel thought that Verity had known more nasty people in her life than nice ones. 'It would do wonders for you to have a holiday,' she said impulsively. 'I'm concerned about sending you off to people I don't know, but if that woman Wilberforce was good enough to take in a slum kid in trouble, she can't be a bad sort. Is there a husband?'

'She's a widow,' Verity said. 'She teaches Ruby at home too. She's old enough to work now, but Mrs Wilberforce wants to bring her up to scratch before she looks for a job. Please let me go, Auntie? I can't face going back to school when Susan doesn't even want to be my friend any more.'

'She was no friend if she turned her back on you so fast,' Hazel said tartly. 'I'll tell you what I'll do. I'll ring Mrs Wilberforce myself tomorrow, and I'll find out what time the trains go to Torquay. You can stay back from school and do a bit of cleaning for me. And if it all works out, you can go on Tuesday or whenever Mrs Wilberforce says.'

Verity leaned over her aunt and hugged her, and for once she didn't recoil as if bitten by a snake.

'I'll miss you, of course,' Hazel said gruffly. 'Just mind you behave!'

It was Thursday when Verity eventually set off for Torquay. Mrs Wilberforce had agreed she could come as soon as she liked, but Aunt Hazel wanted to see her off at Paddington Station so they had to wait for her day off.

Verity was beside herself with excitement from the moment it was arranged she could go. She had to get her holiday clothes washed and ironed while her aunt was at work, and also buy some sandals. The packing took no time at all, because she only had three summer dresses that still fitted her, a pair of shorts and a blouse. Ruby had said she didn't need a swimsuit, as Wilby had several that she could borrow.

It was torturous waiting to leave; she cleaned the house, polished the brass, scrubbed the stone doorstep and pulled up weeds in the garden to pass the time. Even reading – the one way in which she'd always managed to escape from reality or make time go faster – didn't seem to work.

Finally, Thursday morning arrived, the sun was shining and good weather was forecast for the next week. Verity washed, then dressed in the pale green and white cotton dress which had been her mother's and her aunt had altered.

'You look very nice,' Hazel said when she came downstairs to find Verity making toast. 'That dress suits you. Now the train leaves Paddington at eleven, and it doesn't get to Torquay till nearly four thirty, so I'll make you some sandwiches for your lunch.'

When the time came to set off, Aunt Hazel proved surprisingly knowledgeable at getting around in central London. She led Verity down the stairs from Charing Cross to the underground and knew exactly which train to get to Paddington.

They arrived at Paddington with twenty minutes to spare, and Hazel bought Verity a bar of chocolate and a magazine to read on the train.

'I want you to travel in the Ladies Only carriage,' she said. 'And don't do anything you shouldn't do.'

Verity wondered what naughty thing her aunt could possibly imagine her doing on a train, but she said nothing.

'It's going to be very strange without you,' Hazel said just as her train was announced as boarding on platform one. 'Be helpful and polite to Mrs Wilberforce,' she added as they walked to the train, looking for the Ladies Only carriage. 'I'll telephone at the weekend to see if everything is as it should be.'

Aunt Hazel walked away the moment the guard blew his whistle, and Verity suspected that was because she was struggling not to cry.

As the train chugged out of Paddington Station, past the backs of shabby houses and glimpses into mean streets where some of the poorest people in London lived, Verity could almost feel the cares and anxieties she'd been harbouring for so long now leaving her. School and any problems there might be with friends were put aside for now, and there would be no more neighbours pretending kindliness just to inveigle their way into a confidence. She wouldn't have to see that look of hurt and bewilderment on her aunt's face for a little while, and there'd be no need to fake grief for Ruby.

The sadness she felt was not exactly because her mother was dead. It was more because she'd realized that their feelings for one another had been very limited. When had they ever really shared anything? Or talked about anything important? When had they ever laughed together till their sides ached? Or for that matter cried in each other's arms? How could any child respect a parent who crumpled at the first sign of trouble? How could she truly love her mother when she didn't believe her mother ever knew what it was to love her?

In a way she was glad her mother was gone, even though that was an absolutely terrible thing to admit to. If she'd lived, Verity knew her mother would always have been hanging on to her coat-tails, always been a liability, a problem she would have had to find the answer to.

She was free now. She might have to go back and live with Aunt Hazel for another year, but that was fine. She respected her, she was grateful for all she'd done.

And maybe that odd little feeling she got when her aunt was sweet, or made her laugh, was actually love.

Verity relished everything about the train journey. There were three elderly ladies in the compartment with her until Reading, but they got off there and she had it all to herself. Once out of London everywhere looked so beautiful in the sunshine: sparkling rivers winding their way through meadows, herds of cows chewing the cud as they looked with interest at the train passing. There were vast fields of ripe golden corn, wheat and barley, much of which was being harvested. She marvelled at how the farmhands were cutting it, binding it and standing it up in stooks, presumably to dry off. Small children were helping, she even saw one little girl, probably no older than six, riding a big shire horse, and it reminded her that all she knew of farming and country life was when they had Harvest Festival at school.

The gentle motion of the train and the warmth of the sun through the windows lulled her to sleep, and she woke with a start as the train stopped at Bristol.

Two ladies got on there, and the way they spoke made her smile. Despite being very elegantly dressed, they sounded the way farmers did when they spoke on the wireless. A little later, when they offered her some home-made chocolate cake, she discovered they were from a village outside Torquay. They were only too eager to tell her all about the seaside town, and that the address she was bound for was in Babbacombe, a village up on the cliffs, a short bus ride from Torquay.

'It has a funicular that takes you down to the beach,' the bigger of the two ladies told her and then proceeded to explain that this was a kind of train carriage, like a lift, which carried about eight or ten passengers down or up the cliff face. 'And would you believe? There was a terrible murder there once.'

'Indeed there was,' the second woman chipped in. 'The terrible beast of a man strangled the old lady, stabbed her and then set fire to the house. They tried to hang him three times but failed. Up there in Babbacombe they call him "the man they couldn't hang".'

Verity liked this story – she bet Ruby did too and would fill her in with even more details. 'Fancy that!' she responded. 'I hope he was locked away in prison?'

'He certainly was, though some say he can't have done it or he would've hung. I think his wife and children still live around these parts.'

After Exeter the track ran right along beside the sea. Verity could hardly believe her eyes at such a sight, waves breaking on the shore just feet away from the train. Through the open window a lovely intoxicating smell wafted in.

'That's the smell of the seaside,' one of the women informed her. 'It's seaweed and saltiness. We don't notice it much, because we live here, but they say it's good for your lungs. That's why folk come here to convalesce after they've been ill.'

Verity was glued to the view. The sea was turquoise blue, and the sun on the water made it look like a million diamonds had been sprinkled on the surface. There were lots of boats, mostly small yachts, but some bigger ones too with no sails – like the steamers she'd seen on the Thames.

As the train went through a place called Dawlish there were dozens of people swimming in the sea, small children paddling holding their mother's hand, and she saw a man building a huge sandcastle.

She had seen pictures of the seaside in books and wished she could see it for real dozens of times, but the reality of it was far, far better than she expected. She couldn't imagine why anyone would want to live in a grimy city when they could live here.

Finally, the train arrived at Torquay. Saying only the briefest of goodbyes to her travel companions, Verity opened the carriage door and leapt on to the platform with her suitcase.

She didn't recognize the girl with the wide grin on her face walking towards her as Ruby right away. She still had the image in her mind of a pinched, dirty face, shabby clothes and untidy red hair. But this girl had shiny curls and freckles, a pretty blue dress and a smile as wide as the River Teign she'd just crossed on the train.

'Verity!' she yelled joyfully. 'I thought you'd never get here!'

Nothing felt as good as her friend's warm hug and the way she jumped up and down holding Verity. Somehow, it told her that the misery of recent weeks was behind her now and that the future was going to be so much better.

'I've lain awake for the past few nights too excited to sleep,' Verity said. 'But I hardly recognized you! You've changed so much.'

Ruby took her arm and walked her out of the station. 'Wilby has transformed me,' she giggled. 'First with a bath, new clothes, good food, and then on to manners and speaking proper.'

'Properly,' Verity corrected her.

Ruby laughed. 'When I'm excited, I lapse,' she said. 'But tell me you like the new Ruby or I'll change right back.'

'I like the new Ruby even better,' Verity smiled. 'And I'm so happy for you that something good came to you.'

'Seems we've had a bit of a life swap! Wilby told me what your father did. When you wrote and she saw your name, she was reminded of how she'd read it in the paper. Is he still on the run?'

Verity blushed with shame at the thought of Wilby knowing her background.

'Don't!' Ruby put her hand on her friend's arm, sensing what was wrong. 'Wilby don't hold nothing against people – especially someone innocent, like you. Anyways, it's best she knows, then you've got nothing to hide and you can talk to her about it too. Now buck up, we've got to catch the bus, and Wilby will have a special tea waiting.'

Chapter Ten

Archie was very comfortable living with Françoise in her beautiful chateau. It needed a great deal of work doing on it, and the gardens were very overgrown, but in the warm late summer sun, with fruit ripening on the trees in the orchard and the flower beds alight with colour, it was like paradise. She made out to people she was employing him as an odd-job man and that he lived in the room above the stables. When she had visitors, he did sleep in there, but the rest of the time he shared her bed.

Like so many widows he'd met, she was insatiable and really enjoyed wild sex games, tying each other up or getting him to spank her with a hair brush. For a fifty-year-old woman she looked good, with barely a line on her face, shiny coppery hair and a lovely voluptuous figure. He loved it that she often walked around with nothing on, letting him watch as she masturbated in front of him.

For the first time in his life he had exactly what he wanted: a really sexy woman who was ready for anything he desired, at any time. She was a good cook too, with a well-stocked wine cellar, and she didn't seem at all interested in his past, only enjoying the present with him. He even felt he was falling in love with her.

He had been with her for three weeks when, late one morning, while he was fixing a shutter that had been banging in the wind, Françoise drove up the gravel drive in her old Renault like a mad thing. She had gone into Rouen to do some shopping and her usual flower arranging in the church.

Thinking perhaps she had rushed back for sex, Archie hurried forward to open the car door for her.

To his astonishment, she looked furious with him.

'*Tu es un gredin,*' she spat out at him, followed by a volley of French delivered so fast he couldn't follow any of it. But he had understood the first few words – 'You're a scoundrel!' – so he guessed she had found something out about him.

She picked up an English newspaper from the passenger seat and thrust it at him. There, to his shock, he saw a small picture of himself, with the headline above: 'Missing Embezzler's Wife Commits Suicide'.

Françoise could read English better than she could speak it, so there was no point in trying to lie about the news story. It seemed Verity had found her mother gassed in the kitchen. It made plaintive reading: the wife and mother who couldn't live with her husband's crime or the loss of her home.

Yet even as Françoise raged at him, all Archie could think of was that Cynthia and Verity had snatched away the first really good thing that had happened to him in years. He could see by Françoise's anger that she would never forgive him for being married all along and being on the run from the police. Even if he spoke French well, he knew he could never find the right words to talk her round.

'You want me to go?' he asked.

She slapped his face hard. And before he could stop himself, Archie struck her back, twice as hard.

'Get out now,' she roared at him, holding her cheek which was bright red from the slap. 'I hate you!'

He had to run to grab his belongings and get out quickly, because he knew she would call the police. Five minutes later, as he hurried down the drive with his suitcase, with Françoise hurling abuse in rapid French from the front door, Archie cursed Cynthia for stirring up his name again in the press. But he put all his hate on to Verity, just because there was no one else to blame.

Verity opened her eyes and, for a split second, was confused to see a window straight ahead of her instead of the bedroom door. But then she remembered she wasn't at home with Aunt Hazel, but with Ruby in Babbacombe.

She sat up and rubbed her eyes. Ruby was still fast asleep in the bed next to hers. The last thing Verity remembered about last night was her friend telling her the gruesome story of John Lee, the man who had strangled, stabbed and then set fire to the house of an old lady down by Babbacombe Beach. They tried to hang him on three separate occasions but the trapdoor didn't open, so he went to prison. Verity thought she must have fallen asleep then, but she half remembered Ruby telling her she'd show her around the place today.

Nothing about meeting Ruby and Mrs Wilberforce had been as she had expected. Firstly, she had been scared Ruby would be different to how she remembered, maybe shy and uncommunicative. Then she had imagined Mrs Wilberforce to be stern and forbidding, her house to be spartan, the food very plain. But how wrong she was on all counts!

Ruby was even more fun than she remembered. She was really happy, which could have just come from being clean, well fed and nicely dressed, but it was more like she'd found something inside herself to be proud of, and liked her new self.

The house in Higher Downs Road was around the same size as Verity's old home in Daleham Gardens, but not so old. It was detached, with five bedrooms and a lovely big garden. The sea was just behind the houses on the opposite side of the street. They were on the cliff edge, with the sea far below. Ruby had immediately shown her friend how they could see the sea from upstairs, but only had glimpses of it from the rooms downstairs at the front.

The furniture was a mixture of very old and beautiful handed-down items, and modern pieces. Maybe the scores of children who had stayed here over the years had scuffed the paintwork, marked the wallpaper and made the carpets thin, but the house still had a classy, gracious yet very homely appeal.

But as nice as the house and garden were, nothing had prepared Verity for the jaw-dropping, spectacular view of the bay from the Downs, which Ruby had shown her before they got to the house. The Downs was a flat, grassy sort of promenade on the cliff with pretty flower beds and lots of benches for people to sit down and admire the view. The sea below the cliff was turquoise, small yachts scudding around with the wind, the odd fishing boat and pleasure steamer drifting by. The cliffs going down to the beach far below were covered in trees and greenery, though here and there red soil showed through. Ruby told her that sometimes there were rock falls and the sea turned brown with the soil.

Verity thought she could stand and look at that view every day and never grow tired of it.

As for Wilby, she was just such a lovely welcoming lady, the kind Verity had imagined only lived in works of fiction. Ruby said she was over sixty, but she seemed much younger, even if her face was lined. She was tall, a little stout, with snow-white hair and very bright blue eyes, but still very elegant in both manner and dress. Yet the best thing about her was her warmth; Verity felt it wrap around her the moment she walked through the door. Wilby had dedicated her entire life to taking in children who for one reason or another needed a temporary home, and Ruby said she believed she had loved every single one of them.

'She's helping to fund-raise now with a group of people who plan to get Jewish children out of Germany to save them from Mr Hitler,' Ruby had informed her that first evening. She then proceeded to tell Verity all about what a nasty man Hitler was and how he hated Jews.

Verity had heard the news on the wireless back in March that Hitler was threatening to remilitarize, and she knew there was widespread condemnation of this. She didn't really understand what this meant, any more than she understood the rumblings of violence in Spain, or what it would mean if the Prince of Wales continued his affair with Mrs Wallis Simpson. Both items were constantly referred to on the news.

However, she did understand the talk, not just on the wireless or in the newspapers but also on the street, that there might be another war against Germany. She was inclined to dismiss it as just talk, hoping that the problems which were causing this anxiety could be solved. She had often wished there was someone who knew about such things and could explain it properly to her.

Ruby, it seemed, did know a great deal about world events; she said it was because Wilby thought all young people ought to know about such things, and she had explained it all very clearly.

Before they began supper, as Wilby called the evening meal – back home Aunt Hazel had always called it tea – Wilby had included in the grace a prayer for the poor people in America's Dust Bowl.

Verity hadn't known what that was, and asked.

'My dear,' Wilby addressed Verity, 'surely you must have heard about the catastrophic dust storms back in April, which swept across the country from Canada south to Texas?'

Verity shook her head.

'Oh dear, schools are so lazy about important world news,' she tutted. 'Anyway, since then there has been a terrible drought with temperatures rising to 120 degrees in places, resulting in failure of crops and livestock dying. As if it wasn't bad enough that there is no work for so many men! People are dying of hunger, Verity.'

The older woman looked intently from Ruby to Verity, as if checking they'd taken on board what she'd just told them. 'You two already understand a little about inequality and hardship, and I'm going to charge you both to do what you can in life to show others how wrong it is to ignore the plight of those less fortunate.'

She went on to say that she believed that it wasn't just chance that had brought Verity and Ruby together.

'My parents would've claimed it was God's work,' she said with a little chuckle. 'But I'm not inclined to believe in a God who allows innocents to suffer, and the greedy and ruthless to thrive. However, I do believe fate can intervene for a reason. You two girls, complete opposites at the time you met, became friends against all the odds. Verity, you gave Ruby the idea of improving her lot in life. And you, Ruby, showed Verity how the poor live. Imagine, Verity, how much worse it would've been for you when you had to move from your fine house, if Ruby hadn't prepared the ground for you a little. And Ruby, if Verity hadn't influenced you, would you have been able to see I was offering you a lifeline that day in court?'

'Maybe not,' Ruby smirked. 'Verity made me see some posh folk are good sorts.'

Verity nodded too, in total agreement, although she suspected she'd go along with anything this extraordinary woman said. How could she not trust someone who had spent her whole life taking in needy children? Her husband, who she had obviously loved dearly, had died a few years ago, and the only change she'd made since then was to take in older girls, because she felt small children and bigger boys needed the balance of both a man and a woman caring for them.

'You girls won't appreciate this now,' Wilby went on, 'but you are both approaching a crossroads in your lives. Which way you turn will be all important. I think from what your aunt told me, Verity, you don't feel you are worth much, and that might make you take any old job rather than think what it is you really want to do.'

Verity shrugged. 'Maybe, but I don't know what different kinds of work I could do. People say things like, "You'll be married soon," as if it doesn't matter anyway.'

'If there's another war with Germany, and I believe there may be, young women will be needed to keep the factories, transport, banking, teaching and just about everything going. I believe all girls of your age should be prepared for what might come, and now is the time to think on it.'

She paused, then looked at Ruby and smiled.

'Ruby and I have discussed her situation quite a bit already,' she went on. 'She admitted when she first arrived here that she thought she could only survive on her wits. Now she's beginning to read and write better, I think she is feeling more hopeful for the future. But you know, I think you too will cope very well if and when war comes, because you've already faced so many difficulties.'

Wilby moved on then to dish out the supper, macaroni cheese with hard-boiled eggs sliced into it, and extra cheese on top. It was delicious, completely different to the tasteless dish of the same name Aunt Hazel made so often, and Verity had two helpings.

They talked about books as they ate, and Wilby seemed impressed by both the quality and number of books Verity had read.

'Reading is the quickest way to educate yourself. I'm delighted to see that Ruby's reading is coming along in leaps and bounds now,' she said. 'But not quite at the point yet where she can't put a book down.'

'I expect that's because she's still reading too slowly to get the story in her head,' Verity suggested. 'But tell me, Ruby, won't you be starting work soon?'

'I'm going to start in the Palace Hotel next month. Starting as a chambermaid, and waiting on tables, but

I'll work up to managing the place.' She grinned impishly at this, and Verity suspected that was actually her ambition.

She envied Ruby, and even wished she could come and live here and do the same. But she couldn't leave Aunt Hazel yet – and anyway, she had to get back to school to finish her school certificate.

'I believe you could even do that,' she said. 'You've really made the most of the lucky break you were given. You speak better, you've got poise now, I think you could do anything.'

'Yes, she's a little marvel,' Wilby agreed, smiling broadly. 'And you coming to visit, Verity, will make her even more determined to get on.'

It was only once they were in bed with the light off that Verity got up the courage to ask her friend about her mother.

'I don't know, and I don't care,' Ruby said in the darkness.

'I bet you do care,' Verity replied. 'I want to know where my father is, even if I do hate and despise him.'

'She didn't even come to court to see me,' Ruby said in a small voice. 'She was the one who told me to go to that house in Hampstead. She'd been there, you see, with the man who lived there. They got drunk together. He paid her for sex and then passed out, so she took a look around and saw the clock.'

'Really?' Verity couldn't think of anything else to say.

'I wouldn't tell you such a thing if it wasn't true.' Ruby's voice sounded strained, as if it hurt her to admit this.

'So why didn't she take the clock herself? He could hardly call the police, if he'd been with her.'

'He was the kind who's got nasty friends. They would've come after Ma.'

'So she told you about the clock and told you to go and get it?'

'Yup. She said he wouldn't be there during the day, but he was.'

'Are you sure she knew you'd been caught with it? I mean, maybe she never heard.'

'A policeman went round to see her early the same evening. He told her, and she wasn't even drunk then, so she couldn't have forgotten. The truth is, she was just glad to get me out of the way. I reckon, if I hadn't been nicked, she'd have been making me go with men by now.'

'Surely she wouldn't do that,' Verity whispered in the darkness. 'No mother would.'

'Don't you believe it!' Ruby made a snorting noise of derision. 'She'd already made hints about it. Anyways, it were good she never came to court. Wilby wouldn't have felt sorry for me, if she'd met Ma.'

'I bet she would've, and given your mother a good ticking off,' Verity insisted.

Ruby sighed. 'You don't know what a good actress my ma can be. She'd put on her best frock and do her hair all nice, and she'd have the judge and Wilby convinced she'd done her best for me and that I was the wrong 'un.'

There was a hint of pride in Ruby's last statement, and Verity realized that they were the same in this. They both had flawed mothers – some would say terrible ones – yet, despite that, it could be said that both girls loved them.

That was the point when Ruby began to tell her about 'the man they couldn't hang', and Verity must have fallen asleep before the end of it.

The first week in Babbacombe was bliss to Verity. Lovely balmy weather, restful, peaceful and calming. Unlike Aunt Hazel, Wilby didn't go on and on about what chores had to be done, she just calmly pointed out what needed doing, be that laying the table, sweeping the kitchen floor or peeling some potatoes, and she would get on with making a pie or a cake and let them work around her.

Verity had always liked to feel involved and useful but Miss Parsons, and latterly Aunt Hazel, had always hovered over her as she did jobs, implying she was doing it all wrong. Not Wilby, she barely even glanced at what the girls were doing, trusting them to do it well. The only comments she ever made were to compliment them on a job well done.

The structure to each day was comfortingly unchanging: breakfast in the garden, because it was such lovely weather, and then Wilby dished out a few chores. Later, she went shopping and she liked the girls to go with her. The shops in St Marychurch were only a short distance away and much nicer than the ones Verity was used to in Lee High Road, so that was no hardship. And they were always back for elevenses. Wilby made them milky Camp coffee, which seemed very sophisticated.

Ruby had lessons then until one o'clock, but Wilby included Verity in them and made them fun. While Wilby went off to the kitchen to make lunch she would get Verity to help Ruby with her reading.

The current book was *What Katy Did*, an old favourite of Verity's, and each day Ruby complained that they hadn't read enough of it by the time they were called for lunch.

Wilby liked to have a rest in the afternoons, and the girls were allowed to go out on their own. Sometimes they just sat on the grass on the Downs, watched the holiday-makers and talked, but on other days they went down to the beach. It was always a toss-up as to whether to make it easy on themselves by taking the funicular down to Oddicombe Beach, or take the tougher way of walking down the steep path through the woods to Babbacombe Beach. Oddicombe Beach was always in the sun – and there was a little sand, which was easier on bare feet when they paddled – but Babbacombe Beach had rock pools at low tide, which were fun to poke into. And there were boys fishing on the old stone pier.

Boys were something of a mystery to Verity, as she'd never got to know any. But Ruby was very enthusiastic about them, and she coached Verity to look interested in what the boys had caught, and to flirt with them. Ruby was adept at flirting; she had a way of catching a boy's eye, smiling shyly, then turning her head away, so that in no time at all he came over under some pretext to speak to her.

They made up stories about themselves to tell boys: that they were cousins sent down to Devon because of an epidemic of scarlet fever in London, or that they were just visiting their aunt before going off on a steamer to America.

One day, as they walked back up the steep hill, Ruby started to laugh.

'Our real stories are far more exciting than the ones we make up,' she said. 'I almost went to prison, and you are the daughter of a swindler who's on the run. And here we are trying to be so terribly posh.'

Verity laughed too, she hadn't thought of it like that before. 'If we did start telling boys the truth, they probably wouldn't believe us. How daft is that!'

They walked on a little further, panting because the hill was so steep. 'I wish I could stay here with you for ever,' Verity suddenly blurted out. 'Aunt Hazel does her best, and I know she's grown fond of me, but it hasn't ever felt like home. I hate having no bathroom and the lavatory being outside. It's going to be horrible there in the winter.'

Ruby patted her on the shoulder, a silent gesture of understanding. 'When I first got here, I was scared to get into the bath,' she admitted. 'I'd never had one before. I had to wash in a bowl. But I'd hate to go back to that again. If you want, I'll ask Wilby if you could stay?'

Verity pulled a glum face. 'Even if she agreed, I know I can't stay. I need to go back to school and get my school certificate.'

'Maybe you can come back after the exam and get a job here?'

'I owe it to Aunt Hazel to help her out with money for at least a year,' Verity said. 'Anyway, by then you might have met a boy, and we might be bored with one another.'

Ruby looked at her friend, her eyes twinkling. 'I would never get bored with you,' she said. 'And Wilby thinks you're a good influence, which is handy.'

*

Knowing how Wilby felt about her prevented Verity from agreeing to Ruby's wilder schemes. Ruby wanted to slip out the following evening to meet a couple of boys they'd spoken to during the afternoon. They were seventeen-year-olds, and Verity had not only felt intimidated by them but she also knew Wilby was far too smart to believe the cock and bull story Ruby planned to tell her.

'We can't do that,' she insisted, and then explained why. 'Don't spoil what you've got here just to meet a boy.'

Ruby sulked, but she did finally agree she would forget the idea.

'I thought you'd be game for a bit of adventure,' she said, glowering at Verity. 'I didn't expect you to be a goody-goody.'

Verity said nothing. She wished she had the words to tell her friend that being here on holiday with her was the best thing that had ever happened to her, and she didn't dare do anything that might upset Wilby and turn it sour. Nor could she bring herself to admit she was afraid of boys because of what her father had made her do. It was too awful.

There was a slightly strained atmosphere that evening. Ruby didn't chat as she normally did, using the excuse she wanted to listen to the play on the wireless. If Wilby sensed anything, she didn't remark on it and got on with her embroidery. Verity was relieved that the play was a good one and a perfect excuse for keeping quiet.

That night when they went to bed was the first time Ruby didn't talk to her after turning out the light. Verity whispered that she was sorry, but there was no response.

They woke the next morning to the sound of heavy rain.

'Well, that's it, the summer's over,' Ruby announced, bouncing out of bed and going over to the window to pull back the curtains.

'Does that mean I've got to go home?' Verity asked, thinking that was what Ruby meant.

'Of course not, you daft moo,' Ruby grinned. 'Sorry I was mean last night.'

Verity felt like a sunbeam had just shone through the window and tickled her nose. 'You don't need to say sorry, I felt bad because I was being so dull. So what are we going to do today in the rain?'

'You can help me with my reading. There's a Sherlock Holmes book downstairs, I've had my eye on it for a while.'

Verity was thrilled she'd been forgiven. 'Okay, sounds perfect for a wet day.'

Wilby set some sums for Ruby to do after breakfast, and Verity went into the kitchen to help with the washing-up.

'What was all that about yesterday?' Wilby asked.

'Nothing much,' Verity said quickly.

'I bet she wanted to do something you didn't approve of,' Wilby said. She looked hard at Verity, as if daring her to lie.

Verity shrugged, not wanting to admit Wilby was right.

'I expect it was a boy. I've noticed she seems rather precocious in that direction.' Wilby sighed, as if that troubled her. 'Sadly, girls brought up without any love or guidance almost inevitably fall into the arms of the first sweet-talking man who comes along.'

'But you've helped her, and shown her another way to live,' Verity said. 'She isn't going to want to go back to her old life.'

'Of course not, Verity, but young girls – especially ones as hungry for love as Ruby is – are at risk of being used and talked into going further than they intended. In such cases, the girl often finds herself in trouble, and the young man who once vowed he loved her often disappears.'

Verity wanted to show her indignation, to tell the older woman Ruby would never be that easily led, yet as unworldly as she was, she sensed Wilby was right. If Ruby had gone out last night, something might well have happened. Those two boys weren't looking for a girl to just talk to.

'You look shocked, dear,' Wilby said. 'Perhaps you think me hard on Ruby?'

'No, I don't think that,' Verity said. 'You know far more about such things than I do. Is there anything I can do to help Ruby?'

'Just be her friend, and let her be yours, confide in one another, make her know you care for her,' Wilby smiled. 'You've got enough to deal with in your own life, Ruby told me you are dreading going back to school.'

'Yes, I am,' Verity said, hanging her head. 'They'll whisper about my mother gassing herself, and some will know about my father too. What can I say or do about it?'

Wilby gave her a hug. 'Hold your head up high, dear,' she said. 'You've done nothing wrong, remember. People soon get bored talking about someone who doesn't react to it. Now let's see how Ruby has got on with those sums I set her.'

Two weeks after she'd arrived in Torquay, Wilby and Ruby waved Verity off on the London train.

Verity leaned out of the window and waved until she could no longer see them, then slumped down on to the seat and wiped the tears from her eyes. Just the thought of being back in Aunt Hazel's dreary little house made her feel like bursting into tears. Wilby had suggested she came again during the Christmas holidays, but that seemed such a long way off.

Her first period had arrived two days ago, and she had been so glad that Ruby was there to tell her what to do. She thought she might die a death if she'd had to ask her aunt.

Back to school too. Another thing she wasn't looking forward to. But, as Ruby pointed out, it wasn't for much longer.

She must start planning what to do when she left.

Chapter Eleven

1937

'No, Michael, I mustn't,' Ruby said, pushing his hands away from her breasts. 'Besides, it's time I went home.'

It was a miserable, wet and cold evening in October, and Michael had promised to take her to the pictures to see *The Prince and the Pauper* with Errol Flynn but instead he took her to a pub in Wellswood in his car, and then after a couple of drinks brought her down to Meadfoot Beach.

It was high tide, and every now and then a wave came right across the road, almost hitting their car parked opposite under the cliff. Michael said it was romantic, but Ruby had the sneaky feeling he'd only brought her down here to have his way with her.

She had been seeing Michael for six weeks now and she had fallen hopelessly in love with him. He was everything she liked in a man – tall, dark and very handsome – she thought he looked a bit like Errol Flynn, with the same smouldering eyes. He was a reporter, and he'd told her that they wanted him on *The Times*. But that would mean moving to London and leaving her, unless she went with him.

'Just a few more kisses,' he pleaded with her, and his hand slid right up under her jumper before she could stop it.

His kisses made her feel like she was floating away on a cloud, and all at once she realized he'd unfastened her bra.

The touch of his hand on her bare breast was so delicious she lost the will to attempt to stop him.

A few more kisses and he had his hand up her skirt, his fingers finding their way inside her.

'You mustn't,' she said weakly, but it felt so good she was writhing against him, wanting more.

Suddenly her knickers were off and he was pushing her down on to the seat, unbuttoning his fly.

'Michael, no!' she said in alarm. 'I might have a baby.'

'You won't, I'll be careful,' he said, his voice all husky with passion. 'You are so beautiful, Ruby, I must have you. You know I love you, there's nothing to worry about.'

He'd never said he loved her before, and somehow that overrode any further objections.

It hurt a bit, and she was very uncomfortable, because her legs were stuck at an awkward angle while he bore down on her, breathing heavily. But it didn't last very long. He made a loud sort of sigh, and then he was still. Almost immediately he sat up and tucked himself away.

Ruby wanted to say, 'Is that it?' All this time she had imagined something amazing, she hadn't expected just a grubby little fumble, a few thrusts, and it being over in seconds.

But she didn't say anything. She was embarrassed, a bit ashamed, and she felt silly that she hadn't known what to expect.

'Right, I'd better get you home,' he said, lighting up a cigarette before starting the car. 'Are you alright?'

She wanted him to say he loved her again and kiss her. She didn't want to have to grope around to find her knickers and put them on in front of him. She certainly didn't want to be asked if she was alright, when surely he could sense she wasn't?

'Just take me home, Michael,' she said and bit her lip so she wouldn't cry.

Despite getting excellent results in her school certificate, most of the companies Verity had applied to for a job as an office junior didn't even grant her an interview, and those who did were not the least impressed by her only experience being a Saturday job in the canteen at Chiesmans. One company even suggested she should work in catering. After being turned down so many times, she felt she had to take the only job offered to her – as an assistant in a wholesale goods company.

Cooks of St Pauls was a warehouse that supplied general shops with everything from knitting wool and haberdashery to clothing, shoes and outerwear. It was a rather grand old building, though very dusty and dark, right across the road from St Paul's Cathedral. At her interview Verity was told that although her job would mainly be picking out orders, she would be moved to different departments now and then and also given a chance to try invoicing and other office work, so there was the prospect of learning other skills.

The first shock when she started at Cooks was that she had been put in the Corset Department. All the other assistants were men, and she found it excruciatingly embarrassing when they spoke of brassieres, cup sizes or suspender belts, as she'd thought only women knew about such things. But most of the orders were for ready-made corsets – stout, tea-rose pink ones like Aunt Hazel wore – and as they were for elderly ladies, and not the least bit sexy, within a couple of days she was making jokes about them just as the male assistants did.

Working turned out to be nowhere near as exciting as she'd imagined it would be. Each morning the Department Manager, Mr Cushing, handed her a bunch of orders sent in from shops. They were almost always handwritten orders and usually barely readable. They might read:

> 2 Twilfit full cup girdles, size 36 bust. Tea rose.
> 1 Ambrose cream sateen corset, size 40 bust.
> 3 white cotton suspender belts, size 26 waist.

Her job was to pick the items from the shelves, tie the bundle of goods securely with string, attaching the costing note, then drop it down the chute which led to the packing department in the basement. Down there they would be put together with other items from different departments, packed securely, and one invoice including all the different goods would be written up. Then the parcel would be sent to the customer.

During the day there could be dozens of telephone orders too, and Mr Cushing was always praising her telephone manner. He said they had had girls before who could barely speak the King's English, let alone manage to take down an order correctly and politely.

All in all, 1936 had been a sad year, with King George dying in January, and then all the will-he-won't-he stuff of King Edward wanting to marry Wallis Simpson, and people arguing about whether a king could marry a divorcee. Finally, at the end of the year, the King abdicated, which most people seemed to think was a good thing. At least it made more interesting news than the Nazi party dominating the German parliamentary elections, or speculation over Chiang Kai-shek's intentions towards Japan.

Verity had managed to spend a long weekend last New Year with Wilby and Ruby, then a week at Easter, and two weeks in August. They were the highlights of the year, even though Ruby was working at the Palace Hotel a great deal of the time.

The New Year of 1937 had brought in a tangible air of hope as plans for George VI's coronation were made for the 12th of May. People seemed genuinely supportive of the new king, his wife and their two little girls, Elizabeth and Margaret.

Verity helped organize the Weardale Road street party for Coronation Day, and for that day at least the whole of England buzzed with excitement. Ruby came up from Torquay for the celebrations and stayed a whole five days, which they managed to fill with not only the street party but also a dance in Lewisham, a fair on Blackheath and a shopping trip to Oxford Street.

But the coronation bunting had scarcely been taken down, and Ruby was barely settled back home with Wilby, before the newspapers brought back all the doom and gloom. There was the ever rising death toll in war-racked Spain, the explosion of the Hindenburg airship in New Jersey, and reports of Japanese troops taking Peking, Shanghai and Nanjing in the war with China. Then the Duke of Windsor, with his new American wife, made a controversial trip to Berlin and even met Hitler – something that created a great deal of criticism.

Every day without fail there was some reference in the newspapers to Germany, Hitler or the prospect of war, and on top of that they published sad and dreary articles about unemployment and poverty, which was still particularly bad in the north of England. Verity wondered if there was anything going on anywhere in the world that people could be cheerful about.

She and her aunt had made improvements to the house during the last year. Verity had moved into her mother's room at the back of the house after her death, and with Aunt Hazel's help she'd made it more attractive by making new curtains and a patchwork quilt. Her aunt had also paid a man to come in and decorate the hall and stairs; the paper was cream, with a green swirly pattern, and cream woodwork too. And through Verity selling a few more of her mother's treasures they'd managed to buy a new green carpet.

The next plan was to get the parlour done. But her aunt kept stalling, because she couldn't decide whether to get rid of some of her parents' old furniture or not. Verity thought she should, she couldn't imagine why anyone would want to hang on to the Victorian chaise longue. It was horribly uncomfortable and the horse-hair stuffing came through the imitation leather and pricked your legs. It also took up so much room. But she supposed her aunt was entitled to be sentimental about something she'd seen her entire life.

There were only a few of Mother's trinkets left to sell now, but they had done well to eke them out over such a long period. Aunt Hazel was anticipating a pay rise at work soon, as business had increased during the autumn and up to Christmas, which everyone seemed to take as a sign the Depression was ending.

Although by now Verity had got to know almost all the staff at Cooks, and liked many of them, she had made only one really close friend. Sheila worked in hosiery. They had met outside the Personnel Manager's office on their first day at Cooks, and they'd been friends ever since. It was difficult to spend much time together outside work, as Sheila lived right out in Dagenham, but they always had lunch together. In the summer they ate sandwiches on the steps of St Paul's, and in the winter they either had soup in a cafe on Cheapside or went into the staff canteen.

Sheila had five younger brothers and sisters, and she had to give nearly all her wages to her mother to help out. When they first started at Cooks, they only earned fifteen shillings and six pence a week, and Verity had to give her aunt eight shillings of that, so after buying a season ticket to get to work she didn't have much left either.

Since joining Cooks, Verity had been moved around the company learning new skills in all the different departments – invoicing in accounts, working the switchboard, packing – and every three or four months she and some of the other younger girls would be summoned up to the boardroom to help collate pages for the company catalogue. That was an enjoyable job, as they could talk and listen to the wireless while they worked.

As the year drew to a close, Verity considered her future. Sometimes she thought she should use all her new skills and get a better job. But it was easy, undemanding work at Cooks, the other staff were fun, and she got regular pay rises. It might be a lot tougher in another company.

As for her father, he still hadn't been caught. The last time a policeman came to the house to check that Archie hadn't contacted Verity, he said the senior officers doubted they would ever find him now. He said they had some information that he'd gone to South Africa, but that had not been confirmed.

But with all the talk of war, and so many men bracing themselves for a call-up, Verity didn't imagine the police cared much about Archie Wood.

She certainly didn't.

Chapter Twelve

'Happy New Year, dear!' Aunt Hazel raised a glass of sherry to Verity as church bells rang out. A hubbub of shouting and loud banging of tin trays broke out in the street. 'It's too cold for me to join that lot out there – and anyway, we've both got work in the morning. So I'll say goodnight.'

'Happy New Year to you too, and sleep tight,' Verity replied and sipped her sherry. She didn't like it much, but she thought it was a drink she must learn to master.

She listened despondently as Hazel went into the kitchen and struck a match to light her little lantern to take out to the lavatory. There was the predictable gust of cold air as she opened the back door, then the click of the lock when she closed it behind her.

Verity had listened to the same ritual and sounds every night since she got back from her first holiday in Torquay over two years ago. Sometimes she wanted to scream out to her aunt to bang the door, turn on a torch, smash a bowl, wash up a cup, or take a biscuit out of the biscuit tin. Anything to make it different. Tonight Aunt Hazel had drunk some sherry before going out there, but not enough for her to start singing or making cheese on toast.

Verity got up from her chair once her aunt had gone

upstairs, picked up the torch by the back door, which her aunt always ignored, and darted to the lavatory. It was pitch dark, very cold and the wind was getting up. She could hear next door's tin bath banging on its nail by their door. She had politely mentioned to the neighbours that it made a terrible racket in high winds and wondered if they could put something around it to stop the clanging, but nothing had been done and she would hear it all night once again.

Aunt Hazel had put a hot-water bottle in her bed earlier, and as Verity got into bed she cuddled it gratefully. She burrowed into the pillow and closed her eyes, going into her favourite fantasy in which she and Ruby ran a cafe in Babbacombe. In this fantasy they were both older, beautifully dressed and terribly sophisticated. They lived together above the cafe in a lovely flat with a luxurious bathroom, and it was always warm and sun-filled.

Being in Babbacombe with Ruby were the truly happy times of the year for Verity. She lived for the two weeks in summer, and usually tried to get there at Easter and for a long weekend at Whitsun, but it was never enough. If it wasn't for the weekly telephone call to Ruby, and the letters they exchanged, Verity couldn't imagine how she'd cope with living with her aunt.

It was just so terribly dull. Conversations were only ever about what they'd have for tea, who said what at Chiesmans, and speculation about the neighbours. Hazel didn't read books and had never been anywhere – she didn't even like going to the pictures, something Verity adored.

Ruby kept telling her she should make a friend locally, find someone to wander around the shops with, or go to a dance with. But how did you make a friend? You could hardly stop someone in the street and demand they became your friend. From what she knew about the girls at work, their closest friends were from schooldays. But the girls at Verity's school had all been so mean after her mother's suicide. As for Susan, she used to turn her head away if Verity went anywhere near her – it was like she had a nasty, infectious disease.

Even two and a half years on, Verity still felt bruised by her mother's death. She didn't miss her, didn't wish she was still alive, but it was an unfinished tragedy. She knew that local people still referred to her as 'the girl whose mother gassed herself'. She had said to Ruby once that it was a good job they hadn't really caught on about her father, or they'd be calling her 'the swindler/suicide girl'.

Yet Ruby seemed to have cast off her humble beginnings, like a snake sheds its skin. She spoke well, she was bright and articulate, and had become astoundingly pretty. With curly auburn hair, sparkling green eyes, a china doll complexion and the figure of a showgirl, she turned heads wherever she went. She loved working at the Palace Hotel, and it seemed she was very well thought of there. She sometimes stood in as a receptionist, when needed, and Verity knew the minute one of the current receptionists left, Ruby would be applying for that position.

Verity reminded herself to telephone Ruby in the morning, on the way to work, to wish her and Wilby a Happy New Year. Along with working at the Palace Hotel, Ruby was learning shorthand and typing at night school. She had said in a letter that once she got her diploma she was going to do a catering course next.

*

Verity left the house fifteen minutes early the next morning so she could telephone Ruby from Hither Green Station. The wind was really raw and she turned up the collar of her coat and tied her scarf tighter around her neck. The coat had been her mother's and it was a very good camel-hair one, bought in Gorringes. It was lucky that Aunt Hazel had had the foresight to keep so many of her mother's things, because Verity had long since grown out of all her own clothes and there just wasn't any money left each week for what her aunt called 'fripperies'. She was five foot five now, wore size 4 shoes, and to her delight had a presentable 34, 24, 34 figure. Her breasts had been a long time coming – in fact she'd thought she would be flat-chested for ever – but judging by the number of wolf whistles she got, she must be reasonably attractive.

Not that she liked male attention. She associated all men with what her father had done to her, and apart from a couple of kisses under the mistletoe at the office Christmas party she hadn't got close enough to anyone to discover if she was wrong to think this. Sheila had a boyfriend called Jack and went on and on about how he made her feel, which Verity found very tedious. Ruby tended to be much the same too, in her letters there was always someone who put her on cloud nine.

Luckily, last August, when Verity went to stay for a holiday, Ruby had just broken up with Charlie, and claimed to be broken-hearted. It didn't stop her eyeing up other boys, but at least she wasn't rushing off to meet someone all the time – or, even worse, trying to make Verity date one of his friends.

Back in November her letters had been full of a man

called Michael who was twenty-two, and had a car. She thought he was 'the one'. But she hadn't mentioned him in her Christmas letter, so maybe that had fizzled out too.

There was the usual river of bowler-hatted men flowing into Hither Green Station. They mostly worked in the City so caught a train to Cannon Street like Verity. The train was always standing room only by the time it got to Hither Green. She couldn't count the number of times she'd been jabbed with a furled umbrella. But that was marginally better than being face to face with a smoker puffing away, regardless of his close proximity to others.

The telephone box was empty for once, and it was good to get out of the cold wind for a few minutes. She dialled the number, fed in some coins and pressed the button once she heard Ruby's voice.

'Happy New Year,' she said. 'I'm just on my way to work, but I had to catch you before I got on the train. Tell Wilby I rang, won't you?'

'Thank heavens you've phoned,' Ruby said. 'I've got a serious problem and I didn't dare put it in a letter in case your aunt reads it.'

'She wouldn't read my letters,' Verity said. 'But whatever is it?'

There was a slight pause, and Verity imagined Ruby looking round to check Wilby wasn't within earshot. 'I'll have to be quick, Wilby's out in the garden doing something. If I change the subject, it'll be cos she's come back in. Anyway, can you ring back this evening after seven thirty, as she'll be out at a meeting and we can talk properly?'

'Okay,' Verity agreed. 'You make it sound so cloak and dagger.'

'She'll hate me if she finds out. I'm pregnant, Verity. I want you to go to my mother in Kentish Town and get her to arrange an abortion.'

Verity reeled in shock. 'You can't do that!' she exclaimed. 'I thought you loved Michael?'

'Well, he doesn't love me, and he's scarpered,' Ruby said bitterly. 'And I *can* do it. I'm going to do it. I don't want a baby –'

She broke off, and when she spoke again her voice was quite different, the hard edge had gone and she sounded like she was smiling. 'And a Happy New Year to you too, Verity, let's hope it's the best one ever. Oh, Wilby has just come in, I'm sure she'd love to speak to you, but you've got the train to catch. Speak again soon.'

Verity stood there with the receiver in her hand for a few stunned seconds. But someone rapped on the glass, wanting to use the phone, so she put it down and left the warmth of the box.

She couldn't really believe what she'd heard. It had never occurred to her that Ruby might be going that far with her boyfriends. But Ruby was far too worldly to think she was pregnant if she wasn't.

Verity wished she could get on a train to Torquay right now and go and see her friend, but she couldn't. She hadn't got the fare – and she'd got to go to work anyway. Besides, Wilby would be alarmed if she turned up unexpectedly.

It was going to be a very long day at work, her mind constantly on Ruby. What had her friend meant by saying she wanted Verity to go and see her mother to arrange an abortion? Surely having an abortion was dangerous? What kind of mother would arrange it for her daughter?

'You seem very preoccupied,' Aunt Hazel said as she fried some sausages for tea. 'You've been staring at the wall as if you think something is going to come through it.'

They were in the kitchen and Hazel had lit the fire. Most evenings when it was cold they stayed in the kitchen and listened to the wireless by the fire until bedtime. They only used the parlour in summer and on Sundays.

Verity mentally shook herself. She had been thinking about Ruby and what on earth she could say to her. She didn't know anyone else who had become pregnant when they weren't married, but she'd heard people being nasty about girls who had. She didn't believe Wilby would be nasty; upset and disappointed perhaps, but not nasty. However, she doubted Ruby would believe that.

'I was thinking about work,' Verity lied. 'Sorry. How was your day?'

'Busy, we got a big order in for a lady up in Blackheath, new curtains all over her house. She's picked the most expensive brocades, must be lovely to have enough money so you can buy whatever you want.'

Aunt Hazel didn't go out until nearly seven thirty. As soon as she'd gone, Verity ran down the street to the telephone box. Luckily, no one was in it; the cold night was good for something. She balanced her pencil and paper on top of the directories, then rang the number.

Ruby answered after two rings.

'I thought you were going to let me down,' she said.

'As if,' Verity said. 'Now take down this number and ring me back, because I haven't got much change.'

A couple of minutes later they were talking again.

'Now explain,' Verity said. 'I thought Michael was "the one" and he loved you.'

'He said he did.' Ruby began to cry. 'He even said he'd marry me when I told him I was pregnant. But then he disappeared. He was such a liar, Verity. He told me he was a reporter on the local paper so I went there, but they said they'd never heard of him. I'd already been round to his digs, and his landlady said he left owing her a week's money. I even went to the pub he used to take me to, where he seemed to know everyone. It appears he'd told them all a pack of lies too. How he was waiting to be taken on by *The Times* newspaper and he was going to buy an expensive car. I was really taken in by him.'

'Oh dear, Ruby,' Verity sighed. 'Are you absolutely sure? Have you been to the doctor?'

'I've missed two periods, that's enough proof. I'm not going to a doc's, as I'm going to get an abortion. Now have you got a pencil and paper? Cos I'm going to give you Ma's address. You go round there and explain, and tell her she's got to sort it for me. She's got a pal who does them for the tarts around there.'

'You can't do that, it's dangerous,' Verity begged her.

'It's a bloody sight more dangerous to bring a child into the world that you don't want,' Ruby spat back at her. 'I should know, that was me. I can't bring a kid up on my own, it's impossible.'

'But Wilby will help you, and so will I,' Verity said.

'Forget that idea, it wouldn't work. Just do what I ask

and go and see my ma. She'll probably be funny with you, but give as good as you get. Insist she does it, or I'll come back to London and land myself on her.'

Verity was alarmed at Ruby's fierceness, she had seen glimmers of that toughness when they first met, but it had disappeared during her time with Wilby. Somehow, she knew there was no point in going on about the dangers, or the rights and wrongs of it. Ruby was determined, and if her mother didn't arrange it for her, she'd find someone else. That person wouldn't care a jot about Ruby, only about the money.

So Verity took down the address.

'The best time to catch her in is around six, when she's getting dolled up to go out. Her real name is Aggie Taylor, but she makes out it's Angie Taylor. You aren't going to like the way she lives, but you knew that anyway. Please don't let me down, Verity, I haven't got anyone to fight my corner but you.'

As Verity walked home she thought about that last statement of Ruby's. It wasn't strictly true, Wilby would fight her corner in a heartbeat. But not on this, though. She'd say adoption was the answer, if Ruby really didn't want the baby. But if Ruby did want it, she'd help bring the baby up and love it like it was her own grandchild.

Apart from the moral issues, Verity really didn't want to meet Angie Taylor. Any mother who sent her child out to steal was a bad person, and she doubted Ruby would be in this predicament if she'd been taken care of and loved as a child.

The following evening, Verity caught the underground to Kentish Town straight from work. She had looked up Rhyl

Street in the London A to Z and knew roughly how to get there. Once she had turned off the main road into the warren of narrow, terraced streets behind the wide thoroughfare, she felt quite sick with fear.

The houses were small here, mostly two storeys, built in Victorian times for working people. There was fog in the air, not so thick that she couldn't read the street signs, but it made everything look even dirtier and more sinister than it really was in the yellow-tinged street lighting. She thought of Hither Green as poor and dreary, but compared to this part of Kentish Town it was a desirable area.

It was quite obvious that most if not all of the houses were multiple occupancy; many had the front doors open, and she could see prams lined up in the hall. Most houses didn't even have curtains so she got glimpses of meagrely lit rooms with many children and adults clustered around a fire. Furniture as she knew it seemed non-existent. She saw iron beds in some rooms, but there appeared to be little else.

Her flesh began to crawl at the thought of how it must be to live that way. She had been dreading calling on Ruby's mother all day, but now she just hoped she'd be in so she could say her piece and get away from here.

Number 32 Rhyl Street was just as wretched as its neighbours, and two ragged urchins of about eight or nine were huddled in the doorway.

'I'm looking for Angie Taylor,' Verity said. 'Do you know if she's in?'

'I seed 'er come in about ten minutes since,' the slightly older boy said. 'You a street walker an' all?'

'No, I'm not,' Verity said with some indignation. 'Now go on in before you freeze.'

'Can't yet, our ma's workin'.'

Verity gulped, realizing immediately what that work was. She had a sixpence in her coat pocket, she gave it to the boys. 'Go and buy some chips,' she said. 'It'll be warmer in there.'

'Thanks, lady!' The boy who'd spoken before grinned at her. 'Angie's upstairs front.'

The bare wooden stairs hadn't been swept for months, and the whole house smelled of damp, of fried food and something else even more unpleasant which Verity didn't recognize. There was only one door upstairs, at the front of the house, and she rapped on it.

'Who is it?' a voice called out.

'Verity Wood, a friend of Ruby's,' she called back.

'Whatcha want?'

'It's private,' Verity called back. 'Please let me in?'

The door was unlocked. There stood a much older, raddled and plumper version of Ruby. Her red curly hair was loose on the shoulders of a dirty green dressing gown, beneath which was a black petticoat. Verity knew her to be thirty-four, but she looked older.

She beckoned Verity to come in and shut the door. Under the room's central light her red hair gleamed just like Ruby's.

'Where d'you know Ruby from?' she asked, taking a packet of cigarettes from her dressing-gown pocket and pulling out a cigarette.

'We met on Hampstead Heath three years ago,' Verity said. 'We've remained friends. I go down to Torquay and stay with her now and then. She asked me to come to you, because she's pregnant and she wants your help in getting rid of it.'

It hurt Verity to say something so serious in such a cold, uncaring way, but she felt there was no point in trying to be more tactful, best to get it over and done with.

There was no surprise on the older woman's face, or even concern. 'Why ask me? Why the hell does she think I'd even know anyone?'

'She is asking you, because you are her mother,' Verity said, her voice quavering with nerves. The room was a real pigsty, squalid, smelly and strewn with dirty crockery, cosmetics and clothes. The sheets on the unmade bed were so ingrained with dirt they must have been on there for a year, and there was underwear drying in front of an open fire. 'And she knows you have contacts who can help her. She said to tell you that if she can't get rid of it, she'll have to come back here and stay with you.'

'She ain't bloody well doing that!' the woman exclaimed in horror. 'She oughta bin more careful. I told 'er if a geezer put 'er under pressure to do it, to suck 'im off, that way she wouldn't get up the spout. I can't do no more than tell her.'

Angie's suggestion brought back a vivid recollection of what Verity's father had made her do to him, and she gagged involuntarily.

'That is truly disgusting,' she managed to get out. 'What sort of a thing is that to say to your own daughter?'

'A bloody sensible thing,' Angie fired back, coming closer to Verity and prodding her in the chest. 'Once you've got over 'aving one cock in yer mouth it won't ever bother you again. Most men like it better an' all. And you can't catch nuffin, either.'

Verity remembered Ruby's advice about giving as good as she got. So she prodded Angie back, but the older woman's chest was like prodding a huge marshmallow. 'I don't want to hear your vile schemes to avoid pregnancy or disease. I just want you to tell me you'll arrange this thing for Ruby, and quickly.'

'It'll cost yer,' she said, her green eyes, so like Ruby's, narrowing because she thought she was going to earn from this.

'No, it won't,' Verity said firmly. 'You'll get it done for nothing, and done properly and safely, because she's your child and you owe her. It was you who sent her off to that house in Hampstead to rob it, and you never even went to the court to try and help.'

'Good job I never went, as it turned out. She got lucky, didn't she?'

Verity felt sickened by this woman, but she knew she'd got to try and like her enough to get her to agree to help Ruby.

'Yes, she got lucky, and now you've got to make sure her luck holds. It won't, if she has to have this baby. You know she'll come back here to Kentish Town, and before long she'll have no choice but to work the way you do. I don't think you'd want that, would you?'

Verity took a photograph of Ruby from her bag. Wilby had taken it back in the summer. The black and white picture didn't capture the beauty of Ruby's hair and eyes, but she still looked stunning, leaning back against a tree in Wilby's garden, laughing because Verity was pulling faces at her.

She handed the picture to Angie. The older woman made a little gasp.

'She looks lovely, doesn't she? And she's got a great

future ahead of her in the hotel trade. But that and everything else will go, if she has the baby.'

'That Mrs Wilberforce will look after 'er, won't she?'

For the first time Verity heard a note of concern in the woman's voice.

'She would, but Ruby will never tell her, she'd be too afraid of disappointing her. That's what Ruby's like – loyal, loving – and she'd take anything rather than hurt her. Just like she was prepared to get a prison sentence rather than grass her mother up for sending her out robbing,' Verity said.

There was a moment or two of silence. The only sounds were Angie inhaling on her cigarette and the crackle of the fire.

'Alright, I'll arrange it,' she said eventually. 'Tell her to make out to that Mrs Wilberforce she's coming up here to stay with you for a few days. And coming to see me to talk. She can 'ave it done 'ere and stay the night. I can arrange it for next Friday. Tell 'er to be 'ere by four in the afternoon.'

Verity must have looked puzzled, as Angie laughed. 'It don't 'appen straight off,' she said. 'My mate does the thing, then we wait. By evening it will start to work, it'll all be over by midnight, and then we can get our heads down.'

'Ruby said she didn't care about the risks, but I do,' Verity said. 'What are they? Could she die?'

'The risk of dying ain't any bigger than 'aving a baby when you live around 'ere,' she replied. 'My friend knows what she's doing, she's a nurse. If she thinks our Ruby's in trouble, she'll tell me to ring for an ambulance. Course I'll 'ave to lie through me teeth to the doctors there, make out she just started miscarrying, but they'll see to 'er, so don't you worry.'

'Okay, then.' Verity felt sick and faint just at the thought of it. 'I'll tell Ruby. But you must phone her too. Tell her you'll look after her.'

Angie smirked, showing bad teeth. 'Yeah, alright, but I want you 'ere an' all, I ain't dealing wiv her on me own.'

Verity didn't intend to leave Ruby alone with her mother. 'I'll be here,' she said sharply. 'Please put some clean sheets on the bed.'

'Hoity-toity,' Angie exclaimed. 'Who d'you think you are?'

'A good friend of Ruby's,' she said quietly, and wrote the telephone number in Babbacombe on a small card. She wrote down her own name, with the number and extension at Cooks too, and handed it to the older woman. 'Next Friday, then? Telephone Ruby before then. And that's where you can contact me in an emergency.'

'You ought to join the bloody police force,' Angie said, her voice heavy with sarcasm. 'You're bossy enough.'

Chapter Thirteen

'What on earth is the matter with you?' Aunt Hazel snapped at her niece. 'I asked you to keep an eye on the sausages while I paid the insurance man, and you've let them burn!'

Verity was jolted back to reality. 'I'm sorry,' she said, looking at the sausages which were now black, and seeing the kitchen was full of acrid smoke. 'I was thinking about work. But they'll be alright, it's only the skin.'

Tomorrow Verity had to meet Ruby and go with her to Kentish Town. She was frightened for her friend, and scared of what she was going to see. She had told her aunt she was going with Ruby to meet her mother, to act as a kind of mediator, and she would stay the night.

Her aunt had spoken to Wilby on the telephone a few times and thought she was a real 'lady', so she couldn't see any good reason for Ruby wanting to see her real mother, who she referred to as 'a bad lot'. Verity felt much the same so she'd had to invent a plausible story with Ruby to tell both Wilby and Hazel. The one they'd come up with was that Ruby felt that in order to finally put the past behind her, she really needed to know her mother's background – in the hope that it would shed light on why she'd been such a bad mother.

Wilby was entirely convinced, but then she'd suggested many times before that Ruby should meet up with her mother. She was the kind of person who believed any problem could be solved by discussion; Ruby had mentioned that she often had people coming to her house to talk over their problems with her.

But Aunt Hazel was a very different kind of person; she hadn't had Wilby's good education, or her experience with damaged children and their destructive parents. Hazel was a black and white sort of person who saw people as either good or bad, and didn't believe they could change. So she took the view Ruby should keep well away from her mother – and she didn't like the idea of her niece being with her, either. Verity knew if she could see the way Angie lived, she'd be absolutely horrified, so she'd made out she was just a weak, rather dim woman who found it hard to cope.

'I should've told you to bring your friend here to spend the night,' Hazel said. 'But I suppose it's too late to change the plans now. I just hope this woman gives you a decent meal, and the bed is clean and comfortable.'

Verity had a mental glimpse of the squalid room and the filthy sheets on the bed, and wished once again that she hadn't got to spend a night there. 'I'm sure it won't be anywhere near as bad as you imagine,' she told her aunt. 'From what Ruby's told me, it sounds like her mother really is trying to pull herself together.'

'Pity she didn't try when Ruby was still a child,' Hazel sniffed. 'I bet she only wants Ruby back now because she's working; there's a lot of women like that. You tell Ruby not to be stupid and fall for any old blarney.'

'She likes Wilby and being in Babbacombe too much to want to go back to her mother. She just needs to lay a few ghosts, and see how things are with her mum. I can understand that.'

'Times have changed,' Hazel said thoughtfully. 'Back when I was a girl no one would have dared speak out about their parents, not even if they beat them black and blue and half starved them. Our mother was nasty, and our father was as weak as a jellyfish. But we put up with it, it's just the way it was.'

Verity felt terribly sorry for her aunt. She hadn't had much of a life, pushed out by a prettier younger sister, bullied by her parents and then expected to stay and take care of them. It was no wonder she could be so cold and brusque. But just this once Verity wanted Hazel to know she cared, so she put both her arms around the older woman and hugged her.

'You've been so kind to me,' she said. 'Just saying thank you isn't really enough, but I want you to know that you are very special to me.'

'Oh, get away with you.' Hazel pushed her away. Yet her lower lip was quivering, proving she was touched and struggling not to show emotion. 'I only did what anyone would do for their family. Besides, I like having you here with me.'

Verity reached out and patted her aunt's cheek tenderly. 'And I like being here too. So don't worry about me being away for a night, I'm not going to come to any harm.'

Verity left work at two in the afternoon the following day to get to Paddington Station to meet Ruby. She'd said she had a dental appointment to go to. She was carrying a small overnight bag and she'd taken the precaution of adding a small bottle of Dettol, a packet of sanitary towels, soap and a clean towel. She wasn't convinced Angie would have cleaned the place up.

Ruby's train had already arrived when she got there, and she was waiting by the news-stand wearing a dark blue coat, a cream woolly beret and matching scarf. She looked very pale, all her usual bounciness gone. 'Before you ask, I'm not scared,' she said, even before she greeted her friend. 'I just want it to be over and done with. So don't try to talk me out of it.'

'Then all I'll say is that whatever you do, going ahead, or backing away, I'll be right beside you,' Verity said.

Ruby half smiled. 'I knew I could depend on you. Now let's just get there. It's going to be quite an ordeal, seeing Ma again.'

Angie's room in Rhyl Street was marginally improved from Verity's previous visit. The bed was made, clothes had been picked up, and there were no unwashed cups or dishes lying around. Yet it was still dirty; there were balls of fluff on the lino, thick dust on the mantelpiece, and the oilcloth on the small table didn't look as if it had been wiped over in months.

Angie did, however, seem genuinely pleased to see Ruby, admiring her clothes, her hair and how tall she'd grown. But she didn't attempt to embrace her.

'Well, you ain't my little girl any more,' she said, looking her up and down. 'Shame with all that learning and posh talk you got from that snooty woman that you didn't learn to keep your knees together.'

'Well, I've had a lifetime of lessons from you on how to lie on my back,' Ruby retorted, her tone harsh and her face like stone. 'But don't you worry, Ma, I won't make the same mistake again. You get me sorted out and I'll be out of here.'

'I was only teasing, don't you go all snotty wiv me,' Angie said. 'The woman will be 'ere soon, and I got a cheap rate cos you is my kid. So don't come all lah-de-da or she might put the price up.'

They had a cup of tea while they waited for the woman to come. Angie spoke about some people in the road that Ruby used to know, and she said she was worried about what she'd do if war broke out. 'A few bombs round 'ere and the 'ouses'll come down like a pack of bleedin' cards,' she said. 'I reckons I'd be better off movin' out of London.'

Verity saw Ruby's look of panic that her mother might turn up in Babbacombe, and felt she had to chip in. 'You'd be best moving to a small town up north,' she said. 'The Germans will be targeting the ports mostly. In fact I think all places on the coast will be at risk.'

'Is that so?' Angie said. 'I didn't think of that.'

'Anyway, it might all blow over,' Verity said, even though she knew that wasn't likely, not the way things were going.

Angie clearly wasn't very bright, or sensitive, as she launched into telling her daughter how the abortion was going to be done, in very graphic terms.

'She'll get you to perch on a stool wiv yer legs wide open and she gets the end of the enema tube and puts it right up inside. Takes a while cos she 'as to get it right in the neck of the womb. Then she pumps in the soapy water. You know when it's in the right place cos the water don't come out. Then she'll bugger off, and we wait for the pains to start and it all to come away.'

Verity had a dozen questions. Was this enema thing sterile, could the soap cause a violent reaction, how bad would these pains be? And what if something went wrong and Ruby died? But she couldn't ask them for fear of frightening Ruby still more – and anyway, Angie was already talking about how they used to do this procedure with a knitting needle.

'Alright, Ma, shut up now,' Ruby said in a shaky voice. 'I don't want any horror stories. And don't let the woman tell me any, either.'

'The pains are getting stronger,' Ruby whispered to Verity.

Verity had nodded off, even though she'd intended to stay awake lying beside her friend. But at the mention of pains getting stronger she was awake instantly. 'What can I do?' she asked. She looked at the clock on the mantelpiece; it was three in the morning.

'Nothing, just stay there and keep me company. Don't wake Ma up, she gets on my nerves.'

Angie was asleep in an armchair, her slippered feet up on a footstool, and she was snoring for England.

Angie had put a scarf around the central light to make it softer, and the fire had been banked up to keep the room warm, but even if the soft lighting masked how ugly and grubby the room was, what Verity had seen earlier was so ghastly she doubted she'd ever forget it.

The abortionist was called Evie, a small red-headed Irish woman who appeared supremely confident and knowledgeable, but when she got Ruby on the stool and then put her hand right up inside her, talking all the while about how she had to open the cervix, Verity felt sick.

She had already grated Lifebuoy soap into a bowl of boiled water, and she whisked it vigorously until the water was pink and frothy.

Once she was satisfied she'd opened up the cervix, with one end of the enema douche in the soapy water, she slid the other end right into Ruby until she squealed. 'That's it, then,' Evie said. 'It always makes my ladies call out when it's in right – bit like the thing that got you in this way, ducks.'

Angie found that very funny, and poured herself some gin, but Ruby was white-faced and wide-eyed. Verity watched how Evie began squeezing the rubber bulb on the tube, pumping the soapy water into her friend.

'I expect Angie's told you,' she said. 'Soap is an irritant, and it starts up contractions. It'll be no worse than your period – a few aspirins and you'll be fine.'

The whole thing was over in half an hour. Angie paid Evie, and she packed up her enema douche and her cheese grater, and left hurriedly. Ruby said she just felt bloated, nothing more.

It was a very long evening. Angie didn't have a wireless to distract them, and she carried on drinking gin and going on and on about the arguments she'd had with neighbours, how her landlord kept threatening to throw her out, and how the children downstairs made so much noise.

The children were indeed noisy, they appeared to be playing some game in the hall, and their shrill voices were very irritating. There was a baby crying at the back of the house too, and every now and then a man would bellow for it to shut up. But there was noise from the street too: boys kicking a tin can around, women shouting for their children, drunks coming home singing and falling over. But by twelve it grew quiet, and that must have been when Verity fell asleep.

'How bad is the pain?' Verity whispered.

'Strong, but bearable,' Ruby whispered. 'But I think I'm losing a lot of blood. Can you get me another pad?'

Verity hadn't taken off her blue tweed skirt and toning twinset in case she had to rush out to get an ambulance or anything. But Ruby was in her nightdress, and she was lying on the clean towel Verity had brought with her.

As Verity pulled back the covers to help her friend change the pad, she was shocked at how much blood there was, and the smell of Lifebuoy was very strong.

'Don't look so alarmed,' Ruby said. 'You can't make an omelette without breaking eggs, I expected a lot of blood. Just throw the pad on the fire.'

Verity had found it distressing and embarrassing to watch the procedure Evie did, as she'd never seen another woman's parts before, but that embarrassment was gone now, her only concern was her friend's safety. Angie continued to snore as Verity sat beside her friend and rubbed her lower back for her, which appeared to help the pain. But the severity of the pain and the amount of blood she was losing was very frightening, and when Verity saw lumps of what looked like liver coming away she helped her friend on to a chamber pot and prayed silently it would soon be over.

A sudden small splash and the almost immediate lessening of pain suggested the deed was finally done, and it was only then that Angie woke up.

Verity felt nauseous but she managed to tell the older woman she thought it was over.

'I'll check,' she said, helping her daughter off the chamber pot and peering into it. 'Yeah, it's done, you'll feel better now, luv,' she said to Ruby. 'I'll get rid of this, and Verity can make us all a cuppa tea.'

'Do you feel better now?' Verity asked her friend, once Angie had gone out of the room. She helped her to lie back on the bed. 'I'll wash you and put a clean pad on, shall I?'

'Did you see it?' Ruby asked, catching hold of Verity's hand.

'No, I couldn't bear to look.'

Ruby began to cry silently. Verity held her in her arms and cried too, sharing her distress at what had just happened and the tiny life that was now gone.

'What's up wiv you two?' Angie said from the doorway.

Verity hadn't heard her come back, and she turned her head towards the woman, but couldn't bring herself to speak.

'No point in gettin' all soppy about it,' Angie said. 'It's done now.'

Ruby had slept after Verity washed her, and Angie went out saying she needed to see someone. Verity sat in the armchair by the fire and tried to read a magazine. But the light was too dim – and anyway, she couldn't take anything in, because her mind kept constantly returning to what she'd witnessed.

It was still only eight in the morning, although it felt much later, as she'd had so little sleep. Ruby had intended to catch the four o'clock train home, but Verity wasn't sure she should do that. It seemed far too soon to be going anywhere.

She turned to look at her friend sleeping. She was still very pale, but Verity thought that might be because of the poor light in the room. Outside it was a typical cold, dark January day, the street still quiet. Two old ladies emerged from the house opposite carrying shopping baskets, they looked pinched with cold.

The best solution seemed to be to leave Ruby here for another night, Verity thought. She could come back in the morning and go with her to Paddington to see her off. But she really didn't want to leave her friend to Angie and her less than tender mercies.

Should she take Ruby home with her? She wanted to, but aside from the journey maybe being difficult for her, there was Aunt Hazel. She was always quick to sense anything unusual, and even with the best acting skills in the world Ruby wasn't likely to be able to hide the fact that she was recovering from something.

Hearing a little sound, she got up and went over to Ruby. She was awake, but with beads of perspiration on her forehead.

'How are you doing?' she asked. 'You look hot. Shall I get you some water?'

'I think something's wrong,' Ruby said in little more than a whisper. 'I feel really poorly.'

Verity put her hand on her friend's forehead. It was hot enough to fry an egg. 'Do you hurt anywhere?' she asked, suddenly feeling frightened.

'It feels like I'm tender everywhere, even my arms and legs, I can't explain better than that.'

'I'll get you some aspirin and a glass of water. That should make it better.'

'Has Ma gone out?'

'Yes, she had to see someone.'

'Getting away from us more like. She won't come back until we're long gone.'

Verity was shocked that Ruby would think that of her mother, but perhaps she was right. After all, Angie had gone out very early, without a proper explanation. But it wasn't just shocking to think a mother could care so little for her child, it was very frightening too, as Verity had been banking on her help and advice if anything went wrong.

She got the water and the aspirin, and propped her friend up to take them. 'I don't think you can cope with the long train ride home today,' she said sitting down beside Ruby, who had now slumped back down on the pillow again. 'You should stay here another night.'

'You'll stay with me?'

Verity looked down at her friend and, without an ounce of medical knowledge, she knew something was badly wrong. Being very hot was the only obvious symptom, but Ruby's eyes looked cloudy too, and that weak voice wasn't put on.

'Of course I'll stay with you until I'm sure you are okay,' she said. 'But I'm wondering if I should call an ambulance and get you to hospital.'

'You mustn't do that,' Ruby whispered. 'I'll get in trouble, and Ma will too.'

Another hour went past, and Verity sat beside her friend, from time to time wiping her face and neck with a cold wet flannel. But she sensed Ruby was sinking lower, she didn't seem aware of anything, not even Verity bathing her face.

By eleven Verity was beginning to panic that Ruby might actually die if she didn't get her help. Whatever the consequence of that help, it wasn't going to be as severe as death.

'I'm going to slip out and call an ambulance,' she said to Ruby. 'I'll do all the talking for you, I'll say you started to miscarry when you got here to see your mum. If I deny you've done anything, they can't prove otherwise.'

Ruby just looked back at her with vacant eyes, it was clear she had gone past the stage of making a decision for herself.

It was very cold out in the street, especially after the close, stuffy air indoors. Verity had noticed a telephone box the day before, two streets away. She ran all the way to it, her heart thumping with fear.

She told the operator that she feared her friend was having a miscarriage, that she'd lost a lot of blood, and she believed her to have a very high temperature. After giving her name and Ruby's, also the address in Rhyl Street, the operator said she was to go back and wait for an ambulance.

The ambulance took Ruby to the Whittington Hospital in Archway, a hospital Verity had been to once before with her mother when she was about eleven, to visit a sick friend of the family. She had thought it rather exciting to see inside a big hospital. But to go there riding in an ambulance, watching her dearest friend vomiting suddenly and then becoming as limp and lifeless as a doll, was terrifying. She could smell the Lifebuoy soap on Ruby and she was sure the ambulance men could too, she wondered if they would call the police once they were at the hospital.

Once in the casualty department, Ruby was wheeled away and Verity was told to sit in the waiting area. A young nurse came and took some details from her. Verity merely gave her Angie's address, and said that Ruby had come to visit her mother on the previous day, but in the early hours of the morning she'd begun to miscarry. She said that Ruby had only told her she thought she might be having a baby a few days earlier and that was why Verity had come to visit her.

Whether the nurse believed her she didn't know. She made no comment at all, just wrote down the little Verity had told her and then went away.

Verity felt her nerves were at breaking point after two hours passed with no one coming to tell her what was happening. The waiting area was full of people in some kind of distress: men with bloody heads as if they'd been in a fight, and others who had come hobbling in with leg injuries. There were several white-faced mothers holding a sick child or baby in their arms, a man with a young girl who looked like she'd broken her arm, and many old people, some of whom were talking to themselves.

Each time an ambulance arrived their patient was wheeled straight in through the double doors where they'd taken Ruby, so she assumed all the people around her had arrived under their own steam and were not considered such urgent cases.

Finally, at three thirty, Verity plucked up courage to go and ask a nurse about Ruby. She said she would find out, but Verity was to sit down and wait.

But this time she didn't have long to wait, as a doctor came out through the double doors and asked her to come with him. He led her to a small office and then turned to her.

'Who did this to your friend?' he asked point-blank.

'Sorry! No one did anything to her,' Verity said. 'She just started bleeding this morning.'

'Rubbish,' he said sharply. 'Tell me the truth.'

She couldn't, she'd promised both Ruby and Angie. The only way was to act indignant and stick to her story.

'I beg your pardon,' she said, frowning at him. 'I have told you the truth, and please may I know how my friend is? That, surely, is the important thing right now, not persecuting me for bringing her here for help.'

'We had to take her to theatre for an emergency D and C,' he said, his eyes sparking with anger. 'She had lost a great deal of blood and it's touch and go if she'll make it. Maybe you knew nothing of what she'd done, but someone did this to her and they should be horsewhipped.'

Verity felt faint, she slumped back against the office wall, her legs suddenly feeling like rubber. The doctor caught hold of her arm, led her to a chair, and pushed her head down between her knees.

'Take deep breaths,' he said. 'Have you eaten anything today?'

She managed to shake her head, realizing she hadn't eaten anything since a couple of slices of toast yesterday morning.

'Well, I suggest you go and get something, we have enough sick people in here to deal with as it is.'

His brusque tone was evidence he had no sympathy for her. She didn't want any further questions, so she pulled herself upright and slunk out.

She found a bakery close to the hospital and bought a meat pie. At the first bite she remembered the day she had met Ruby for the first time and bought her a pie, and the thought that her friend might not survive made it difficult for her to swallow. But she forced herself to eat – the doctor was right, they didn't need people fainting in the waiting room. And she had to stay strong in case the police came.

Back in the hospital, she waited a further hour, all the time gnawing at her nails with worry. And when she couldn't bear not knowing anything, she burst through the double doors and demanded to know how Ruby was.

It was a sister she asked, a small woman who looked too wrinkled and old to still be working.

'I just need to know,' she begged her. 'I don't know whether to go home, or what. The aunt I live with will be worried about me and she's not on the telephone.'

'Just wait here,' the sister said. 'I'll just make some inquiries.'

The smell of disinfectant and other chemicals turned Verity's stomach as she stood there waiting. There was so much feverish activity and noise too, porters wheeling trolleys with patients on them, nurses scurrying by, a bellowing sound coming from further down the corridor, and close by a child crying.

The old sister came back. 'Tell me, Miss Wood, is Wilby her brother or just a friend?'

'No, it's a lady that she's very fond of,' Verity explained, not wishing to admit Ruby lived with her for fear they might contact her. 'Why do you ask?'

'The nurse who is with her said she kept saying the name when she was delirious.'

That made Verity a hundred times more worried. 'But how is she now?'

'All I can really tell you is that she is in a critical condition. I would suggest that you contact her mother, or this Wilby person, and get them to come here now.'

'As bad as that?' Verity croaked out, her eyes filling with tears. 'But Wilby lives in Devon.'

The sister shrugged. 'If she is able to get here, it may well make all the difference to your friend. Now I must go, I'll leave the contacting to you.'

Verity went back into the waiting room and sat down, her head whirling with conflicting thoughts. If Ruby survived and found out she'd told Wilby about this, she was never going to forgive Verity. But if Ruby died, without Wilby knowing, Wilby was never going to forgive Verity.

Whatever she did, Verity knew she was going to be cast out.

'So what is the *right* thing to do?' she asked herself.

She knew it was to telephone Wilby. And after that she should go back to Rhyl Street and find Angie.

'Just live, Ruby,' she whispered softly. 'I can bear it, if you never speak to me again. But I can't bear the thought of you dying.'

Chapter Fourteen

Verity opened the letter with a Torquay postmark in some excitement, as she had been waiting nervously to hear from Ruby. She felt her friend would only take the trouble to write if she'd decided to forgive her for what she had called her 'betrayal'. If she had anything nasty to say, she'd use the telephone or speak face to face.

But as Verity pulled a plain white postcard from the envelope she gasped. In large capital letters Ruby had simply written:

YOU ARE DEAD TO ME.

There was no explanation as to why Ruby felt compelled to be this brutal, and the starkness of the message was evidence that her heart had turned to stone and there was no way back now.

Verity was too stunned to cry for a few moments. She could only stare at the words in absolute horror. But at the realization that their friendship, which Verity had valued above everything, was now dead and buried, the tears began to flow.

She had of course known when she telephoned Wilby from the hospital that she was breaking her promise to Ruby. But she wasn't telling tales out of spite or for attention, it was a desperate situation. No one – not her, not the doctors or nurses – believed Ruby would last the night.

What sort of friend would she be if she didn't try to contact Wilby, the woman who had done so much for Ruby, so that she could say goodbye?

Or was Ruby so utterly selfish that she didn't know how important such things were to caring people?

If Ruby had died alone in the hospital, the police or Angie would have had to contact Wilby anyway and tell her what had happened. Did Ruby imagine that was a preferable way to hear of the death of someone you loved?

But setting aside the obligation to inform Wilby, did Ruby have any idea what Verity had been through that night? She had stayed at her friend's bedside all of those endless, dark hours when Ruby was barely conscious. She had knelt on the floor by the hospital bed and prayed for her to live. She had even believed God heard her and granted her wish, because around seven o'clock on Sunday morning Ruby finally began to rally.

Wilby arrived at ten in the morning, having driven up from Devon in her old Austin, which didn't even have a heater. She was icy cold, exhausted and stiff from the long drive, yet if she was disappointed in Ruby, or angry with her, she certainly didn't show it. All Verity saw was love and deep concern for Ruby's welfare.

There was no doubt Ruby was glad to see Wilby. She was very poorly, yet she clung on to the older woman like she was a life raft, and she didn't ask how she came to be there. Maybe it would have been better if Verity had stayed there for the rest of that day, so she could explain her actions. But Wilby said she should go home, because she was exhausted, and she said she would make everything right.

As it was, Wilby telephoned Verity at her work the following day, telling her she was staying in a guest house for a few days until Ruby was able to travel.

'She was so foolish not confiding in me,' she said. 'It is true I would never have condoned an abortion. But we could have made plans for adoption, if she felt unable to keep the baby. I don't blame you for anything, Verity, I know how forceful Ruby can be when she wants to do something.'

Verity cried then, telling the older woman how scared she'd been and that she was afraid Ruby would hate her for calling Wilby.

'I'm afraid Ruby does think you betrayed her at the moment, Verity,' Wilby said gently, her voice cracking with emotion. 'But that will pass once she's a hundred per cent again. I have told her that I thank you from the bottom of my heart for calling me, I can't bear to think how I would have felt if I hadn't got to see her one last time. I stressed that you did the right thing, the only thing. If there is anyone to blame, it's her own mother, who hasn't even been to see her. It's difficult to believe anyone can be that callous.'

Verity had believed then that Wilby was right and that once Ruby was on the mend she would be ashamed she'd ever spoken of disloyalty.

How wrong she was! Two months had passed, Ruby was completely well again and back at work. This ought to have been an apology, and a plea for her to come to Devon as usual at Easter, but instead it seemed their close friendship was over, and Ruby hated her.

The only reason she had come up with for her friend's

nastiness was that Ruby believed Verity was jealous of her relationship with Wilby. Maybe she imagined Verity had implored Wilby to come to London in the hope that she would look saintly while Ruby looked wayward and bad. It didn't seem possible that Ruby could be crazy enough to believe Verity would try to turn Wilby against her, or that she was spiteful enough to send such a horrible message, but it was the only thing that made some sense.

Verity wished she could confide in Aunt Hazel and get her opinion, but she knew that wasn't an option. Hazel had been very suspicious after that weekend, because Verity was so withdrawn, and her endless probing questions almost drove Verity mad. But she couldn't, and wouldn't, tell her aunt or anyone else, as it had been a hideous, pain-filled experience.

No one had come out of it well: not Verity for agreeing to ask Angie to arrange the abortion, not Angie for putting her own child in such danger, and not Ruby, either, if she could turn on the one person who had tried to do the right thing.

Verity felt much the same as she had when her mother committed suicide – a similar burden of guilt, anger too, and a terrible loneliness.

The months passed, Easter came and went, reminding her of Easter egg hunts in Wilby's garden, going down to Oddicombe Beach and daring each other to paddle in the icy spring water.

Whitsun came, and then the summer holidays, recalling all those things they did on sunny days: water fights in the sea, the competitions to see who could eat an ice cream cone the fastest, or running full tilt through Brixham to catch the last ferry of the day back to Torquay. There had been the boys they'd flirted with, rides on the bumper cars, eating winkles, drinking a bottle of cider between them and then walking home, because they were too drunk to get on a bus. Happy, golden days. It had never mattered if it rained, or if they had no money. They could have a good time together just sitting chatting and giggling in a bus shelter.

Verity ached to be back there with her friend, she wanted to smell the sea air, hear waves crashing on the shore, and feel the wind in her hair. Her life was so dull and empty now. She didn't think she would ever laugh again, or ever be as close to another human being as she'd been to Ruby. With nothing to look forward to, no one to share her hopes and dreams with, she even thought of doing as her mother had done, ending it all in the gas oven.

The only reason she didn't do it was because of Aunt Hazel. Even if her sister had been a trial to her, Hazel had been devastated by her death. Verity knew her aunt really loved her, and she couldn't put her through more tragedy.

So she did her best to hide her sadness, she went to work as normal, talked to her aunt over their tea as she'd always done, and went to bed early so she could read. Reading was always a way of shutting out unwanted thoughts, of escaping to a better, kinder world.

All through the spring, summer and autumn, every Saturday morning when her aunt was at work she cleaned the house from top to bottom and then took herself off to the library. She would choose a couple of new books, but then she'd go into the reading room and read newspapers and magazines until the library closed.

She liked the reading room, the sloping wooden desks, high stools, the peace and quiet, and the huge trees which surrounded the building. Even in bad weather, when old people came in from the rain to get warm and the air became thick with the smell of wet clothes and body odour, it was still her place of safety and tranquillity.

The rumbling threat of war and what was happening in Germany fascinated her, and she wanted to know everything. Even if she'd bought a newspaper every day, she still wouldn't get a broad picture of what was happening elsewhere in Europe and around the world – for that she had to read a cross section of newspapers and specialist magazines, and the library had them all.

In March she read how German troops crossed the border into Austria, defying the Treaty of Versailles which had forbidden the union. In May she read about how Hitler and Mussolini met in Rome, in June how all Austrian Jews were given a fortnight's notice to leave by their employers, and in August that Germany had mobilized its armed forces. The civil war in Spain was still continuing. Meanwhile, the leaders of Britain, France and Italy met up with Hitler in Munich for talks which lasted until the early hours. They emerged with a settlement which allowed Hitler to take control of portions of Czechoslovakia. On the 30th of September, Prime Minister Neville Chamberlain arrived back in England waving a piece of paper which he said would guarantee 'peace for our time'. On the 1st of October, Hitler led his troops into Sudetenland. The Czech Prime Minister described it as 'the most tragic moment of my life'.

Many people, including Aunt Hazel, still believed war

could be averted, but Verity didn't. In November, when she read about *Kristallnacht*, the 'night of broken glass', when synagogues were bombed or burned out, and the shops and homes of Jewish families were ransacked, she found herself weeping openly about man's inhumanity to man.

But while Verity was thinking about what war would mean for her and Hazel, and encouraging her aunt to lay in stocks of tinned food, Hazel was more interested in finding her niece a young man. 'It isn't right that such a young and pretty girl spends every evening at home listening to the wireless,' she said plaintively on a weekly basis. 'Why haven't you got any friends? What is wrong with you?'

Verity had no ready explanation. All through the year Aunt Hazel had regularly asked if she was going to have a holiday in Babbacombe. And why didn't Ruby write to her any more? Verity's response that it was because Ruby was courting now, and she had no time for anyone else, seemed to appease Hazel. But she did say waspishly that girls who forgot their old friends the minute a boy came into their lives were not real friends at all.

Verity wished so much that she could forget Ruby, but it just wasn't possible. So many things reminded her of her friend: books they'd read together, magazines they both liked, the sight of another girl with curly red hair in the distance, a raucous laugh like hers on the train going to work. The song 'September in the Rain' was always on the wireless, and Ruby had loved it. Meat pies, fish and chips, chocolate eclairs; sometimes Verity thought that there wasn't anything in the world which wasn't connected in some way to her friend.

She wanted to telephone Wilby and beg her to tell Ruby just how sad and alone she felt, but she was too proud to go that far. It would only make her look pathetic.

On the 23rd of December, Verity arrived home from work to find a policeman ringing the doorbell. She knew even without being told that something had happened to her aunt.

'I'm so very sorry,' the policeman said once they were inside. 'Your aunt, Miss Ferris, was taken ill suddenly this afternoon at her work. They called an ambulance but I'm afraid she died on the way to the hospital. It was a heart attack.'

Verity felt as if she'd gone into free fall down a deep pit. It couldn't be true, surely. Hazel wasn't that old, she always seemed fit and healthy. And why should it happen at Christmas? The very worst time in the whole year to lose someone you loved.

The policeman put the kettle on, he even offered to light the fire, and he hugged Verity when she cried. He was a kind man, probably in his fifties, with a lined face and tired-looking eyes. He said he was Sergeant Michaels and that he lived by Hither Green Station. He suggested that he get a neighbour to stay with her, but Verity said she'd rather he didn't.

'I'm best on my own,' she said. 'It gives me time to sort out my thoughts.'

'But you're too young to be alone, and it's Christmas Eve tomorrow,' he pointed out.

Verity just shrugged. She had helped her aunt decorate a small tree for the parlour and put up some decorations last Sunday. Verity had pretended excitement to please Hazel, she'd even bought some new red and gold baubles for the tree to convince her. She'd bought her aunt a red wool dressing gown with satin reveres. If she'd bought it in a shop, it would have been very expensive, but as she'd got it from Cooks – at wholesale price, less staff discount – it had been a real bargain. She had gone to great pains to wrap it beautifully, and tied it with red satin ribbon, before putting it under the tree. Aunt Hazel had joked that she'd be creeping down in the night to shake and prod it.

'I have to go to work tomorrow. It's the Christmas party too,' Verity told the policeman. 'I won't want to be at that, of course, but it will give me a chance to tell my boss I might need some time off after Christmas.'

'I will knock on your neighbours' door and tell them what has happened,' Sergeant Michaels said, his tone firm like a school teacher. 'You'll need someone to tell you all the things you must do when arranging the funeral and your aunt's affairs. And they will keep an eye on you too.'

Verity nodded. 'Fair enough, but please tell them to leave me tonight, I really couldn't cope with anyone fussing round me.'

He insisted on lighting the fire before he left, and urged her to put a hot-water bottle in her bed for later. 'Now make sure you eat something,' he said, patting her shoulder as he prepared to leave. 'This couldn't have come at a worse time, you won't even be able to busy yourself with arranging the funeral until after Boxing Day. But you make sure you keep warm, and if you need some help or advice you can always come to the police station. We'll be open all over Christmas.'

After he'd gone, Verity sat by the fire with another cup of tea and stared into the flames. She felt curiously numb, as if she was looking through a window and watching someone else's problem. She thought how she would never again hear her aunt's bedtime ritual of lighting her lantern before going out to the lavatory. Neither would she wake tomorrow to hear her riddling the ashes in the kitchen fire, and coaxing it back into life with some kindling and paper. She wanted such thoughts to make her cry again – that would be normal, and to be expected – but no tears came.

Verity didn't go to work on Christmas Eve. She wanted to, because being in the house now Aunt Hazel was gone was unbearable. But she knew if she did go to work, everyone would think she hadn't cared about her aunt.

So she telephoned Cooks from the phone box and said she'd ring them again after Christmas, as soon as she knew when the funeral was. Then she went to register Hazel's death in Lewisham.

Christmas fever was in full swing in the high street, with so many people shopping it was hard to get through the crowds. The market was always busy at any time of year, but today it needed sharp elbows and determination to get from one end to the other. Verity had always loved the market. Last Christmas Eve she and Aunt Hazel had come down here just before it closed. All the stalls were lit with hurricane lamps and the heaps of tangerines and apples on the greengrocers' stalls looked like treasure troves. They had bought a Christmas tree, a big chicken and a whole bag of fruit, and walked home carrying the tree, Aunt Hazel holding the top end and Verity the bottom. They'd laughed every step of the way.

They had said at the time they'd get the tree earlier the following year, because it was too hard doing all the decorating on Christmas Eve. They had done that; the tree was in its pot right now, sitting in the parlour window all decorated. Hazel's present was beneath it. But she wouldn't open that present, or see her niece light the candles on the tree. Tomorrow Verity would open the present her aunt had bought her, alone. There would be no chicken, as they'd planned to come down here again today, at the close of the market, to buy it. Verity had no intention of buying a chicken to cook and eat alone.

Verity didn't get out of bed the next morning. She heard church bells ringing, but she pulled the covers over her head and tried to get back to sleep. Later she heard someone knocking on the front door, but she ignored that too as she knew it would be Mrs Purcell from next door inviting her in to share Christmas with her family. She knew they didn't really want her there, they barely knew her. And who would want someone so recently bereaved spending Christmas with them? They were kind people, but not thinking straight. With luck, they would think she'd gone out already and would forget about her as they enjoyed their day.

She stayed in bed until twelve, and only got up because she knew she'd never sleep at night unless she had some exercise. So she dressed, pulled on her coat, a woolly hat and gloves, and left the house. She walked briskly up to Blackheath, right across the heath to Greenwich Park, down through the park to Greenwich and the river. It was a grey, slightly foggy afternoon, and there were not many people about. She guessed most were still sitting around the table eating, drinking, pulling crackers and laughing. Her mind slipped back to the last Christmas at Daleham Gardens. She'd had amongst other presents a beautiful sewing box which opened to reveal four drawers on either side, and in them were many reels of cotton, pins, needles, scissors and embroidery silks. It must have been left in the house when they moved away, as she didn't have it now. But then the pleasure she'd got from the gift was spoiled by her father later that same day, when he came to her room.

She hadn't thought about what he did to her much since they left the old house – having Ruby in her life had helped to numb the painful memory – and she supposed it had jumped into her mind again now because it was Christmas Day. She knew a bit more about sex these days, even if it was only through Ruby and the other girls at work. From what they said, it was quite ordinary for a man to get his girlfriend to hold his thing and rub it. She had the idea they even liked to do it. And Ruby's mother had said that awful thing about taking it in the mouth to avoid getting pregnant. But Verity knew with absolutely certainty that it was a wicked and perverted thing for a father to make his daughter do such things to him. Just the thought of it made her flesh crawl, and she still had that smell of him in her nostrils as he'd pushed it into her mouth, nearly choking her.

How she wished she could get on a train now to go and see Ruby and Wilby. For a moment or two she was resolved to find a telephone box and ring them to say Aunt Hazel was dead. She knew Wilby would be so sympathetic, she would tell her to get on the next train, but she couldn't risk Ruby refusing to speak to her, that would tear her apart.

Once down by the river she lingered because she loved the Thames, especially on days like this when the water was choppy and the silver glinted amongst the grey. She thought she would like to get on a boat and sail right down to the estuary at Gravesend and out into the open sea. She had the idea that would wipe out all the sad and nasty things that had happened to her in the past few years.

But it occurred to her then that, as miserable, sad and scared as she was now, without one relative left, apart from her hateful missing father, it also meant she was now answerable to no one. That was actually quite a nice thought. She could stay out as late as she liked, go anywhere she liked.

She owed no explanations, excuses or promises to anyone.

Chapter Fifteen

'Well, Miss Wood, I take it you have searched the entire house and found no legal papers, other than these?' Mr Platt the solicitor asked. He patted the small pile of old, yellowing papers Verity had brought in.

'That's right,' Verity said. 'My neighbour told me I must look for my aunt's will, but I've searched the attic, every box, cupboard and drawer, and I can't find one. I found those old papers in a box under her bed, and as they had your address on them I kind of hoped you'd have her will.'

It was now early February. After a post mortem to confirm Hazel's death was the result of a heart attack, she had been buried in the same churchyard as her parents and sister during the first week of January. It had been a bitterly cold day with flurries of snow falling. But despite that, the funeral had been well attended by staff from Chiesmans and many neighbours.

Verity had taken today off work to come to Simmons, Platt and Friedman Solicitors in Lewisham. Amongst the old papers she had found was a copy of her grandmother's will, leaving the house in Weardale Road to Hazel.

'Sadly, your aunt didn't make one, at least not with us. But as she had these papers and knew the deeds of the house were with us, I am fairly certain we would have been her first port of call.'

'I suppose she thought she had plenty of time – she was, after all, only fifty-one.'

'I wish we could make people see such assumptions are folly,' Mr Platt sighed. 'If you die intestate, the government can take the estate if there is no heir. Even if there is an heir, probate is held up while searches are done to find the closest relative.'

'That will be me,' Verity said. 'She wasn't married, she had only one sister – my mother, who is dead. I'm the only person left.'

Mr Platt looked at her thoughtfully over his glasses. 'Well, my dear, that's as may be, but we still have to make absolutely certain. It wouldn't do to hand over a property to the wrong person. But you can continue living in the house until such time as it either becomes yours, or we find another rightful beneficiary. But even if it is yours, you will have to wait until you are twenty-one to legally inherit it.'

Verity had assumed that would be the case, but she was relieved she didn't have to leave the house.

'I paid for her funeral with some cash I found in her bedroom and her final wages from where she worked,' Verity admitted. 'Was that wrong?'

'For someone so young I think you've handled everything very sensibly. But legally you cannot sell or dispose of her jewellery, silver or any other valuables until probate is settled.'

'She didn't have anything of value,' Verity said. 'The cash I found was money she saved to have a bathroom put in.'

'Will you be able to afford to carry on living there alone?' he asked.

'Just about, I think,' Verity said. 'But with war looming none of us knows what's going to happen, or how we'll manage.'

'That is very true, Miss Wood. I am still hoping it can be averted, but it seems most people are resigned to it now. We've had many clients coming to us to discuss moving out of London for the duration. Personally, I think such action is unnecessary. But tell me, you said your mother died, but where is your father?'

Verity gulped. She hadn't said anything much about her own circumstances. She certainly hadn't expected to be asked about her father.

'He walked out on Mother and me, a long time ago now,' she said quickly. 'Our house was repossessed and we had to come and live with Aunt Hazel. Mother died a while back too.'

'I am sorry to hear that.' Mr Platt's face softened in sympathy. 'You certainly have had a tough time of it. But I would be a poor legal advisor if I didn't point out that, if he has heard of your aunt and mother's deaths, he could come back and insist on moving in with you. As your father, while you are under age, he can exercise that right.'

Verity's heart sank, this was the last thing she had expected to be told. 'I won't let him in,' she retorted. 'He's a violent, nasty man.'

Mr Platt frowned. 'I'm sorry if I struck a raw nerve,' he said. 'Under the circumstances all I can suggest is that, if he does turn up, you telephone the police if you feel you are in danger. But meanwhile I will act for you in dealing with your aunt's affairs, if that is what you wish.'

Verity left the solicitors' office feeling very anxious. It

had been bad enough finding there was barely enough money to bury her aunt. She had expected there to be some kind of insurance policy to cover the funeral expenses, but there wasn't. All she had now was her own wages, and with electricity and gas to pay she was already struggling. She had come to see Mr Platt in the hope that, even if there was no will, she would at least feel comforted by knowing she had put all her aunt's affairs in order. She had never imagined that her father would even be mentioned, let alone that she would hear he had rights over her still.

Looking at the situation logically, Mr Platt didn't know he was on the run, and that therefore her father was extremely unlikely to do anything which would risk him being arrested. Also, he'd always wanted to have the best of everything, so Verity doubted he'd ever contemplate living in a house with an outside lavatory and no bathroom.

So she might as well put him out of her mind.

In the evening of her visit to the solicitors, Verity began a massive sort-out of her aunt's house. It was partly to distract herself from unwelcome thoughts of her father, but also because it occurred to her that if she got a lodger in, that would solve some of her problems.

Hazel had been a hoarder; she kept everything from old postcards to stockings with holes in them. Every drawer in her bedroom was filled, and there were dozens of full boxes under her bed, piled on top of the wardrobe, and even more in the attic.

Verity made several piles. The best clothes and shoes for a jumble sale, the rest in old pillowcases for the rag and

bone man. All the worthless items she put out for the rubbish collection, and she made a bonfire with the hated
chaise longue, despite having been told she wasn't to
dispose of furniture, as she was sure no one would ever
want that. And she threw on to the fire all the old cards
and letters.

It took four evenings, working solidly after she got in
from work until late at night. While sorting things she
came across a few belongings of her mother's that she and
Aunt Hazel had forgotten about. There was a very stylish
silver cigarette case, a gold and garnet bracelet and a silver
and turquoise necklace.

It was almost as good as finding a crock of gold, and it
lifted her spirits considerably. She thought, if she got
enough money for the items, she might go ahead with
Aunt Hazel's dream of putting a bathroom in. The man
her aunt had asked to call round to give her a quote said it
would be easy to install a bathroom in the small box room
that used to be Verity's when her mother was alive.

That find, and all the increased space as a result of clearing out Hazel's worthless clutter, had a surprisingly
therapeutic effect on Verity. She found herself getting
excited by thinking about the many small improvements
she could make to the house herself. She could easily give
Hazel's bedroom a lick of paint, even try her hand at wall-
papering. She would move her things into that room and
then make her old one nice for a lodger.

All at once she found her evenings busy when she got
home from work, and weekends no longer seemed to be
so long and lonely. With something creative to do she
found she wasn't dwelling on the absence of her aunt,

Ruby or her mother so much. Early March also brought some very mild, sunny days, and that made her think of what she could do to make the back garden nicer so she could sit out there in the summer.

She took her mother's cigarette case, bracelet and necklace up to Rosen's, the jeweller's in Blackheath, one Saturday afternoon. During her periodic visits to the shop she had struck up a rapport with Mr Rosen, the owner, and this time he greeted her very warmly like an old friend.

'I keep hoping you'll come in with a young man one day to buy an engagement ring,' he said teasingly. 'You really should ensnare one soon before they all get called up for the war.'

Verity laughed, and all at once realized she had been finding quite a lot of things funny in the last couple of weeks.

'There is no young man to ensnare, I'm afraid,' she said. 'I need some cash to put a bathroom into my house. Perhaps, once I've got that, I'll find Mr Right.'

He looked at the goods for some little time. 'Ten pounds,' he said finally.

'I can't accept that,' she gasped in horror. 'I was expecting at least thirty.'

'I'm sorry, my dear, if that offer disappoints you,' he said with a shrug. 'But times are getting very hard for me. I still haven't sold the silver pheasant I bought from you, and I doubt I will until this threatened war is over. Many of my best customers are worried about it and moving out of their homes here in Blackheath. The last few weeks I've hardly sold a thing.'

'Why are they going? We don't even know for certain there will be a war,' Verity said with some indignation.

He looked hard at Verity and made a resigned face. 'I think we all know it's inevitable, my dear. People say it's better to find a safe place now and get settled before it begins. I say to them, "Who will look after your fine house and stop burglars and looters getting in?" They don't say I am a silly old man, but that is what they think.'

'So you mean these people are just shutting their front doors and going away?' Verity asked incredulously.

'Just so,' he said. 'Just this morning as I came up Lee Park I saw Mr and Mrs Solway, next to the doctor's, they were putting suitcases in their car, ready to go. They told me they were going to the Lake District where they own a cottage.'

Verity agreed to accept the ten pounds he'd offered, because she needed money now, and she doubted anyone else would give her more. She stayed for a little while, chatting about what the war might mean for them. Like her, Mr Rosen had been following the news closely, and they spoke of the awful way the Germans were treating their Jewish population.

'I have a feeling it is going to get much worse for them,' he said. 'Many of the wealthier ones have left for America and other safe places, but the rest will become trapped there. And goodness knows what will become of them.'

Verity could see his eyes filling up, perhaps thinking about friends or family he had over there, so she changed the subject to conscription and said she'd read that in April men of twenty and twenty-one would be called up.

'Thank goodness I'm too old this time,' he said with a weak smile. 'I went off so willingly last time, not even waiting to be called up, just like so many others. But I lost most of my pals, and for a time I thought I'd lost my mind too. I pray this time it won't be so bad.'

After leaving the jeweller's Verity bought some fruit, and a loaf in the baker's. As she walked back through the village she wondered if ten pounds was enough for a bathroom, as she couldn't remember what Aunt Hazel had said it would cost.

It wasn't exactly sensible to get it done, not until she knew for certain the house was hers. But on the other hand, it would make life so much more comfortable for her and a lodger to have a bath, hot water and an inside lavatory. Could she really go another couple of years without them?

As she got to Lee Park she stopped to look at the Solways' house, wondering how they could bear to leave it. It was one of those elegant, detached Georgian houses, with a central front door beneath a fancy portico, and lovely long windows, arched at the top, of which there were so many in Blackheath.

Aunt Hazel had made most of the curtains for the couple, and she had often talked about how beautiful the house was inside.

Verity looked over the gate, noting they had closed the internal shutters across the windows. Then she saw a young man sitting on the lawn under a monkey puzzle tree.

He had a small suitcase with him, and he was slumped over, almost as if he was crying. Assuming he was a relative of the Solways, and he had arrived after they left, she felt she had to speak to him.

'Excuse me!' she called out. 'If you are looking for Mr

and Mrs Solway, I've been told they left for the Lake District this morning.'

He looked up at the sound of her voice, and wiped his eyes with the back of his hand. 'Yes, I know,' he said, getting to his feet. 'I was their gardener and they gave me notice today.'

He was an unusual-looking man, slender and tall, with a bony but rather beautiful face, a thick thatch of unruly fair hair and duck-egg-blue eyes. She guessed him to be in his mid-twenties, and though his clothes were old and worn he sounded very well bred.

'Gave you notice just like that?'

He walked over to her and stood behind the gate looking at her. Close up he looked even more interesting. He had chiselled cheekbones, and his eyes were lovely, with thick, long dark lashes. Not handsome in a conventional way, but there was something fascinating about his face.

'That's right. Called me in just after ten, handed me my wages and said they were closing up the house and leaving. I asked if I was to stay on to look after the house and garden – I have a room above the old coach house, you see – but they said that wasn't necessary, I was to go.'

He *had* been crying. Verity saw his eyes were red.

'That was very mean of them,' she said. 'Had you been with them long?'

'Six years. The garden was nothing until I came, I breathed life into it and made it what it is today. The daffs are all coming out now, in another few weeks it will be a picture, and they just chuck me out like I did nothing for them.'

His voice was quavering, and she wasn't surprised he was upset – anyone would be.

'Can you go home to your family?' she asked.

'No, I don't have any –'

He stopped short, and Verity noticed he'd turned very pale and was wavering.

'Are you alright?' she asked.

To her shock, without answering her, he just crumpled in front of her eyes, falling down on to the gravel drive. Verity hastily opened the gate and went in. She crouched down beside him, not knowing what to do.

Thankfully, he opened his eyes after a few moments, so clearly he'd just fainted, or maybe it was shock. He tried to sit up.

'Sorry,' he said haltingly. 'I don't know what happened there, I felt whoozy and then suddenly I was on the ground.'

'I think you just fainted,' Verity said, helping him to sit up. 'It might be shock, especially if you haven't eaten anything today.'

'Just before you came along I was telling myself I ought to go to a cafe. I haven't eaten since yesterday.'

'Eat this for now,' she said, getting one of her apples out of her bag. 'Then I'll come with you to the cafe. There's one down the bottom, on Lee High Road.'

In Fred and Ada's cafe he ordered beef stew with mashed potatoes, while Verity just had a bacon sandwich. She waited until he'd begun to eat before she asked him any questions.

It was apparent he was very hungry, and she was reminded of the day she bought Ruby a meat pie. The difference was that this man's manners were impeccable, no stuffing his food in or not using cutlery.

'I'm Verity Wood,' she said. 'I live close by, I'm sixteen and I work in a wholesaler's in the City.'

'Well, I'm Miller Grantham. I'm twenty-five and as of today jobless and homeless.'

'Miller! What an unusual name,' she said. 'But you'll soon find another job and home.'

He gave her a weak smile. 'Of course I will, just feeling a bit sorry for myself, as it was so unexpected. Miller is a family name, my father and grandfather both had it as a second name.'

'I like it,' she said. 'And it kind of suits you.'

'You don't think I need to be covered in flour dust to carry it off, then?'

Verity laughed. 'No, not at all. You said you had no family, I haven't either. What happened to yours? You sound very top drawer.'

He smirked and raised an eyebrow. 'An expensive boarding school,' he said. 'My father had a government position in India, but he and my mother got yellow fever and died out there when I was ten. I was already at boarding school here. So I stayed, even through the holidays, under the care of Matron. That's when I started gardening, as I used to help out the school groundsman. Along with caring for the cricket pitch, he had a vegetable and flower garden too. A lovely man, he died a few years ago and I still miss him.'

'What would he tell you to do now?' she asked.

Miller laughed. 'For a girl of sixteen you are very direct and adult.'

'I've had to be,' she said, telling him briefly she'd lost her mother and her aunt recently and was now on her own.

'First thing, I need to find some cheap digs,' Miller said. 'Then look in *The Lady*, to see if anyone needs a gardener. But from what I've heard, all young men will be called up soon, so maybe I should just jump into that instead of waiting to be pushed. I quite fancy the air force.'

'You'd suit the uniform,' she said. 'I think you'd look quite dashing.'

'Are you flirting with me?' he said with a warm smile. 'Or just trying to cheer me up.'

'A friend told me I was useless at flirting,' Verity admitted, blushing because that wasn't what she'd intended. 'I'm usually tongue-tied with boys. I think I was trying to help you see the positives. But surely joining up is a bit mad, when you haven't had time to think it over?'

'Well, the money I've got won't last long without a job – even the cheapest room and buying food will soon eat it up. And who will want a gardener now, not with war imminent?'

'That's all true, but you need to give yourself a couple of weeks' breathing space,' she said. She paused for a moment, an idea spinning around in her head. 'Look, I've got a spare room you can have.'

The moment those words came out of her mouth she wished they hadn't. She couldn't have a male lodger, it wasn't right. She knew nothing about him, he could be an escaped murderer for all she knew, and she was living alone. On top of that she still had things to do in the room. But yet, when she saw his expression – surprise, delight and relief – how could she back down?

'Of course it would be just for a couple of nights, until you've thought things through,' she said quickly. She wanted to warn him off any funny business too, but she didn't know how to say that.

'If you are sure,' he said. 'It's a wonderful and kind offer, Verity, and you can rest assured I won't take advantage of your generosity.'

Verity thought it ought to feel awkward as she brought him into the house and showed him the spare room and explained about the lack of a bathroom, but it didn't.

'I didn't have one in the coach house, either,' he said. 'So I'm quite used to going to the public baths, or sluicing down in a big bowl. And as you said, it's only for a couple of nights.'

By the time Verity went to bed that night she felt she'd done a good thing bringing Miller home. He was easy to be with, he washed up after supper without even being asked, and fetched more coal from the back shed when it got chilly. They sat by the fire talking until quite late; he told her his memories of India, before he was sent to school in England, about being taken on to train as a gardener at Hever, the old Boleyn house in Kent, where he stayed for three years, then a chance meeting with Mr Solway, which brought him to Blackheath.

'Mr Gordon, the head gardener at Hever, advised me against it. He said Solway would just get me to do all the donkey work of creating a beautiful garden, then kick me out when it suited him. He did point out there was no real security in working in a famous garden like Hever, either, but at least there was some kudos in having trained there, and people with huge estates would search you out to work for them. But I thought if I missed Hever, I could always go back as a visitor.'

'So the head gardener was right about the Solways?'

'Yes, sadly he was. In fact, looking back, they never cared about the garden the way I did. It was just something to show off to their friends. They paid me a pittance, the coach house was cold and damp, and I was very lonely sometimes, as I'd been used to working with half a dozen other chaps. I suppose I should feel quite excited about embarking on something new now, but all I can think about is that it's heartbreaking to leave a garden I created from scratch.'

'I can imagine,' Verity said.

His eyes looked shiny with unshed tears. 'It was like a field when I began. Weeds five foot high, and overrun by brambles, such back-breaking work in all weathers.'

Verity reached out and patted his arm in sympathy. He smiled weakly, as if he was gulping back tears.

'Maybe tomorrow I'll take you up there, before it becomes overgrown again, I need to rescue my tools anyway. Would it be alright if I brought them here and put them in the little shed to keep them safe?'

'Of course,' she agreed. 'I can't wait to see the garden you created.'

'I built a pond with a waterfall, winding paths with arbours, big herbaceous borders, planted all the trees and sowed the lawns. I used to wake up every morning burning to get out there and care for it. It never seemed like work, just love made visible.'

Verity thought 'love made visible' was the most poetic phrase she'd ever heard. And so apt for a beautiful garden.

'I'd like to say I fully understand, but the truth is I've never done any gardening,' she admitted. 'We had a lovely one in Hampstead, but I was too young to think about who created it. But maybe you can inspire me here? The back garden is a mess. I was thinking I'd like to make it nicer so I could sit out there.'

'I'll have a look tomorrow,' he said. 'After you being so kind to me, it's the least I can do.'

Miller was, she decided, a perfect gentleman. She already knew she wasn't going to be in a hurry to make him move on.

Chapter Sixteen

The next day Miller took her up to the Lee Park house to get his tools and show her the garden. He was so honest, he even felt guilty at taking the Solways' wheelbarrow to carry his forks, spades, shears, hoes, rakes and other gardening tools back to her house. But as he pointed out, it was the only way he could transport them – and the Solways wouldn't even know they had a wheelbarrow.

'They only had poor quality tools,' he explained as he loaded up. 'As the handles fell off, or the blades grew blunt, I replaced them with good ones I bought. That was part of the reason I was so upset yesterday when you saw me; I was wondering where I could store them till I got another job. You, Verity, have been a lifesaver.'

She was too shy to admit then that she thought he might save her life too, because suddenly everything looked rosier. She'd discussed her plan with him of getting a bathroom put in, and he'd said he'd help in any way, as he was good with his hands. But the bathroom was just the start of it, really, there was redecoration needed all round. The only thing holding it up was money.

The garden he'd created and maintained for the Solways was the most beautiful Verity had ever seen. Although it was too early in the year yet to get the full picture of how it would be in full bloom, there was enough blossom on the trees, camellias, hellebores, daffodils and other early flowers to imagine what it would be like in a few months. She hadn't known what the beautiful rose-like flowers in red, pink and white were, until he said they were camellias. The winding stone paths and the fantastic pond with huge rocks would look splendid when the water was turned on, but of course it had been stopped for now. The lawn, like a bowling green, also took her breath away. She knew then that a man who could do all this could be trusted.

As they trundled the wheelbarrow home, Miller told her about friends of the Solways who had already left their homes to go and live in the country. 'Just upped and went. Of course some of the wealthier ones already had homes in the country. But the rest were like sheep, convinced that if the Germans invade down along the south coast, they'll be straight through Blackheath on the way to the heart of London, burning, looting and killing as they go.'

'I suppose if they do invade, that's exactly the way they'll come.' Verity felt a pang of fear at the thought.

'Do you really believe we'll let them invade us?' he said, looking at her incredulously. 'I believe we'll fight to the last man and woman standing to keep them out. You have to believe that!'

He let go of the wheelbarrow handles for a moment, and put his finger under her chin to lift it. 'But if by some chance the Germans do invade, no one can guarantee people's safety, however much money they've got, whoever they are, or wherever they go. Okay, so if bombs drop that's more likely to be on the big cities and ports. But just the same you might stay safe in Lee Green but be bombed out in Hither Green, it'll be like a lottery. So what's the point of moving out?'

'None, if you put it like that,' she agreed. 'But all these

rich folks in Blackheath who've cleared out, have they left their homes intact?'

He nodded. 'I assume they've taken their jewellery and any stuff that's easy to move, but I think most are the same as the Solways, running in panic, and haven't even considered that their homes could just as easily be looted by locals as by Germans. Yesterday I even thought I might break into their house and stay there, drinking their wine and brandy, sleeping in their big bed and reading all their books. I mean they haven't even turned the electric off. It would be like a swish holiday.'

Verity laughed and he joined in. 'But you aren't going to, because?' she asked.

'Well, they might come back for something. Imagine being stretched out on their bed with a big glass of expensive claret, and in they come?'

That second day together Verity cut the pork chop she'd bought for herself into two to share, and roasted lots of potatoes to make up for the small amount of meat. With cabbage, carrots and tasty onion gravy, followed by rice pudding, it turned out to be an excellent lunch.

'You are a very good cook,' Miller said appreciatively as he scraped his pudding bowl clean. 'I'm fairly useless, I do a good bacon and eggs, and cheese on toast, but that's about it. But unless you want me gone tomorrow, I'll go and buy some food for dinner, maybe sausages or something, and I'll have it ready for you when you get home from work.'

'I don't want you gone,' she admitted. 'It's good to have you here, and you've no idea how good it sounds to come home to a meal I haven't had to cook.'

After lunch Miller went outside to clear the little potting shed. It had nothing but ancient paint pots inside, some rusty tools and a great many cobwebs. She watched him sweep it out, then hammer some long nails into the sides so his tools could hang up tidily.

He stayed out in the garden for some time after he'd stowed away his tools, and when he came back in he sat down and drew a little plan of the ideas he'd had for it. 'We should pave over that patch of mud and weeds in the centre,' he said. 'I know where there are some broken paving stones which will be perfect for crazy paving. I thought a nice arbour with honeysuckle growing on it, backing on to the scullery as that's south facing, so a good place to sit. Then dense planting down the bottom to hide the ugly fence.'

It wasn't until the washing-up was done and they were sitting by the kitchen fire listening to the wireless that Verity decided to tell him how she felt about having him here.

'It's nice having your company,' she said. 'Obviously, you'll need to get some work, and maybe that will be somewhere else so it won't be possible to stay here. But I'm really hoping you can find something locally and stay.'

His broad smile told her how pleased he was. 'I'll pay you rent, and help with the bills of course. I thought I'd go and see if they need anyone in Greenwich Park,' he said with excitement in his voice. 'At this time of the year they usually take on more men.'

Verity went out of her way to tell the biggest gossips in the street that she'd taken in a lodger, as she was struggling to make ends meet. If they thought she had gone off the rails and was living in sin with Miller, they said nothing to her face. But she didn't care what they thought, for the first time in months she was really happy.

Miller got work in Greenwich Park and bought an old bicycle to get there and back more quickly. He paid her five shillings a week rent, and they each put six shillings into a pot for food, coal and the gas meter. He went to work before her in the mornings and was back earlier, so he mostly bought meat or fish on the way home and started getting their supper ready. Verity loved coming home to find him busy in the kitchen. He often brought back a few flowers from the park to put on the table, which delighted her too.

'I'm surprised you haven't got a girlfriend,' she said one evening.

'I was crossed in love at Hever,' he said with a grin. 'She was a maid there and one day I caught her kissing one of the other gardeners. I was livid at the time, but a couple of months on I realized it would never have lasted. I lusted after her, but I couldn't talk to her, and I think real, lasting love is a combination of both those things. What do you think?'

'I've never lusted after anyone,' she admitted, hardly able to believe she could tell him such a thing. 'And I think you are the only man I've ever really talked to. I mean I talk to the men at work, have a laugh and a joke with them, ask them about their wives, girlfriends and kids, but it's all lightweight stuff, not deep or meaningful.'

She'd told him about her mother gassing herself soon after he moved in, and a week or so later she told him about how she and her mother came to be here and her father's part in it. But it was only the previous weekend that she'd told him about Ruby.

He listened carefully, making no comment until some little time after she'd finished the story and had wiped a few emotional tears away.

'I'd say she behaved like that towards you because she was afraid you'd always remind her where she came from.'

'No, it wasn't that or she would have broken friends with me long before,' Verity said indignantly. 'I would never say anything about her past, she knew that. I didn't even talk about my own, because there was nothing to be proud of.'

'I didn't mean she thought you would blab about it. More that you were a reminder that she'd been given a second chance in life, and she'd messed it up and lost Mrs Wilberforce's trust in her. Like you said yourself, the only logical explanation for her nasty note was that she feared you had tried to get between her and Mrs Wilberforce. But I bet anything you like she's regretted it dozens of times, and is missing you like crazy.'

'Should I write to her, then?'

'No, Verity. She was the one who was in the wrong. If she's too bull-headed or ashamed to get in touch and apologize, then that's her funeral. You mustn't let anyone walk over you, Verity, get tougher. You are a truly lovely person but, sadly, many people will take advantage of that.'

In April, just as they'd already heard, it was announced that men of twenty and twenty-one were to be called up, and Miller saw that as a sign he must join up now. That way he stood a better chance of getting into the air force, rather than waiting until he was called up and being put into the service of the government's choice, not his.

'Let's face it, they won't want gardeners anywhere for the whole of the war,' he said. 'So I'm going to take next Friday off to enlist, then go and spend the weekend with my aunt and uncle in Surrey. I haven't seen them for over a year, and if the air force do want me I might not get a chance to see them again in a long while.'

Verity didn't like the thought of losing Miller at all, but she was happier about him going into the air force than the army or navy. He had no flying experience, and therefore she thought they would make him ground crew, which didn't sound very dangerous. But she hadn't realized until Friday evening, when she found herself alone at home, just how much she now depended on him for company.

She busied herself changing the sheets on his bed and ironing a few things. Then, feeling at a loose end, she wandered out into the garden. Miller had wasted no time in digging up the central area and laying crazy paving. He'd also dug out old shrubs that were not particularly attractive, and he'd brought new plants back from his work and some from the Solways' garden – but he was so honourable that he'd only dug up those that needed dividing up. Although it was all still very new, it was beginning to take shape as the new plants filled out.

He had made a start on the arbour seat too; just last night he'd said he would finish it after the weekend. It was already looking good, with an almost Gothic aspect to the latticed, pointed top. Once the honeysuckle and jasmine he'd planted beside it got going, it would be a lovely sweet-smelling place to sit.

It wasn't only his company she'd come to depend on, either – the five shillings a week rent would be hard to live without. As much as she'd hoped she could save a bit each week for decorating, repairs and the bathroom, so far she'd had nothing left over to save. So she was going to have real difficulty in making ends meet when Miller left.

The thought of all those abandoned homes up in Black-heath popped back into her head. Their owners clearly cared nothing for their possessions, if they'd just left them. Why shouldn't she have them? She didn't have to be greedy, just a small bag of stuff which would probably never be missed.

Ruby had told her how she used to get into houses without breaking windows. She said she used a thin, bendy blade which she slid along the middle strut of sash windows to push the catch back, and then she'd climb in. She'd said French windows were usually easy too.

Going indoors, Verity looked in the drawer where she kept cooking implements, took out a palette knife and looked at it reflectively. A thin blade, bendy too, and strong enough to withstand a little force.

As Miller had named three families who had abandoned their homes it was simple enough to walk down to the telephone box at the end of the street and look up their addresses in the directory. After finding them, she rang the numbers too. There was no answer from any of them.

What had started out as a mere fantasy suddenly became real. She actually wanted to burgle one of these houses, she even felt excited at the prospect of it.

When it was close to sunset on Saturday evening she walked up to Blackheath to make absolutely certain there wasn't anyone in the houses, and checked out each of them for lights as it got dark. The address in the Paragon was in a terrace, but she found the way to the back service alley and peered through the gate. She didn't think she'd attempt to rob that one, it would be too hard. But Blackheath Park and The Glebe both looked like good possibilities, with side gates leading to gardens that had trees to hide her from view. She settled finally on the one in The Glebe and decided it would be at daybreak the following morning, with enough light to see what she was doing, but yet too early for anyone to be about on a Sunday morning.

Verity's heart was pounding as she got to the house in The Glebe early the next morning. She was so nervous she almost walked away, but the side gate wasn't even padlocked, and after slipping on her gloves she was through it and into the garden in seconds. Internal shutters were closed at the front of the house, but not at the back, and the trick with the palette knife worked like a dream on a small scullery window. She was through the window and on to a draining board in seconds, then with just the briefest glance around the kitchen and laundry room, where clearly no one but a maid or housekeeper came, she went up the stairs to the main rooms. In the drawing room she took a pair of handsome silver candlesticks and a silver bonbon dish. There was masses of silver in the dining room, mostly large tureens and heavy cutlery, but she took only a small jug, and nothing at all from the study at the front of the house.

She went upstairs then to the master bedroom, where she found a ruby brooch sitting in a drawer, and an old-fashioned big silver locket. She looked in the wardrobe, purely because both her mother and her aunt had been in the habit of putting a little cash away in theirs. To her complete shock, there in a shoebox was a wad of five-pound notes.

It seemed to justify what she had done, and because of it she put the jewellery back where she'd found it, and returned the candlesticks and bonbon dish to the dining-room table. She had said she wouldn't be greedy – and anyway they were bulky and heavy to carry.

She went out the way she came in, using her knife to close the latch again. A few moments later she was walking down the road again, her mission accomplished.

On arriving home she opened her handbag to count the money. But to her surprise, along with the money was the small silver jug, which she'd forgotten to put back. That pulled her up sharply, making her see the enormity of what she'd done. Burglary was a crime you got sent to prison for.

She sank down on to a chair, head in hands. It was a terrible thing she'd done, and she felt very ashamed that she'd allowed greed to overcome her conscience. Later she counted the banknotes and discovered there was fifty-five pounds, more money than she'd ever seen at one time before. Somehow, she felt alright about the money – money could easily be replaced, if you were rich – but the jug could have been a wedding present from someone dear to the owners.

Ruby looked up from her seat in the garden as Wilby came out. 'Come and sit with me for a few minutes,' she said.

The blossom on the cherry tree was just opening up in

the sunshine, and all the new leaves on the trees and shrubs were the sharp acid green of spring.

'Something wrong?' Wilby asked.

'I just had a funny little feeling about Verity,' Ruby admitted.

'Sorry you cut her off? I did tell you that you'd regret it.'

'I was too vile to expect her to forgive me now,' Ruby shrugged. 'I'm too ashamed to even admit to you what I said. But this feeling I had was more like a premonition. Like something was happening to her.'

'Then you should stop being so pig-headed and drop her a line,' Wilby said sharply. 'That girl is the reason you are alive today. I don't think you ever appreciated just how poorly you were.'

'Sometimes things are broken beyond repair,' Ruby sighed. 'I really don't ever want to see my mother again, I don't regret telling her that. But I've left it too long now to even hope Verity might still care about me.'

'Don't you think with war likely to break out soon that people should say what is in their hearts?' Wilby said. 'In the last one everyone I knew lost someone, and I heard many women, including my own mother, speak of their regrets at not telling the person they'd lost how much they loved them.'

Chapter Seventeen

Miller came back on Tuesday evening looking dejected. His shoulders were slumped and his eyes had lost their usual sparkle. 'They don't want me,' he said, dropping his overnight bag to the kitchen floor.

Had he not looked so miserable Verity would have expressed delight that he didn't have to go away.

'Why on earth not?' she asked. 'You're young and fit, what else do they need?'

'It seems I've got a heart murmur. First I've heard of it, I've always been as strong as a horse.'

'I'm so sorry,' she said. 'And dreadful to be told you've got something wrong with your heart. That is very worrying.'

Miller shrugged. 'I won't worry about something I can't do anything about. But what I *am* concerned about is what I can do now I'm exempted on medical grounds. There won't be any gardening jobs going, and I doubt any farmers will take me on if they don't think I'm fit.'

'I read in the papers they are going to dig up parks to grow vegetables for the war effort, and they are telling ordinary people to turn their gardens over to do the same. So maybe they'll keep you on at Greenwich Park – and if not, there's Hilly Fields and Chinbrook Meadows too, all within cycling reach.'

'Umm, yes, but I dread people thinking I haven't joined up cos I'm a coward.'

He sighed and turned away, and Verity sensed that he felt as if he'd been cut off at the knees, and was no good to anyone.

That evening, they barely spoke. Miller was brooding on what exemption would mean for him, and she was still full of guilt at breaking into the house in The Glebe. She had salved her conscience a bit by telling herself she would never do it again. And anyway, it would help the plumber she was getting to install the bathroom, as he had four children to feed.

Yet there still remained a little voice at the back of her head telling her that she was just a common thief, and a low-down one at that for robbing someone when they were away from their home. She had no way of silencing that voice, either.

Spring slipped into summer and war was now a certainty, the only unknown was when it would start. Gas masks and ration books were distributed. As it was against the law not to carry your gas mask, Verity covered hers in some bright blue velveteen that made it look like a chic handbag. Everyone was talking about rations, wondering how much food they would each get. They also discussed the merits of the sandbags being stacked against public buildings; some people thought they were an unnecessary eyesore, almost as pointless as boarding up Eros in Piccadilly. Kerbs, lamp posts and other obstacles were being painted with white stripes to help people see their way during the blackout, and that was another cause for amusement. Everyone seemed to be debating whether to have an Anderson shelter in their back garden or a Morrison shelter which was like a reinforced cage, with a table top you kept indoors.

Drapery shops advertised blackout material for windows, reminding everyone it would soon be an offence not to have it, and many government buildings were already taping up windows. Yet despite all this activity in preparation for war, most people were very relaxed and enjoying the hot weather.

Verity could hardly wait to get home and sit out in her now pretty garden. Miller had rescued a little table from beside a dustbin in Blackheath, and painted it bright yellow. Using two stools from the kitchen, they ate outside most evenings, lighting candles when it became dark.

Having a real bathroom and constant hot water was a never-ending delight too. The plumber had done a fine job, and Miller and Verity had put up white tiles together and painted the walls above pale green. With some pretty curtains and a couple of plants on the windowsill, it looked lovely. Verity had told Miller she had used the bit of money her aunt had left her to pay for it, and she had even managed to convince herself that was true.

Miller was still working in Greenwich Park, but he had received word from the Department of Agriculture that he was likely to be transferred to another location on the outbreak of war.

'They are already building air-raid shelters in Greenwich Park,' he told Verity. 'I heard a whisper too that the military might use the park for the duration. I wonder if they'll kill the deer for food?'

It seemed very strange that despite the country almost holding its breath for the moment war would be declared, everyone was so light-hearted. They knew the evacuation of children would start soon, and that food would go on ration, yet most people talked quite casually about where they would go if their house was bombed, often laughing about it as if it would be a huge adventure.

At Cooks of St Paul's, however, it was very plain that England's shopkeepers were not taking any chances, and sales rocketed as they stockpiled goods. Verity was now working permanently in the office doing invoices, rather than in a specialized department, so she saw these increased sales daily and noted which items were the biggest sellers. She found it amusing that corsets were barely ordered any more, yet women's sanitary products, knitting wool, haberdashery and clothing were all flying out of the warehouse.

At the end of July, when Verity was called into a meeting along with all the other staff and the departmental managers, she assumed Mr Smailes, the Managing Director, was going to tell them Cooks was closing down. She didn't actually mind; there had been so much talk about women taking over men's jobs when the men were called up that she was quite excited at the prospect of change. However, Mr Smailes was adamant that the wholesale business would continue elsewhere, further out of London, where there would be less risk of bombing.

'I'm sure you can appreciate that St Paul's Cathedral is likely to be a target, and sited so close to it as we are, we think it would be folly to take the risk and stay here,' he began. 'We have found suitable premises in Hertfordshire, and so between now and the end of August I ask that you tell your departmental manager whether you want to move with us, or not. All of our young men have already been called up, and I am sure many of the older ones will enlist in the coming months. But for those of you who are left, this is the time to make your mind up, move with us and start a new life in a safer place, or leave our employ and stay in London.'

A buzz of conversation broke out, people looking to one another, nodding or shaking their heads with either pleasure at the prospect of a new life, or horror at leaving London.

Mr Smailes clapped his hands to get their attention again. 'Your departmental managers will be able to answer your questions, and rest assured that those who don't wish to go with us will all be given references and will leave with our best wishes for the future.' He paused and smiled at all those in front of him. 'When it is all over – and providing this building, which has been housing Cooks of St Paul's for over seventy years, is still standing – we will open again and we will welcome back all of you.'

'I bet he won't welcome Sweaty Betty back,' Marilyn whispered. She was a new friend that Verity had made since she'd been sent upstairs to do invoices. Although she was quite a bit older than Verity – over thirty – and a plump, plain girl, she was great fun, always making Verity laugh.

Verity giggled. Sweaty Betty was a real stinker. She worked in haberdashery and it was said that the manager had taken her to task several times for smelling bad and putting customers off. Clearly she had a medical problem, because there had been no improvement. Even now Verity could smell her, even though she was three rows back.

It was raining at lunchtime, so Verity and Marilyn went up to the canteen for their break. 'I'm gonna go, if they help us find somewhere to live,' Marilyn said. 'Dave and I have decided to get married before he enlists, and Hertfordshire has got to be a better place to live than Dagenham. What about you?'

'I think I'll stay put,' Verity replied. It seemed to her that it would mainly be the married women with children who would want to get out of London, and they could be a dull bunch sometimes. 'I fancy doing something exciting, like driving a train or putting up telephone wires.'

'Driving a train!' Marilyn exclaimed. 'I don't think they'll be letting women do that. Anyway, how's that lodger of yours? Jumped into his bed yet?'

'No, I haven't and I wouldn't,' Verity said indignantly. 'We are just friends, and it's nice.'

'Bit of a pansy, is he?'

'No, not at all,' Verity retorted, wondering why everyone seemed to think that of any man with good manners and who spoke correctly. 'He's a gentleman.'

'Some of the "gentlemen" I've met were the randiest, pushiest blokes ever,' Marilyn said with a shrug. 'Actually, I quite like that in a man, it shows they're normal.'

On the way home that evening Verity thought about what Marilyn had said. She *had* thought of Miller in a romantic way on many occasions; she loved his sparkly eyes, the dimple in his chin, and the way his hair started to curl if he left it too long between visits to the barber. When he took his shirt off in the garden the sight of his muscular chest and arms, now tanned a shiny golden brown, made her feel quite weak at the knees. She was guilty of lying in bed wondering what his kisses would be like too, or how he'd react if she stole into his room and climbed into bed with him. She wouldn't, of course, attempt to do the latter. She could never be that forward, especially as she had no way of knowing if he ever had similar thoughts about her. She assumed he didn't, because he'd surely have made some kind of move by now, if he was interested in that way.

Just two days after Mr Smailes had talked about Cooks moving to Hertfordshire, Miller got home from work to find a letter from the Department of Agriculture.

'Well, blow me down,' he said as he read it. 'They are ordering me up to Scotland to work for the Forestry.'

Verity was horrified. She had been so certain they'd find him a position somewhere local. 'Do you have to go?' she asked, feeling as if she might cry.

'I think it's an order, not a request,' he shrugged. 'But forestry work is fine by me, I'd rather that than working in an abattoir, or at a sewage farm. Mind you, I'm not so sure about chopping trees down, I like to plant them.'

'What will I do without you?' she said, trying to keep her tone light.

'You should get another lodger,' he said. 'You'll need company when the nights draw in, not to mention when the bombing starts.'

Verity had to turn away and pretend to be engrossed in shelling some peas so that he didn't see her eyes filling with tears.

That night in bed she cried silently into her pillow.

Miller had almost filled the hole in her life that Ruby had left. He was funny, good-natured, he helped her with chores around the house, and she could talk to him about almost anything. The prospect of being alone again filled her with dread. It seemed to her that she was jinxed, that everyone she was fond of left her. She was nearly seventeen now, but she hadn't had a proper boyfriend, she didn't even go to dances like other girls her age because she had nobody to go with.

She and Miller had been going to the cinema together every week since he came here, and they often caught a bus on Sundays out towards Farnborough to walk across the fields to Downe and have a bite to eat in the pub there. He was interested in so many diverse things, from animals and plants to ancient civilizations, and psychology too. He had once told her he'd studied several convicted murderers in an effort to discover why they did such appalling crimes. She had told him about the murderer John Lee in Babbacombe, 'the man they couldn't hang'.

'I read up on him, absolutely fascinating,' Miller replied with real enthusiasm. 'A complete bad lot – or a madman – to strangle and stab the poor woman and then set fire to her house. I couldn't find one redeeming quality in him, at least not in all the books and journals I read. He's now the local legend.'

'Ruby and I used to pretend his ghost hung around Babbacombe,' Verity giggled. 'But then someone told us he went to America when he got out of prison, and I think he's actually still alive.'

'Not a person I'd like to live close to,' Miller said with a smile. 'We should go to Madame Tussauds one day, the

Chamber of Horrors has all the famous murderers in there.'

They never got around to going there, like so many other things they'd talked about doing, and now Miller was telling her to get another lodger – as if anyone else would fit in here as well as he had.

She was very quiet the following morning as they ate their breakfast. She was tempted to tell him how much she was going to miss him, but yet afraid that was too forward.

'You will write to me?' he asked suddenly, looking at her anxiously. 'I'd hate to lose touch with you.'

A wave of joy flooded over her. 'Of course I will,' she smiled. 'As long as you write back and don't find a Scottish girlfriend who wants to keep you all to herself. There will always be a bed for you here too, even if I do get a new lodger.'

On Saturday the 27th of August, Miller was to leave for Glasgow. Verity walked with him to Hither Green Station to wave him off. She could barely speak, she felt so sad, and when she did it was just trivialities to break the silence.

The platform was crowded with people, many of the women crying as they saw their husbands or sons off. Such a public display of emotion made the impending war so much more real.

'You will come back and see me sometimes?' she asked anxiously.

Miller put a hand on each of her shoulders and smiled down at her.

'Why are you looking so worried for me? I'll be safe where I'm going, and of course I'll come back to see you.

It's you I'm concerned about. Promise me you'll run to the public shelter the minute you hear the siren?'

She managed a wobbly smile, afraid she might cry at his concern for her. 'I promise,' she said.

He moved his hands from her shoulders to either side of her head, tilting her face up to his. 'I don't think you know how much you mean to me,' he said, his eyes looking right into hers. 'All this time I've been too scared to say anything as I've sensed you've had a bad experience with a man. But I must speak out now, Verity, before I leave. You are the girl of my dreams.'

His lips came down on hers before she could even express delight at his words, his gentle, lingering kiss sending delicious shivers down her spine.

She heard the train coming into the station and her arms came up involuntarily to cling to him.

'Oh, Verity,' he whispered, their noses still touching. 'I wish I'd been brave enough to do that before.'

'I wish you had too,' she admitted.

There was no time left for further declarations of feelings, or any promises. The carriage doors were open and the guard was yelling, 'Hurry along!'

Miller had to pick up his bag and, with just the briefest peck on her cheek and a squeeze of her hand, he pushed his way on to the already packed-to-capacity train.

Verity waved until the train was in the distance, even though Miller had been elbowed too far down the carriage to see her out of the window. But once the train had disappeared from view she couldn't hold back her tears, and she joined a throng of other crying women walking down the slope to the subway, many of them carrying babies or with children in tow. It ought to have made her feel less alone, but somehow it made her feel even more isolated.

When she got back into the house and saw Miller's raincoat gone from the peg in the hall and his work boots, which usually sat beneath it on some newspaper, missing, she cried again.

Last night he'd spent a couple of hours polishing his boots till they looked fit to go on parade. She'd laughed at him and said the other foresters would think him odd wearing polished boots.

'It's kind of the same as having a clean shirt and a haircut,' he claimed. 'Besides, I've never seen you go out of the front door without putting on some lipstick. Why do you do that?'

Last night she'd had no answer to that, but right now she didn't think she'd want to put lipstick on ever again until he came back.

As she made a cup of tea the walls seemed to be pressing in on her. Any day now, war might be declared, and she felt she must be the only person in the country who was totally alone.

She took her tea out into the garden, but that was just another reminder of Miller. The two stools were still by the garden table, but she wouldn't be eating her dinner out here now she was alone. Sitting on the arbour seat, she leaned back on the cushions, feeling the sun's warmth on her face, and relived his kiss. She felt a little twinge of something low in her belly which she knew was desire, even though she'd never felt it before today.

He said she was the girl of his dreams, and that was the most wonderful thing she'd ever heard. But how was she going to be able to deal with never knowing when she'd see him again?

He was all around her, here in the garden; bright dahlias, asters and big yellow daisies were like his sunny disposition, and the jasmine, honeysuckle and pink climbing rose which had spread themselves right along the side fences were evidence of his tenacity and reliability. Sitting in the arbour she could be in the depths of the country, not surrounded by houses, but then that was what he'd set out to create.

She didn't know how much longer she had at Cooks of St Paul's. Some of the stock and office equipment had already been moved to Hertfordshire, the rest would go when war was declared. She'd had an interview with the Post Office and was waiting to hear back from them, but then it seemed like the whole world and his wife were waiting for something.

On the 1st of September, four days after Miller had left, it was announced on the wireless that Germany had invaded Poland, and that unless they withdrew a state of war would be declared.

On Sunday morning, Verity switched on her wireless for the message from the Prime Minister that all of Britain was waiting for. Shudders went down her spine as she heard Chamberlain's measured tones laying out that Germany had not backed down from invading Poland, and as Britain had made an assistance pact with the Poles, we were therefore now at war with Germany.

It had been entirely expected, the country was ready for war, but still it was terrible. Then an air-raid warning siren went off and sent people running out on to the street, half expecting to see German soldiers marching along Lee High Road. It was a false alarm, of course, or just a practice run – but just the same, it was frightening.

Verity stood out in the street with everyone else, but the babble of voices meant nothing to her. The only question repeating in her head was how was she going to get through a war alone?

At the same time that Verity was standing outside her house feeling very alone, Wilby and Ruby were preparing Sunday lunch for themselves and the three evacuee children Wilby had taken in the previous day.

The children were from North London – two sisters, Helen and Sandra, aged eight and nine, and ten-year-old Joseph. They had experienced a terrible long journey by train, arriving in Torquay late in the evening, and then had to suffer the indignity of waiting for someone to pick them out to take them home. No one, it seemed, wanted sisters, or a boy with red hair. Although Wilby had only intended to take in one child, when she saw the anxious expressions on the three small faces as, one by one, their friends were picked out, she felt she must take them.

She had given the three children the game of Ludo to play with after Chamberlain's speech on the wireless, as she felt the three of them needed a distraction. They had been told they would be safer away from London, but their first question after the speech had been to ask whether their mothers would be safe if the Germans bombed the city. And Helen, the younger of the two sisters, had started to cry.

The children were calm again now, sitting on the floor in the sitting room, engrossed in the board game.

'Will you go back to the Palace tomorrow?' Wilby asked Ruby when they were alone in the kitchen.

Ruby was one of the receptionists at the hotel now. As she had planned, she'd worked her way up through being a chambermaid and a waitress, and she was popular with other staff, and approved of by the management. They had been told some time ago that the hotel was to be requisitioned by the War Ministry and would be converted into a hospital for RAF officers in the event of war.

'Oh yes, I've been promised a job,' Ruby replied. 'You'll remember me telling you almost all the young waiters have already joined up, and a lot of the girls are going into the Land Army. As for the older female staff, they all seem to want to work in factories, as the money is better than in a hotel. But I'm not sure what the older men will do. A few might be kept on as porters, I suppose.'

'Civil Defence, I expect,' Wilby said. 'Everything from Home Guard to fire watching and rescuing people if there are air raids.'

'There won't be much call for that around here, surely?' Ruby asked. 'Plymouth and Portsmouth perhaps – the Germans are likely to target docks, after all – but there's nothing for them here.'

Wilby shrugged. 'Depends if they want to bomb everywhere just because they can,' she said. 'But I agree, I can't see us being in the front line of it. However, I can't help worrying about people in London, they are far more likely to be singled out. I wish you'd contact Verity and see how she is faring.'

Wilby half expected Ruby to round on her and tell her to mind her own business, but she had sensed that since the day back in the spring when they'd spoken about Verity, Ruby had spent some time considering how she could make amends with her old friend.

The trouble was, Ruby had had to fight for everything since she was born, and that had made her remarkably stubborn, never wanting to go back on anything she'd said or done.

But after what seemed an interminable time, Ruby sighed. 'At the risk of you telling me "I told you so" I think I cooked my goose there,' she admitted, looking rather sad. 'I doubt even the most grovelling apology would work.'

Wilby had to curb the desire to shout 'Praise the Lord!' and dance around the kitchen.

'I don't agree,' she managed to say, as if she didn't care either way. 'Verity was always a very understanding girl, and she loved you. I believe you loved her too. Love doesn't die, it just gets buried sometimes.'

'Buried as deeply as I buried it, I must have squashed all life out of it,' Ruby said, looking decidedly crestfallen.

'War being declared will change people's feelings about many things,' Wilby said. 'Write to her – or better still, take a trip to London and call on her. To save face you can make out you're just checking she's okay. But from what I remember of Verity, she'll just be so glad to see you she won't even think about how mean you were to her.'

'I was very mean to her,' Ruby admitted and hung her head. 'She didn't deserve to be treated that way. I'll never be able to forgive myself for that.'

She turned away then and walked into the next room. Wilby smiled to herself.

Ruby looked down at the three children engrossed in playing Ludo on the sitting-room floor. She thought it was amazing how quickly they'd adjusted to their new home. Yesterday, totally confused at having to leave their mothers, they had been upset by the long journey to a strange place, and even more disturbed when they didn't get picked for a new home straight away.

But after a night's sleep they looked like they'd always lived here. Ruby knew how that felt, as it had been the same for her when Wilby brought her here.

She had, of course, been in a far worse state than these three – she really didn't understand now what that had all been about – but a good meal, a soft warm bed and a house that somehow told you nothing bad could ever happen here was enough for most children, even Ruby. And these children had got the best to come yet, when they learned that Wilby was reliable, fun, understanding and generous with her love and time.

'Fancy a walk down along the Downs before lunch?' Ruby asked the children. 'You can see the sea below, but unfortunately we aren't allowed on the beaches any more, they've blocked them off with barbed wire.'

All three turned towards her, their pale faces suddenly flushed with excitement. 'The sea is that close?' Sandra asked.

'Just around the corner, at the foot of the cliff. There used to be a magic railway down the cliff,' Ruby said, 'but that's closed too now for the war.'

'Why?' Sandra asked.

'To stop Germans coming up on it,' Ruby laughed. 'If they had to climb up the cliff, they'd be too puffed to fight anyone, so they won't bother trying now.'

Wilby watched Ruby walking down the road from the front window. She was holding the two girls' hands, and Joseph was just in front of them, hopping over cracks in the pavement. It was absolutely terrible to think England was at war again. After the last one, with so much destruction and appalling loss of life, she had believed the men in power would make absolutely certain it never happened again.

But even so, the touching scene she was watching was a kind of evidence that good things could come out of bad. She'd got these three children to care for, and that would make her feel useful again. And with luck Verity would come back to the house again too.

Wilby turned back to the kitchen to continue with the lunch. Ruby had changed in many ways since her abortion. She was quieter, no longer impulsive, and there was a sadness in her that nothing seemed to dispel. She'd also, understandably perhaps, grown harder towards young men. A handsome face and sweet talking didn't lure her any longer, she barely glanced at groups of men congregating on the Downs on warm days, and rarely went to dances with girls from her work.

Wilby was fairly certain that Ruby had devised her own mental list of requirements for prospective suitors, and only those who matched up got a date with her, and there had been no more than three or four of those in the last year.

But while Wilby approved of her becoming more discerning, she was concerned that Ruby had lost that wonderful spontaneity she used to have. She weighed up everything now: risk, cost, time, effort. Wilby just hoped that meeting the right man and falling in love would bring back the part of her she'd lost.

'Contact Verity soon,' she murmured to herself. 'We all need a special friend, and you, Ruby, more than most.'

Archie Wood was broke and miserable and had spent the last three nights sleeping in a barn just outside Dover.

He had realized a few weeks ago that war was inevitable and that it was probably safer for him in England than staying in France. But as soon as he got on the ferry to Dover, he regretted the decision. What he should have done was go right down to the south of France and hunker down with some amenable woman. Life was easier for him with people who didn't speak the same language; details of where he was from, his past and, indeed, where he was going could all be fuzzed over when communication was difficult.

He'd thought he was on to a winning streak with Mrs Carol Onslow, the landlady of a guest house in Folkestone who had rented him a room. Her husband had been called up, and on his second night there, after sharing a bottle of gin with her, he got her into bed. She was rather plain, a little overweight, the wrong side of forty, with straight brown hair and bad teeth. But he liked that she was eager for sex, and he thought after a few weeks with her, during which time he could find out where she hid her savings, he'd then be ready to move on, with those savings.

But he reckoned without her skills as an interrogator. The questions began on their third night together.

'What were you doing in France, Archie?' she said, almost before he caught his breath after orgasm, and lighting a cigarette.

'I'm in import and export.' He gave his standard answer to such a question.

She leaned up on her elbow beside him, and he noted how flabby her breasts were. 'Importing and exporting what? Farm machinery, food, furniture, guns?'

'Chemicals mostly,' he said. That usually shut women up.

But not her. She wanted to know if they were chemicals for medicines or fertilizers.

'For all kinds of things at different times from different companies,' he said.

'You didn't show me your identity card,' she said suddenly. 'By law I'm supposed to ask to see everyone's who comes here to stay. Did you forget, or haven't you got one?'

'I think you just forgot to ask me,' he said. He hadn't got one, and one thing he needed to do was get a forged one.

'Well, get it now,' she suggested.

'No, I will not. There's better things to do right now than study identity cards.'

She laughed, and he thought that would be the end of it. It was for that night, but the next day the questions came even thicker and faster.

Was he married? Had he got children? Where was he born? Was he in the army in the Great War? Why was he hanging around in Folkestone?

He replied – the truth to some, lies to others – and said he was hanging around in Folkestone waiting for a fellow importer to contact him. Then she asked him for his identity card again, and he made an excuse to go to his room. He packed his bag, but as he came back down the stairs she insisted on seeing the card.

He lost his patience and punched her in the jaw. She fell to the floor, banging her head hard, and Archie ran for it.

That was how he came to be in the barn. She was bound to have called the police, and although he'd told her his name was Ivan Dunstable – the name on the false passport he'd acquired in France – they might show her pictures of wanted men, Archie Wood amongst them. But there was an even stronger likelihood, particularly in view of his vague answers to Carol's questions about what he had been doing in France, that the police would think he was a fifth columnist, recruited by the Germans to spy or spread sedition.

That was far more serious than being wanted for embezzlement.

Chapter Eighteen

1940

'I love these light evenings,' Verity exclaimed to her friend as they came out of the telephone exchange at nine in the evening. 'No more tripping over things in the dark on the way home when we work late.'

'Remember what hell it was back in the winter?' Amy said. 'That bitter cold snap in January? You just couldn't see the ice on the pavements. It was either sidle along cautiously like an old lady or rush to keep warm and risk landing up on your backside.'

Verity laughed. She had been laughing a great deal since joining the Post Office back at the start of the war.

The Phoney War was what the press called it. But most people, amused by the lack of drama or activity, said, 'What War?' Until quite recently nothing appeared to be happening, at least not in England. Many of the children who had been evacuated to the countryside last September were back home with their mothers by Christmas, because there had been none of the expected air raids. Sugar, butter and bacon had gone on ration back in January. But apart from that irritation and the hated blackout, life was much the same as before the war began.

Other countries weren't having it so easy; there were some awful stories circulating about what the Nazis were doing to the Poles, and Denmark and Norway had been invaded at the start of April. Now Germany's troops were smashing their way through the Low Countries with columns of massed tanks, motorized infantry and backed up by aerial bombing. Even the most optimistic people couldn't fail to realize that it was actually possible that England could be invaded soon too.

Chamberlain had resigned as Prime Minister and his place had been taken by Winston Churchill. It was thought he was the man to pull the country together in its adversity.

Verity was still just as interested in world news, but since going to work for the Post Office she didn't have much time to go off to the library and read all the papers. Now she had to rely on the wireless and the odd glance at a daily paper. Although she had been taken on as a telephonist, she was also being trained for outside maintenance and installation work. This had previously been men's work, but with so many of them joining up, women had to be pressed into service. Young ones like Verity were nimble enough to shin up telegraph poles and didn't mind heights.

It was this new work which was making Verity happy. Each day was different, and she liked the challenges of the job and feeling she was doing something useful for the war effort. She even enjoyed donning her dungarees and tying a scarf around her hair to climb up telegraph poles. Back at Cooks nothing had been vital, or even important, and there was no social life with the job. The other staff had been friendly, but no one really met up after work or at weekends.

It was quite different at the Post Office. In the main the

other girls lived in or around Lewisham, and they wanted to socialize. Hardly a week went past without someone inviting her to their home, for a drink or to a dance.

Amy was Verity's new lodger. A twenty-year-old buxom brunette with a heart of gold, until she met Verity at the Post Office she had been staying in digs in New Cross. She had hated it there and missed her family in Southend badly. Verity had expected it to be hard to adjust to someone taking Miller's place, but it hadn't been. Amy was easy-going, enthusiastic and fun, they had a lot to talk and laugh about, and when they were working on the same shift it was so nice to have company on the way to work and coming home, especially when it was dark.

But it was light and warm this evening, and Verity thought they could sit out in the garden with a fish and chip supper, the way she used to do with Miller.

He wrote to her every week, always funny, interesting and affectionate letters. He was very happy in Scotland. The other foresters were a mixture of men too old for call-up, some who, like Miller, had been turned down because of a health problem, and some were 'conchies', men who for religious or moral reasons would not join up.

Verity noticed from his letters that it was the 'conchies' who Miller appeared to get on best with. He said the old men tended to be bossy, far too keen on boasting about their abilities as young men. Those exempted on medical grounds were often very lazy and found fault with everything, but he admired the conchies' commitment to their beliefs, and that they were cheerful and worked hard.

*

'You go and sit in the garden,' Amy said when they got home. 'I'll pop down the fish and chip shop to get the grub.'

Verity put some knives and forks, the pepper, salt and vinegar on a tray and took it outside in readiness for Amy getting back. She sat down with a contented sigh, still thinking about Miller.

He'd only come back to London once, and that was at Christmas. She'd only had one full day off to spend with him, but it was still wonderful.

She understood now what people meant when they talked about 'getting carried away'. If it hadn't been for Amy in the house, Verity was pretty certain they would have spent that whole day in bed.

She smiled as she remembered how they kept stealing kisses every time Amy's back was turned. Each one sent Verity's heart pounding.

Amy had fallen asleep by the fire in the parlour after Christmas dinner, and Verity and Miller went into the kitchen intending to wash up. But instead she sat on his lap by the kitchen table for more kisses.

'It's so hard being away from you,' Miller said, stroking her face with such tenderness. 'I go to sleep thinking about you, and wake up with you still on my mind. Just having a few days like this with you isn't enough, but what can we do?'

'Everyone says the trains are terrible now, so very slow and crowded with servicemen,' Verity said. 'You mustn't try it again until later in the year when the weather improves, it's too difficult. Or maybe I could get a week's holiday and come up there to see you?'

'I could book a hotel room for Mr and Mrs Grantham?'

he suggested, and blushed scarlet. 'I don't mean to, well, you know, presume. I just want to hold you.'

She almost told him she loved him then. He was wearing a ridiculous yellow and red spotted bow tie she'd made him for a joke present, and a paper hat from a cracker. He was looking at her with puppy dog eyes that made her feel they could be this happy together for the rest of their lives.

But she didn't say she loved him, or even that she'd risk booking into a hotel with him. He was her first boyfriend, and she was mindful that she had to be absolutely sure of him and her own feelings first. She longed to ask someone's advice but the girls at work were all the kind who would laugh at such a question. Most of them had boyfriends they said they loved, who were away in the forces, but that didn't make them all faithful. Even some of the married women with husbands away went dancing up the West End now and then. Verity found this very puzzling, she didn't want to dance with or kiss other men, and although she went to dances with Amy sometimes, the girls always outnumbered the men, so they danced together.

Besides, she felt a girl was supposed to let the man talk of love first. Miller might have said she was the girl of his dreams, that he fell asleep at night thinking of her, but that wasn't the same thing as declaring his love. So until he did say that, Verity wouldn't allow herself to dream of anything more than kissing him; she certainly wouldn't hope for an engagement or marriage. She remembered how Ruby with all her experience of boys had allowed herself to be fooled into thinking she'd found the perfect man who would love and protect her for ever. And look what happened to her.

Thinking of Ruby again brought Verity up sharp. She

wondered if she was still in Devon with Wilby, and what she was doing. She also wondered if she ever regretted their falling out. Time and even Miller, or her new friend Amy, hadn't erased the hurt and injustice of it for Verity. Yet right now, while she was feeling happy and contented, she could only really think about what they'd meant to one another before it all went wrong.

She knew that if Ruby was to contact her, the hurt would be wiped out immediately. It was obvious Ruby had made that terrible statement in a moment of fear that she'd messed up her life for good and would lose Wilby's love. It was understandable; Wilby was the first adult who'd ever cared about Ruby, she had in fact become a mother to her. But Verity hoped Ruby realized now that she'd cared just as much as Wilby, and it was she who had sat by her friend's bedside afraid Ruby was going to die.

The front door banged, disturbing Verity's reverie, and Amy came out into the garden.

'I almost opened the paper on the way home, I'm so hungry. But then I remembered you said it was common to eat in the street,' Amy said as she put the two newspaper parcels down on the table.

'Did I say that?' Verity grinned. 'I'm a fraud, then, as I've been known to eat fish and chips in the street occasionally. My headmistress used to rage about us eating while in school uniform. She once said, "There is nothing worse than a large girl licking a lolly." We all used to mimic her.'

'You are quite posh,' Amy said thoughtfully after they'd been eating for a little while. 'You always put the milk in a jug, I think that's pretty grand.'

'We've got more important things to think about now

247

than whether to put milk in a jug,' Verity said, sprinkling a little more vinegar on her chips. 'I caught a bit of the news today at lunchtime and it sounds bad. Our boys and the French army seem to be on the run from the Germans. They can't retreat much further cos they are already right by the coast, near Dunkirk in France. They say ships will be sent to rescue them, but there are so many men.'

Amy never read the newspapers or even listened to the news. She called Verity 'Major News Reporter', and relied on her for information.

'I'm sure Mr Churchill will come up with a plan,' she said, getting to her feet and screwing up the paper from the fish and chips in her hands. 'And my plan is to go to bed now, I'm bushed.'

'I'll stay out here a little longer,' Verity said. 'Goodnight, sleep tight.'

It was good to be alone in the garden as it got dark. Before the blackout there had always been some light, from windows and street lighting. But now, once it was pitch dark, the stars and moon seemed so much brighter and nearer. She could smell the honeysuckle and see the glint of white roses just coming into flower.

Amy didn't seem to understand the implications of the retreat from France. Sweet as she was, she was a bit dense, and actually imagined the English Channel as some impregnable moat which the Germans could never cross.

She had been just as dense when their Morrison shelter had been dropped off. 'They expect us to sleep in that?' she said indignantly as Verity finished putting it together. 'It's just a cage with a table top!'

'Yes, it is, but it's reinforced steel, which makes it far safer than being in our beds during an air raid,' Verity explained patiently. 'We'll put a mattress, pillows and blankets in it, and if the siren goes off we needn't go to a public shelter.'

The girls put the kitchen table out in the garden and covered it in oilcloth to prevent it getting ruined in the rain, and then they hung a tablecloth over the shelter. It was far bigger than the real table, but then it had to be so they could lie down. Amy took some persuading to try it out, but once she was in it claimed it felt like the camps she and her brothers had made in the woods when they were children.

She was stubborn about learning how to use the stirrup pump too. 'How do they think we can put a fire out with one bucket of water and that?' she complained. 'Surely it's easier to chuck the whole bucketful at it?'

'The idea is to aim at shrapnel and cool it down,' Verity had to explain. 'Apparently, shrapnel is little pieces of red-hot metal which come off a bomb, and if we don't soak them with water they could start a fire.'

A sudden knock at the front door startled Verity. But assuming it was the officious little man who strutted around the street at night checking no lights were showing at windows, she felt she must answer the door. She hadn't drawn the curtains in her room this evening, and maybe Amy had switched on the light to look for something in there and forgotten about the blackout.

'I'm sorry, is there –?' she began as she opened the door, but stopped short when she saw who it was calling so late. 'Father!' she exclaimed, her legs turning to jelly with fright. 'What are you doing here?'

'Forget the twenty questions,' he said, barging his way past her. 'I can't stand on the doorstep breaching the blackout rules.'

She felt faint with shock, and she couldn't believe he had the cheek to come here. 'You aren't welcome here,' she blurted out. 'Please go now, there's nothing I want to say to you.'

'There's plenty I need to say to you,' he said. 'Now shut that front door, put the kettle on and take that look off your face. I'm not a murderer but your father.'

Verity had always thought of him as tall, with wide shoulders, but she didn't remember him filling space the way he was now. Granted there wasn't much room in the kitchen now with the Morrison shelter in the centre, but he took it all up. He didn't look smart the way she remembered, either. His dark hair was long and untidy, with touches of grey, he hadn't shaved, and his moustache was no longer trimmed and waxed. In a crumpled dark suit and a shirt with grubby collar and cuffs, he could have been sleeping rough.

Yet it was his face that had changed the most. He'd always looked so suave and well cared for. But now his face was bloated, and there was a redness to it which wasn't sunburn. Even his eyes were bloodshot, with bags beneath them. He made her think of the man who was always waiting outside the Tiger's Head at Lee Green for it to open at lunchtime. He was a drunk, and she'd been told he was often found out cold on the pavement outside after closing time. She could smell drink on her father too, so perhaps that was why he looked the way he did.

She put the kettle on, so nervous she had difficulty

lighting the gas. 'What do you want?' she asked, quaking inside.

'Want?' he repeated, his voice suddenly very loud and harsh. 'Is it a crime for a man to wish to see his daughter?'

'It was a crime that made you run away,' she said more boldly than she felt. 'And you half killed me before you left. Mother and I had a terrible time, forced to come here cap in hand to Aunt Hazel. So I ask you why you would imagine I'd want to see you?'

He took a couple of steps towards her. Thinking he was going to strike her, she flinched and backed away.

'Don't flinch from me, I'm not going to hurt you,' he said, holding out his hands towards her. 'Hear me out! You can have no idea of the forces that brought me to that point,' he said. 'Your mother was a spendthrift, I was under terrible strain. I'm not that person any more. I want to make it up to you.'

'I'm glad to hear that. But whatever kind of person you are now, I still don't want you near me,' she said defiantly. She pointed angrily at the oven. 'Mother put her head in that because of you. Aunt Hazel might not have had a heart attack and died, if she hadn't been put under so much strain. As for me, I had to deal with girls at school whispering about you, the police calling here all the time, and the stigma of having a swindler for a father.'

'Cynthia gassed herself?'

'Yes, she did, and I bet you knew that already. And that Aunt Hazel died, or you wouldn't have come.'

He didn't answer immediately, just looked at her with a slightly hangdog expression.

'You think that little of me?' he said eventually.

'I think nothing of you,' she snapped back. 'So get out now.'

'Oh, Verity,' he said, his voice suddenly very soft. 'I am sorry I hurt you this badly. Let me make amends now and help you. It must be lonely living here all alone.'

His sympathetic tone affected her momentarily, but she reminded herself of what he was. 'I don't live alone,' she glowered at him. 'I have a friend as a lodger, and I have a boyfriend too. I don't need you or want you in my life, so get out now or I will telephone the police and tell them you're here.'

'You can, if you like,' he shrugged. 'They aren't looking for me any more, I sorted it all out before I went off to South Africa. If I look a bit rough, it's just because I came rushing back to see if you were alright now the war seems to be heating up.'

She was just going to tell him that made no difference to her feelings for him, and she didn't believe him anyway, when Amy came down the stairs in her dressing gown, looking curiously at him.

'This is Archie Wood, my father,' Verity said. 'He's just leaving, aren't you?'

Dense as always, and not picking up on a strained atmosphere, Amy smiled and held out her hand to him. 'I'm so pleased to meet you,' she said. 'Verity and I work together, but it's late to leave now. I could go in with Verity, and you could have my bed.'

Verity gritted her teeth. 'Amy! I just said he's leaving.'

'I'm glad my daughter has friends with good manners,' Archie smiled. 'Verity promised me a cup of tea which hasn't transpired yet, and as it happens I think I've missed the last train too.'

'Then I'll make you the tea,' Amy said, going over to the kettle which was just coming to the boil. 'When I heard the door, then raised voices, I was afraid it was that warden again. He's told us off many times for not closing the curtains properly.'

Verity knew she'd lost this battle. Amy didn't know what her father had done, and this wasn't the time to spill family secrets.

She'd just have to go along with it and let him stay till the morning.

Half an hour later, Verity and Amy were lying side by side in bed with the light out.

'You never told me anything about your dad,' Amy whispered. 'Why not? He seems so nice.'

'He's not, he's a real snake,' Verity whispered back. 'And thanks to you he's got a foot in the door. So you are going to help me boot him out tomorrow before we go to work, understood?'

'Okay,' Amy muttered. 'I'm sorry.'

Amy fell asleep almost immediately, her breathing deep and steady, but Verity lay awake rigid with tension. However much he might deny it, she sensed that the only reason he'd come here was because he'd fallen on hard times and had nowhere else to go. That would make it hard to get rid of him.

Was he speaking the truth about the police no longer looking for him?

It was true they hadn't come round here to check up for a very long time now, not since Aunt Hazel died, and they had said they thought he was in South Africa. So perhaps he had sorted it all out, or even had a spell in prison. Yet even if he had been punished for his crime, he still didn't deserve any loyalty or sympathy from her.

Ninety-nine per cent of her brain was telling her he was bad news, that he might hurt her again, but the remaining one per cent was telling her to give him a chance, that he was the only family she had left, and maybe it was her mother's greed and idleness that had caused him to go wrong.

She barely slept and shortly after six o'clock she got up, tired of tossing and turning. After washing and dressing very quietly, she slunk downstairs and took a cup of tea into the back garden to drink it.

It was a beautiful morning, the sun already rising in a clear blue sky, birds singing merrily. Normally such a morning would make her feel joyful and invigorated. She probably would have written a letter to Miller, sharing her thoughts. But her father's presence upstairs was worrying, and she knew that she really did need to make him leave today.

She and Amy had to leave for work by twenty to eight, so she needed to act now if they were not to be late. She drank the remainder of her tea and went inside to pour some for her father and Amy, then carried the cups up the stairs.

Amy got hers first; Verity shook her awake and hastily told her she was to get washed and dressed quickly. Then she went into the other room and flicked back the curtains.

'Wake up, Father,' she said sharply.

He had undressed down to a vest which looked grey

with wear, and he had thick dark stubble on his chin. People had always said he was a good-looking man back in their days at Daleham Gardens, but no one would say that now. Seen in broad daylight, his nose and cheeks were covered in red broken veins, and his shoulders and bare arms were white and flabby. He also smelled sour.

'Amy and I have to leave by half seven for work, and you can't stay here.'

He opened one eye and looked at her. 'Why can't I?'

'I told you, we've got to go to work. And anyway, this is Amy's room and she only allowed you to stay in it for one night.'

'I'm not going anywhere,' he said. 'As you are not twenty-one yet, I am still your legal guardian and therefore entitled to stay here.'

'Then I shall have to go to the police,' she said firmly. 'I won't have you here, Father, I have the law on my side. You abandoned Mother and me, you can't just come back when it suits you and throw your weight around.'

He sat up in bed, calmly picked up his tea and took a long drink of it. 'Oh, can't I?' he said eventually, his lips twisted into a sneer. 'We'll see about that. Suppose I tell the police you were using this house for immoral purposes?'

'That's ridiculous,' Verity retorted. 'Do you think they would take the word of an embezzler?'

'That, my dear, is all stowed away now. I gave myself up a couple of years ago and sorted it all out and paid back the money. And it isn't ridiculous for me to say you are being immoral. I know you had a young man living here last year, and now it seems you've got a girl in here, and you could be running a little business on the side.'

'We're doing no such thing,' Verity gasped indignantly. 'Amy is a friend from work and my lodger. That's all.'

Her stomach gave a sickening lurch to think he had been spying on her. The insinuation that she was using the house for immoral purposes was hideous, she wondered if that fat busybody down the road had said something.

'Run along to work now,' he said, grinning broadly as if he knew he'd taken the wind out of her sails. 'Why should you mind your old dad being here anyway? It's quite normal for a father to want to visit his daughter now and then.'

'You aren't normal,' she blurted out. 'You've only come here because you've got nowhere else to go. I'll let you stay today, just because I haven't got time now to fight with you, but when I get home tonight you must leave.'

She turned and fled the room, because she was afraid she was going to be sick. Instinctively she knew he was going to stay for as long as it suited him, whatever she said or did.

All day long at work she could think of nothing else but her father. She guessed he would spend the day searching the entire house for something he could use against her, and although she couldn't think of anything there that could be useful to him, just the thought of him searching through drawers and cupboards was alarming.

It hadn't helped that Amy had thought it exciting that he'd turned up. She really was a chump sometimes. But then Amy's father was probably a kind, caring man who could never harm anyone.

Chapter Nineteen

'Fancy Amy leaving the Post Office!' Beryl remarked to Verity. 'Do you know why?'

Both girls were putting on their dungarees in readiness to climb telegraph poles and check the wiring for faults. Beryl was twenty-five and an experienced driver, so she drove the van and they took turns in doing the pole climbing, the one on the ground holding the ladder steady.

Verity was puzzled at Beryl's remark. 'She hasn't left. She went home to Southend to see her family for a few days, but she's coming back.'

'She isn't, she handed in her notice a week ago.'

'No! That can't be right, she's due back tomorrow or the next day. She would've told me, if she was leaving.'

Beryl shook her head. 'Well, all I can say is that Miss Haig asked me last week if you two had had a falling out, because Amy had given in her notice and would be leaving at the end of the week. I told her that, as far as I knew, you were still as thick as thieves. Then she asked me not to talk about it, not even to you, as Amy didn't want anyone questioning her.'

Verity just stood in shocked surprise, the braces on her dungarees still dangling down unbuttoned. She couldn't really believe what Beryl had said, but as Beryl was neither a troublemaker nor a liar, and Miss Haig was the supervisor, it had to be true.

It did make sense of why Amy took so much stuff with her last Friday. She'd claimed it was just her winter clothes, which she was going to leave at her parents' home to make more space, and Verity hadn't noticed if everything else was gone too.

But why did she go? Was it because of having to give her room up for Archie?

Amy had seemed to get on well with him, better than Verity did. It was she who started calling him by his Christian name, and Verity followed along with it.

Could he have said or done something she didn't like? Verity squirmed at the idea, as memories of what he made her do to him came back to her. Yet even if he did something truly horrible to her, and she ran off because of it, why leave her job too? Besides, surely if he had assaulted her in some way she would have said something to Verity, if only a vague hint?

'Oh dear, you really didn't know, did you?' Beryl said, in concern. 'How strange this is! Amy has always been one for blabbing everything out. If she had a grievance, the whole world would know. I can't imagine how she managed to keep this under her hat.' She paused for a moment, seemingly deep in thought. 'Maybe it's family problems, like her mum's ill or getting hysterical about the bombing. Southend is, after all, likely to get a hammering being on the coast and on the way to London.'

Verity was too shaken to reply. Beryl was what Ruby would have called a 'Posh Bint'. She came from one of the huge houses up in Blackheath, her father was a judge, and she had that poised, polished look of a *Vogue* model. Slender, with sleek dark hair and sharp cheekbones, her eyes were a strange and beautiful amber colour which made everyone take a second look at her.

Verity loved being her work partner, because she had a great sense of humour, she was interesting and worldly, and more than that she was very accepting of people, whatever their background. Verity liked that and wished that there were more like her, especially now that it looked as if England was about to witness what war really meant.

The evacuation of the retreating troops from Dunkirk in the days before the 4th of June had been a sobering warning of just how much better equipped the German army was. A flotilla of boats rescued 215,000 British troops and 102,250 French from the beaches while the Luftwaffe strafed them with continual gunfire. With somewhere in the region of 11,000 men losing their lives, it must have been hell for every man there.

Verity had seen Pathé News at the cinema and the sight of thousands of different kinds of craft – fishing boats, pleasure boats, ferries and even rowing boats – sailing gallantly out from England's coastal towns to Dunkirk, their owners intent on doing their part in rescuing men, had everyone in the cinema crying with pride at their courage and endurance.

But then the whole retreat from Dunkirk was played out by the press as a triumph of courage over adversity, evidence of the bulldog spirit. They didn't print the numbers of soldiers who died, perhaps because they wanted to keep up morale, but the news soon leaked out. Apparently, there were over a thousand civilian casualties in the town of Dunkirk on just the first day too.

There was, however, a mention of ninety-seven prisoners

of war, massacred at La Bassée Canal, lined up against a barn and shot. Only two men survived, and perhaps they released this story as a perfect piece of anti-German propaganda. As all the British tanks, trucks and heavy artillery had to be left behind in the evacuation, the whole country could appreciate that it was going to need a monumental effort on everyone's part to rearm, to build new trucks and tanks, to say nothing of rebuilding the faith that the Allies could win the war. Right now it looked as if the Germans might invade England at any time.

It was partly because of Dunkirk, and the events that followed soon after, that Verity didn't force Archie to leave the house. Hundreds of wounded soldiers were being brought back to London hospitals to be treated, Paris fell to the Germans on the 14th of June, and then there was the first daylight bombing in London in early July. In the face of so much tragedy, it seemed cruel to turn her father out when he had no home. She also thought, as things were looking so black and scary, perhaps she and Amy needed a man around the house.

Whatever her misgivings about letting her father stay, he had his good points. Back in Daleham Gardens, as she remembered, he'd been sarcastic, lacking in humour, and had little in the way of conversation. She wondered now, as an adult, if that was because of her mother's constant carping, and how she was never satisfied with anything, because he showed no sign of those traits any more.

He was actually very good company, making both her and Amy laugh and taking an interest in their work. He was handy too, doing little repair jobs around the house, and he had a knack of being able to get black market goods.

Just a week ago he'd come home with some fillet steak and tins of salmon. He hadn't been at all nasty to Verity, even making supper for her and Amy occasionally before disappearing to the pub.

Sometimes he had money, but Verity had no idea where he earned it. But at those times he was generous, treating both her and Amy to dinner out, or the cinema. Once he'd even given Verity a ten-pound note to help with the housekeeping. But when he had no money, he could be a little grouchy, often asking her to lend him some.

The main problem with him being in the house wasn't so much Verity's old grievances against him, although she certainly hadn't forgiven or forgotten, she just had too much else to think about to dwell on them. The problem was the lack of privacy, and having to share the bed with Amy. Verity missed not being able to read at night, not having a room just for herself, and she had concerns that if Miller wanted to come to London, he couldn't stay with her.

But even the question of Miller didn't worry her too much, as she was planning to travel up to Scotland at the end of August for a two-week holiday. Miller knew a couple who would be glad to have her as a paying guest.

Now to hear that calm, easy-going Amy had rushed off without so much as an explanation, or even a goodbye, was very odd. Verity wasn't so much concerned about losing her rent, even though she relied on it to pay the bills, she wanted to know what had made her friend leave a job she liked, and the person she called her best friend.

Verity also didn't relish being alone in the house with her father, but thinking on that made her realize he must have had a hand in Amy leaving. Did he want to be on his own with her? And if so, why?

She recalled that when he first arrived, she'd got the idea he had something up his sleeve. Unfortunately, he'd lulled her into a false sense of security recently, and she'd stopped watching him so closely.

'Are you going to stand there gawping all day, or do I have to be a contortionist, climbing the post as well as holding the ladder?'

Beryl's sarcastic remark made Verity realize she'd been lost in thought for some time and still hadn't buttoned up her dungarees. 'I'm sorry, I was pondering on why Amy has skipped off. She used to tell me everything, I can't believe she'd go without so much as a goodbye.'

'Forget Amy for now. Up the ladder with you,' Beryl said, holding it in place for her. 'I can see a broken wire from down here, you might need to put a whole new length in.'

Verity climbed to the top of the ladder and then used the footholds on the pole to reach the top to check the wiring. She liked this part of the job. Well, at least on a warm, sunny day like today, when she could see for miles over rooftops. They were close to Crystal Palace today, and the trees in the big park there looked like a forest from up here. She didn't think it would be so pleasant in the pouring rain or in icy conditions, though. So far she and Beryl hadn't been sent out to restore telephone wires after a dropped bomb, but they both knew that was going to come any day now.

Their supervisor had informed them recently, 'Telephones are a vital form of communication during wartime'.

As Beryl had said, 'Trust her to state the bleeding obvious.'

The Battle of Britain that Winston Churchill had promised would follow the Battle of France had begun. On Pathé News, at the pictures, they saw the dogfights in the sky above Kent and Sussex between the British Spitfires and Hurricanes and the German Messerschmitts. It brought tears to Verity's eyes to think that those brave and dashing young airmen gambled with their lives each day to try and keep England safe. After their example she didn't think it would be fitting to whinge if she was sent out to mend telephone wires in a bit of rain.

'Do you know Amy's home address in Southend?' Beryl asked as Verity climbed down.

Verity shook her head. 'There was no reason for her to tell me it. I wish she had, I'd write and ask what I did wrong.'

'Maybe it's a man,' Beryl said with a smile. 'I'm becoming much more impulsive, especially about men. I've noticed many women are. I suppose it's because we could be killed by a bomb tomorrow, and we don't want to die wondering what it was all about.'

Verity laughed, because she was sure Beryl already knew everything about men and sex.

She was considered a femme fatale by the staff in the Post Office because of her admirers. Only a few days ago, a handsome American colonel came to meet her from work and took her for dinner at The Ritz. Beryl just laughed when asked about him and claimed he was an old family friend. That may have been true, but she always had a quiet confidence about her that suggested she could get any man she wanted.

'I hope my father didn't make her run off,' Verity blurted out. She had promised herself, after Susan Wallace was so mean to her at school, that she would never, ever tell another person about her family. She had, of course, told Miller some edited parts, but he was different, she somehow knew he would never use anything against her.

All she'd told Amy was that her father had left her and her mother, and they'd come to stay in Weardale Road with her Aunt Hazel. She said that her mother died a year later, and her aunt another couple of years on. Amy was so dizzy most of the time that she probably forgot the details almost instantly, and she wasn't one for asking questions anyway.

'Do you mean you think he might have made a pass at her?' Beryl asked.

'I certainly hope not,' Verity said. 'But he can be devious, and I think he might have wanted her out of the way because he has some kind of plan. You know how dumb Amy could be, it would be easy enough to scare her off.'

Beryl stared hard at Verity. Her eyes looked as if they were boring right into Verity's mind and reading what was in there. 'When you are ready to tell me the whole story about your dad, I'll be all ears.'

Verity gulped. She wanted to spill it out, but she didn't dare. 'There's nothing much to tell,' she lied. 'He's a bit of a bounder, that's all. I expect all it was with Amy was homesickness, and she couldn't bring herself to admit she wanted to be with her mum.'

'Maybe.'

Beryl raised one of her perfectly shaped eyebrows, and Verity knew then she didn't believe her.

*

Verity didn't get home that evening until after nine. While on the bus she heard there had been a bomb dropped that morning on the docks in East London. She knew the RAF were off on bombing raids at night over Germany now, and wondered how long it would be before the Germans retaliated with force. She suddenly felt really scared.

'You're late tonight,' Archie said as she walked in. 'I've kept your dinner hot for you. It's bangers.'

Verity barely glanced at the dinner plate on top of a saucepan of hot water, with the saucepan lid covering her dinner. 'What did you do or say to Amy to make her leave? She's left the job too, probably because she couldn't face me.'

'I didn't say or do anything,' he said, his eyes wide as if he was entirely innocent. 'She told me her mum was a worry guts, that she was terrified they'd start dropping bombs down in Southend and she might be buried under the rubble. Amy asked what I thought she should do.'

Verity was pretty certain Amy had never said such a thing to him; she'd always claimed her mum was a very tough woman. 'So I suppose you said she must go to her poor, scared mum?' she spat at him.

'No, I didn't, I only said she ought to do what she thought was right. She said she couldn't travel into London to work from Southend, but I said the Post Office would need people down there too.'

'You're lying, I know you are,' Verity roared at him. 'If you'd had that conversation with her, she would've told me and asked my opinion too. She would never have handed in her notice in secret, or left here pretending she was going home for the weekend, that wasn't her way. So tell me how you forced her hand and why.'

There were a few moments of complete silence before he spoke.

'The truth is that she's afraid of you,' he said eventually in a quiet, steady voice. 'She always did what you told her to do, she admitted that to me a while ago.'

'That's not true!' Verity exclaimed. 'No one is afraid of me.'

'No? Well, that might have been true in the past, but you've got a backbone of steel now, and it would be a brave person who would go against you,' he said with a shrug. 'I noticed it as soon as I came back here. I guess having to deal with moving from Hampstead and the way your mother was had a lot to do with it. Your Aunt Hazel was a difficult woman too, God only knows how you put up with her. Look at what you've done here: got the bathroom put in, decorated the rooms, new carpet on the stairs and stuff. You're still only a kid, but you did all that on your own.'

His admiring tone made her anger fade. She hadn't expected that he would remember what the house had been like when Aunt Hazel lived alone, much less notice that Verity had improved it. She hadn't expected him to appreciate the difficulties with her mother and aunt, either.

He picked her plate of dinner off the stove and put it down on the table for her. 'Eat up, you've had a long day,' he said.

He hadn't given her a real explanation about why Amy left, but right now she was very hungry and had expected to have nothing more than cheese on toast for supper, so it was really good to be given a hot meal. The sausages, fried onion and mashed potato smelled wonderful and she began to eat.

'Was Amy really scared of me?' she asked after a little while.

'Not scared like she thought you'd hit her or anything like that, but aware she seemed stupid next to you with all your reading and knowledge of world affairs. I told her you never thought of her like that, but I think she'd already made up her mind she'd be happier going home to her mum, and she didn't tell you in case you were cross with her.'

'Why would I be?' Verity felt a bit bewildered. 'I can understand her wanting to be in her own home. I never really understood why she came up to London anyway.'

Archie shrugged. 'She was like most young girls, she wanted adventure and independence, but she soon found out it isn't all it's cracked up to be. Now let's see if we can get along better, love. There's hard times coming soon.'

Upstairs in bed later, thinking on what Archie had said, much to her surprise Verity felt a warm glow. It was good to think he was admiring of her, and she especially liked him saying she had a backbone of steel. He'd never seemed to like anything about her when she was a child. She wondered what Miller would make of it all. He'd once said she sometimes reminded him of a puppy who had been ill-treated, shying away from people, always wary and on her guard, but at the same time so much wanting to be loved.

She wished she did know Amy's address in Southend so she could write and say what a good friend she'd been and how, although she was going to miss her, she was glad she was home where she'd be happier. She didn't like to think of anyone imagining they were inferior to her.

Before she fell asleep she reflected that in a day or two she'd have to make Archie see that he'd got to contribute towards the household expenses. It was all very well him getting a bit of black market food now and then, but she needed a regular sum from him.

Worries about Amy and Archie no longer ranked as important when night-time bombing of London began. Night after night it continued, throughout September, people starting to call it the Blitz, as the newspapers had used the world 'blitzkrieg' to describe saturation bombing.

At first it was utterly terrifying, like all hell had been let loose above. The deafening bangs, the fires that flared up wherever shrapnel fell, the way the very earth shook made people want to run from it, yet at the same time their legs often became leaden with fear, so they couldn't move.

Verity had been told by several people that they had been caught outside a bomb shelter when an air raid began and all they did was crouch down, their hands over their heads, as if that would save them.

Although they had the Morrison shelter at home, and Verity and Amy had practised getting in there many times, now Amy was gone Verity wouldn't use it. She left it to Archie and took herself off to the brick-built public shelter on Lee High Road when the siren went off. She thought it was preferable to be with her neighbours and have a hand to hold, or some chatter to distract her, rather than be squashed into the cage with a man she still didn't entirely trust.

People said you could get used to anything, and that

was certainly true of the bombings. As the weeks passed, everyone became far less fearful. They learned to identify by the sounds outside how close a bomb was, and some became so good at it they could almost pinpoint the road it had hit. They learned to take little comforts with them: a deckchair, blankets, food and a hot drink in a Thermos. Some women were organized enough to have a primus stove with them. Verity often played cards with the bigger children because, if left to their own devices, they tended to squabble or pester their mothers.

It wasn't until the night Hither Green Station was hit that they fully experienced the real perils of bombing. The noise was deafening – not just the bomb but the ack-ack guns too. The shelter shook, and brick dust and plaster rained down on them all.

Cowering in the shelter, they believed the bomb had landed right outside in Lee High Road, and even feared that their shelter was covered in rubble and they'd been buried alive. It was such a relief, when the all-clear finally came and the ARP warden opened the door, to see daylight – even if the air was full of smoke and dust, like thick grey talcum powder all over everything.

Someone came along then and told them the station had been hit and that a whole row of terraced houses in Fernbrook Road next to it had been flattened. While everyone in the shelter was very glad the bomb had missed them, many of them had a friend or relative in Fernbrook Road, and went straight there to see what they could do.

As it happened, Verity and Beryl were sent there the very next morning to mend the telephone wires, and the destruction they saw was truly terrible.

Just a few parts of the interior walls remained, with bits of broken furniture, mirrors and pictures strewn around. Rugs and clothes were in tatters, strewn across the still-smoking rubble, waving in the breeze like some kind of weird confetti.

Some of the people who had lived in the bombed houses were just standing there motionless, white-faced and red-eyed, so stunned to see their homes flattened and their belongings buried in the rubble that some couldn't even respond to questions. Four adults and two children had been killed. Two of the adults had been in a shelter but had run back to their homes to get something. The other little family had been in their own Anderson shelter in their garden, but it hadn't survived the direct hit.

Verity and Beryl had only been at the site for half an hour mending the telephone wires when the Civil Defence men dug the bodies out. The two children were so small they put them on one stretcher, and both men carrying it had tears washing a clear path through the brick dust and plaster on their cheeks.

In the days that followed, it soon became clear that it was London's docks and the railways that the bombers were keenest to target. They could follow the gleam of the River Thames in moonlight; Verity imagined that, from above, it was almost as good as a floodlit runway for the pilots. She supposed railway tracks gleamed almost as brightly. But that certainly didn't mean people could feel safe if they weren't living by the docks or a railway.

The bombers dropped their loads indiscriminately.

So no one was safe.

Chapter Twenty

Archie was feeling quite content in Weardale Road, especially now he'd got rid of that silly goose Amy. She was another one who asked too many questions. Verity didn't, in fact she didn't talk that much at all. She worked long hours, and most nights she went to the shelter, which he liked because it meant he could go to a card game, or have a few drinks without her even knowing he'd left the house.

But he needed to find some real money so he could move on. Despite what he'd told Verity, he was still wanted by the police, but he felt smug that they were just too tied up with war-related crime to concern themselves with looking for him. If he could get enough money, he could go to Ireland until the war ended, then he would go to South Africa, for good.

He had a plan for that. It had come to him just a couple of days earlier as he was walking up through Blackheath. He had intended to go down through Greenwich Park to the Isle of Dogs to see an old pal who always knew where the good card games were.

Quite by chance he glanced into a jewellery shop window, and to his surprise saw the big silver pheasant that had been given to him by his parents. It was possible it was merely an identical one. But his father had always claimed it was unique and pointed out his father's initials GLW – Gerald Lawrence Wood – right by the hallmark underneath.

Archie had assumed that all the silver and other valuables were seized by the bailiffs when the house was taken. But it seemed Cynthia must have been cannier than he thought, if she'd kept a few things back.

He went into the shop, and told the little Jewish shopkeeper that he'd had a silver pheasant just like this one stolen from his house five years earlier.

'Of course, I'm not saying that it is my pheasant,' he said, not wishing to alarm the old man. 'Mine had my grandfather's initials GLW engraved on it.'

The old man opened the catch on his shop window and took the pheasant out. 'It's a beautiful piece, but I shouldn't have bought it, people don't have the money now for such frivolities.' He turned it upside down and gasped. 'My goodness me, it has got those initials on it. I shall have to contact the police, I have never knowingly bought stolen goods.'

'I certainly didn't wish to bring any trouble to your door,' Archie said. 'I was just surprised to see it. Can you remember who you bought it from?'

'I do indeed,' said the old man. 'It was a very pleasant young lady, she said she and her mother were having money problems. I bought many things from her, all of them sold a long time ago now, except the pheasant. I can't believe she could be a thief.'

'She might not have been, maybe she had been asked to sell it for someone else. Does she live around here?'

'I did assume so. It's usually local people who bring me things to sell.' The old man paused, as if suddenly remembering something more. 'Oh dear, I think it is possible I may have been duped a second time by that young lady!

You see, a couple I know well came in to see me a couple of months ago and mentioned in passing that someone had broken into their house in The Glebe while they were away. A silver cream jug was taken, along with some cash. And that young lady with the pheasant sold me a cream jug too.'

Archie's heart soared. An idea was forming in his head which could be the answer to all his problems. 'What did she look like?' he asked.

'A pretty, blonde girl. But when she brought me the pheasant she was wearing a gymslip, so she could only have been about thirteen. I cannot imagine such a sweet-faced girl breaking into a house. And where did you say your house was?'

'Over in Highgate,' Archie lied. 'Some of the slum children around Holloway are adept at burglary from the age of nine or ten. She was a smart girl to bring it over here to sell.'

'Oh, she was no slum child,' the old man said. 'She was very well spoken and polite. But what shall we do about this? I bought the pheasant in good faith. Shall we call the police to decide what is to be done?'

'I don't think that's necessary,' Archie said. 'You might find yourself being charged with receiving, and I wouldn't want that on my conscience. Suppose you either give me back my pheasant or twenty pounds for my loss, and we call it quits.'

He saw the old man's face tighten and his eyes narrow, and fully expected him to say that he was going to call the police. But instead he sighed. 'I'll give you the money,' he said. 'I have a good reputation in Blackheath, and I wouldn't want anything to spoil that.'

Archie left the shop with a spring in his step. He had something to hold over Verity now, and twenty quid. A good day's work, all in all.

Verity's plan to go to Scotland had to be postponed once everyone became aware that the Blitz wasn't going to stop within days. The bombers came every night that the skies were clear enough for the pilots to see. That meant there would be many telephone wires needing mending or replacing the next day, and Miss Haig wasn't giving anyone time off for anything as frivolous as a holiday.

Many people couldn't bear the noise or the danger and left their London homes to go and live in the countryside. Other less fortunate folk merely packed their children and a few provisions into a pram or cart and walked out of London to spend the nights in fields or woods. Even being cold or wet was preferable to waiting for a bomb to drop.

Verity could understand that degree of fear. She realized from talking to people that everyone had their own mechanism for dealing with it. Some people stayed in their houses, claiming if a bomb had their name on it nothing would save them. Others went into open spaces or parks, convinced they'd be safer there. Verity's way was to run to cower in the shelter, surrounded by people she would never have chosen to spend a night with, and she blocked out the terrifying bangs and thuds by pretending she was in Babbacombe, going down to the beach through the woods.

If she concentrated hard enough, she could recall the smell of damp soil, taste salt on her lips, and feel the wind in her hair. In such moments Ruby was always there grinning at her, slender in her blue shorts and white blouse, her hair a storm of red-gold curls. She would imagine them both racing down the last hundred or so yards to see the sea, and once Verity had that view before her of turquoise water, black rocks and small boats bobbing on their moorings, she could hold it there in her mind regardless of what was going on around her in the shelter. She didn't smell the baby with the dirty nappy, or hear the man in the corner coughing his lungs up. She didn't even mind that the old lady sitting next to her had fallen asleep on her shoulder.

Sometimes the vision was strong enough for her to believe that Ruby would eventually contact her and that Archie would get bored and move on somewhere else.

It was only in the early morning, when the all-clear sounded, that her spirits flagged and made her face the truth that Ruby was never coming back, and Archie was never going to leave.

One Sunday morning in early October the all-clear siren went off at five, and Verity staggered out of the shelter with stiff legs and an aching back. The weather was surprisingly mild for October and although it was still dark, it felt warm. But drifting smoke coming from the east suggested it was the City of London which had got a pasting last night. The smell was one Verity had grown used to after air raids. A combination of smoke, brick dust, plaster, gas, often mixed with sewage when a bomb had damaged the pipes, it was acrid and caught the back of her throat.

The smell was strong enough that she half expected somewhere close by had been bombed. But as far as she could see in the gloom, the houses and shops in Lee High Road were undamaged, and there was no rubble in the road, or air-raid wardens and Civil Defence men gathering to rescue people. She breathed a sigh of relief, as she did every time she came out of the shelter to find she still had a home. As it was Sunday she could get a few hours of proper sleep, before tackling Archie.

People called out goodbye and, 'Enjoy your Sunday!' to her as she crossed the road to go home. She hadn't spoken to any of these people before the air raids began – most of them she'd never even seen before. She wasn't much of a talker, at least not when she could hear bombs dropping close enough to make the shelter quiver, but she listened to her neighbours and they'd become almost like family members. If one of their number missed a night in the shelter, they discussed where he or she might be. When Vera Friar, a rather bossy woman, was reported to have been hit by a bus on a very wet day in August and taken to Lewisham Hospital, a small party from the shelter, Verity included, went to see her.

Archie scoffed at community spirit. He said it was nosiness, not concern, and he bet these same people who she felt were her friends had been nasty about her mother killing herself. Verity thought he was probably right about that, but people were pulling together now when it was needed, and that was what counted.

Verity found Archie was still fast asleep in the Morrison shelter, lying on his back, snoring, his mouth gaping open, still fully dressed. He usually went back to his bed upstairs when the all-clear sounded, but by the stink of whisky coming from him she knew he'd got drunk last night and fallen into such a deep sleep that he didn't hear it.

That made her angry. Whisky was difficult to get hold of, even for people with money, and if he could afford to buy it, then he could pay for his keep. She filled the kettle, making as much noise as possible, even kicking the shelter as she walked past it to get the milk from the pantry. She had put the milk bottle in a bowl of cold water with muslin draped over it to keep it cool, yet despite her efforts it had gone off. That made her angry too, because it meant she'd have to use tinned milk and she hated the taste of it in tea.

There had been half a bottle of Camp coffee in the cupboard. Beryl had snobbishly called it 'poor man's coffee', because it was a coffee essence made from chicory, but Verity quite liked it, especially made with tinned milk. But when she found that was gone too, her anger spilled over.

'Wake up, you useless good-for-nothing,' she snarled, banging on the shelter. 'The milk's gone off and you've used all the Camp. When are you going to do something for the common good?'

He woke up with a start and as he sat up, banged his head on the table top.

'What's all the commotion about?' he asked, rubbing his head. 'Why aren't you in bed?'

'Because, you great lump, I was at the shelter all night, because bombs were dropping. I get home here to find the place stinking of whisky. And I can't have tea, because the milk's gone off, and I can't have Camp, either, because you've used it all.'

'The milkman will be here soon,' he said. 'Can't a man have a couple of drinks without his daughter shouting the odds?'

'If you can afford whisky, you can afford to give me money for your keep,' she raged at him. 'You tell me why I

277

should work all week just to keep you! What've you ever done for me?'

'I kept you in luxury and gave you a good education until you were thirteen,' he retorted. 'How easily you forget that.'

'I can't forget that you swindled people and that you beat me within an inch of my life before you ran away like the pathetic coward you are,' she shrieked at him. 'I shouldered the burden of looking after mother and trying to appease Aunt Hazel all the time. You've got no idea what kind of hell I had to go through.'

He stood up, and suddenly he looked so big and frightening she thought he was going to hit her. She backed away towards the door to the garden, wishing she hadn't been quite so reckless.

'Was it such hell that you felt compelled to rob a house up in Blackheath?' he said, his voice steady but with a hint of menace. 'You sanctimonious little thief.'

Verity felt a cold shiver go down her spine. How could he know about that?

'No good looking like you don't know what I'm talking about,' he said with a sneer. 'I know what you did. You sold that silver pheasant that came from my family to the jeweller's in Blackheath. I knew straight away it was mine, and I went in to ask about it.'

'There was nothing wrong with us keeping a few valuables back from the bailiffs,' Verity said indignantly. 'We had nothing to live on, I was too young to work and mother wasn't capable.'

'Nothing wrong with keeping those things, nothing at all,' Archie said and came closer to her, bending a little so his face was right up to hers. 'I admire that kind of resourcefulness. But I got chatting to the jeweller, and he told me the little hard-luck story the girl who'd sold it to him gave him. Then he went on to tell me about a silver jug that turned out to be stolen from a house in The Glebe.'

Verity suddenly felt very faint.

'You'd better sit down, my dear. You've gone chalk white, and it would be beastly if you fainted,' Archie's voice dripped with sarcasm. He pulled out a kitchen chair and nudged her on to it. 'First rule of thieving is that you don't try and sell the goods in the area you stole them from,' he said. 'You are very lucky he assumed you lived miles away, otherwise he would've called the police. I didn't, of course, enlighten him that I knew the culprit. I said my pheasant was stolen a few years ago.'

'Why didn't you say something before?' she asked.

'Because, my dear, I was actually impressed that you could be so resourceful. One could say a chip off the old block. I thought that in the fullness of time, once I'd got to know you all over again, we could pool our resources and work together to become rich.'

She stared at him, her mouth agape. Surely he couldn't be suggesting they robbed houses together?

'I can't do that,' she said, shaking her head. 'I only did the one burglary because I needed money, after Aunt Hazel died. I felt really bad about it.'

'Not so bad you gave it to charity? Instead, you had the bathroom installed,' he said, raising his eyebrows. 'Yes, I found the receipts for that, and for all the other little jobs you had done. Very sensible, really, most girls of your age would've spent it on frivolous stuff like clothes.'

He had her cornered, and she knew he wasn't going to let her off lightly. What a fool she'd been to think he'd changed and that he cared about her.

'You see why I encouraged Amy to go away?' he smirked. 'My dear, resourceful little daughter, how lucky it is that you are in a job where you can find out who has cancelled their telephone because they've gone away.'

'I can't get that information,' she said in horror.

'You can,' he laughed. 'Dopey Amy even mentioned that it is part of your job to disconnect a line when it is not in use. Not that I would be so stupid as to encourage you to rob a house where you had been the person to do that. But I know you can easily look at someone else's work sheets.'

'I won't do it,' she said firmly. 'You can't make me.'

He threw back his head and laughed. 'Is that so? Believe me, Verity, I have many different ways of making sure you obey me. You won't like any of them.'

Her heart was racing with panic, she felt sick and scared out of her wits.

'How could you say such a thing to your own daughter?' she asked.

He laughed again. 'I wonder your aunt didn't tell you. You aren't my daughter. I never wanted any children. Your mother was pregnant when I met her, only she omitted to tell me that. I thought she was smart and sexy, and that together we could go places. It turned out she was neither of those things, just a lying, greedy, self-centred gold-digger. But by then I'd made the mistake of marrying her.'

Chapter Twenty-One

February 1941

A letter from Miller was still lying on the doormat when Verity came home from work, which meant Archie hadn't been back to Weardale Road for three whole days. She thought it would be marvellous if he'd cleared off with a woman, fallen under a train or even been killed in a bombing raid. But she couldn't be that lucky. He'd been saying they were going to start their 'new business' any day now, and as she'd managed to get him a list of disconnected telephones in Kew and Putney, he could even be away checking out the addresses right now.

The house felt like an ice box. At least when he was there she came home to a fire blazing. Waiting for him to turn up again was nerve-racking. She felt unable to relax, knowing he could walk in the door at any moment. And there was always the threat, if she said the wrong thing or did anything he didn't like, that he would hit her. He had struck her at Christmas, that was for saying she was going to spend Christmas Day with a friend from work. He'd slapped her round the face so hard she fell over, and told her she wasn't going anywhere.

It was so very tempting to go to the police, to throw herself on their mercy and spill out the entire sorry story. But she had burgled the house in The Glebe, and she'd sold valuables from Daleham Gardens when they were supposed to be left in the house for the bailiffs. But what the police would do to her didn't frighten her half as much as Archie did.

He was as sly as a fox, the most plausible liar she'd ever met, and he could twist things to make himself look like the most tender-hearted father to any onlookers, and her the ungrateful, troubled daughter. Then there was the violence. She knew he was more than capable of giving her the kind of beating he had given her back at Daleham Gardens. And worse still there would be no warning when it came.

It had been a shock to be told he wasn't her real father; to have believed he was for so many years seemed a terrible thing. Yet it was also a relief to know they shared nothing more than a name. One she intended to change the minute she could get away from him.

She picked up the letter from Miller, and just looking at his big, sprawling handwriting made her feel warm inside. She hung up her coat and took the letter upstairs to read it, just in case Archie came in.

Three weeks had gone by without a letter, which made this one even more precious. In his letter just after Christmas he'd suggested that she come up to Scotland for Easter.

She had the feeling that once she was with Miller, she would be able to tell him everything about Archie, and he'd find a way out of her problems. Of course she didn't want to admit she'd burgled a house, that was shameful, but she felt Miller would take into consideration how much pressure she'd been under, and help her.

Just holding his letter in her hand made her feel less alone and frightened. Maybe she could even pour it all out in her next letter to him and get it off her chest.

She savoured opening the envelope, leaning back against the headboard of her bed, knowing in a few moments she would be transported to his world of forests, wild animals and wide open spaces. She started to read.

Dear Verity,

This is a very difficult letter to write, but I must do it, for to leave it any longer would be so wrong . . .

Verity frowned. This sounded like it was going to be a confession about something bad.

But surely not, Miller wasn't that kind of man.

I am afraid I have met a girl up here. Because of that I must end our friendship, as she wouldn't understand me writing to you. And besides, it wouldn't be right to string you along thinking you were going to come up here at Easter for a holiday.

May I explain that I came to a different world up here, and I've found I'm not the man I was in London. I want different things now, another kind of life, and my new girl is a quiet wee thing who fits into the forest like a rabbit or a pheasant.

I have so many things in my head that I want to tell you, to make you see why this came about and where I am going, but all that will do is make me feel justified, and it won't lessen your hurt and sorrow.

But I do think you need a very different man to me, and I sincerely hope you find him and have great happiness.

I thank you again for giving me shelter in your home, for being a good friend too, perhaps the best I've ever had.

Yours,
Miller

Verity let the letter drop on to her lap, and for a moment was transfixed with shock. Miller was the one good thing in her life, and he didn't want her any more.

She sat there for some time before she could even cry. Only Miller could let a girl down so kindly; she could imagine him, pen in hand, trying to find the words that would hurt the least.

But however he dressed it up, she'd been abandoned for someone he liked better. She hoped his 'quiet wee thing' would turn out to be stultifyingly boring, and he'd be tormented in his dreams of all the laughs they used to have and those passionate kisses at Christmas.

It was ignoble to think bad thoughts about his new girl, but she couldn't help it. Miller should have been her man, her future husband and father of her children. Now she had absolutely no one to turn to for help with Archie.

So she'd just have to go along with his plans.

Chapter Twenty-Two

1942

Ruby came out of Hither Green Station and for a moment just stood still outside, looking towards the Railway Hotel, the big pub on the corner which Verity had mentioned once while she was down in Babbacombe.

Ruby had been told while on the train from Charing Cross that Hither Green Station and the street next to the railway embankment had been bombed during the Blitz. Repairs had been made to the station, but from where she stood she could see the bombed street, the rubble only partially cleared, and she felt a pang for all those who had lost their loved ones and their homes.

The *Daily Mail* had reported just a short while ago that Torquay was a funk hole, where cowardly people were hiding from the war. Ruby very much resented that, as did most of its residents. So maybe there hadn't been any really serious bombing incidents yet, but factories there were providing all kinds of goods needed for the war, and the locals worked very hard to reach targets, often above and beyond the call of duty.

Many of the hotels had been taken over by the military too; they used them for specialist training and for billeting men before shipping them off to the fighting. The Palace, where Ruby had worked before the war, was the main hospital for RAF officers. She had been kept on as receptionist, and was in charge of the men's medical records.

She had seen airmen with such terrible injuries that she now knew exactly what war was all about, and it had changed her. Gone were the days when she thought of nothing but going dancing and what dress she was going to wear. In her off-duty hours now she practised first aid, helped Wilby with the evacuees and collected old clothes door to door. These clothes were for people who had been bombed out, and she helped sort them into men's, women's, children's and babies' in a storeroom above a shop in Reddenhill Road.

This change in her had also made her see how badly she'd treated Verity, and she'd already been up to London twice, once in the late summer of 1940, and then again last year. Both times she'd seen Verity from a distance but hadn't spoken to her.

Wilby said it was daft to get so near, then to back off. All she had to do was write a letter and apologize. But Ruby had put pen to paper so many times, and yet she could never find the right words to explain herself.

Today she was determined to speak to Verity, even if she had to stay another night in London to do so. She'd come up this time to check on her mother. A well-meaning air-raid warden had reported to the police that she was in a bad way, and they in turn had telephoned Wilby.

The air-raid warden had found her huddled in an alley with a black eye one very cold night, and he'd got the idea she couldn't go home because of a violent husband. In fact she was just drunk and confused, she couldn't even remember who had hit her. When Ruby saw her, she read her the

286

riot act about looking after herself, then cleaned up her room and left.

She had no sympathy for her mother. There were so many people in real difficulties all over England, and most of them were grateful for any help. Ruby saw no reason to waste time or energy on a woman who would never change her ways, even if she was her mother.

The first time Ruby had come to Hither Green, in the summer of 1940, to see Verity, she was attending a three-day medical course in New Cross. It was far more intensive than basic first aid, intended to train civilians like her in case there should be a very serious incident where they needed to pull in extra people with medical knowledge and practical skills to help.

She had gone to Weardale Road on an impulse, because the course ended earlier than she'd expected and her train back to Torquay didn't leave Paddington till seven in the evening.

Reminders of Coronation Day and the Weardale Road street party came to her as she approached the house. Everything still looked much the same, but shabbier.

She knocked on the door, but there was no reply. She was still standing there, wondering if it was worth coming back a bit later, when a fat middle-aged lady spoke to her.

'You won't find anyone in till later,' she said. 'Both of the young ladies work for the Post Office and they work shifts. I saw them going off before six this morning, giggling like they was going on a fun day out.'

Ruby sensed this woman with a sour face didn't approve of anyone who enjoyed life. She also sensed she was the street gossip and it would be wise not to give her any ammunition.

'I wasn't looking for a young woman,' she said. 'It was Miss Ferris I was looking for. I suppose she's at her work too?'

'Didn't you hear, love? She died a couple of years back. She'd turn in her grave too if she knew her niece had had a male lodger since then, and now this brassy blonde with her tight skirts and her bright red lipstick. Heaven only knows what the two of them get up to alone in that house without supervision.'

Ruby hadn't known about Verity's Aunt Hazel dying, and it made her feel sad that she hadn't been in touch to comfort her old friend. But she wasn't going to let that slip. 'I'm sorry to hear about Miss Ferris,' she said, determined not to rise to the woman's spiteful remarks about Verity. 'I was just hoping she'd make some curtains for me. What did she die of?'

'A heart attack at her work,' the older woman said. 'Hardly surprising, really, what with the trouble of having that sister of hers turning up uninvited with her kid and expecting poor Miss Ferris to take care of them. That lazy good-for-nothing never did a thing for her sister when she was living in a posh house and the kid was at private school. But as soon as that crook of a husband of hers disappeared and the woman fell on hard times, she came here expecting handouts.'

'How unpleasant for Miss Ferris,' Ruby said. She thought the woman's venom against Verity's mother was harsh and unnecessary. She wondered if she was the same gossip Verity had spoken of sometimes.

'Then her sister went and stuck her head in the gas oven!'

'Did she really?' Ruby exclaimed. She knew already, of course. She'd seen how much it had affected Verity too, but she wasn't going to say anything that would blow her cover. 'Well, thank you for your help, obviously I'll have to find someone else to make my curtains.'

Ruby walked away; she had the feeling if she talked to that unpleasant woman for any longer, she'd say something she'd later regret. She was very shocked to hear of Aunt Hazel's death, poor Verity must have felt very alone, with her mother gone too. Ruby wondered about the male lodger. Was he her boyfriend? She just hoped, if he was, it hadn't all gone wrong for her.

Ruby thought that if Verity had gone to work at six this morning, she'd probably finish at four, so she went to a cafe in Lee High Road, right across from the end of Weardale Road, ordered tea and a sandwich, and waited.

She had read an entire local newspaper, including the obituaries, and was just about to give up and leave when Verity jumped off a bus, with another girl.

The pair of them stopped almost outside the cafe and it looked as if they were discussing whether they needed anything from the shop before going home. It gave Ruby the chance to get a good look at her old friend.

She looked very pretty, and far more womanly now; she'd only ever had the tiniest of breasts before. Ruby remembered how she used to despair of them ever growing. But they had now, and she was radiant, her blonde hair plaited around her head like a crown, and her face tanned. She was wearing a blue polka-dot shirtwaister dress Ruby remembered. The wide navy-blue belt around her waist made it look tiny. She had white socks and plimsolls on her feet, and her legs were very brown, so she must have been outside a great deal during the summer.

Ruby's whole being wanted to run out of the cafe and hug her, but Verity had her head thrown back, laughing heartily at something the other girl was saying, and Ruby felt she had no right to intrude.

Whatever the gossip of Weardale Road had said about this friend, she looked nice, with a generous mouth and a wide smile. Ruby hoped she'd be a better friend to Verity than she had been.

So Ruby didn't try to speak to Verity that day. She told herself she would write and explain that she'd seen her but was too afraid of rejection to speak.

But the war kind of took over just after that. Dunkirk, the Battle of Britain, and then the Blitz brought so many wounded men to the hospital in the Palace, and she found herself working eighteen-hour days, with no time to think of anything but the suffering all around her.

The second time Ruby came to London was last year, when she accompanied two airmen on crutches who were going home to the north of England, and needed assistance with changing trains in the city.

Ruby could scarcely believe the changes in London with bomb damage everywhere, boarded-up windows, great gaps in the rows of houses around Paddington, and people looking weary and grey. The so-called Blitz might have ended, in as much as the bombing wasn't every night like it had been back then, but Ruby heard from people that when the bombers came back it was still terrible. There were shortages of everything from paint to petrol, people were living on next to nothing, and it showed in their lean bodies and drawn faces.

Down in Devon, they could still get butter, cheese and meat from various sources. Even strictly law-abiding Wilby didn't mind a bit of black market produce, so she could feed what she called 'her family' – the three evacuees, along with Ruby. They also kept chickens and grew vegetables in the garden, so their diet hadn't changed that much.

Ruby didn't get as far as Verity's house in Weardale Road the second time. She had just come out of Hither Green Station when she saw Verity walking towards her, with a man. She darted into one of the telephone boxes outside the station and watched them. He looked about fifty, a big good-looking man with wide shoulders and greying hair. He fitted with what Verity had said about her father. But surely it couldn't be him? Verity had always claimed she'd never have anything to do with him again. They appeared to be arguing about something. And it looked to Ruby as if Verity didn't want to go with him, because he caught hold of her wrist and practically dragged her into the booking hall.

Ruby came out of the telephone box to follow them, hoping for some sign she should engage with them. But the man bought train tickets and then, still holding Verity's wrist, he headed straight for the tunnels that went up on to the platforms.

He was going on a southbound train out to Kent, but Ruby's ticket was a return back to Charing Cross. She was tempted to throw caution to the wind and follow them, but she decided that approaching Verity on a busy train when she was accompanied was hardly likely to result in a successful reunion.

So Ruby decided to let it go.

When she got home, she asked Wilby what she thought. But Wilby just pulled a pained face. 'I've told you a dozen times to write to her,' she said. 'Last time you went, you discovered her aunt had died and I told you then that you should send her a letter of condolence. But you didn't listen. Tell me, you silly girl, how many more years is this going to go on for?'

Ruby knew Wilby was right, and that night she lay in her bed crying. Not just because of Verity and what had passed between them, but because of all the sadness, everywhere in the world, since then. Little evacuees had come here from London, poorly dressed, underfed and crawling with lice, yet they'd cried for their mothers and wanted to go home. One of them, Jack, lost his mother when their home was bombed last January in Stepney. Wilby had kept the boy, hoping to adopt him, but just when she thought no relative would ever claim him, his grandmother did.

There were the wounded airmen at the Palace too. Some with terrible, disfiguring burns. They acted tough and brave, but she'd often gone into the wards at night and heard them crying. They knew, as everyone did, that they were unlikely to marry and have children, most would have difficulty in even getting a job. What sort of a thank you was that for someone who had given his youth and health to defend his country?

Daily, Ruby spoke to young women whose husbands

were away at the war. Their lives were one long round of anxiety, afraid that any day they would get a telegram to say their man had been killed in action. Some of them had been pregnant when their husband left, others had two or three small children, and they had a hard time coping with everything all alone.

Some of the married women who worked at the Palace kept telling Ruby to make the most of the opportunities this war offered. She had the job other women envied, because they just saw her as a pretty face behind the reception desk. In fact her role was not just ornamental, as they seemed to think. Aside from keeping all the patients' records, she was the sympathetic ear when distraught relatives arrived to see badly wounded airmen. She made bookings for these people to stay in nearby hotels, arranged transport for them. She relayed messages to everyone, from surgeons down to cleaners, and every memo pinned up in the canteen, every instruction on what to do if there was an air raid, and even the menu of the day, was typed up by her and distributed to the right place.

The hospital manager had told her on several occasions that she was a 'treasure'. This was because she had earned the reputation for sorting out any problem. But when older women told her to make the most of opportunities, they didn't mean furthering her career but finding herself a good husband. The Palace probably was an ideal hunting ground, not just amongst the officers who were patients but also the doctors, friends of the patients, and men who were in administration.

But Ruby just wasn't interested in luring any man, not an officer, bus driver or air-raid warden. Even she thought it was odd that a girl who had once been such a flirt didn't attempt it any more. She had lost the desire for men ever since her abortion. Sometimes, if she drank enough at a dance, she could flirt a little with dance partners, perhaps even kiss them and fake some passion. But no amount of drink could ever make her go further than kissing. Sometimes she felt she was dead inside.

Now as Ruby stood at Hither Green Station with her hands in her pockets, a bitter January wind biting through her coat, she felt completely resolved that this time she was going to speak to Verity. She turned up the collar of her coat against the wind and began walking towards Weardale Road.

She paused outside number seven before knocking. The paint was very chipped, and it looked as if someone had forced the door with a heavy boot. It felt scary to be back here again, not full of anticipation as she had been for the coronation, but afraid of being rebuffed.

It seemed ages before she heard someone coming, and her pulse quickened. The door was opened just a crack, with the chain still on, but even so she knew it was Verity.

'Open up, it's me, Ruby,' she said quickly. 'That is, if you'll speak to me!'

'Ruby?' Verity's voice was very quiet, almost a whisper.

'Yes, it really is me. Not before time too!'

'Oh, my goodness,' came the startled reply.

Ruby expected the door to be flung open wide, followed by either a volley of abuse or a warm hug. But when the door didn't open wide she assumed her belief that, once her old friend saw her, everything would be alright was misplaced.

'I know I was awful to you, but I wasn't thinking straight back then. I've come here twice before and seen you, but lost my nerve.' The words just poured out in a nervous torrent. 'Please let me in so we can talk.'

'I can't,' Verity whispered. 'I want to, but I can't.'

All at once Ruby realized her friend was in some kind of difficulty. She assumed it was a man; she'd met many who didn't like their girl having friends.

'Okay, but can I meet you in a cafe? There's one at the end of the road.'

'Not there, go back to the station. There's one just by it. Wait there.'

'Verity!' A deep and loud male voice rang out from inside the house. 'Who is at the front door?'

'Go,' Verity whispered, but reached out one small hand through the crack in the door to touch Ruby's cold cheek. 'Wait for me!'

'It's only the postman,' Verity called back. And then, first putting her fingers to her lips like she was going to blow a kiss, she shut the door.

Ruby walked swiftly down the road without looking back, just in case the man she'd heard was looking out of the window. The situation brought back a few memories of scenes from her childhood. It was men coming to the door then, and she had to get rid of them when her mother had another man with her upstairs. She would keep the chain on the door and play dumb, saying her mother had gone out and she mustn't let anyone in. Sometimes they got nasty, because they sensed the truth, and sometimes they tried to cajole her. She had grown up wondering why, when her mother had so many men who seemed to adore her, she also had so many who hit her.

She learned by the time she was ten that these men gave her mother the money for drink. Yet she never really discovered why men who wanted sole use of her hit her so often. Why would violence go hand in hand with sex?

Ruby just hoped that man upstairs in Verity's house wasn't beating her.

Chapter Twenty-Three

'Who did you say that was at the door?' Archie called out from his bedroom. His door was open, and as Verity turned to look at him she got the same sick feeling that came so often when she was near him.

He was sitting up in bed, wearing a vest, and a smell of stale sweat and unwashed feet wafted out from his room. She hated him so much now that she often dreamed of killing him to escape his clutches. There was a time when she'd been afraid of losing her home in the bombing, but now she longed for it to happen, a direct hit, with him inside it. As he still never went to a public shelter, it was possible. But then he had the luck of the devil.

'It was Beryl. I'm wanted at work, lines down in Catford. She was going to wait, but I told her to go on and I'd follow in a few minutes.'

'Haven't they got anyone else? It's your day off.'

'Seems no one else is available,' she called back as she went into her bedroom. Looking at herself in the dressing-table mirror, she saw the delight at Ruby turning up had brought some colour to her face. She felt there was a glimmer of hope now, as Ruby was the only person in the whole world who was likely to fully understand what had brought her to the life she'd been living for nearly two years.

Aside from the colour in her face, she could see nothing

else to feel good about. She was very thin, gaunt in fact. This was due to rationing, in part, but she felt it had more to do with the pressure she was living under. Her blonde hair had lost its shine, and each time she brushed it she was alarmed how much came out. She never slept well any more, yet she was bone tired.

She took off the drab grey woollen dress she was wearing and changed it for a dusky pink one that was more flattering. Even as low as her spirits were, she was too proud to let Ruby see her looking quite so bad. She brushed her hair and, leaving most of it loose, pinned up the sides on either side of her head with two pretty pink hair slides. A bit of face powder, a touch of Vaseline on her eyelids and some mascara improved her, then she finished off with the last of her pink lipstick.

'There's no more where that came from,' she murmured to herself, putting the empty lipstick case down. 'Unless you steal some!'

Just the idea of stealing another woman's lipstick made a lump come up in her throat. Somehow, it seemed worse than taking a ring or a bracelet.

Pushing her feet into her best shoes, tan leather with a two-inch heel, she was ready apart from her coat. She just hoped that Archie wouldn't notice that she was dressed up. She rarely made an effort with her appearance any more.

'What time will you be back?' he called out as she went down the stairs.

'I've no idea, it depends on the emergency,' she called back. 'There's sausages in the meat safe, but you'd better cook yours in case I'm late.'

It struck her as she put on her navy-blue coat and her felt hat of the same colour that anyone overhearing the dialogue between her and Archie would never imagine she hated him. But Verity had realized the first time he hit her, after he'd got rid of Amy, that appeasement was a smarter way than challenging him.

Slipping out quickly, Verity ran up the road towards Hither Green. It was good luck she'd had the day off today; if she'd been at work when Ruby called, Archie would never have told her. She hoped that her good luck would hold, because she hadn't had any for a very long time.

Since Miller sent her that last letter telling her he'd got another girl, nothing in her life seemed worth anything. She went to work each day, and she maybe fooled all her old friends most of the time into believing nothing was wrong. Yet there were questions sometimes about why she never wanted to go to the pub after work or to a dance. Beryl once said it was like a light had gone out inside her, and asked if it was to do with her father. Verity almost broke down then and told her the truth, that he was a thieving blackguard who blackmailed her into burgling houses. But how could she confide in Beryl? She would take Verity straight to the police station. And she couldn't expect any sympathy from them, because she'd got in too deep.

Ironically, Archie claimed she brought him good luck. But that was only because the information she got about cancelled telephone lines was always good. Verity mostly had Wednesday afternoons off, and that was when Archie liked to do the jobs. He felt marching up people's garden paths in broad daylight attracted much less attention than being spotted at night. Not that he did anything more than force the window locks and stand guard, Verity took all the risk.

Her heart was pounding at the thought of seeing Ruby. It didn't matter to her how long they'd been estranged or why. Just the knowledge that there was a possibility they could pick up where they left off, was enough.

Mick's cafe by the station was a grubby little place used mainly by railway workers and other workmen. The windows were streaming with condensation, so it was impossible to see in. But to Verity it was as good as The Ritz, because it was a place of safety for a little while.

As she opened the door Ruby came rushing towards her, arms wide to embrace her friend. 'I'm sorry, I'm sorry,' she whispered against Verity's hair. 'I was so nasty.'

Verity took a step back, holding Ruby's forearms, and smiled. 'None of that matters. We're together again now.'

They took a table right at the back of the cafe, and Ruby went up to the counter to order fried spam sandwiches and tea.

'I was sort of hoping they might have bacon and egg,' she said as she came back to the table. 'But they do say there's a war on.'

Verity giggled. 'I've grown to like spam. And they fry the bread here too. I've heard it's becoming quite a delicacy and talked about in every major city,' she joked.

For a moment the girls just looked at each other across the table, the years apart falling away. Verity moved first, reaching out to touch one of Ruby's unruly curls which had escaped from her beret and looked like a little corkscrew. 'You look so sophisticated,' she said. 'And even lovelier than I remembered.'

'That's a super thing to say,' Ruby said, her eyes shining. 'Completely untrue, of course. And now I'm probably going to upset you again by saying you are too thin, you've lost your bounce, and I sense something bad is going on in your life. You are going to tell me everything.'

Verity loved Ruby more than ever for that blunt appraisal. She needed to unburden herself and she was glad she hadn't fooled Ruby she was fine by just sticking a couple of pretty hair slides in her hair and a slick of Vaseline on her eyelids.

'My dad is the problem. He's back,' she began. 'I don't call him Dad, just Archie, and it turns out he isn't my dad at all. Mum was pregnant when she conned him into marrying her.'

Ruby nodded. 'When I came here last, I saw you with a big man, I thought that might be who he was. But he looked as if he was dragging you into the station against your will.'

'He probably was,' Verity shrugged. 'But for you to understand how it all came about I'd better go back to when Aunt Hazel died.'

'A neighbour of yours told me about that, that was back before the Blitz began,' Ruby said. 'I'm so sorry. I should've written then, but I couldn't find the words.'

Verity reached across the table and put her hand over Ruby's. 'Please, no more apologies, we must draw a veil over all that and forget it. I was in financial difficulties when Aunt Hazel died. I needed to get a lodger, and that meant sprucing up the house and getting a bathroom put in.'

As clearly and quickly as she could, she told Ruby about how when her mother was alive she'd sold various valuable items from their old house to a shop in Blackheath. Later, after Aunt Hazel died, she'd gone back with some more things and Mr Rosen had told her about people running off and leaving their houses, because they were afraid of what war might bring.

She stopped there, not sure if she could go on.

'Don't stop, Verity, you need to tell me,' Ruby said. 'I won't judge you, whatever you did.'

'What he said about people leaving their homes gave me an idea.'

'To break in and rob them?' Ruby whispered.

Verity nodded. 'Well, I didn't do it right away. You see, I met this lovely man, Miller, a gardener. He'd lost his job and home cos the people he worked for were some of those lot who moved away. So he came as my lodger.'

'Just the lodger?' Ruby smiled.

Verity smirked. 'Yes, just. He never became anything else, not until I was waving him goodbye when war broke out. He was turned down for the forces, as he had a heart thing, so they sent him to work for the Forestry up in Scotland.'

Verity went on to explain that her aunt had always intended to put a bathroom in, and she wanted one desperately too. Miller went off one weekend to see some relatives and she decided she was going to burgle a house while he was gone to get the money for the bathroom.

'I remembered stuff you'd told me when we first met, and so I just did it. Only the one house, I didn't take much, just a silver jug, and I found some cash in a box. That paid for the bathroom to be put in.' She paused then, because the waitress was coming with their tea.

'I didn't feel bad about it, Ruby, at least not then,' she said once the waitress was out of earshot. 'I kind of justified it to myself. I told Miller it was some money Aunt Hazel had left, and we did the tiling in the bathroom ourselves. Later that summer, when it was obvious war was going to come any time, and Miller got sent to Scotland, Cooks of St Paul's – where I was working – moved out of London. So I applied to the Post Office and got myself trained up to fix telephone cables. I still work there.'

'So you did this burglary before the war. Never again?'

'That's right. I came to be really ashamed of doing it. Then Amy became my lodger. I worked with her at the Post Office.'

'The buxom brunette girl I saw you with?'

Verity looked askance at her. 'You saw me again? And didn't speak.'

'That was the first time I called. I waited in the cafe on the main road and you got off the bus with Amy. Maybe if you'd been alone I'd have been brave enough to speak. Then the second time was when I saw Archie pulling you into the station. How could I approach you then?'

'It's a good job you didn't.' Verity shook her head, as if bewildered by the evil he was capable of. 'You see, he turned up when Amy was there and he'd obviously fallen on hard times, so I let him sleep in Amy's bed and she came in with me. Then one day she just left, both my house and her job, with not a word of farewell, nothing. Archie said she was afraid of me.'

Ruby snorted with laughter. 'Afraid of you? Who could be afraid of you?'

'That's what I thought. But he said I'd changed because of Mother and Aunt Hazel dying, and also he maintained that Amy was intimidated by me because I was clever, reading and knowing about world news and stuff. I suppose I felt a bit flattered, really, it stopped me thinking he'd got rid of her for his own ends.'

'So just to interrupt, have you heard from or seen Miller since he went to Scotland? That's a strange name, by the way. What was he like?'

'He was kind, funny, easy-going. And he made my garden so pretty,' Verity said, and her eyes filled with tears. 'He wrote to me every week. He didn't actually say he was in love with me, but there was a kind of understanding that we had something special. I hear women say all the time how the war altered everything, and that's just how it was. I couldn't rush off to Scotland to be with him, and he couldn't come down here, either. Then Archie turned up and Amy went. The Blitz started, and suddenly I get a letter from Miller saying he's sorry but he's met someone, and it wouldn't be fair to her to keep writing to me.'

'Oh no!' Ruby exclaimed.

Their fried spam sandwiches arrived, and for a few moments neither girl spoke while they took their first bites.

'This is seriously good,' Ruby said with her mouth full. 'I shall have to train Wilby to make it like this. Though she'll probably say so much fat isn't good for you. But to get back to Miller, at least he told you the truth, so few men do that.'

'I know,' Verity agreed. 'I just wish we could've had a bit more time together before he wrote me off. I really thought he could be "the one".'

'Look how many times I thought I'd found "the one",' Ruby smirked. 'But we've got sidetracked. Now let's get back to Archie. Did he go to prison? Or is he still on the run?'

'I don't know anything about him, at least I don't know the truth. When he turned up, I told him to go or I'd call the police and turn him in. But he said they weren't looking for him any more, because he'd sorted it all out with them. He implied he'd paid back the money he took.'

Ruby raised both eyebrows.

'I know,' Verity sighed. 'Only a fool would believe that. But if he is still a wanted man, he doesn't hide himself away. Okay, he told the neighbours he's my uncle, Gerald Wood, but the police have never been back to ask if I've seen him. Maybe he did wriggle out of it. Anyway, to get back to the point, one day I got a bit tough with him, because I needed a lodger who paid their way, and that's when he blackmailed me. Seems he got into conversation with the jeweller I sold Mum's stuff to, because he still had the silver pheasant that came from Archie's family in his shop window. The jeweller described me, and told Archie I'd also brought in a silver cream jug which sounded like it was taken from a house in Blackheath.' Verity paused, hanging her head in shame. 'I don't need to go into all of that, but the gist of it is that Archie realized what I'd done and saw he could use it to make me do anything he wanted.'

'Just a minute. Does the jeweller know who you are or where you live?'

'No. If he did, the police would have been round by now. I expect he thinks I came to him from miles away.'

Ruby just sat back in her chair for a moment looking at Verity, then she shook her head in dismay.

'It was a bit daft selling the stuff from the house you robbed more or less on their doorstep!' she said. 'I should've given you my expert advice on how to burgle efficiently!'

Verity knew that was supposed to be a joke, but she couldn't laugh. Instead she looked rueful. 'I know it was daft, I should've thought it through. But in my defence at least that proves I'm not a habitual criminal.'

'So is Archie making you rob more houses?'

Verity nodded. 'He hand picks the right ones. I get him the addresses of people who've cancelled their telephone connection. He checks the houses out. But I'm the one who goes in, while he stays outside and keeps watch. It isn't every week – he staggers the jobs, and in different areas – but I'm a bag of nerves with it.'

She couldn't even begin to tell Ruby how terrifying she found it. She couldn't eat or sleep for days before, and she never really trusted Archie to warn her if someone was coming. He was far more likely to run for it. It was so wrong to be going through people's things looking for valuables and cash, but she knew if she came out with nothing he'd only make her do another house on her next day off.

The nightmare didn't end with the completed job, either. When she closed her eyes at night she imagined being caught red-handed, handcuffed and taken to the police station cells. She had terrible pictures in her head about what prison was like, and she felt so sorry for the people she robbed. Archie said it served them right for leaving their homes, but she didn't agree with that. Then Archie often hit her for not getting enough valuables, and it wasn't as if she benefitted from any of it; he took the goods to fence them, and spent the money on gambling and drinking.

'The absolute bastard,' Ruby hissed, sounding much as she did when Verity first met her. 'He needs stringing up. Look, Verity, come home with me now. Don't go back there. I can fix you up with clothes and things.'

For a brief moment Verity felt her nightmare was finally over. Nothing could be better than being back in Babbacombe and free of Archie. But she'd barely begun to imagine sharing that lovely bedroom with Ruby again before reality set in.

'I can't come,' she said sadly. 'There's my ration book, my job, all those little bits and pieces that I need.'

'They aren't important,' Ruby said. 'Well, I suppose your ration book might be, you don't want to leave a trail he can follow down to Babbacombe. So okay, not today, but soon. You can give in your notice at work; tell them you are going to Scotland to see Miller. Gradually sort out the stuff you need to bring, maybe pack it in a case or bag when he's out and put it in a left luggage office. There's one at Charing Cross Station. Then act like you are off to work one day and just get on the train and come to me. I can get you a job at the Palace, where I work. It was a hotel, but now it's a hospital for wounded RAF officers.'

'If he gets wind of anything, there's no knowing what he'll do to me,' Verity said fearfully. 'And what if he goes to the police and tells them about the robberies?'

'If he does, he will only incriminate himself,' Ruby said. 'Does he know anything about me? Like where I live, or that you used to come down and stay with me?'

'I don't think so. I've never talked about you to anyone, because I felt so sad about it. But he's a snoop, Ruby. Once he'd found out I'd taken silver to sell at that jeweller's he searched the house and found the receipt for getting the bathroom put in. He could've found a letter from you. I thought I destroyed them all when we fell out, but I can't be sure. But Ruby, what about Wilby? How can I face her? She'll be so shocked, if she finds out about any of this.'

'She's the least of your worries,' Ruby said. 'I've never seen her fazed by anything, and she's fond of you, always begging me to write and apologize to you. If the worst came to the worst and you did get found out, she'd fight your corner. As I would too. Leave that vile man, start a new life.'

'But it's Aunt Hazel's house and once I'm twenty-one, if her solicitor hasn't found a closer relative, it will be mine.'

Ruby sat back in her chair and just looked at Verity.

'A bomb could drop on it tonight,' she said after a bit. 'It's bricks and mortar, that's all. Your life, safety and happiness are worth far more. Walk away; leave all the sadness you've had while living there behind you. You and I together can make new, happy memories and a good life.'

Verity thought that sounded so wonderful. But she'd been under Archie's thumb for so long, she didn't really believe she could get out from under it. Ruby would never understand just how devious and manipulative Archie was. He could disappear again and inform the police anonymously about her doing the burglaries. It would be an open and shut case. She had access to the addresses from the Post Office, and all the houses were entered through small windows, too small for an average-sized man. Even the neatness of the jobs suggested it was the work of a woman.

If she tried to tell them Archie Wood forced her to do it, they'd ask why she didn't call the police. Somehow, she didn't think being afraid of him was likely to stand up as a good reason.

'Oh, Ruby, you make it sound so tempting. I'll think it over. But I haven't asked you anything! Is there a boyfriend? What adventures have you had?'

'No adventures. I've just worked and turned myself into Miss Boring of Babbacombe. But if you come back, maybe I can change that.'

The girls chatted on, having several more cups of tea and a slice of apple pie each. Once started, there was so much to say, on both sides. But finally Ruby glanced at her watch and reluctantly said she must go and catch her train.

Once outside the cafe, they embraced, and for Verity it was hard not to burst into tears, as she knew planning her escape and going through with it was going to be the hardest thing she'd ever done. If Archie suspected anything, he would make her pay. She'd had so many beatings from him, been burned with cigarettes, he'd even held her head down in a bath full of water, nearly drowning her.

'If you write anything down – like my phone number, or address – change one of the numbers or the words, so he'll never know the right one,' Ruby insisted. 'Get everything sorted slowly and calmly, don't strip everything out of drawers and wardrobes. That way he won't suspect. On the day you leave for good, make it look like you are just going to work. But if in a month's time you aren't down in

Babbacombe with me, I'm coming back for you. And I'll bring some muscle with me to teach him a lesson.'

'Could you really do that?' Verity asked.

'For you I can do anything,' Ruby said with a smile. 'But I'm serious. You must get out of that house, as quickly as possible. I hate the thought of you having to go back there now.'

Verity hated the thought too. She'd spared Ruby the details about the injuries he'd given her. He'd broken her wrist, ribs, dislocated her shoulder, and there was barely an inch of her body he hadn't punched. But he was always careful to avoid her face – once he even pointed that out to her, as if she should be grateful for it.

If he got wind that she hadn't gone into work today – and, even worse, had met an old friend – she would be punished. Last week she accidentally burned one of his shirts while ironing it, which resulted in him taking away all her bedclothes. It was below freezing and she could only huddle under her coat, unable to sleep because she was so cold. But burning a shirt was a minor misdemeanour to him. Planning to run out on him would warrant life-threatening injuries.

Verity put on a brave smile, promised Ruby she'd be with her soon, and wished her a safe and quick journey home. Train journeys were a trial of endurance now in wartime, stopping and starting all the time, with no heating in the carriages. And with the windows covered over with blackout material, you couldn't see out, either.

'I hope the journey home isn't too bad,' she said.

Ruby laughed. 'I'll close my eyes and dream of the summer and us going swimming, and going to dances together. That will keep me warm.'

Verity stayed until Ruby had gone into the station and then reluctantly turned towards home. She doubted Archie would have gone out; he stayed in most days and then went out at night, all dressed up in his best suit and often a bow tie. He played cards. Where, he never said, but when he had a big win, sometimes he would come back the next morning in a good mood. Once or twice he'd even bought her flowers, but she knew now that was more for the benefit of nosy neighbours, who would then think he was her doting uncle.

She had to assume gambling was how he'd made a living ever since he ran away from Daleham Gardens. She seemed to remember her mother making remarks about him throwing money away before that too. Verity often wondered why her mother had never revealed anything really bad about her husband, even after the embezzlement business. But perhaps he kept her quiet by violence and cruelty too.

While it was possible that it was going on the run and mixing with other crooks and villains that had made him so evil, Verity was sure now he had been born that way. He could be very charming when he chose; her mother must have fallen for this side of him, and when she found out about his other side, she put up with it because of the lovely house and the money. That could explain why she had always seemed so jittery and distant.

Verity felt jittery as she walked home. She knew in her heart that Ruby was right and she must leave as quickly as possible, but Archie always seemed to sense when she was lying or hiding something, and if he couldn't get it out of her by trickery he used his fists. She would need to be very strong for as long as it took to arrange her departure.

*

311

'They didn't need you for a full shift, then?' he called out from the kitchen as she hung her coat up in the hall. He was sitting in the easy chair by the fire, his feet up on a stool, wearing a shabby, dark red dressing gown over his underwear.

This was something which made her hackles rise, a man sitting around all day not dressed properly, she felt it was indecent. He hadn't done it back when Amy was here, and she was fairly certain he only did it now to try and rile her.

'No, someone had made a mistake on the shift rota. It got straightened out when the right girls came in later than expected. I wasn't needed any more.'

He got out of his seat just as she was about to go upstairs and change.

'Since when do you wear a dress and high heels to climb telegraph poles?' he said, standing in the kitchen doorway, looking at her.

She had been wearing slacks to work for the last couple of years, because it was mostly maintenance and repair work. The only time she wore a dress or skirt was when she was going to be working inside.

'I only had to stand in on the switchboard,' she said, as casually as possible, her heart fluttering with fear that he suspected something.

'You're lying,' he said in a low, even voice. 'You haven't been to work at all. I know, because I rang the Post Office.'

She was certain he hadn't, because he'd have got dressed to go to the phone box.

'Whoever answered your call probably just looked at the rota and saw it was my day off,' she said. 'There's an awful lot of girls there, and in different rooms. Some of the newer ones don't even know me, as I work outside mostly.'

'Liar!' he said and swiftly moved forward to punch her in the stomach. 'Now tell me who called here earlier and where you met up with them. Was it that Miller bloke?'

His punch had winded her, and she remained bending over holding her stomach.

'No, of course not, you know he ended it with me. It was just Beryl, like I told you.'

From her bent-over position she lifted her head to look at him. His face was darkening, the way it always did when he was in a violent rage, and he was clenching his fists.

'Archie, please! Don't be like this,' she pleaded.

'Like what?' he snarled as he kicked her side, knocking her over on to the floor. 'You think you can lie to me and I'll do nothing about it?'

Even though he was wearing long underwear under the dressing gown, she noticed as he kicked her again that he was wearing proper shoes. What sort of man would put them on purposely before she got home, just to kick the life out of her?

He kicked her twice more, then dragged her up to her knees.

'Now for the thing you hate most,' he said, grinning at the pain she was in. 'You, my dear, are going to suck my cock.'

She gagged involuntarily as he released it from his long pants. It was already hard, as if beating her excited him. It wasn't as big as she remembered from the previous time, but as he brought it close to her mouth it smelled of mouldy cheese.

It was no good trying to move back to escape him, as he had moved his hand from her shoulder to the back of her head, and holding her hair he forced her head forward so she had no choice but to obey him.

She gagged again as he thrust it into her mouth, and while she thought of clamping her teeth down on him, she knew if she did he'd make her suffer even more.

'Just endure,' she thought to herself as he moved her head backwards and forwards on him. 'It will soon be over.'

It was mercifully quick. With a loud gasp and his whole body jerking, the fluid shot into her mouth and he let go of her. But as she spat out the disgusting stuff in her mouth and attempted to wriggle away, he kicked her again in the side.

'Filthy bitch!' he yelled at her, and in a frenzy he kicked and kicked at her.

The last conscious thought she had was that this time it was the last. He was going to kill her.

Chapter Twenty-Four

Ruby was on the underground on the way to Paddington Station when she suddenly got a bad feeling about Verity. She tried to convince herself that she was overreacting, because she knew Archie Wood had hurt her friend in the past, but the closer she got to Paddington the stronger the feeling became that Verity was in difficulties.

On the concourse at Paddington she looked at the departure board for her train and saw the four o'clock was already in on Platform Three. It was due to leave in fifteen minutes. She rushed to a public telephone and rang Wilby, blurting out that she was afraid for Verity and didn't know what to do.

'I'm sure you *are* overreacting,' Wilby said in her usual calm, measured manner. 'Why should her father hurt her just for meeting a friend? But obviously you know more about the girl's situation than you are telling me. But I'd say that if you ignore your fears and it turns out something has happened, you are going to feel terrible.'

'So you do think I should go back?'

'Staying in London one more night isn't the end of the world, not if it puts your mind at rest,' Wilby said. 'If you are going to be there, you could pop into Foyles in Charing Cross Road tomorrow morning and see if you can get me a copy of *Frenchman's Creek* by Daphne du Maurier. I haven't had any luck getting it in Torquay.'

Ruby agreed she would try to get the book. She thought she would go out to Hither Green and, if everything was alright, then come back and stay at the Charing Cross Hotel for the night.

As so often happened since the war had started, the underground train stopped suddenly just before South Kensington, and the lights went out. A gentleman sitting next to Ruby informed her that it often happened on the District and Circle lines, because large sections of the track were in fact above ground.

'We count ourselves lucky if it stops at a station, at least we can get out and walk the rest of the way, or get a cab. But I haven't heard anything about a bomb dropping today, so it might just be signal failure or something similar.'

Emergency lighting came on after a few minutes, not bright enough to read, but enough to make it less scary. A guard came through the carriages explaining it was a minor fault on the line, and if they all sat tight it would be put right within half an hour.

In fact it was an hour before the train moved, and by the time Ruby got up to Charing Cross Station it was rush hour and packed with office workers going home. That train too was held up for half an hour at New Cross and as she'd had to stand, because the train was so packed, by the time she got to Hither Green she was wishing she hadn't been so impulsive.

She was also worried that if she had been wrong about Verity being in trouble, she might actually cause some by calling at the house. It was just after six thirty now, and as she made her way through the dark, icy-cold streets to

Weardale Road, she was racking her brain for a plausible excuse to give Archie for calling.

The idea she came up with was to pretend to be doing a survey on what magazines women read. If Archie opened the door, she'd say that she needed to speak to any women in the house.

She had a notebook in her hand luggage in which she jotted down things to remind herself when she wrote her diary at home. She thought holding that would look official enough. But she would have to tuck her hand luggage under a bush in a front garden nearby.

Rapping firmly on the door of number seven, she mentally rehearsed the opening lines of her pitch about the survey. But no one answered the door. She knocked again, louder this time, but still there was no response.

Ruby bent over and peered through the letter box. There was no light anywhere, so she shone her small torch in. The door straight ahead, which she knew led to the kitchen, was closed, and for some reason this sent chills down her spine.

She went to the front-room window and shone her torch in there. To her surprise the blackout curtains hadn't been drawn, and she could see into the parlour. The only reason anyone didn't draw their curtains in a small house like this was because they'd gone out before it was dark and hadn't been back since. She and Verity had parted at around two thirty. It had been dark by four and Verity had said she must get back to make Archie's tea, because he went out most evenings. She had also mentioned she rarely went out in an evening any more, unless there was an air-raid warning and she went to the shelter.

The prickly feeling down her spine was growing stronger; she felt certain Verity was in some kind of danger. Standing there by the sash window to the parlour, she remembered Verity saying she'd learned how to get into houses from her.

Quickly going back down the road a few yards, she retrieved her hidden overnight bag from under the hedge where she'd left it, and rummaged around in it until she found her nail file.

Back at number seven, she slid the file into the central part of the window frame, where the catch was. She fully anticipated the catch would be stuck down with old paint and dust, and too stiff to move, but to her surprise it did move. She was able to unlock it and slide the bottom window up.

She checked first that no one was coming down the road but it was such a cold night, with frost already glinting on the pavement, that she doubted anyone would venture out unless they had to. Groping inside the room, she moved the small table in front of the window to one side and then climbed in, closing and locking the window behind her.

She tiptoed across the room, her heart going like a steam hammer in case Archie was in the house and caught her. When she reached the kitchen door, she turned the knob very quietly, opening the door cautiously. A strange metallic sort of smell which she didn't recognize made her fumble for the light switch.

As light flooded the room, she gasped.

Verity was lying in the Morrison shelter, literally soaked in blood.

It was only her blonde hair which really proved it was Verity. She looked for all the world like a huge lump of meat which had been partially covered in some blood-soaked cloth.

Ruby was no stranger to awful injuries at the hospital, but this beat anything she'd ever seen.

'Sweet Jesus!' she exclaimed, dropping to her knees to help her friend. But then she saw that a chain and padlock were securing the door on the shelter, and she thought Verity was dead.

Putting her hand through the mesh, she took Verity's hand to feel for a pulse. To her relief there was one, but it was very weak. And Verity was icy cold, as there was no fire in the kitchen. It looked as if she'd been hit hard on the side of her head with something heavy; her blood had congealed on her hair and neck. It was difficult to see where, or how bad, her other injuries were because of the amount of blood everywhere.

'Verity, can you hear me?' she said. 'I'm going to run to the corner to call an ambulance. If you can hear me, just squeeze my hand.'

There was no movement, not even a flutter of her eyelids.

Leaving the front door on the latch, Ruby tore down the road to the phone box. She knew it was there, because Verity used to say it took twenty-five giant strides to reach it, to ring her. She even remembered the number – Lee Green 3578 – because she used to ring Verity back to save her feeding change into the slot.

'Police and ambulance,' she said when the operator answered. Within seconds she was telling the woman that her friend had been badly beaten, that she was unconscious, losing a great deal of blood and was locked inside a Morrison shelter, so they would need bolt cutters to free her.

After giving the operator the address and her own name, she rushed back up the street to number seven. As a precaution against Archie returning before the police and ambulance arrived, she put the chain on the front door and checked the back door was locked too.

Verity's eyelids did flutter momentarily but they didn't open, so Ruby told her help was on its way and that she was getting her out of the house to safety in just a short while.

Ruby darted upstairs and, seeing a suitcase on top of Verity's wardrobe, she pulled it down and hastily threw in a few of the nicest clothes she could see. There were a bundle of letters in the dressing-table drawer, presumably from Miller, and she packed those too, along with Verity's cosmetics, some odd bits of jewellery she found, and a green leather box which was full of assorted documents.

There didn't appear to be anything else of importance, other than Verity's handbag, so she carried them downstairs and added the blue coat and hat her friend had been wearing earlier in the day to the suitcase, ready for it to be taken when they went in the ambulance.

At the sound of the ambulance bell Ruby felt she could breathe again. She took the chain off the door and went out into the street to flash her little torch with its mere chink of light, all that was allowed in the blackout, so at least she could direct them to the house.

The police arrived just a couple of minutes after the ambulance, just as one of the men was using bolt cutters to slice through the chain on the cage.

All the men looked dumbfounded by what they saw in the kitchen.

'I'm Sergeant Reilly,' said a policeman who was well over fifty, with a round, shiny face and pale blue eyes. 'Can you tell us who did this?' he asked.

'I believe it was her stepfather,' Ruby said, giving him Archie's name. And then she told him a little of the meeting between her and Verity earlier in the day and how Verity had admitted Archie often hit her. 'I think he must have suspected she wasn't at work like she'd told him. I was on my way back to Paddington Station when I got a feeling she was in trouble. Thank God I came back.'

'I doubt she'd have lasted the night in this cold, if you hadn't,' one of the ambulance men said grimly as he unscrewed the side of the cage-like shelter to get Verity out without hurting her further. 'She can count herself lucky, having a friend like you.'

Sergeant Reilly said he would come down to Lewisham Hospital later that evening to get more details from Ruby.

'The poor kid,' he said, shaking his head. 'Fancy living in fear like that. But we'll get him, have no doubt of it. As if there isn't enough pain and destruction in this war, without family members turning on one another.'

At Lewisham Hospital the doctor who examined Verity said she had three broken ribs, one of which had punctured her lung, and a broken arm. These injuries, along with the blow to her head, had been inflicted with a length of lead piping. She'd also been punched and kicked repeatedly all over her body. She was whisked off immediately to the theatre for surgery.

Sergeant Reilly arrived to talk to Ruby around an hour later, and he told her the lead pipe used to hit Verity had been found under the next-door neighbour's front hedge.

'If he was just trying to get Verity to admit who she had been with earlier in the day, why didn't she just tell him it was you?' he asked.

'I expect because she didn't want to involve me,' Ruby said. 'Maybe she was afraid that he'd search me out and do the same to me. But he didn't need a reason to hit her, from what she told me he could fly off the handle over anything.'

'I've never seen such injuries on a woman before,' Reilly said, wincing as if remembering what he'd seen. 'She was probably still conscious when he bundled her into the Morrison shelter. He wanted to ensure she couldn't get help.'

'It's a wonder she's still alive,' Ruby said. 'If only I'd insisted she came home with me when she told me a little about how he treated her. But I just caved in and let her go back there to him.'

'You weren't to know he would react like that,' Sergeant Reilly sighed. 'But what I can't understand is why she'd stay there with him, if he was violent. And why didn't she come to us for help?'

'Few policemen are as enlightened as you,' Ruby said. 'Most men believe a husband or father has the right to control his wife or daughter however he sees fit. I've met at least a dozen women who have asked the police for help in a domestic situation, and they've been told to go home and be a good little wife.'

'Maybe there's a few in the force like that,' Reilly agreed, 'but it is changing.'

Ruby realized then that the police hadn't yet found out that Archie was once, and perhaps still was, a wanted man. So she told Reilly all she knew about his embezzlement.

'They lost everything – their house, Verity's private education – and were forced to throw themselves on her aunt's mercy,' she explained. 'Mrs Wood never accepted the sudden change of fortune, and finally she put her head in the gas oven. Then Verity's aunt died,' Ruby said. 'I was estranged from Verity at that time and I think she must have been very lonely. That's probably why, when her father turned up, she was willing to forget the past, because she needed someone in her life. You see, back then she thought he was her father, but like so many other cruel things he did to her, he told her he wasn't, and that his wife had been pregnant by someone else when he married her.'

Sergeant Reilly left then, saying he'd be back the next day when Verity was able to talk to him. He seemed quite disturbed by what Ruby had told him, and she expected he was in a hurry to get back to the police station to check the records.

Ruby stayed the night at the hospital, sitting in a chilly corridor on a hard bench, with Verity's suitcase and her overnight bag beside her. Verity had come out of theatre just after midnight but the starchy ward sister wouldn't allow Ruby to see her, or even sit by her bed. All she would say was that Miss Wood was stable.

If nothing else, the long night in that chilly corridor made Ruby understand how it must have been for Verity when she spent the night at Whittington Hospital praying her friend would make it. She knew now that if she thought

Verity might die, she'd do absolutely anything to save her, even something she'd promised she would never do.

Her thoughts turned to what would happen when the police found Archie and he decided to spill the beans about how he and Verity burgled houses together. Would Verity be sent to prison?

She wished she could believe the police would be enlightened enough to understand he'd forced her into it. But she couldn't; her own experiences with the police when she was a girl had left her very wary of them. So her plan was to keep all she knew under her hat, and hope that Archie Wood didn't admit to burglary with Verity as an accomplice.

'Miss Taylor!'

Ruby woke with a start at the nurse shaking her shoulder.

She was an older woman, with a heavily lined face. 'Your friend has regained consciousness,' she said quietly. 'I told her you'd found her, come in with her and were still here waiting in the corridor, and she begged me to let you in. Now I've got to tell you that it is against the rules. It's almost six, and we'll be waking the patients very soon, but I'll let you in for two minutes, as long as you are very quiet.'

'Thank you so much,' Ruby said gratefully. She thought the nurse had kind eyes. 'But how is she?'

'She came through the operation on her lung better than was expected, but she is still very poorly. I recommend that after you've seen her, you leave the hospital. We can't have you sleeping in the corridor all day.'

'No, I suppose not.' Ruby half smiled. She was as stiff as

a plank and very cold too. 'I'll get out of your way just as soon as I've seen her.'

Ruby's eyes filled with tears as she approached Verity's bed in the corner of the big ward. It was still pitch dark outside, and the only light was a small one above Verity's bed and another on the ward sister's desk further down the room. All the other patients appeared to be asleep, faint snoring was coming from a couple of the beds.

Verity's head was swathed in bandages, but even in the faint light it was possible to see that the exposed part of her face looked like raw liver.

'Hello,' Ruby whispered. 'I've had orders I can only stay two minutes. They tell me your operation was a success.'

Verity's eyes were hidden by swollen, bruised flesh, but her eyelids moved just enough for Ruby to know her friend could see her.

'I tried willing you to come back. It worked,' she said, so quietly that Ruby had to bend to hear.

'So how about that! We don't need telephones to contact each other,' Ruby whispered. 'Don't try to speak now. You just lie there and rest. I've got to go and find somewhere to stay, but I'll be back for visiting this afternoon. I packed some clothes for you and I've got them with me, so when you are well enough I shall be taking you home to Babbacombe. I told the police that Archie was an embezzler. So if he was still on the run, I'm sure they'll catch him this time.' Ruby paused, thinking hard.

'I don't want you worrying that he'll tell the police about what you did. I can't see him doing that without incriminating himself further. Don't you dare confess anything, either. If push comes to shove you can deny anything

Archie tells them. Now concentrate on getting better, and dream about all the fun we'll have together soon.'

She saw her friend's lips move into an attempted smile.

'Bye now.' Ruby bent and kissed her forehead. 'Go to sleep, precious one.'

The nurse came out with Ruby. 'She'll be better for knowing you are near,' she said, putting one hand on Ruby's arm comfortingly. 'She couldn't have a more staunch and reliable friend.'

A lump came up in Ruby's throat, knowing she didn't deserve such praise. 'I'll be back this afternoon,' she managed to say.

Ruby had to wait in a transport cafe, the only place that was open so early in the morning. It was grimy but at least it was warm, so she ordered tea and toast, and asked the friendly woman owner if she knew of a hotel or guest house close to the hospital.

'It ain't posh enough for a real 'otel around here,' she said with a wide grin, showing a mouthful of decaying teeth. 'But our Lil, she takes in paying guests, 'specially when they is waiting for someone in the 'ospital. She's in Mount Pleasant, and she keeps a tidy house. Trot round there now, love, and see what you think. You look all in.'

Ruby decided as she made her way to Mount Pleasant, just a couple of hundred yards along the main road, that short of the place being a complete slum, she'd jump at anything on offer. She was too tired to tramp around looking anywhere else.

Lil, it transpired, was the sister of the cafe owner and had equally bad teeth, but she did keep a tidy house. She also had a single room free at the back of the house, which was clean and comfortable, if a little chilly.

'You look like you're dead on your feet,' Lil said once they'd agreed terms. 'I'm gonna make you a nice cuppa tea and put a 'ot-water bottle in yer bed so you can 'ave a kip before you go back to the 'ospital.'

Ruby's last thought as she drifted off to sleep was that the world wasn't such a bad place if a stranger could fill a hot-water bottle for her and tell her she was welcome to come and join her family in the living room later, where she had a big fire.

Ruby stayed with Lil for four days. On the second day it snowed, and she thought that would cause problems when she wanted to go home. As it was, she'd had to telephone the Palace and say she couldn't be sure when she was coming back, as she didn't want to leave Verity until she was certain she was on the mend.

But on the third day the snow began to melt, and Verity was well enough to talk.

The part of her face not hidden by the head bandage was still livid with bruising, but it didn't look like liver any more.

'You must go back to Babbacombe,' she said haltingly. Her jaw was very sore so speech was difficult, and so far she could only manage liquid food. 'It's daft you staying up here in lodgings just to see me for an hour in the afternoon.'

'I'm scared to leave you,' Ruby said, stroking her friend's hand tenderly.

'He won't come here,' Verity said.

The ward sister had already told Ruby that everyone in

the hospital was on alert for Archie turning up and had orders to telephone the police immediately if he should come.

'I wasn't scared of him coming, only of you being lonely,' Ruby said.

'It is nice not to have to speak. To just lie here and be looked after,' Verity said. 'Besides, Wilby will need you.'

Ruby knew Wilby could manage perfectly well alone with Colin and Brian, her newest evacuees, but it didn't make much sense just hanging around in Lewisham with nothing to do. She was needed back at her work, and the police had secured Verity's house, so she couldn't even go up there and clean it. Archie hadn't been caught yet, so she wasn't even about to be called as a witness.

'I'll go, if you are absolutely sure,' Ruby said.

'I am, and I can lie here dreaming of Babbacombe,' Verity said.

Ruby smiled down at her, thinking how brave she was. Several of the nurses and the ward sister had all remarked on her being the perfect patient, so well mannered, so appreciative of their kindness and help. Some of the other women on the ward were tyrants who never stopped complaining about the most trivial of things, and there was Verity – so badly beaten, it was a miracle she had survived – trying to smile and not even admitting she was in pain.

'Okay, then, I'll take all your stuff from Weardale Road back with me, and just leave you a clean nightie and an outfit to wear home.'

'Home,' Verity said in little more than a whisper. 'That sounds so good.'

'And Wilby said you are to think of it as your home for

ever, if you want it to be. Back sharing a bedroom with me, like old times. We'll go dancing, swimming, and walking along the Downs, and all this will be just a distant memory.'

She saw a glint of something in Verity's eye; a terrible sadness, because she felt she would never be completely healed. She would walk to the lavatory again soon, eat proper meals, talk, maybe dance and swim too, but she doubted her friend would ever forget the pain she'd endured both during the beating and even now in hospital.

Or stop being afraid of Archie.

Chapter Twenty-Five

Summer 1942

Ruby came out into the garden and approached Verity, who was lying in a hammock suspended between a fence post and an old apple tree. She was wearing her blue and white spotted swimsuit and looked very relaxed.

'Stay there any longer and you'll look like a prune,' Ruby said waspishly.

'You're only jealous because you burn,' Verity said, squinting in the sun and swinging her hammock harder. 'Of course I go a beautiful golden shade you can't compete with.'

'I hope you fall out of that hammock and break your leg,' Ruby said. 'Oh, come on, you lazy devil, let's go for a walk, I'm bored.'

Verity laughed. Ruby was easily bored. She had said over breakfast that she was going to laze around in the garden all day, as it was her first day off this year when the weather was hot and sunny. But now, at only three in the afternoon, she'd had enough.

It was true that she tended to burn if she wasn't careful, redheads usually had that problem. She seemed to think blondes ought to share it. But Verity tanned easily, despite her hair colour, and she couldn't resist teasing Ruby with it.

'Walk to where? We can't go to the beach, as it's all blocked off. Surely you don't want to walk into town?'

'No, just a little stroll along the Downs, make eyes at a few servicemen, buy an ice cream.'

'But I'd have to get dressed,' Verity protested. 'I didn't want to until we went out tonight.'

'Gosh, I'm asking so very much of you,' Ruby said in exasperation, giving her a withering look. 'In years to come, when you are an old, fat spinster, you'll look back and wonder why you wasted your youth and beauty lying in a hammock when there were handsome young soldiers milling around, any one of whom could be the man of your dreams.'

'Put like that, I'd better go and get changed, then.' Verity swung her legs out of the hammock and stood up. 'My tan is going to make my turquoise sundress look amazing. Are you sure you won't feel inferior to me?'

Ruby sniggered. They were always teasing each other, making out that they were a couple of femmes fatales. Neither of them really believed it of themselves. But since Verity had come here to live, after her discharge from hospital, this act and the laughter that came with it had helped both of them to overcome their problems.

It had taken Verity a long time to get better. Two weeks in Lewisham Hospital might have been long enough to set her broken bones and heal her pierced lung – the bruises and lacerations were much better too – but she had terrible nightmares, screaming out in her sleep about Archie. Then a particularly nasty bout of flu, which brought on a bad chest infection, laid her low again. It was only towards the end of April, when the weather grew warmer and she was able to go out in the garden, that she really began to recover physically. But both Wilby and Ruby were afraid the mental scars were never going to fade.

Archie Wood hadn't been found by the police. Like before, he had disappeared into thin air, and not knowing if he might turn up in Babbacombe hadn't helped Verity's recovery. Wilby tried her best to convince her that, even if he managed to find out her address, he would never dare come to the house. Verity acted like she believed that, but Ruby knew it was a pretence. As the girls shared a room, she had soothed her friend out of too many nightmares about him to believe she was over it.

But brothers Colin and Brian, the evacuees from Bristol, age nine and seven respectively, helped with her recovery by making her laugh and waiting on her when she was unable to get about much. They adored her because she read to them, played board games and helped with their model making. To them she was like a big sister, one who always had time for them.

By May she was well enough to go back to work and was taken on by the Post Office doing outside repair and maintenance on telephone lines, just as she had in London. Wilby was delighted when she began to put on a little weight too, as she had been painfully thin.

It was once Verity was back at work, paying her way and feeling useful, that she began to revert to the twenty-year-old she really was. It started with taking more interest in her appearance, curling her hair, putting on make-up, revamping some of her clothes, and making a new dress out of material Wilby had put by long before the war. Then, just last week, she had suggested she and Ruby go to a dance.

Verity's poor state of health had been a perfect excuse for Ruby to avoid going out. But now that her friend was listening to shop girls talking about all the airmen in and around Babbacombe, and what fun they were at the local dances, she wanted to see for herself. Ruby felt she had to pretend to be enthusiastic, even if she wasn't interested.

They now called the Palace, where Ruby worked, RAF Hospital Torquay, and along with the many wounded officers being nursed there, there were dozens of other servicemen working in roles as diverse as doctors through to maintenance men. On top of that, since June 1940 there had been hundreds of airmen coming to Babbacombe for the No. 1 Initial Training Wing. This initial training for pilots, observers, wireless operators and air gunners took place in the local hotels. As most of these men were billeted in and around Babbacombe, no one could fail to notice them, even if Ruby ignored them.

Last December, when Pearl Harbor in Hawaii had been bombed by the Japanese, America finally entered the war, and began sending troops to England. Some of them came to Torquay when they were off duty, and Verity came home from work with tales from other girls that the Yanks were perfect gentlemen, that they were extremely generous and, in the main, much more fun than their English counterparts.

Under duress, Ruby had agreed they could try the Saturday night dance at the Baptist Church Hall in St Marychurch. It was tonight, but Verity had talked of nothing else all week, and what they would both wear.

She had a pink and white candy-striped dress with a sweetheart neckline, a full skirt and short sleeves, which was very flattering and made her waist look tiny. She planned to curl her hair and leave it loose in a style copied from Veronica Lake, the Hollywood actress who many people thought she looked like.

Ruby hadn't felt inclined to even think about what she would wear. But Verity had rummaged through her clothes and found a slinky, emerald-green satin dress which she'd never seen before and demanded Ruby try it on.

'I can't wear that, I look like "brass" in it,' Ruby said dismissively.

The real reason she was reluctant to wear it was because she'd worn it on her last evening with Michael, the man who had got her pregnant. She'd told him about the baby that night, and had been so certain he would promise to marry her right away.

'Top brass?' Verity joked, knowing quite well that Ruby meant it made her look like a prostitute.

In fact she looked like a film star in the green dress; it clung to her curves, and the colour enhanced her green eyes. But Verity guessed she was afraid of wearing it again in case it brought back all the memories she'd tried so hard to erase.

'Don't try to be funny. If I say I can't wear it, I mean it,' Ruby snapped.

Verity wasn't going to give up. 'You can and you will wear it. It's wartime, clothes are rationed and hard to get. You can't possibly relegate a dress as nice as that one to the back of the wardrobe because of some sad associations. Besides, I bet you wowed everyone who saw you in it the last time?'

Despite her reservations, Ruby couldn't help but half

smile, remembering how every male head in the room had turned to look at her that night.

'That's settled, then.' Verity held out the dress to her friend, with an expression that suggested it was best not to argue. 'Put it on and be glad you've got something so nice to wear, most girls our age are looking quite shabby.'

'What made you suddenly get so bossy?' Ruby sniped at her friend.

'When I saw you were becoming drippy,' Verity replied. 'And I'll get even bossier, if you don't pull your socks up!'

At seven that evening Wilby watched the girls walking up the road to the dance from her bedroom window, and she felt her heart swell a little with joy. She knew that the time and trouble they'd spent on their appearance this evening meant they were both finally turning a corner. She'd been concerned about Ruby since the start of the war. It just wasn't normal for a young woman to wrap herself up in her work to the exclusion of any social life. She wouldn't discuss it, always saying she was fine, and refusing to acknowledge she might have a problem.

It was easier to understand Verity; she had lost her mother and her aunt. Her best friend wouldn't speak to her, and then her stepfather marched in with cruelty and humiliation, and her boyfriend found someone else. Yet she had begun to laugh again before her wounds were even healed. She looked ahead with hope for the future. She was a whole lot stronger than she looked.

Wilby hoped that tonight both girls would let their hair down and have the kind of fun that had been missing from their lives for so long. She actually pitied the other girls going to the dance tonight, as her girls looked like beauty queens, and she didn't think anyone else would get a look-in with these two outshining them.

'Have a great time, and let's hope there are no air raids to spoil it,' she murmured to herself as she turned away from the window to go and tuck Colin and Brian into bed.

They hadn't been troubled too much in Torquay by bombs so far. There had been many air-raid warnings but most were false alarms. The first serious one had been in April of last year, while the Plymouth Blitz was going on. A house in the Warberries was destroyed and two children killed. In May, thirty-one high-explosive bombs were dropped by Luftwaffe pilots leaving raids in Plymouth and jettisoning their bombs before returning to their bases in France and the Low Countries. Luckily, there were no serious casualties.

With so many evacuees arriving in Torquay from Bristol to escape the terrible air raids there, and because Plymouth was being hammered almost daily, there was a general fear that Torquay might be next. Back in June, the town had been attacked by four aircraft, and although there were no casualties, people saw it as a warning.

So when the air-raid sirens sounded, there was anxiety, and a scrabble for the nearest shelter. Just recently the Council had delivered Anderson and Morrison shelters to everyone. But Wilby didn't need one, as she had a cellar. She'd put chairs, camp beds, blankets and a big supply of candles down there some time ago. But so far they'd never had to stay in there for more than an hour before the all-clear sounded. This was much to Colin and Brian's dismay; they actually wanted to sleep down there.

Wilby had had three different sets of children since the start of the war. The first two girls and little Joseph went home for Christmas in 1939 and didn't come back. The second bunch, three sisters from Stepney, came when the London Blitz began, but their mother wanted them home again when the bombing eased. There was also the little orphaned boy Jack, who she had wanted to keep and perhaps adopt. But that wasn't to be, and now she had Colin and Brian. It looked like they might stay till the war ended, because they were very happy in Babbacombe and were getting on well at school. Their mother came down on the train once a month to see them, but as she was working in an armaments factory and had no other family to help with the boys, she felt they were better off in Devon, however much she missed them.

The boys had wormed their way into everyone's affections. They were funny, loving and enthusiastic about everything, from helping turn the handle of the mangle on washing day to feeding the chickens, or dancing.

The dancing had begun because Ruby teased them and said they had to learn to do the waltz. She had gone to ballroom dancing lessons back when she first came to live here, and loved it, but she imagined the boys would be horrified and run a mile. But to her surprise, when she put a record on the gramophone and made Colin hold her, he looked so eager it actually brought a lump to Wilby's throat.

Brian was equally enthusiastic and, in just an hour, both boys had learned the basic waltz steps. Since then, they'd practised every night, and now they'd moved on to the quickstep and the foxtrot.

Wilby often thought that, of all the bad things there were about war, there were some good ones too. Young evacuees like Colin and Brian were learning about a world beyond their own home, with different food, people and values. They would return to their mothers with a wealth of new experience under their belts. Rationing, although universally hated, was teaching people to be frugal, less greedy, and more imaginative too. People were doing things for the common good, rather than just for them-selves. Many were much kinder to strangers, because they hoped their loved ones would be treated well while they were in strange towns or countries.

'I've been blessed,' Wilby murmured to herself as she made her way down the stairs. 'Two lovely girls to care for as if they were my own; and the little boys to borrow for a while. How lucky am I to hear laughter and chatter every day, and know I'm needed.'

'I can't imagine actually dancing with a grown man,' Ruby sighed as they walked up the road. 'I've got too used to Colin as a partner and him only reaching my chest.'

Verity giggled. She'd had dancing lessons at her school in Belsize Park, but she hadn't kept it up when they moved to South London. When she worked at the Post Office there, she had gone dancing with the other girls. But it was rare to get a partner who could do anything more than shuffle around the floor, so she'd forgotten almost every-thing she once knew.

Little Brian had insisted on coaching her as soon as she was well enough to stand and move around. She found it hilarious that a small seven-year-old could be such a good dancer. He'd told her one day that he wished he could have tap dancing lessons so he could become as famous as Fred Astaire.

'I'll settle for anyone taller than me tonight who doesn't step on my toes,' Ruby said. 'Though I draw the line at bad breath and sweaty hands.'

Verity glanced at her friend. Ruby really had no idea how lovely she was, with those coppery curls, her creamy, lustrous complexion and her devastating green eyes. Just a couple of days earlier Colin had asked why Ruby didn't have a sweetheart, when she was so beautiful. Verity couldn't tell him the real reason; that her friend had hardened her heart towards all men after her abortion. But aside from Ruby's indifference to men, Verity knew many men wouldn't even try to win her round, as they would assume they'd never stand a chance with such a beauty.

'She's just waiting for her prince to come riding by,' she'd said to Colin.

'Will she know he's her prince when he comes along?' he asked, big brown eyes looking intently at her.

'Oh yes,' Verity assured him. 'One special look, that's all it takes.'

That seemed to satisfy Colin right then, but a little while later he asked if she was waiting for a prince too. 'Because you are just as beautiful as Ruby.'

She tickled him under his chin and told him she was waiting for him to grow up. But she felt sad afterwards, remembering how sure she'd been that Miller was 'the one'.

She wasn't bitter that he'd found someone else. She blamed herself for not making more of an effort to go and see him in Scotland, and for not fanning those little sparks of desire into a big fire when he came back on leave to Weardale Road. But all the same, she did wonder if she'd ever meet anyone again who she would find as easy and comfortable to be with.

'Love isn't about being comfortable,' Ruby had said when she'd asked her opinion. 'It's more like being caught up in a whirlpool, or jumping blindly from a great height. You get comfortable with a dog or a brother, not with the man of your dreams.'

Whatever Ruby said, Miller had been – and still was – the man of Verity's dreams. But she kept that to herself and just hoped that tonight, or another night soon, a new man would come along who she would like as much.

The organizers of the dance had made a real effort to make the little hall more attractive. Twisted garlands of crêpe paper were looped around the walls, and above the stage they'd fixed branches of evergreen shrubs in an arch. Many of the lights had Chinese paper lanterns over them, which created pools of different-coloured light on the dance floor beneath. The band was already playing and Ruby gave a snort of derisive laughter, because it consisted of only two men and a mere boy. The pianist had to be at least seventy, with a boy of about sixteen on drums. The third member was a saxophonist who was sitting in a wheelchair.

'Don't be cruel,' Verity whispered. 'They play well, whatever they look like.'

'Fancy attempting a Glenn Miller number with only three of them,' Ruby whispered back.

Verity ignored her, she thought they were making a

good job of 'A String of Pearls'. And how could anyone expect a big band like Glenn Miller's to play a church hall in Babbacombe?

About half a dozen girls were dancing together by the stage. At the far end of the hall a sprinkling of men in uniform, mainly RAF, lounged against the walls smoking and watching the girls.

'Let's get a drink?' Verity suggested.

The bar was a trestle table covered in a royal-blue cloth, but it served soft drinks only. Ruby bought two orange squashes. 'Come out to the lav?' she said.

Assuming she had something to say that she didn't want overheard, Verity followed her.

'Hold your glass still,' Ruby said, and pulled a small bottle from her handbag. 'It's gin. I managed to get it from a porter at work,' she added as she poured some of it into both their glasses.

Verity loathed gin. But she took a couple of sips and then a big gulp, as if it was medicine.

'Well done,' Ruby said, doing the same. 'I might even enjoy the evening, if I'm plastered.'

'Don't be a killjoy,' Verity said softly, but she reached out to touch her friend's cheek affectionately. 'Give it an hour. If you still hate being here, we'll go home.'

The band were playing 'Tuxedo Junction' as they came out of the Ladies. Verity's head was spinning, because she'd downed the rest of her drink in one go.

'We may as well dance together,' Ruby said, putting her hand on Verity's waist and leading her out on to the dance floor. 'It would be a shame to waste all that practising we've done. Besides, I need to show off a bit as the sharp-faced blonde in the pale blue chiffon number was nasty to me when I was trying to find Michael.'

Verity glanced over at the girl in question as she danced. 'She's got a rat face,' she said and giggled. 'No threat to you in any way. She looks cross already, because there are two airmen watching us like hawks.'

'I'm not going to look, it's beneath me,' Ruby said. 'But you can describe them.'

'Your one looks like he's spent too long in the sun today. A bright red, shiny moonface, he's not very tall, about five foot six I'd say, with sandy hair which will blend well with yours.'

Ruby giggled at the unflattering description. 'Lovely, almost worth taking a look. What's yours like?'

'Now he *is* a bit scrumptious,' Verity said, looking over Ruby's shoulder. 'Slender, tall, very dark hair, suntanned face, small moustache. His teeth look really white, but he's too far away to see the colour of his eyes.'

'I'll spin you round a bit more, so I can see them without being obvious,' Ruby said.

The girls went round the dance floor several times, and before the number ended Ruby was making jokes about 'her' man, calling him Walter and saying she knew he was a sweaty-hand man, just by his red face. Unfortunately, the dark-haired airman had turned his face away from the dance floor to speak to another man, so neither girl could get a good look at him.

The MC, an elderly man with a red waistcoat, got up on stage to say the band were having a short break. After getting a couple of glasses of squash, Ruby suggested they went to the Ladies to add some gin to it.

By the time they came out, more people had arrived, many of them older couples, some of whom the girls had met at church and through Wilby's fund-raising work.

Ruby didn't make any comment, but Verity felt her stiffen in the way she always did when she'd decided she was bored, or that it wasn't her 'thing'.

The band struck up 'Don't Fence Me In', and some of the men began singing it. The girls just stood at the edge of the dance floor, not wanting to dance to that number.

'I feel quite squiffy,' Verity admitted.

'Me too,' Ruby said. 'But then we aren't used to drinking gin.'

All at once Verity noticed the two airmen she'd seen earlier were walking around the dance floor in their direction. She knew they could be making their way to some other girls – there were at least twenty sitting on the chairs at the side of the hall, and more standing by the dance floor, just as they were – but she sensed the men were coming to ask them to dance. She didn't draw Ruby's attention to them, in case she was wrong, and deliberately turned slightly so she wasn't watching them.

'Would you ladies care to dance? Well, at least the next number, this one's awful.'

The girls turned simultaneously at the sound of the rich, deep voice. To Verity's surprise it was the one with the sunburned face who was speaking, not the very handsome dark one.

His good-looking friend was staring at Ruby, almost as if he was dumbstruck by her.

'We'd love to,' Verity replied. She felt she must be polite, as Ruby had said nothing and was looking just as hard at him, as he was at her. 'I'm Verity Wood. This is Ruby Taylor.'

'Bevan Arkright,' the red-faced airman said, shaking Verity's hand. 'And my friend, who appears to have been struck dumb, is Luke Moore.'

'I'm sorry,' Luke said, holding out his hand. 'Please forgive me, I was distracted. I'm very pleased to meet you, Verity. That's a pretty name. And Ruby, so well named, your hair under that light really is the colour of rubies.'

Verity half expected her friend to say something cutting about insincere flattery, as she had on many an occasion to men who tried to engage her in conversation. But not this time. She was smiling at him, really smiling, and it was very clear to Verity that, even though it had only been a joke when she said the dark one was hers, it was quite apparent that was no longer the case.

She didn't mind being left with Bevan. His voice was lovely, and close up he wasn't so bad-looking. 'You've been out in the sun today?' she said.

He smiled ruefully. 'Yes, I'm afraid so. I do it every summer, even though I tell myself I won't. You obviously don't have the problem of burning, you have a nice tan.'

'Don't Fence Me In' ended and the band struck up 'I'll Get By' by Harry James.

'Shall we?' Bevan asked. And taking her hand, he led her out on to the floor.

He was a very good dancer, light on his feet and leading her superbly. He told her he was in Babbacombe to train as an air gunner, and that he came from a village in the Cotswolds.

As he whirled her round, Verity saw that Ruby was dancing with Luke. They seemed much closer to each other than was usual for a first dance, and they were still looking into each other's eyes.

'I've never seen Luke react like that to a girl before,' Bevan said thoughtfully. 'It's like she's a girl from his past. But she can't be, can she?'

'Where does he come from?' Verity asked. 'Ruby has lived here since she was fourteen, and before that in London.'

'He's from Cheltenham, we met at school there,' Bevan said. 'And he's never been to Devon before we got sent here for training.'

'Then maybe we're just witnessing love at first sight,' Verity said with a light laugh. 'How romantic!'

'Yes, indeed,' Bevan chuckled. 'Well, Verity, it looks like we're on our own now. They don't seem to have eyes for anything but one another.'

Ruby couldn't believe what she was feeling. She was dancing with a total stranger who so far had only said a few words to her, yet all she wanted was to stay on the dance floor with this man's arms around her.

The touch of his fingers on the small of her back, his other hand holding hers, felt so good, sending tingles down her spine. His cheek wasn't quite touching hers yet, but she knew it soon would be, his breath was soft on her face and he smelled faintly of lavender. As for his body, that wasn't actually pressed to her, but she wished it was, and the closeness of him was making her head spin.

'Have you been to a dance here before?' he asked.

His voice was melodic, with no trace of a regional accent. Once she would have called it a posh voice, but she was too used to English spoken correctly these days to remark on it.

She looked up. The top of her head only reached his shoulder, so she had to tilt her head back to see him properly. Dark, shiny hair slicked back from a suntanned, bony face, a narrow, neatly trimmed moustache and eyes that looked almost black. He was a handsome man, there was no question about that, and he wore his RAF uniform well.

'No, never,' she said. 'I live close by. But work, commitments at home and suchlike have turned me into a bit of a hermit.'

'A very beautiful hermit,' he said. 'Tell me now if you've been crossed in love and this is the reason you've been a hermit.'

Ruby thought hard before she answered. 'There was a man who disappointed me. He wasn't who I imagined he was,' she admitted. 'But I certainly haven't been pining for him. I think I had a lucky escape.'

All at once she felt like a bird that had been released from a cage.

She wasn't going to spend another moment brooding on Michael or what had happened to her.

She was free!

Verity liked Bevan. He was a real gentleman, funny, warm and very quick-witted. The sort of man she knew Wilby would totally approve of. She hoped he'd want to see her again after tonight too.

But she didn't think she was going to melt when he kissed her.

They had danced lots of dances, and sat a few out for a proper conversation. She knew now he was one of four boys, that he'd got a degree in chemistry, and after the war he intended to work for one of the big pharmaceutical companies. His mother sounded like the ideal mother, cooking, doing the garden and fussing over her boys. His father was a vet and he'd gone off to the first war just as Bevan had been born. But he was one of the lucky ones, as he'd come home unscathed. The two brothers next to him were in the army, safe so far, but had been out in North Africa. The youngest brother was still too young at sixteen to be called up.

Everything he'd told her so far had painted a picture of a well-adjusted, happy man. He even seemed very excited about his gunner training, and couldn't wait to have his first flight and put the training into practice.

'Aren't you scared of being shot down?' Verity asked him.

'It's better not to think about that,' he said lightly. 'A friend of mine from school was a pilot in the Battle of Britain, and he bought it after only three sorties. Terrible, but back then it was common. The planes are better now, though, or so we're told.'

'Well, I think you are very brave,' she said. 'I was in London during the Blitz and that was very scary at times, but there were shelters to run into. Miles up in the air, in a plane with someone firing at you, that's a whole different thing.'

He smiled, a little sadly she thought, but didn't respond.

'That was a tactless thing for me to say,' she said hastily. 'I'm sorry.'

'Don't be,' he said. 'We've all got our part to play in this war. Now why don't you tell me what your part is?'

Verity looked around later as the band struck up and saw Ruby and Luke were still locked together on the dance floor, not really dancing but shuffling around with their arms around each other, clearly oblivious to anything but one another.

Bevan chuckled. 'This is a new Luke to me, he usually keeps a very cool head. I'd say they were smitten with one another, wouldn't you?'

Verity nodded. She wished she didn't feel a tiny bit jealous. Bevan was a perfectly nice man, but she didn't think he could ever make her feel the way Ruby looked right now.

'I don't remember people falling so fast for one another before the war,' Bevan said.

'Neither do I,' Verity agreed. 'I suppose it's because we don't know what's around the corner. Will you and Luke be going off somewhere else soon?'

'Next week, I think,' he said. 'We don't even know to which airfield, either. Luke and I hope it's down this way, but we could be sent to Somerset, Kent or even East Anglia.'

'I hope you don't get sent that far away,' she said.

'I'd like to think that's because you want to see me again,' he said with a grin. 'But I've got a sneaky suspicion you are speaking for Ruby.'

'Partly. But I would like to see you again, Bevan, you're nice.'

He groaned and made a theatrical gesture of despair.

'Girls always use the word "nice" when they mean you are about as exciting as their brother.'

Verity laughed. 'I haven't got a brother.'

'Well, that's a relief,' he said. 'I wouldn't want some overprotective chap lying in wait when I come calling.'

They got up then for the last dance. The song was 'Until the Real Thing Comes Along' which, as Bevan put his arms around her and his cheek next to hers, she thought was very ironic. But he really was a very nice man. And even if he wasn't making her pulse race, it felt good to be wanted.

Chapter Twenty-Six

'He's wonderful,' Ruby whispered as she turned off the bedside light. 'I didn't think I was ever going to feel this way again.'

'I'm really glad for you, but let's talk in the morning, I'm too tired now,' Verity whispered back.

The girls had strolled along the Downs with Luke and Bevan after the dance ended. It was still warm, with a full moon glinting on the sea and the sound of waves breaking gently on the shore below the cliffs.

Luke said in an awed voice that he thought it was paradise, looking at Ruby as he said it. Verity knew then that this wasn't going to be a five-minute wonder for them, but the start of a real love affair.

She and Bevan went on ahead, chatting and laughing as they went. Each time she looked back Ruby and Luke were wrapped in each other's arms, kissing like it was their last night together for all eternity.

Bevan kissed her at the gate. A perfectly pleasant kiss, but not one that made her knees shake or her heart beat faster. But as Wilby was so fond of saying, not all relationships start with fireworks, and one should never discount the slow burner that creeps up on you.

Verity wanted it to turn out that way, as she really liked Bevan. And he clearly felt the same, as he'd asked her to the pictures on Monday evening. She went indoors while he set off for his digs, and left Luke to follow later.

Ruby was over half an hour later coming in. Her eyes were glowing, her cheeks were flushed, and Verity knew if she didn't pretend to be half asleep Ruby would go on about Luke all night.

So they both lay there in the darkness, Ruby no doubt reliving every moment of the night. Verity wasn't thinking about Bevan but Miller, and how they had been together.

She wondered how long it took to forget a person you really cared for. Sometimes she didn't think about Miller for days, then just when she thought he'd been permanently erased, something would trigger a memory and she was back where she started. She'd have that pain inside her, her eyes would well up, and she'd feel utterly miserable.

She wished she could forget Archie permanently too. There was no good side of him to reminisce about and miss; everything that came into her mind about him was nasty and frightening. She wished she knew where he was and what he was doing, at least that way she wouldn't imagine him standing across the street here, gazing up at her bedroom window and plotting to get hold of her.

Wilby and Ruby had driven up to Weardale Road while she was still in hospital. They had packed all Verity's personal belongings into the car, thrown away anything that belonged to Archie, and cleaned the house from top to bottom. A locksmith came and put new locks on both the back and front doors, so Archie could not get in again. Finally, they contacted an organization who found homes for people who had been bombed out, and asked them to find a tenant for the house.

The person they found was a Mrs Robinson. Her husband was in the army, and she had two school-age daughters. So far the rent money had come every month bang on time, which meant that Verity was able to put that aside for a little nest egg.

Everything was in order, really, and she knew it was extremely unlikely Archie would try to muscle his way back into her life. But the thought was there in the back of her mind, like a splinter too small to get out of your finger.

As Verity was wishing she could forget Archie for ever, he was lying on a bed in a swelteringly hot, dirty room in Limehouse, the smell of drains wafting up to him through the open window. He was drunk, but he hadn't had enough to anaesthetize him from his surroundings, and he was trying to think how he could lay his hands on some money to move somewhere more congenial. All he had left was ten pounds and some loose change, but if he didn't do something soon that ten pounds would be gone.

It was fortunate for him that he hadn't returned to Weardale Road the night he'd locked Verity in the Morrison shelter. He had intended to, but he went on a bender and it was three days before he was sober enough to remember what he'd done. He had found himself on the floor of a partly bombed house in New Cross with a couple of rough-looking men who, if he'd been sober, he would never even have spoken to.

He was walking back to Weardale Road when he saw a

picture of himself on the front of a newspaper. The headline was: 'Wanted Embezzler Attacks and Imprisons Daughter'. He read on to find out that Verity was seriously injured in hospital. That was a shock, as he didn't think he'd hurt her that badly. But even worse for him was the discovery that the police had joined up the dots and knew he was already a wanted man. He had a feeling that this time they would leave no stone unturned to find him.

He couldn't risk going back to the house, not even to pick up a change of clothes. That made him very angry, and he blamed Verity for it.

Fortunately the picture of him in the newspaper was at least ten years old. He didn't want to admit it, but his face was far more lined now, with bags under his eyes, and his once jet-black hair was greyer, and thin too.

He went straight into a backstreet barber's and had him shave off his moustache and cut his hair very short. When he looked in the mirror afterwards, he thought that even his now dear departed mother wouldn't recognize him.

He guessed that the police would concentrate their search for him in his old haunts. It was well documented that he had expensive tastes, so they would be looking for him in the West End drinking and gambling clubs. He thought he'd better hole up in the East End.

That was why he'd ended up in Salmon Lane. It was vile, a filthy hovel of a house without even the most basic of amenities, but it was cheap, and people didn't ask questions.

It was an area teeming with people of all nationalities, there was constant noise and confusion. Being the poorest of the poor, they had plenty of problems of their own, without poking their noses into anyone else's business. They'd lived through months of nightly bombing during the Blitz, seen whole streets razed to the ground, friends and neighbours killed. Many of their children who hadn't been evacuated were now feral. For many, drink was the answer to the miserable conditions, and to some it was opium, as there were dozens of dens along the dockside where they could find oblivion for a few hours.

Archie liked the escape of opium himself, but he limited his visits to a den for fear of becoming an addict. Almost every day he told himself that he ought to get right away from here, as he could feel himself getting pulled further and further into the mire, but then he'd buy a few drinks and for a while he could blot it out.

Yet whether he used drink or opium to escape from his situation, his mind kept turning back to Verity. The way it appeared to him was that she was responsible for everything that had gone wrong in his life. He could take it right back to her birth, the child who had been foisted on him by her conniving mother. All through her childhood he felt pressured to stay with Cynthia and go through the motions of fatherhood. He should have got out then, found a new life with a woman who really loved him, instead of a leech with her offspring. But he thought getting richer was the answer, and that had led to embezzlement.

He and Verity could have done very nicely out of the burglary business, if she'd just put some effort into it, not constantly whinging that it was wrong. Why was it wrong? She had her aunt's house coming to her, for which she'd done nothing at all. But he had nothing to show for all his years of hard work. Nothing at all. And now Verity had turned grass and put the police on his trail.

He would have to find her one day and punish her for that.

When Archie woke the next morning it was already noon, his head ached, and he was aware he hadn't eaten for two days, but what troubled him more was that his own smell was turning his stomach.

He'd always been so fastidious: polished shoes, clean white shirt with a starched collar, and a neatly pressed suit. Another thing to blame Verity for.

He needed money fast, and he knew the only way he could do that was to get himself cleaned up, then do what he'd done before when the chips were down: catch a train out to one of the more affluent suburbs, and find a house to burgle. The thought of it made him hate Verity even more. When she'd done it for him and he'd just stood watch, it was easy.

Without Verity he couldn't get the valuable proof that people had left their houses, and he couldn't squeeze effortlessly through windows the way she had. He also had to admit she had been a little marvel at sniffing out hidden valuables. She never stayed long in a house, but always seemed to find something worthwhile.

Archie dragged himself down to the public baths, where he bathed, shaved and put on a clean shirt and fresh under-wear. He had helped himself to a quantity of men's clothes and a leather briefcase at the last burglary he did in Hampstead and even had the audacity to pack them into a suitcase he found in the hall cupboard. He particularly liked the Harris tweed sports jacket, it fitted him perfectly and made him look like a country gentleman. The brief-case was, to his mind, the perfect accessory to make him look businesslike and trustworthy.

By the time he came out of the baths it was nearly three in the afternoon, he had a quick meal in a cafe, then caught the underground to St John's Wood. It was not as far out of London as he would have liked, but time was getting on.

He always approached his burglaries in the same way. He went for houses that had lots of trees and bushes in the garden, so he wouldn't be seen by a neighbour. And he liked working in broad daylight, as he could pretend to be a surveyor charting any damage done to houses during air raids if he was challenged.

He would ring the bell first and, if someone came to the door, he would ask them if they had any damage to their house. Sometimes this meant he had to pretend to inspect real damage, which wasted his time, but on the plus side he could ask about their neighbours, and sometimes they told him about ones who were away.

He was brisk and purposeful. A quick, clean entry to the house, straight to the sitting room to look for small items of silver, upstairs to the master bedroom for jewel-lery and hopefully cash, then straight out again, with the spoils in his briefcase.

At the first house he called at that afternoon, a maid answered the door and said he'd have to call back when her mistress was there, but at the second house no one was in, and they had obligingly left a side window on to the kitchen open. He was quickly through it, but when he saw a five-pound note tucked under a sugar basin on the kitchen table he knew immediately this had been left for someone, probably a cleaner or housekeeper. As the window was open, they might have just popped out to get something and could come back any minute. He snatched up the five pounds and let himself out of the side door.

Disappointed that he'd gone to all the trouble of smartening himself up yet got so little in return, he went into the first pub he saw and bought a pint of beer. One led to a second, and by then he knew it would be folly to attempt another burglary. But he didn't want to go back to Limehouse. The crowds, noise, putrid smells and the all-abiding sense of extreme poverty depressed him, but the little money he'd got would soon vanish in St John's Wood. He knew too that if he had another couple of pints he wouldn't be able to find his way home.

As it was, he did get lost on the walk from Whitechapel to Limehouse. He stopped in two more pubs to get directions, which meant he had a pint in each.

By the time he got to the Ropemakers Arms, which was close to Salmon Lane, he was drunk – not falling down drunk, but he'd lost his usual cautiousness. There was a woman sitting on a stool by the bar and she looked round at him, as if she knew him.

He didn't think she had played any part in his former life. She was far too rough, probably close to fifty, with dyed red hair that stuck out every which way, like a scarecrow. Her face looked battered, not by fists exactly, just with poverty, lack of good food and too much drinking. Likewise her clothes were very poor, a navy-blue cotton dress that was patched in places, bare legs mottled like corned beef, even her shoes looked too big for her.

'Do I know you?' he asked, thinking perhaps she lived in the same house as him, and however rough she was it would be rude to ignore her if they were neighbours.

'No, sir,' she said in a ridiculous simpering voice. 'But I couldn't 'elp but stare at you cos you is the spit of my Stephen.'

'Oh, really,' he said, intending to get a drink and move away. But when he asked for a pint she insisted on paying for it, and went on to tell him her Stephen had been killed in the Blitz.

Archie wasn't the least bit interested in her tragic story about this man who had been killed. But he'd found in the past that when people opened up to him and told their story, it often benefitted him.

Her name was Mildred Find, and he reckoned she was simple. She told him herself she couldn't read or write. But even if she hadn't divulged that, he would have realized she wasn't the full shilling by her cackles of laughter at inappropriate moments, the loud way she greeted people, and the way she didn't appear to notice they steered clear of her.

Stephen wasn't her brother or son after all. She said she was an orphan and she'd gone to work for Mr and Mrs Lyle in Whitechapel when she was just fourteen, straight from the orphanage.

'They was so good to me,' she said. 'I was what you call a maid of all work, and I 'ad a nice room up in the attic. Their boy Stephen was only a few years older than me, and he was always kind to me. He looked just like you, same 'ight, same 'air colour, and a gentleman like you too.'

She just kept on and on about how like Stephen he was,

and how upset she was when the air-raid warden told her he'd been killed in the Blitz. ''E come straight round to me, cos it 'appened only a few streets away from me. The bloke knew me and that I'd worked for 'is folks, 'e thought Stephen must've been trying to get to me.'

'Why didn't he get Mr and Mrs Lyle?' Archie asked.

'Cos they's dead,' she said. 'Mr Lyle popped off about eight years ago, and then Mrs Lyle she went four years ago. Stephen was workin' up north then, he paid me off and shut the house up. But every time he come back 'ere 'e'd look me up, always telling me I didn't eat enough.'

Archie was getting more interested now, so he bought her a glass of port and lemon and asked what had happened to the house in Whitechapel now Stephen was gone.

She just shrugged. Clearly wills – or buying and selling houses – were well above her level of understanding. 'I dunno. But why don't you come back to my place and I'll show you some pictures? I've got all the stuff 'e had on 'im when 'e was killed.'

He made a joke about gentlemen not going to a lady's house late at night. Then he thanked her for her company and said goodbye. It was dark now, and as he walked down the street his mind was whirling. If Stephen Lyle really did look like him, maybe he could steal the man's identity. He'd been calling himself John Widdicombe, but he had no papers to back that up – and no ration book, either.

As he got to the house in Salmon Lane he saw the woman in the downstairs front room looking out of the window. She had annoyed him before with her prying. But he was aware that it was always useful to have an alibi if embarking on something which might prove to be against the law, so he bowed extravagantly to her and blew her kisses. He saw her smile so, making a big show of being staggering drunk, he went inside and made a noise going up the stairs.

Excitement seemed to have sobered him up. Locking his door, he climbed out of the window, on to the lean-to washhouse beneath. From there it was easy to reach the narrow alley behind. He just hoped Mildred hadn't left straight after him, because she hadn't told him where she lived.

Luck was with him, she was just coming, somewhat unsteadily, out of the Ropemakers Arms as he got there. She put her right hand on the wall of the pub to steady herself, and he presumed she was waiting for her eyes to get used to the dark before moving on. Archie stayed back in the shadows, watching her.

When she finally moved, he followed her, keeping well back. There were few people on the streets now, just a few drunks lurching home. The blackout had been his friend since the start of the war, and it was again tonight; in a dark suit, and with a suntanned face, he was virtually invisible.

She stopped to unlock a door at the side of a boarded-up corner shop, only five minutes' walk from the pub. It was hard to tell in the dark, but it looked as if the shop was bomb-damaged. With just a quick look to check no one was watching, Archie came up behind her.

'Hello, Mildred, thought I'd take you up on your offer, if that's okay,' he said quietly.

'Jesus, you made me jump!' she exclaimed, putting her

hands over her mouth. 'But come on in. A gent like you won't like the way I live, but I can't 'elp it.'

She was right, Archie didn't like the room she took him into. He smelled filth even before she lit the gas light and he saw how dirty it was. The few bits of furniture and the strange collection of household items strewn around suggested she spent her days scavenging on bomb sites. Her bed in one corner was just a mattress with a few ragged blankets. He knew he wouldn't be staying here any longer than he had to.

She took what seemed like for ever to find the photo of Stephen, opening boxes, pulling out envelopes and making even more mess than there had been before.

But finally she found a shoebox, and pounced on it gleefully. 'This is it. I put all the stuff in 'ere what the air-raid warden found on 'im, after they dug 'is body out. But I don't know what to do with it.'

'I expect I can tell you,' he said, wondering if she'd even taken advice about registering his death.

''Ere 'e is!' she said, pulling out a photograph.

She was right, Stephen did look a lot like him. He had a very similar square jaw, their noses were almost identical, very straight and narrow, even their smiles were alike. Archie had been told his was more of a self-satisfied smirk, but Stephen's was the same. It was very odd, staring into the face of someone so similar. 'My goodness!' he forced himself to smile at Mildred. 'You must have got quite a start seeing me tonight.'

She gave one of her cackling laughs. 'You is just like 'im, but I ain't so daft I thought you was 'is ghost. He used to come and visit me every time he come back 'ere, and often gave me a few bob to help out.'

'What line of work was he in?' Archie asked, sitting down on a rickety stool and taking the box of papers from her.

''E used to be an insurance man, like his dad, but he gave that up after 'is ma went. Last time I saw 'im 'e said 'e were strapped for cash but 'is ship was coming in soon. Did that mean 'e was going to sign on a ship for foreign parts?'

Archie thought it sounded very much as if Stephen Lyle and he had more in common than just looks. 'I don't know, Mildred,' he said. 'But let me look at these papers, there might be something in here to tell us what he was planning.'

She sat down heavily on an upturned crate, wobbling because she was so drunk.

Archie took no more than a cursory look at the contents of the box, as the light was very dim, but he saw a passport, a ration book, a set of keys and what looked like deeds for the house in Whitechapel. He wondered why the man had been carrying around so many private papers, especially deeds for a house. It could be that he'd been calling at a solicitor's earlier, but to Archie's mind it suggested he was up to no good.

'Did you get a death certificate for him?' he asked.

She shrugged, her face blank. 'The air-raid warden gave me a bit of paper and told me to go to the address on it about Stephen,' she said. 'But I couldn't read it. And anyways, I was so upset I went and 'ad a drink and I must've lost it.'

'What about his funeral? Did his relatives see to that?'

Again she looked blank. ''E didn't 'ave no folk, not that I knowed about anyways. Don't know about a funeral neither. No one told me when it was or nothing.'

Archie felt a little shiver of excitement run down his spine. He didn't know what the procedure was when people were killed in air raids. As he understood it, they usually took bodies to the nearest hall for them to be formally identified. But on a night when many people were killed, it had to be very difficult to match the dead to living relatives.

It sounded like the air-raid warden believed Mildred was a relative, maybe he even took her back to the bomb site to identify him, and that was when he gave her this piece of paper she mentioned. That air-raid warden obviously didn't realize she wasn't the full shilling and wouldn't understand legal requirements or how to arrange a funeral.

In peacetime this would never have happened, but during the Blitz the emergency services, hospitals and all the many voluntary organizations who did their utmost to find family members and offer support to the bereaved, were so overstretched and snowed under by deaths, that it was easily possible for a body to go unclaimed by anyone.

Of course Stephen Lyle's body must have been held in the morgue waiting to be claimed, but if no one came forward after a time, he supposed there was no choice but to put the person in a mass grave.

'I tell you what, Mildred,' he said. 'I'll take these papers home and read them properly and I'll come back and explain them to you in a day or two.'

He fully expected her to agree immediately, but to his

shock and surprise she sprang to her feet. 'Oh no you don't,' she said. 'That's all I've got of 'im. You ain't takin' nuffin.'

'Don't be silly, Mildred,' he said, trying not to get angry with her. 'The light in here is too bad to read them, and it's late and you need to go to bed. I'll bring them back.'

'No, you can't take them,' she shouted at him. 'I don't know you. You said a gentleman wouldn't go in a lady's house at night, but you must've followed me 'ere, so you might be going to rob me.'

She was edging towards the door and he was afraid if she got out into the street she'd start shouting. He couldn't let that happen, he had too much to lose.

'Oh, Mildred,' he sighed, as if hurt by her, edging his way towards her, hands outstretched as if pleading for her forgiveness. 'I didn't follow you here at all, I took the wrong turning in the dark and all at once I saw you. I was really glad too, because I like you, and I was a bit afraid I'd hurt your feelings by not agreeing to come with you.'

She half smiled, as if she believed him, but as he took a step nearer her, she let out a piercing yell.

Archie couldn't bear women screaming, it grated on his nerves. Cynthia used to do it, and so did Verity. He reacted instinctively to it, leaping forward and grabbing Mildred by the throat. But the moment his thumbs pressed into her larynx, he had to squeeze. She squirmed to get free, her eyes began to pop and her face turned from red to purple, but he couldn't let go, he just pressed harder and harder until she was still.

He let her slump down on to the floor, then he reached down and felt her pulse. There was none, she was dead.

'Why didn't you just give me the box?' he said aloud. 'I didn't want to kill you for it.'

For a few brief seconds he was stunned by what he'd done, just as he had been with the other women he'd hurt, and when he'd beaten Verity and locked her into the shelter. But remorse wasn't in his nature. He quickly pulled himself together, opened Mildred's purse and took the contents. There was only a ten-shilling note and some silver to pocket, but that way it would look like a robbery that had got out of hand.

Then, using an old rag that was lying on the floor, he wiped the purse clean of fingerprints, and dusted the stool he'd sat on in case he'd touched it. Then, picking up the box of papers, he tipped the contents into a canvas shopping bag which was hanging on the door. Still using the rag, he selected several old china ornaments, a couple of hairslides and a picture postcard from Southend. He put them in the box, wiped it down thoroughly and then tucked it under a pile of old newspapers. Stopping only to wipe the outside of the door down for prints, he left.

He hesitated at the back of the houses in Salmon Lane. It was late, he wanted to sleep, but common sense said he must get away from here immediately, as the landlord at the Ropemakers Arms would give a description of the man Mildred had been talking to earlier in the evening. Someone in the pub might know where he lived, so the police would come here.

But they weren't likely to find her body straight away, so why not climb into his room the way he came out, get his stuff together and leave for good in the morning? To walk the streets around here at night with a suitcase was asking to be stopped by the police. The morning was soon enough.

'Anything exciting in the paper?' Ruby asked Wilby.

Wilby looked at Ruby as she poured tea at breakfast and smiled. Ruby's happiness wafted out of her like the sweet scent of honeysuckle. She was deeply in love with Luke, and it seemed he was equally smitten with her. Wilby had only one nagging fear and that was that when his training was complete, and he began going on bombing raids over Germany, the plane he was in might just be shot down. But she kept that fear to herself, for now it was just a delight to see Ruby so happy.

'I didn't read anything about a red-hot romance in Babbacombe,' she replied to Ruby's question. 'Well, at least it's not on the front page.'

'It should be,' Verity chuckled. 'After all, she's broadcast it so much it should have reached Fleet Street by now.'

Wilby was also happy to see Verity looking bouncy and joyful. Maybe she wasn't going to fall in love with Bevan, but having fun with someone she liked and felt safe with was just what she needed.

Wilby turned back to the newspaper. 'The Germans have captured Sebastopol,' she said. 'With luck they'll march on up to Moscow and freeze when winter comes. That happened to Napoleon's army, they had to retreat when they had no more food or warm clothes. Russia's saviour is General Winter.'

Ruby pretended to yawn. 'What about the society page? Any flamboyant, fabulous weddings? Any scandal?'

'Thieves broke into a garage in Surrey to find more than

they expected; it was stacked to the roof with tinned food. It seems the owners had been stockpiling for years before the war. It took so long for the thieves to load it up, the police came and arrested them.'

'So were the owners prosecuted for being greedy? Or were they allowed to throw tins at the thieves?' Verity asked jokingly.

'It doesn't say. I bet the police snaffled some of it for themselves,' Wilby said. 'I wish I'd had the sense to start stockpiling years ago.'

'You'd have only given it away to people you felt sorry for,' Verity said. 'Isn't there a good murder in that paper? We never seem to get them any more. Is everyone behaving properly because of the war?'

'A woman was found strangled in Limehouse,' Wilby said. 'They think she'd been dead in her room for over a week before anyone missed her.'

Ruby pulled a face. 'How awful. Have they arrested anyone for it?'

'Doesn't say. Her name was Mildred Find, mid-forties, no family. A neighbour reported she was a little simple. The police think robbery was the motive, and are still making inquiries.'

'It's funny how real life carries on all around us, despite the war. Murder, stealing, road accidents, babies being born, and weddings too,' Verity mused. 'When the war started, I kind of had the idea that would all stop. Silly of me, but I did.'

'I certainly never expected to see the glamorous Palace Hotel turned into a hospital, or imagined that I would ever be able to look at an open wound without fainting,' Ruby said. 'Tell me, Wilby, are we going to win the war? It would be absolutely terrible if, after all we've been through, we lost.'

'We won't lose,' Wilby said firmly. 'We have Churchill at the helm, and he'll get us through it. In a couple of years the barbed wire will be taken from the beaches, signposts will be back, lights will go on. And you two will be married and living happily ever after.'

Chapter Twenty-Seven

October 1942

'I wish I hadn't got to work tomorrow,' Ruby sighed. She was sitting in an armchair, her legs over the arm.

Verity was busy embroidering some flowers along the edge of a cardigan to try and make it look new. She looked up at her friend. 'If Wilby catches you sitting like that, you'll get a rocket for being unladylike,' she said. 'But why don't you want to go? Luke hasn't got any leave, tomorrow is likely to be as grey and chilly as today, and you've always claimed Sunday is tedious with Wilby insisting we go to church.'

'I don't know why I don't want to go, I've just got this weird feeling about it,' Ruby said, and giggled a little. 'One of my famous premonitions, like when I got the feeling you were in trouble. Okay, that makes me sound cuckoo, doesn't it? I usually love working Sundays, the patients are all happy because they get visitors, dinner in the canteen is good, and it's by far the jolliest day of the week all round. But I just don't want to go.'

'Well, you have to,' Verity said. 'As you are very fond of telling me, no one else can do your job.'

Ruby threw a cushion at her. 'It happens to be true, I've made myself indispensable.'

Verity snorted derisively. 'And so modest, as well as beautiful!'

Ruby grinned. 'Do you ever get these feelings about things that you can't explain?'

'Only to wonder why it is I like you,' Verity said.

'I'm serious,' Ruby said.

'Well, I do get feelings about Archie sometimes,' Verity admitted a little sheepishly. 'I feel he's thinking about me and planning some hideous revenge. But it's daft to think he'd track me down here, he'll only get himself in deeper water.'

A local police inspector had called to see her in Devon about a month after she was discharged from Lewisham Hospital. He had been asked by the London police to check that Archie Wood hadn't tried to contact her. She told them he hadn't and that, as far as she remembered, she hadn't told him about her friends in Babbacombe, so it was extremely unlikely he'd turn up here.

The inspector said that all their efforts to find Archie had failed, but that more often than not, men on the run got themselves caught eventually because they returned to their old home or a family member. He said the Lewisham police were keeping an eye on Weardale Road, and if she had any reason to believe he was in Babbacombe, she must contact the police station immediately.

She would, of course, in the blink of an eye. But Archie wasn't likely to show himself in advance of pouncing on her. But she never admitted that thought to Ruby or Wilby.

'Too much time has passed now,' Ruby said comfortingly. 'He'll be long gone, either tucked in with some woman daft enough to trust him, or even gone abroad. One of the airmen at the hospital was telling me the other day that men who want to hide, whether that's from the police or trying to escape their past, are signing on with the merchant navy. All they need is a fairly good false identity. It would be easy enough then to jump ship in another country.'

'I can't imagine which country would be good to be in right now, with the war going on almost everywhere,' Verity said. 'But I suppose a man like Archie would see a war-torn country as a place of opportunity.'

Colin and Brian came bursting into the room and interrupted the girls' conversation. With their freckled faces, sticking-up hair and soft brown eyes they were very appealing. 'Will you play Monopoly with us?' Brian asked. 'We helped Wilby make some rock buns, and now she's told us to clear off out of the kitchen and leave her in peace.'

Both girls laughed. The two boys were bundles of energy. On a grey, miserable day like today, when they couldn't go out to play, they could be a bit much for Wilby.

'I think we could do that,' Verity agreed, packing away her embroidery. 'And maybe we'll have some dancing practice later too.'

'Oh, goody!' Colin clapped his hands together. 'I danced with my teacher the other day, and she said if I kept it up I might end up like Fred Astaire.'

Ruby arrived at work the next morning just before nine. Sundays were always calmer than weekdays, because there were far fewer service staff working, and many of the convalescent airmen took exercise around the grounds or went to the church just further down the road in Wellswood.

When the hotel was first converted into a hospital they had only 48 beds, but the number had been gradually increased since then to 249. They hadn't needed to make huge alterations to the building to turn it into a viable hospital. Four bedrooms on the second floor had been changed into a theatre block, but there were always complaints from the nursing staff about there being too many single rooms scattered about. One of the biggest advantages of the former hotel was the amount of sporting facilities, including a gymnasium and indoor tennis court, all of which were invaluable for rehabilitation.

Most of Ruby's work that morning was to file any case notes which had been left on the wards for the doctors to see, to chase up copies of any correspondence to do with patients, and file them. She also had to start files for patients who had been brought in on the previous day, which involved typing up the notes made by the doctors both at the time of their injury and on their admittance here. Then there were a few discharge notes to type up for patients going home either today or Monday.

It was around twenty to eleven when Ruby got an internal phone call from the medical quartermaster, who asked her to come over to the east wing and collect some requisitions for drugs and equipment.

She was almost there when she stopped to look out of a window at a group of Home Guard marching off in the direction of Walls Hill. It made her smile, as some of them were quite old men, who had probably done service in the first war and were proud to think they were doing something worthwhile in this one.

Suddenly, without any warning, enemy aircraft came

swarming over the cliff from the sea, strafing the hospital grounds with machine-gun fire. The air-raid siren hadn't gone off.

Shocked to the core, Ruby initially dived to the ground. But as the planes wheeled off, she got up to look out of the window again and was pleased to see the group of Home Guard had run into the woods, and there were no casualties outside that she could detect. She was undecided what to do, whether to run back downstairs and take shelter, or to continue to the quartermaster's office. But before she could act, there was a massive bang, the whole building shook and she was knocked down by something heavy.

A searing pain shot up her back and she tried to call out for help. Her last thought before darkness blotted out everything was of Luke and that she wouldn't get a chance to say goodbye.

Wilby and Verity were preparing the vegetables for dinner when they heard the droning noise of aircraft. With no siren warning them of an air raid, they assumed it was English planes. Until they heard machine-gun fire.

'Boys! Shelter!' Wilby shouted, running to the sitting room where they were playing.

Verity ran to them too, grabbing each of the boys' hands, and flew with them to the cellar.

'Is that the Germans coming?' Brian asked, brown eyes wide with fright.

'Not coming to us, just their planes overhead, but let's get down those stairs quickly,' Verity said.

Once Wilby was down in the cellar with them, they all

listened carefully. 'It sounds like they are firing closer to Torquay,' Wilby said. 'It's not here in Babbacombe.'

Then came the bombs, and Wilby blanched at the massive bangs.

The boys were excited, not scared. 'I want to see what they bombed,' Brian said. 'When can we go out and look?'

'You little ghoul,' Wilby said, but her tone was affectionate rather than cross. 'People may have been hurt, or even killed. It isn't something you go and gawp at.'

When the all-clear sounded, they went back upstairs. Verity went up to the bedroom to get her embroidery. When she glanced out of the window, she could see a plume of black smoke or dust rising up to the right. It was in the direction of Torquay, but she didn't think it was that far away.

All at once she remembered Ruby saying she didn't want to go to work. As the hospital was the only really big building between here and Torquay, it could have been hit.

'Oh no,' she gasped, all at once feeling as if her heart was being squeezed hard.

She ran downstairs. The boys had gone back into the sitting room, and she told Wilby what she feared.

'They wouldn't bomb a hospital, surely?' Wilby said. 'They painted a huge red cross on the roof!'

'Since when did they care about niceties like that?' Verity said with a shrug. 'I must go down the road and just check. If it wasn't the hospital, I'll come straight back.'

'Make sure you do, dinner will be ready at one thirty.'

Verity leapt on her bicycle and whizzed off down the road. As if in confirmation of what she feared, a truck went past her full of rescue workers. She could hear ambulance sirens too, but they were coming from Torquay towards her.

She was at the RAF hospital within five minutes, and to her horror the spiral of black smoke was coming from the east wing of the building. There was that all too familiar, throat-constricting smell she'd grown so used to in London, of brick dust, plaster and burning. By the time she'd propped her bicycle up against a wall, Babbacombe Road was clogged with rescue workers, air-raid wardens, police, firemen and ambulance men, along with a great many local people.

Verity made her way towards the main entrance, but a burly air-raid warden prevented her going any closer. She told him Ruby worked in reception and that she had red curly hair. She pointed out that Ruby ought to have been first out of the door.

'I haven't seen anyone that fits that description,' he said. 'But the patients and staff who are unhurt are all coming out now,' he said.

He waved his hand towards a trickle of people leaving the building. They all looked as if they were in shock, and some of the women were crying. 'Your friend should be among them. But don't worry if you don't see her, she might be helping to get patients out.'

He went on to explain that the bomb had dropped on the south side of the east wing, by the Milk Bar. 'Thank God it's Sunday and it wasn't open,' he said, crossing himself. 'Usually, at eleven in the morning, it's packed with patients and staff having elevenses.'

Verity waited and watched as a steady stream of people came out, nurses pushing men in wheelchairs, and cleaning and kitchen staff wearing overalls or aprons. There were men on crutches, others with arms in slings or bandages around their heads, most of these led by nursing staff. There were rescue and ambulance men going in as others came out, and soon some of the injured appeared. The first ones had what looked like minor injuries, small lacerations on the face, or were supporting an arm which was hurt. But then the more badly injured began to come, holding a dressing over an eye, a shirt or trousers soaked in blood.

Yet still there was no sign of Ruby.

The ambulance men were bringing the seriously injured out on stretchers, but she had no need to rush forward to see each face. Ruby's red hair was enough to identify her, even from a distance.

Fear started to bubble up inside Verity. She wanted to rush into the hospital and search for her friend. But each time she stepped forward the burly man pushed her back.

'Marilyn!' she yelled out, seeing a woman Ruby was friendly with, coming out with a man on crutches. She had come to the house several times, and Verity knew she worked alongside Ruby. 'Have you seen Ruby?'

The man was directed towards a bus which was taking some of the patients to another hospital, and Marilyn left him and came over to her. 'She should be out by now,' she said. 'As far as I know, the only people left are those trapped under rubble and –' She stopped short, and it was clear she had nearly said 'the dead'. 'Of course, she could've come out another door round the back and be helping with patients. Have you looked there?'

Verity thanked her and ran back to the road, then down

the drive on the other side of the building which over-looked the sea. The grounds of the old hotel were huge, and there were crowds of people standing up on the banks at the side of the garden watching the rescue work.

The damage to the building was horrendous; the bombs had gone down through the roof to ground level, shatter-ing everything in their path. If Ruby had been on that path she couldn't have survived.

Verity found another girl she knew slightly, and asked her if she'd seen Ruby.

'I did before the bombing,' she said. 'She passed me on the stairs going up to the second floor.'

'What time was that?' Verity asked, her heart sinking even further.

'Just before –' The girl stopped, her eyes wide with alarm. 'Oh, I'm so sorry, how tactless of me! But I'm sure Ruby's fine, go and ask that big man with the dark hair. He's in charge of the rescue team.'

That was how it was for almost an hour. Passed from one person to another, and no one could say whether Ruby was still in the hospital or not.

By now the death count had risen to ten. She heard there were more inside, and Verity was sure the next body brought out on a stretcher with a blanket over them would be Ruby.

Verity knew the part of the building where the bombs had dropped quite well, because Ruby had taken her to the Milk Bar several times and shown her the operating the-atre too. She decided she was going in to search for her friend. The worst that could happen was that she'd be ejected forcibly. But as volunteers, both male and female, were arriving to help in the rescue, she saw no good reason why she shouldn't be one of them – although, in an ordinary coat over a skirt and jumper, she wasn't exactly dressed for rescue work.

Seeing a group of rescue workers going in from the back of the building, she tagged along behind as if part of their group.

The staircase they made their way up was intact, but windows had been torn out beside it, and there was broken glass, chunks of plaster and lumps of brick everywhere, so they had to pick their way through it carefully. The leader of the group asked that they all remain silent once they went into the corridors approaching the bombed section, so they could hear any cries for help. He also warned them to watch where they were walking, as the bombing may have loosened beams. If they should come across a person trapped by fallen beams or masonry, they were to call for help, but not try to get the person out alone until the experts had assessed the situation.

As one girl had said she'd seen Ruby on the second floor just before the bombing, when the group reached that level Verity let them all go on up further, then made her way gingerly along the corridor towards the point where the bombs had created a void down through the hospital.

A cold wind was coming in off the sea, blowing loose plaster, odd sheets of paper and even small items of clothing around. At one point a blue hospital gown flew towards her, flapping in her face.

She wrestled herself clear of it. 'Ruby!' she called out. 'If you can hear me, shout or bang something.'

She stood still and listened. She could hear the wind,

creaking timbers, and glass showering down somewhere, but no cry for help. She called again and again, each time edging nearer to the void.

When she was finally within a yard of it, she stopped short, suddenly aware how dangerous it was. From a distance the floorboards looked safe, but close up she could see they were merely held together by a couple of nails at her end; to step on to them would be like walking the plank. The walls of some wards were still intact, some with a patient's notes still hanging on a hook above where the bed had been. Peering down, she saw a bed two floors below, the iron twisted and buckled like it had been crushed by a giant fist.

'Ruby!' she called out. 'Ruby, if you can hear me, make some noise!'

Then suddenly she heard something, a faint sound that was almost like a mewing cat.

'Ruby!' she called again. 'If that's you, try to do better.'

Again the mewing sound, and in a flash of intuition she realized whoever was making it was just terrified and unable to really speak.

'That's better, I understand you are really scared, but keep making some kind of sound so I can work out where you are,' she said, edging forward and keeping close to the corridor walls, as she thought the floor was probably safer there.

A step forward and the floorboard shifted under her feet, hanging down precariously. If she'd taken a bigger step, she saw she would have slid down to where the twisted bedstead lay two floors below.

But she could now see to the right of the void, into a room with its far wall blown away.

'Ruby, or whoever you are!' she called again. 'I'm right on the edge of a huge hole. Try to say something, to help me find out where you are. I can't move any further forward.'

'Here . . . at back of hole,' a faint but familiar voice called back. 'Blown here by blast . . . trapped under heavy joist.'

'Ruby, thank God you're alive!' Verity exclaimed. 'Hold on, I'll go and get the rescue team. Are you badly hurt?'

Again the mewing sound, and Verity realized it had taken all Ruby's strength and willpower to say where she was. She was obviously badly hurt, or she would have cracked a joke.

'Just be brave a little longer,' she called back. 'I'll soon get you out.'

Verity retraced her steps and ran full tilt down the stairs and outside. She saw the big, dark-haired man who she'd been told was head of the rescue team, and went straight to him.

'My friend, the receptionist, is trapped up on the second floor by the void the bomb made. She's badly hurt. I can't see her, but she said she was thrown by the blast and is trapped by a joist. Please save her?'

'There are many people trapped,' he said. 'I'll get to your friend as soon as I can.'

Verity caught hold of the sleeve of his overalls. 'I don't think she can hang on much longer. She's a brave person, but she's making this horrible mewing sound which I know is because she daren't shout out in case everything comes down around her. So please, please go to her now!'

He looked down at her, and half smiled. 'You put forward a good case for her. Okay. Second floor, you say?'

She went to follow him and another two men who went with him, but he ordered her back. 'Stay there!' he shouted. 'And what's her name?'

'Ruby,' she called back. 'She's got red hair.'

Verity went round to the part of the garden where she could see right into the destruction the bomb had caused. The ground at the bottom was a mound of still-smoking brick, plaster and timber debris. She craned her neck up to see if she could spot Ruby on the second floor, but she couldn't. But she saw a glimpse of the big rescue man; he was standing where she had stood, and he appeared to be giving his companions instructions.

Then to her astonishment she saw him flipping over the edge of the floorboards. She gasped involuntarily, thinking he had fallen, but when he suddenly stopped in space, swaying in the wind, she realized he was tied to a rope and looking for Ruby.

There was so much noise all around her, she couldn't hear what was going on up there, and not knowing was agony. She knew she ought to find a telephone and ring Wilby, who would be frantic by now, but she couldn't bring herself to move away.

She could see the big man pointing to something at the back of the void, and then he was gesticulating as if giving instructions to his companions.

It looked as if a rescue was really in hand.

It was another two hours before they finally got Ruby out. It was three thirty by then. She was the last of the forty-five injured to be brought out, and there were nineteen dead.

Service casualties were taken to Melksham, but Ruby, being a civilian, was taken to Torquay's general hospital, where it was found she had a serious back injury, a broken leg and a broken arm, along with many lacerations all over her body from flying glass and masonry.

Wilby hugged Verity when she got back home at just after five. 'How is Ruby now?' she asked, her voice shaking with emotion.

'Very poorly,' Verity sighed. 'But she's alive, and we should be so grateful for that. Apparently, she was wedged against a wall just by a joist. If it had moved, she'd have dropped down on to the debris on the ground floor and almost certainly been killed. I wanted to stay at the hospital with her, but they wouldn't let me.'

Verity had eventually telephoned Wilby while she was waiting for Ruby to be brought down by her rescuers. Wilby had walked down to the Palace to collect Verity's bicycle, and Verity had gone with Ruby in the ambulance.

'She drifted in and out of consciousness in the ambulance,' Verity went on to say. 'When she did come round, she said she was afraid she'd never dance with Luke again. I'm terrified she might never walk again.'

'Did they say she might not?' Wilby's eyes widened in horror.

Verity nodded and began to cry. 'They were taking her in for an operation as I left. They said it all depends on what they find.'

'Don't cry, sweetheart.' Wilby pulled her into her arms, but she was crying too. 'I can't believe God could be cruel enough to take the use of her legs when he's just fixed her up with the man of her dreams.'

'We have to telephone Luke,' Verity said, her voice muffled because her face was buried in Wilby's chest.

Neither of them spoke again for some time. They just stood there in the kitchen, wrapped together crying. Both of them knew Ruby would never accept having to spend the rest of her life in a wheelchair. The chances were she'd drive Luke away too, because she'd never believe he was staying with her out of anything but a sense of duty.

A series of snapshot pictures kept running through Verity's mind as she held on to Wilby. The hungry, ragged girl she'd met on the heath who seemed to know so much more about life than her. There was the fun-loving extrovert who dazzled her when she came to stay with her and Wilby. She didn't think about the interlude when Ruby wouldn't forgive her, but moved on to how it was Ruby who saved her life by getting her out of that Morrison shelter and to the hospital.

Then there were these last couple of years here together. They'd healed each other with laughter and love, and recently Ruby had allowed herself such big dreams for her future with Luke.

Surely fate couldn't be savage enough to snatch that from her?

Chapter Twenty-Eight

February 1943

'Just one more go,' Wilby urged Ruby. They were in the dining room, which Wilby had turned into a bedroom for Ruby when she came home from hospital a week before Christmas. They were unsure then if she would ever walk again, despite the best efforts of a Mr Ernest Clitheroe, a top surgeon and spinal injuries specialist.

Ruby wasn't paralysed; she could move her legs when lying on the bed. And yet back in hospital, when she had tried to stand, her legs had just given way. Clitheroe was baffled. He hadn't expected her to be able to walk immediately – her leg muscles had atrophied during her three-month stay in hospital – but he believed the exercises he had given her would strengthen them.

Wilby insisted on bringing her home for Christmas. She felt certain that most of the problem was in Ruby's head. While in hospital she had grown very insecure and depressed, she didn't believe she would ever walk again, and feared that Luke couldn't possibly love a girl in a wheelchair.

It didn't help that Luke was now stationed somewhere near Cambridge, and he'd only managed to get one thirty-six-hour pass to travel to see her, back in December. It was just too far and too complicated a journey to attempt on a twenty-four-hour pass. Yet there was absolutely no evidence he was beginning to back away from Ruby; he wrote to her almost every day, and since she'd been back home he telephoned every night when he wasn't on duty.

Wilby and Verity had made the dining room into an attractive bedroom, so Ruby could be wheeled easily into the kitchen, and outside the house once the weather improved. There was a downstairs lavatory too. But they had no intention of allowing Ruby to think she would stay in the wheelchair, or have to be helped into bed and on to the lavatory for ever. Wilby had got a pair of sturdy parallel bars made so that Ruby could practise walking.

This was what they were doing this morning. Wilby sat Ruby on the edge of the bed, and then lined the bars up in front of her. Supporting her weight on her hands, she had to take steps forward. She had managed just one step the first time, rising to three or four since, but today she had actually walked to the end of the bars. She couldn't seem to turn to walk back, and she hauled herself back to the bed using her hands and arms.

'I can't do it again,' Ruby insisted. 'My legs just stopped working, and it hurts my hands and arms too much when they have to take my weight. But I'll try again tomorrow.'

Wilby was disappointed. Once she'd got Ruby to take a couple of steps she'd expected that, within a few days, she'd be walking everywhere. But she couldn't let the disappointment show.

'You did marvellously. Luke is going to be so thrilled when you tell him.'

Ruby's mouth drooped. 'Wouldn't it be kinder to let him go?' she sighed. 'I love him so much, but I'm no use to man nor beast.'

'That is a really stupid thing to say,' Wilby said briskly. 'Luke loves you, and we all know you are going to walk again. You just have to believe that. Now I'll just help you into the wheelchair, and we'll do a few leg lift exercises.'

Wilby went to the kitchen after she'd finished helping Ruby. She left her sitting in her wheelchair by the window, just staring into space.

She was seriously worried about the girl. Brian and Colin were at school, Verity was at work, but when they were home Ruby seemed brighter and more positive. Wilby had realized now that this was an act, and she was very afraid Ruby was slipping into a state of complete apathy which she might never come out of.

It had been touch and go for her in the first couple of weeks after the bombing, and while under sedation for the pain she'd said some very odd things. The general gist seemed to be that she believed she had bad blood. She didn't know her father, and her mother was a drunken prostitute who thought of no one but herself.

Wilby sensed that inside Ruby's head a small voice was telling her she had no right to a happy future. She suspected this voice had always been with her, but after she rescued Verity and they were so happy to be back together again, the voice was silenced for a time. This terrible accident had brought the voice back, and to Ruby it must seem that being unable to walk was her punishment for daring to think she could ever escape the fate that had been planned for her.

This was, of course, all absolute hokum. But Wilby knew that when people got such ideas into their head, they were difficult to remove. She thought what was needed was a distraction, to get Ruby thinking about something – or someone – other than herself and her predicament.

But what?

Verity appeared to be the most likely person, but she hadn't got any problems that needed solving. Bevan was in Cambridgeshire too, and Verity was delighted when he telephoned. They exchanged letters almost as often as Ruby and Luke, and she looked forward to him getting leave and coming here. But she wasn't in love with him, and no help or advice could make that happen, either.

Verity loved her job too. She was in her element climbing telegraph poles, she didn't mind how cold or wet it was, she took a pride in keeping telephone lines working. Recently she'd taken up a real interest in wirelesses too, and she'd enrolled in an evening class to learn how they worked, and to repair them. She'd mentioned that once the war was over she might open an electrical goods shop and do wireless repairs on the side.

The only thing Wilby could think of which wasn't quite right in Verity's life, apart from her stepfather, was this chap Miller. She often spoke of him, always with affection, and from what she said it seemed entirely out of character for him to take up with another girl.

As for the stepfather, Wilby often thought there was more there than Verity had ever admitted to. She was terribly cautious with men, as if she'd experienced something really bad in the past. She had, of course, had all those beatings, but Wilby didn't think it was that, she thought it went back much further, to when Verity was still a child.

As Wilby began making some pastry for a pie, she thought opening a discussion about Verity with Ruby might be a smart move. Anything was better than seeing Ruby with that blank expression on her face, as if she felt there was no light left in her life.

Archie Wood picked up the poker and prodded the fire viciously to warm up the icy room. He was staying in a run-down boarding house in Ipswich, and he knew it was time to move on because Pearl Marlowe, the landlady, kept asking him more and more questions.

He wondered why women always had to know every last thing about a man once they'd slept with them, and claimed to be in love. When he'd just been her lodger, renting the back room on the first floor, she'd been bright and funny, happy to have a drink with him when he came in, laughed at his jokes, brought him up tea and toast in the mornings, and didn't appear to want to know anything about him.

He'd been Stephen Lyle for months now; sometimes he even forgot it wasn't his real name. He had his identity card, his ration book, and a few old photos of Stephen's mother and father too to add weight to his new identity. He'd even got himself a job as concierge at Drury's Hotel in Ipswich. At least he told people he was the concierge, as it sounded rather grand – in point of fact he was the only male help in the hotel, and so he opened doors, carried in coal and luggage, and did anything else the female staff found difficult. Dressed in a good suit and highly polished shoes, he created the impression that although the hotel was rather shabby, it had class.

The pay at the hotel was abysmal, but there were perks: a hot meal every day, amenable and attractive staff, and he was in the warm. Furthermore, he often heard items of interest. One of the most useful was that a wealthy widow living alone about ten miles out of Ipswich had been taken into hospital for an emergency operation. The two people he overheard discussing it were concerned that the house might be broken into in her absence. She'd never had help in the house and so there would be no one popping in to keep an eye on things now.

He went out there the following morning, got in effortlessly through a side door which wasn't even locked, and found nearly a hundred pounds in cash in her wardrobe and a beautiful sapphire ring amongst her costume jewellery.

There was a great deal more in that house that he could have taken, but it made him feel quite virtuous not to be greedy. Besides, fencing silver and jewellery was always a risk, the sort of people he dealt with were just as likely to grass him up.

It was the same night that he ended up in bed with Pearl his landlady too. He'd managed to get his hands on a black market bottle of brandy; they had a few drinks together, and one thing led to another.

He'd thought she was just another dumb blonde back then, amusing, sexy, warm and fun, but not very bright. She was, after all, almost an iconic seaside-postcard woman, with her bleached hair, big bust and low-cut, tight dresses. He liked her wide blue eyes and her mouth like a scarlet gash. She was his kind of woman, she would never answer him back or volunteer an opinion.

Before Christmas he'd done a few jobs that had brought in quite a bit of money. He'd gambled some of it, and while on a winning streak he'd bought Pearl a fox-fur stole. She was delighted with it, but smilingly asked why – if he had enough money to buy her such an expensive gift – was he staying at her sorry little place?

He got himself out of that one by telling her he'd cashed in some shares he'd been holding on to for years. She appeared to believe that, but it wasn't long before there were many more questions. Sometimes the questions came right after they'd been making love. Did he have any children? Was his wife dead? If so, what did she die of? The questions went on and on, it was as if she wanted his whole former life charted out in front of her.

At first he thought it was just plain jealousy, because she felt he'd had some kind of grand, privileged life. She had been married to a surly fisherman at seventeen, brought two sons up on next to nothing, only for them to join the navy as soon as they were old enough.

The fisherman husband had died in an accident at sea back in 1937, and she got just enough insurance money to furnish this rented house and let out rooms.

But as he got to know Pearl better, he realized he'd been wrong in thinking she was just a dumb, lonely widow reaching out for the love and security she'd never had. He'd seen flashes of sharp intellect now and then. Indeed, it was probable that she suspected he was on the run, perhaps he'd even let something slip when he'd been drinking, and that she intended to use it to her advantage.

Pearl wanted money, that much was plain, and she thought he had it but wasn't sharing it with her. It was only a matter of time before she revealed her hand, and if he disappointed her there was no telling what she'd do. So there was nothing for it but to leave. And that was a shame, because he liked it here, especially his job at the hotel.

He heard the key turn in the lock and sighed, because now he'd have to wait another day before going. Another day of telling her he loved her, that once the war was over he could claim his inheritance from his parents, and that together they could start a new life.

'Why are you sitting there by the fire, Stephen?' she asked as soon as she was through the door. 'You said you'd paint the window frames in the back bedroom.'

He looked up at her. She was wearing a midnight-blue coat and a black beret-style hat perched on the side of her blonde curls. As always, she looked lovely; few would guess she was forty-five, she could pass for thirty.

'I wasn't feeling too good,' he said. The truth was he'd forgotten, but he wasn't going to admit that. 'I thought paint fumes would make me feel worse. And besides, I've got a shift at Drury's at four this afternoon.'

'I find it funny that you only have spells of not feeling good when I've asked you to do something for me,' she said waspishly. 'I might start feeling poorly myself instead of making the tea, or washing and ironing your shirts.'

'Don't take that tone with me,' he said, jumping to his feet, anger welling up inside him.

'I'll take whatever tone I like,' she said, tossing her head defiantly. 'This is my house and you already get far more privileges than any of the other guests.'

'Sleeping with you? Is that a privilege? I've heard that you sleep with any of your guests who you think might have a few bob.'

The moment the words were out of his mouth he

regretted them. It might possibly be true, but it wasn't wise to make her angry.

'You've had the privilege of me not going down to the police station and asking them if you are on their wanted list,' she fired back. Her blue eyes sparkled with malice, and the speed with which the implied threat had come out of her mouth suggested she'd had it on her mind for some time.

'That's a ridiculous thing to say,' he blustered. 'As if I'd take a job in a hotel if I was wanted!'

'You could with a false identity. The police are too busy right now chasing up black marketeers, deserters and local criminals to check out the Londoner in the smart suit hiding away in their town.'

Archie sprang forward and caught her by the throat, pressing his thumbs on to her windpipe. 'How dare you speak to me like that,' he raged at her. 'You're just a cheap little tart, stuck in a dirty little town, even your sons don't come back to visit you.'

She kicked his shin, and it hurt, but that made him squeeze her throat harder and harder. All at once her eyes were popping, her face turning purple, until her bucking body became still.

He let go of her and she slumped to the floor, her coat and dress riding up to show her stocking tops.

For a few moments he just stood there, panting and looking down at her, shocked that it had all blown up so quickly and that he'd lost his temper.

He didn't feel remorse exactly. He was glad she was dead, because now she couldn't talk to anyone. But he would have preferred to kill her away from this house, at least make it look like it had been done by a random madman.

Pulling himself together, he closed the door through to the hall. He didn't think there were any guests in upstairs, but someone could come back at any time. Then, opening the door which led down to the cellar, he lifted Pearl up, slung her over his shoulder and carried her down the cellar steps.

She stored apples and potatoes from her garden, bottled fruit and jams down here. Shelves lined the walls, food stuff in one area, paint in another, and coal at the far end beneath a hatch that lifted up outside for deliveries. There was an old pram too, which must have been used for her boys. The sight of that made him wish he hadn't taunted her about them not coming home. She didn't really deserve that.

He laid her down on a pile of old sacks, and saw her stocking tops were visible again. He put one hand on her plump, soft thigh, and felt a sudden arousal. But he shook it off, pulled her coat and dress down over her knees and went back up the stairs.

Locking the cellar door, he poked the key down through a crack in the floorboards. With luck she wouldn't be missed for a few days, and it would be even longer before a search was organized.

His fingerprints were everywhere. But it would be pointless to try and wipe everything clean, as he'd be bound to miss one or two. All he could hope for was that the police wouldn't question that the prints belonged to Stephen Lyle. They might find out he was thought to have been killed in the Blitz, they might even connect him with the murder of Mildred Find too. But that should keep them busy enough. And with London being bombed again now, they were unlikely to find any thread to connect Stephen Lyle with Archie Wood.

Now he must pack his clothes and leave. London first. He'd have time on the train to plan where to go next, and how he was going to find a new identity.

Chapter Twenty-Nine

'Wilby, are you really suggesting we poke into Verity's private letters? Shame on you!' Ruby said in her most haughty voice, but then grinned because Wilby looked so guilty.

'In my defence I will say she's told us in the past that they weren't soppy ones,' Wilby said. 'It just strikes me as odd that a man as level-headed and kindly as Miller sounds, who in his own words said Verity was "the one", should suddenly write and say he'd met someone else. Neither of us met him, we can only go on what Verity has told us, but if we read his letters to her, we'll get an understanding of what kind of man he is.'

'She's read bits of them to me,' Ruby said. 'I had hoped for something more titillating, they were lovely, very poetic letters, but not passionate.'

'So does that mean you think he found passion with someone new?'

Ruby screwed up her forehead as she considered the question. 'Maybe, but if he had, wouldn't the "Dear John" letter have alluded to that? I mean wouldn't he say something like, "I thought it was the real thing with you, but now the real thing has come along I see you were just a very good friend." That's putting it a bit bluntly, but you get the general idea?'

'Yes, I do,' Wilby said. 'Mind you, that's a hard thing for

anyone to say, especially if you are trying to let someone down gently.'

'Then let's do it,' Ruby said, suddenly looking animated in the way she used to before the bombing. 'We won't read all his letters, just a random selection, and compare it with the final one.'

'Okay, I'll get them,' Wilby said, getting to her feet. 'This is a bit cloak and dagger, isn't it? Verity would be furious, if she knew.'

Ruby looked up at Wilby, suddenly feeling a surge of love for this woman who'd done so much for her. Under normal circumstances she knew Wilby would never sneak a look at anyone's private letters, but Ruby sensed this was a ploy to get her involved with something as much as it was about sorting things for Verity.

Half an hour later, the pair of them were reading a selection of six letters from Miller, and then the Dear John one.

'You are right, Wilby,' Ruby said 'The Dear John has got a different tone. He should sound apologetic, sad even, but instead he sounds hurt. That line, "I came to a different world up here, I've found I'm not the man I was in London." Even when he says about falling for this other girl, she is "a quiet wee thing who fits into the forest like a rabbit or a pheasant". What kind of barmy talk is that? What man wants a girl like a rabbit or a pheasant?'

Wilby laughed, Ruby had always been good at saying exactly what she meant. 'Yes, it doesn't sound as if he lusts after her, and surely the only thing that would make a man throw a girl like Verity over is red-hot lust!'

'Ooh, Wilby,' Ruby said, pretending to be shocked. 'What would you know about such things?'

'I've had my moments,' Wilby said, folding her arms and trying to look fierce. 'So if Miller's heart wasn't really in it, why would he pack Verity in?'

'Because he wanted to see other women without guilt?' Ruby suggested. 'Or he just got cold feet at the thought of this leading to marriage? Or he did it to save face, because someone told him something about Verity?'

'Who could tell him something about her? Did he have friends in London who might have been watching Verity?'

Ruby shook her head. 'I don't think he knew anyone much in London except her.'

'What motive would anyone have for splitting them up?' Wilby asked.

'Maybe Verity had a girlfriend who was jealous?'

'Or a man who wanted Verity for himself?' Wilby said.

'The only person she's ever mentioned to me as being a special friend was that girl who shared her house. I think she said she was called Amy,' Ruby said. 'But she didn't become pals with her until after Miller had gone to Scotland.'

'Maybe this Amy wanted her pal to go out dancing and suchlike, but Verity wouldn't out of loyalty to Miller?' Wilby suggested. 'That could be a reason to split them up!'

'From what Verity said about Amy, I can't see her being that devious. Besides, she shot off one day, left the house and her job without giving Verity a reason. That was after Mr Wood came back and moved in.'

'Ah ha,' Wilby exclaimed. 'Mr Wood! Doesn't everything seem to come back to him?'

Ruby shrugged her shoulders. 'I don't see how he could have had any part in Miller dropping Verity. Mr Wood never met Miller, as far as I know.'

'Just suppose Mr Wood threatened Amy to get rid of her, because he wanted to be able to control Verity. Wouldn't he want to get Miller out of the picture too, in case he turned up and got in the way?'

'So how would he do that?' Ruby asked. 'It wouldn't be any good just writing to Miller and threatening him, Miller wasn't the kind to accept that.'

'What if he wrote him a clever letter telling him something really bad about Verity, and suggested Miller save face by writing her a Dear John?'

'It sounds a bit implausible to me,' Ruby shook her head. 'Do gentle souls like Miller care about saving face?'

'Well, it depends what that rat wrote. He could have told Miller she was pregnant by another man, or that she'd caught a social disease – anything, really.'

'A social disease, what's that?' Ruby laughed. 'Is it like "Come-to-tea-itis"?'

Wilby spluttered with laughter. 'No, it's one of those nasty diseases you get from sex. Soldiers get them in brothels.'

'Oh, you mean syphilis and the like?'

'Yes, dear, but let's not dwell on that sort of thing, it's so very vulgar.'

Ruby smiled. 'Well, why don't we write to Miller ourselves? Tell him a bit about what Verity's been through and say we have our suspicions that Archie Wood may have thrown a spanner in their works. If Miller did really want to pack Verity in, he'll just ignore our letter. But if not, and he's still pining for her, he might write back. It's worth a try!'

Wilby looked at Ruby's flushed cheeks and the new sparkle in her eyes and felt that anything which made her look so animated was a good thing. It might not work out. Miller might be happy with his little woodland rabbit. Verity might be furious at them for interfering. And Bevan was likely to be cross that they didn't consider his feelings, either. But as Ruby said, it was worth a try.

Archie decided on the train to London that he would call himself David Close. The name had come to him out of nowhere, but he liked it. He pondered for some time on how to get some kind of proof of identification together. It was an offence not to carry an identity card, and although he hadn't been asked by the police to show his yet, it was likely to happen before long. He needed a ration book too.

On the one hand, with the Luftwaffe making night-time raids on London again, he could probably get around unchallenged, or even unnoticed, but on the other hand he did have a contact in Bermondsey to get a forged identity card. But he didn't fancy staying in London; the police were sharper, people were naturally suspicious, and if he was forced to go into a bomb shelter he'd have to endure questions.

So where else could he go?

The north of England, the Midlands or Wales were out of the question. The natives were always curious about someone who didn't share their accent. Bristol was a possibility, a big city and a pleasant one. There were docks there too, people constantly coming and going, which was good. He would go there, but first he'd go and see the man in Bermondsey for his identity card.

Ruby took her time writing to Miller, as she wanted to get the tone exactly right. She needed to make it quite clear

Verity knew nothing of her inquiry, as she'd accepted he had a new lady in his life. She felt she must also point out that Verity had suffered a great deal at her stepfather's hands, and she suspected the man had in some way engineered Miller to call it off with Verity, so that he could more easily control her.

She didn't belabour the point of the physical and mental abuse Verity had suffered, leaving that to his imagination when she said she and Wilby had brought Verity to Babbacombe when she was released from hospital. But she said Verity was now working for the Post Office in the Torquay area.

The letter was rounded off by saying that if Ruby had got her wires crossed, and if he had indeed wanted to end it with Verity, she was sorry for contacting him, and wished him well for the future.

'Well done,' Wilby said after she'd read it and put it in the envelope. 'I'll pop out and post it in a minute, and then we just have to wait.'

With his new identity card in his pocket in the name of David Close, and his address as 14 Culverley Road, Catford, South East London, Archie arrived in Bristol. He had put down his occupation as being a surveyor, and he'd claimed to be fifty-five, three years older than he really was.

He'd had to pay twenty-five pounds for the card, which had left him a bit short, but he thought he could easily rectify that. As he recalled from his last visit to Bristol, there were some very nice houses on the other side of Clifton Down, and he was fairly sure some of the residents would have moved out to some funk hole for the duration of the war.

It was icy cold as he came out of Temple Meads Station. He had intended to catch a bus and book into one of the many boarding houses in Clifton. But the prospect of a chilly boarding house, and having to go out to get some supper, decided him. He hailed a taxi and asked to be taken to The Grand.

He had only been to the hotel once, long before Verity was born, and he'd liked the plush comfort of it so much he'd promised himself he'd come back.

It was something of a shock to see how badly Bristol had fared in the bombing raids, especially in the old part of the city, in Wine Street and High Street. There were many gaping holes where once there had been fine buildings. Living in London tended to make people feel they were the only ones affected by the war. But he was glad to see St Mary Redcliffe Church was still intact. Tomorrow he would take a walk around and see how the rest of the city had fared.

'How long were you planning on staying with us, sir?' The man behind the reception desk at The Grand in Broad Street looked at least sixty, with so much loose skin around his eyes it was astounding he could still see, and he was as skinny as a rasher of bacon.

'I'm not sure, it depends on how my business goes here,' Archie replied. 'But at least four days, I imagine.'

He handed over his identity card, signed the register, and the reception clerk handed him a key. 'Enjoy your stay with us, Mr Close, your room is 212 on the second floor. Your luggage will be brought up in a few minutes.'

'No need for that,' Archie said, picking up his suitcase. 'I'll take it with me.'

The room looked a little tired, but then that was the same everywhere since the war began. But it was warm, the bed felt soft, the heavy curtains were drawn, and it had its own washbasin. Pearl's house had been cold, often chaotic and mucky, and there was never enough hot water. One of the things Archie dreamed of quite often was having a really deep, very hot bath. With the wartime restriction of two inches of water, a bath was no longer a pleasure, just a necessity.

As he put his clothes away he wondered how long it would be before they found Pearl's body. He would have to find some way of changing his appearance, as no doubt a picture of him – or at least Stephen Lyle – would soon be plastered over every newspaper.

He lay down on the bed, suddenly feeling exhausted. As good as it felt to be in such a pleasant room, he knew he couldn't really stay for more than a couple of days. He didn't intend to pay for his stay anyway. He'd just pack a few things in a shopping bag and make off, leaving his suitcase and some clothes here to fool them into thinking he was coming back.

But changing his appearance was going to be tricky. A moustache and beard took too long to grow, and as he wore a trilby all the time there was no point in dying his hair. Maybe he could put a patch over one eye? People always noticed that and nothing else.

All at once he felt angry about his position, and once again he brought it back to Verity being to blame. 'Why did she have to lie to me about meeting a friend?' he thought bitterly. 'Everything was alright back in Weardale Road, but she had to ruin it.'

He went down to the bar, sat on a stool and got very drunk because he'd had nothing to eat. He didn't speak to anyone, not even the barmaid, just downed one brandy after another. He couldn't understand why, when he'd arrived at the hotel feeling fine, had been delighted with his room and was looking forward to a nice supper, suddenly Verity had to pop into his head and spoil it.

'I think you've had enough now, sir,' the barmaid said when he asked for yet another brandy. 'Why don't you go up to your room now?'

The barmaid was around thirty, plain, with straight dark hair, thick-rimmed glasses and no breasts. He was about to tell her that The Grand must be desperate for staff if they employed someone as plain as her, but he stopped himself just in time. They would probably throw him out of the hotel, and might even call the police if he didn't have enough money to pay his bill.

'I'm sorry. I had some bad news today,' he said, slurring his words. 'No excuse, I suppose, but please accept my apologies.'

Archie woke the next morning with a thundering headache, and feeling anxious. He regretted being so impulsive as to book into The Grand. The staff in good hotels were trained to be observant; he'd known concierges who sensed what a guest wanted, be that female company, a game of cards or theatre tickets, just by looking at them.

He thought he ought to leave now, before anyone became suspicious of him or got his face firmly fixed in their mind.

Looking out of the window, he saw it was snowing. That made him even more anxious.

He got up, washed but didn't shave, and dressed, putting on two pullovers, long john pants and two pairs of socks for extra warmth. He got some sheets of brown paper and a ball of string out of his suitcase, and began to make a parcel. He couldn't put too much into it, just a spare pair of shoes, a couple of shirts and underwear. He looked at his tweed sports jacket and his cavalry twill trousers still hanging in the wardrobe and for a moment considered packing his suitcase with everything. But he knew that the risk he'd be taking in leaving the hotel with a suitcase was a huge one. However much it grieved him to leave most of his stuff here, it had to be done.

He tied the parcel up firmly with string. He had done this trick many times before, even a sharp-eyed concierge wouldn't think a guest with a brown paper parcel under his arm was jumping ship without paying his bill.

All his papers and his toothbrush went into his briefcase, and he put the torch and penknife in the pockets of his overcoat. With his shaving gear left on the washbasin, and yesterday's shirt slung over a chair, it didn't look like he'd gone for good.

It was heavy going, taking the steep hill up to Clifton in the snow, but it looked as if the buses had stopped running. Archie cheered himself with the thought that cold weather was good for something: unoccupied houses had no smoke coming out of their chimneys.

He went into a chemist's and bought an eye patch and a tin of sticking plasters. Not a perfect disguise by any means, but he hoped all anyone would remember about him was that he looked like he'd been in a bad accident.

Last time he'd come to Bristol and had walked from the centre up to the Downs, it had seemed just a short stroll, but then it had been in summer. It seemed endless this time, his face stinging with icy snowflakes, his shoes already leaking, and he had to stop every now and again to brush snow off his hat and tuck his parcel more securely under his arm.

He stopped at a cafe at the top of Whiteladies Road to get a hot drink and some breakfast, knowing there were no shops near the big houses on the other side of the Downs. A fried egg, fried bread and a very small portion of baked beans barely touched his sides, but at least the tea warmed him through.

A newspaper had been left on the table, and he read how German Field Marshal Paulus had surrendered to the Russians at Stalingrad. It was a good sign that the Germans could be defeated, but ironic that it was more to do with extreme cold than superior soldiery. Glancing out of the cafe window at the driving snow, he could almost sympathize with the Germans. But the young, blonde girl behind the cafe counter made him think of Verity, and he felt a surge of anger that it was she who had brought him to this. No home, everything he owned in a brown paper parcel, and the police on his tail.

He was going to make her pay for this! He might as well get hung for a sheep as a lamb.

Chapter Thirty

'Psst! A letter has come!'

Ruby was just attempting to use her parallel bars when Wilby hissed at her from the hall.

'Addressed to me or her?' she whispered, guessing Verity was in the kitchen and could hear.

'You. But I've hidden it for now.'

Ruby realized Wilby was taking this precaution because Verity might recognize Miller's handwriting. And if the letter wasn't what they hoped, she would just get upset for nothing.

'Okay, later,' she whispered back. 'Now I'm going for six steps, turn, and six steps back. Possibly doing it twice,' she added in a loud voice.

'Bully for you,' Wilby said. 'Want me to stand and cheer?'

'No, I don't,' Ruby said. 'You put me off.'

Wilby went back into the kitchen with a couple of bills in her hand.

'What were you two whispering about?' Verity asked, looking up from the breakfast table.

'I was just teasing her, she claims I shout at her for not exercising enough,' Wilby said. 'So I whispered.'

'She seems to have bucked up a bit,' Verity said. 'Maybe the spring-like weather has helped?'

They'd had a lot of bad weather in February and early March, including some snow, unusually for the south coast. But for the last few days the sun had shone, making the crocuses in the garden open up at last and even some of the daffodils.

'Yes, I do believe she is brighter,' Wilby agreed. 'Sunshine makes us all feel better.'

'Well, I must get off to work,' Verity said, getting to her feet. 'Shall I go up and wake the boys first?'

'Don't worry, I'm going up there now anyway. If I don't bully them, they'll forget to wash.'

Verity smiled, getting the boys to wash and clean their teeth was an ongoing battle. 'I'm working down in Plymouth today, so I might be late back this evening.'

Wilby went to the door with her, and watched her wheel her bicycle out of the garden, then leap on to it in the road, turning her head just briefly to wave. She looked so pretty; she'd plaited her blonde hair and wound the plaits around her head like a crown. With a bright pink scarf tied around her neck, even the threadbare old coat she wore for work looked good.

Wilby scuttled back indoors, snatching up the letter from its hiding place under some papers in the hall. 'Right,' she said as she rushed back into the dining room to see Ruby.

Ruby was standing by the bed, wearing a smile of triumph. 'I did both ways, twice,' she said. 'Just wondering if I can manage a third.'

'That's absolutely wonderful, but you mustn't exhaust yourself,' Wilby said, handing over the letter. 'Now sit down and read this letter to me.'

Ruby lowered herself gingerly into an armchair. 'I hope you are prepared for disappointment,' she cautioned, playing with the envelope in her hand. 'I think if it was good news he'd have written back by return. It's been nearly four weeks.'

'That's true. But he's a good-mannered lad to write anyway.'

Ruby smiled. Wilby set great store by good manners.

She opened the envelope, pulled out the single page and began to read.

Dear Miss Taylor,

I was very surprised to get your letter, in fact so much so I found it hard to think about anything else for several days, and the delay in replying is partly that, and also because it's a very busy time felling trees at the moment.

Verity often talked about you, I knew she was very saddened by you becoming estranged. So I am very glad you are friends again now, but was very shocked to hear how and why this came about.

I can't even begin to tell you how horrified I was to hear Verity was badly treated by her stepfather. I did know he was something of a rascal, and he had, after all, left Verity and her mother in financial difficulties, but I had thought he was her real father. Perhaps I was mistaken about that?

To backtrack, yes, your assumptions/suspicions are correct. Mr Wood did write to me, and told me that Verity had met another man, and indeed was expecting his baby and planning to marry as soon as it could be arranged. Whatever I'd heard about him from Verity, he did sound absolutely genuine, a caring father who was trying to sort out a mess without anyone getting hurt even more.

I didn't consider for one moment that it might not be true, and his request that I let Verity off the hook gently seemed so very thoughtful. He said she was sick with worry about admitting the truth to me, she thought I would be devastated. As I was, of course. Yet we all know now that this war has thrown all kinds of problems at people. So how could I judge Verity for not waiting for me, when I'd never even admitted I loved her?

So the upshot was I wrote to her, doing just what her stepfather asked, even though it hurt to make out I had another girl. Verity was, and still is, the only girl for me . . .

Wilby's sharp intake of breath made Ruby break off and look at the older woman. Tears were cascading down her cheeks.

'Don't cry, Wilby,' she said. 'Everything will be alright for them now.'

'Will it?' Wilby said. 'That beast of a man is responsible for so much pain and humiliation. She may seem to be alright to us, but she learned to cover things up at a very early age.'

'Maybe so, but I have every faith in her self-healing powers,' Ruby said staunchly. 'Now am I going to finish reading this letter?'

'Yes, go on,' Wilby sniffed, wiping her eyes on her apron. Ruby read on.

So what do I do now? My heart tells me to get the next train down, but what if you are wrong and her feelings for me have died? I'd only cause her more embarrassment, wouldn't I? I know if I'd been a real man I should have gone straight to her when I got Mr Wood's letter to have it out with her, and been prepared to fight for her if necessary.

I need a couple of days to sort things at this end anyway. As I said at the start, we're felling trees at the moment and I'm needed.

So if it's alright with you, please say nothing to Verity for the moment. I suppose the sensible thing is to write to her and leave her to decide if she wants to see me again. But I took the sensible option last time, and look how that turned out.

So if I decide to just come, I'll telephone you or send a telegram when I'm about to board a train. I can't thank you enough for intervening. And if all goes well, I shall be meeting both you and Wilby soon.

Yours with high hopes,
Miller

'He sounds such a nice, sensitive lad,' Wilby sniffed, still wiping her eyes on her apron. 'Bevan is going to be upset, though!'

'He'll be fine,' Ruby said. 'I think he's always known Verity was only ever going to be a friend. Now what do we do? It's going to be torturous waiting until Miller appears.'

'You can practise walking,' Wilby said with a smile. 'If I could see Verity happy in love and you walking again, I would be one happy lady.'

While Wilby and Ruby were talking about happiness, Archie was seething with resentment at being cold, hungry, penniless and wanted by the police. His luck had left him as he arrived in Bristol. It seemed no one had left their homes here to stay somewhere safer.

He had prowled the area beyond Bristol's Downs, up and down every wide avenue of gracious-living detached houses, and it seemed all of them were full of people. Some, it seemed, had been requisitioned by the government for civilians involved in war work, because he noted domestic help going in early in the mornings and coming out at dusk. If it wasn't for the blackout, he had no doubt he'd see people dancing in drawing rooms, warming their backsides at roaring fires, and lounging in well-stocked libraries.

He had found a semi-derelict house, boarded up, but he'd had to resort to sleeping in the garden shed for one night, because he had no tools to prise off a board and get inside. It was so cold that night, he thought he would freeze to death. The next day he managed to get into the house, but there were no pleasant surprises for him there. A mattress on a bed was a nest for hundreds of mice. He just touched it and dozens ran out; it stank and was wet with their urine. He couldn't light a fire, because the smoke would give him away, and although he did find some old blankets in a tin trunk that the mice hadn't managed to get into, this didn't cheer him because he was too hungry to sleep.

With only the suit he stood up in, and nowhere to bathe, wash his shirts or underwear, he knew that before long his neglected appearance would make people suspicious of him. Each morning he walked to the library to warm himself up in the reading room, and so far he hadn't seen anything about Pearl's murder in any of the national newspapers.

Yet he couldn't be complacent; it didn't mean her body hadn't been found. With the paper shortage, newspapers concentrated on big stories, and while the Eighth Army had captured Tripoli and the RAF were bombing Berlin in daytime, a woman's body in a cellar in Ipswich wasn't that newsworthy.

Yet for all he knew every police station in England could have been alerted about Stephen Lyle; they possibly knew now that was an alias, and he was really Archie Wood. Furthermore, the manager at The Grand had almost certainly reported to the police that a guest called David Close had disappeared without paying his bill. The police would immediately have asked for a description, and so it was possible, even probable, that the hunt for him was centred on Bristol now. Even with his eye patch and the newly grown beard and moustache he knew a sharp-eyed detective would see through the disguise.

Having no money meant he was not only hungry and dirty, but he couldn't catch a train to another town. He was so desperate that he stole a woman's purse one day in broad daylight. She had left it on the top of her shopping basket, and he snatched it without even checking if anyone was watching.

There was nearly three pounds in it. It kept him from starving for a few days, but it wasn't enough for a few nights in a guest house so he could clean himself up and buy a train ticket.

He blamed Verity for his present plight. If she hadn't been so sneaky, going off to meet that friend of hers, he wouldn't have hit her and they'd still be in Weardale Road and doing fine. Why couldn't she have appreciated that she owed him for bringing her up and sending her to a private school? They could have made a great team, if only she hadn't kept coming out with that mealy-mouthed whinging about it being wrong to steal from people's homes.

He blamed Cynthia too. He told her when she said she was pregnant that he'd never wanted children, that he

412

didn't even like them. But she twisted his arm into marrying her, and as soon as they were married he found out it wasn't even his.

Looking back now, he didn't know why he ever got involved with her. The Great War had taken so many young men, and a tall, handsome man from a good family, like him, could have found a society girl with money. But Cynthia was pretty and sexy, and he liked her drive, the fact that she aspired to the middle classes. But perhaps what endeared her to him most was that she didn't turn a hair when she found out he'd been cashiered, dismissed from the army for suspected theft from another officer.

Of course he insisted to her that he had been set up, and that the reason he wasn't court-martialled was because there was no proof. But the truth of the matter was that he had stolen money several times, and although there was no absolute proof, such as catching him with marked notes in his wallet, he was the only man who had the opportunity to do it. So he was cashiered, and he got a vicious beating from his fellow officers. It could have been prison, if there had been a trial. But the war had just ended, and perhaps no one had any stomach for something which would only sully the regiment's name.

It turned out Cynthia hadn't actually believed he was innocent, but she had few morals herself, and perhaps was even too dumb to understand what a disgrace being cashiered really was.

But they made a good team in those early years. For three years they ran a hotel in St John's Wood for the owner, who lived in South Africa. By not declaring a good half of the bookings, and skimping on the guests' breakfasts, domestic staff and redecoration costs, they bought the house in Daleham Gardens. Finally, they had the status they both felt was owed to them.

At the hotel Verity was usually left with one of the staff, so Archie had little to do with her, but there was something about the way she looked at him and tried to get his attention that really irked him. In front of guests he'd always tried to play the loving, affectionate father, and this obviously confused her when he switched it off.

When they moved to Daleham Gardens, he got taken on by a new construction company who were building large estates of new housing, part of the plan for 'a country fit for heroes'. He set up and ran their accounts department, and he worked long hours, so Verity was mostly in bed by the time he got home. But at weekends and holidays there she was, trying to get close to him in any way she could. And the harder she tried, the more it annoyed him. He wanted to hurt her, and although he mostly controlled himself, sometimes he did slap her far too hard.

If he had just stuck to syphoning off small amounts of money from the construction company into his bank account, he might never have been found out. He had, after all, devised the system, and knew how to play it. The directors of the company were really just builders, they knew everything about construction, but not bookkeeping and accounts.

But as his gambling habit grew, Cynthia's need for smarter clothes and jewellery grew too, and there were Verity's school fees, the housekeeper, and quite often he had a mistress who he wined and dined. So he was taking larger and larger amounts from the company.

He still often thought of that day when the whole thing came out. He had come back from a long, late lunch with his lady friend to spot auditors in his office with the company books spread all over his desk. He knew immediately what this meant and panicked. He fled home, intending to pack a bag, grab money he had stashed away there, get his passport and be on his way to France before the auditors conferred with the company directors and called in the police.

He hadn't expected that Cynthia would already know what he'd done. As always when she thought she might be inconvenienced, she screamed at him like a fishwife. In the midst of all that the police brought Verity home for being in league with some thieving guttersnipe.

Maybe he shouldn't have taken out his anger at being discovered, or his fear of going to prison, on Verity. But when he hit her once, he couldn't stop. He got some wild thrill out of it too, almost as big as the one he'd got the previous Christmas when he made her take his penis in her mouth.

Maybe that was why he'd eventually killed two women. That thrill he got from hurting Verity – both back then and, more recently, when he ended up shoving her into that Morrison shelter – he'd tried to duplicate it with other women he'd hit. But it was never as satisfying.

It had taken strangling Mildred and Pearl to replicate it, and there was something about the risk that made it all the sweeter.

He had always enjoyed risk. Whether that was stealing from other officers in the army, embezzling company funds, gambling, having an affair right under his wife's nose, or forcing a child to perform a sex act on him.

He'd taken even bigger risks after he was forced to go on the run. Most of that time, before he tracked Verity down at her aunt's house, was spent in France where he lived by theft, confidence trickery and gambling. The impending war brought that to an end. He'd had to get back to England while he could, and with no money or home, he turned to Verity as a last resort.

It didn't take much to bring back the oh-so-eager-to-please girl with the puppy-dog eyes. All it took was a bit of praise, patience and guile. Separate her from her friends, then a spot of blackmail to keep her in line. She was on the hook and he could reel her in any time he liked.

He didn't, of course, reckon with that pal of hers breaking into the house and getting Verity out. And Verity had to tell the police all about him, didn't she? Since then it had been downhill all the way, and Verity was to blame.

'You'll pay,' he murmured aloud, pulling another blanket over him. He was so cold and hungry, he knew he wouldn't be able to sleep tonight. There was nothing worse than lying awake in the dark with just bitter thoughts for company.

Yet as he lay there, hunched up against the cold, he suddenly recalled Verity telling him it was a place called Babbacombe where she used to go and stay with her friend. She had spoken of the Downs that had the best view of the sea in England.

'I'll find you,' he murmured to himself. 'You just wait.'

Chapter Thirty-One

Archie went into the post office and made out he was filling out a form at the bench at the side of the office, while keeping one eye on transactions being made with each of the four assistants behind the metal grilles.

Most were posting parcels or buying stamps, but what he was hoping for was someone withdrawing money from a post office book. He had tried loitering in a bank for the same reason, but his scruffy appearance had made one of the bank tellers come and ask if he needed help. He knew that was a thinly veiled suggestion that he should leave the bank.

Post offices were less picky about their clientele. Since he'd been standing here he'd seen everything from a priest buying a postal order to a burly builder, encrusted in mud and brick dust, posting a parcel. In between these extremes he'd seen men in uniforms, little old ladies, children and housewives.

Then just as he was thinking he'd have to give up for the day he saw notes being counted out to a lady of about sixty. It was quite a pile of notes, and she hastily put them into her handbag and quickly left.

Archie followed her. The post office was in Corn Street, in the financial centre of Bristol, and the woman walked up to High Street, which had been badly damaged by bombs, then over Bristol Bridge to Victoria Street.

She had her handbag, an oblong brown leather one, securely on her right arm. She was neatly dressed in a tweed coat, a brown felt hat with a narrow brim, and sturdy brown lace-up shoes. She walked quite briskly for a woman of her age. He wondered if she was going to catch a train at Temple Meads, as people just going home or returning to the office tended to amble.

He would have to make his move soon in case she was going to the station, as it was always busy there and he could be easily caught. Victoria Street, however, was fairly quiet mid-afternoon, as it was mainly offices, and there were streets turning off it which would make it easier for him to make his escape.

Archie didn't like this method of getting some money; he'd used it quite a bit in France years ago, and it was fraught with unexpected problems. You had to hit the person hard enough to temporarily incapacitate them, grab the wallet or handbag, and then run like the wind to get away. Often someone you hadn't even noticed before gave chase, or someone coming the other way could see what you'd done and block your path.

He was strong enough to incapacitate a sixty-year-old woman, but he could no longer run very fast.

Luck was on his side. Once they were well over Bristol Bridge and past the few shops and the brewery on the left-hand side, he couldn't see anyone else on either side of the road. There were quite a few bomb sites along the road too, so few windows overlooking the road.

He picked up a bit of speed, looked over his shoulder to check no one was behind him. A car and a van went past, but now it was clear both ways. He had in his pocket a short length of lead piping. He gripped it tightly, keeping it to his side, then once he was just a yard behind the woman, he pounced, bringing the pipe down hard on her right shoulder. She gasped rather than screamed, and began to keel over. The handbag slid off her arm to the pavement.

Archie snatched it up in one fluid movement and ran. Mitchell Lane was just a few yards ahead on his right-hand side. The woman was screaming now, and he thought he heard a car stop, but he didn't look back. He ran into Mitchell Lane, and seeing a semi-cleared bomb site, he ducked into it, scrambled over some debris until he reached the back and hid behind a wall which was still standing. Panting with the exertion, he got the wad of notes out of the handbag, stuffed it into the inside pocket of his over-coat, then emptied the contents of her purse into his outside pocket. Then he poked the handbag and the piece of lead piping under some ivy growing on the wall.

He was reluctant to leave what seemed a safe place, as his heart was still racing, but if a car had stopped for the woman the police would be with her in minutes. Keeping to the back of the bomb site, he found an old doorway through bomb-damaged walls on to a road which ran in front of some old warehouses overlooking the floating harbour. There was no one about and he walked quickly up to Redcliffe Way, then doubled back on himself towards Queen Square.

It was only on reaching Queen Square that his heart stopped thumping with fear, because there were plenty of people around for cover. He strolled through the square, suddenly aware the sun was shining and there was even some early blossom on a couple of trees. What he really wanted was a stiff drink, but the pubs weren't open yet – and besides, he had to do something about his appearance immediately.

Two hours later, Archie got off a bus outside Temple Meads Station. He had been to a barber's and had his beard and moustache trimmed and his hair cut. His overcoat was in dire need of a good brush, his shirt collar was filthy, and he badly needed a bath. But he no longer looked like a tramp or an escaped patient from an asylum.

He had been back to the derelict house to collect his things. And when he counted the notes he'd stolen, he found it was twenty-five pounds – more than he'd expected. His plan was to go as far as Exeter tonight, find cheap lodgings and then go on to Torquay tomorrow.

Babbacombe and Verity were just a few miles from there.

Wilby watched Ruby's face as she spoke to Luke on the telephone. She had wheeled herself into the kitchen for supper and was still there when Luke rang.

'I've walked backwards and forwards on the bars three times today,' she told him excitedly, her eyes sparkling and her cheeks flushed. 'My legs ache a bit now, but that's a good sign the muscles are waking up.'

Clearly Luke had made some joke, as she roared with laughter, and then went on to say that by the time he got leave to come and see her, she intended to be able to dance again.

This was the first time Wilby had heard her being so

positive, only a week ago she'd said she was doomed to spend the rest of her life walking with sticks. Even that had been a significant improvement on what she'd said when she first got home from hospital, that she'd spend the rest of her life in a wheelchair.

Wilby finished off drying the supper things. Verity wasn't home yet, so hers was being kept warm. Colin and Brian were in the sitting room doing a jigsaw.

It suddenly occurred to Wilby just how much her life had changed since she was widowed. Yet at the time she had believed it was the end. She and Douglas had married in 1898, when she was twenty and he was twenty-four. Douglas was an articled clerk then, but he became a solicitor a couple of years later and eventually was made a junior partner and saw his name added to that of Reid and Quigley, to become Reid, Quigley and Wilberforce. They lived with his widowed mother in an old house in Wellswood.

Eunice voluntarily helped at the local primary school, and although she had no teaching qualifications she was highly thought of, and the children loved her. That was when she first got the nickname Wilby. It wasn't just an abbreviation of Wilberforce, as most people assumed, but because she had a habit of saying, 'What will be, will be.' And so it stuck. She much preferred it to Eunice anyway.

Just after Douglas left for France in the first war, Wilby found she was pregnant. But to her heartbreak, at nearly five months she lost the baby and she was told she was unlikely to carry another baby full term.

That was the point when she realized, if she wasn't to spend the rest of her life grieving, or becoming bitter, she must help other children. For the duration of the war, through a military charity, she took in war widows in difficult circumstances and their young children, to give them not just a holiday by the sea but a chance to adjust to a life where their husband and father was not going to return to them.

Douglas was wounded at Verdun, but Wilby and his mother considered themselves lucky to get him home again, when so many of his friends had been killed.

Later in the 1920s old Mrs Wilberforce died, and Eunice and Douglas bought the newly built house in Higher Downs Road in Babbacombe because it was close to Douglas's office in St Marychurch. It was also large enough for Wilby to take in more children in need of help. She chose to help children who had been drawn into criminal activity because they had no choice. She insisted that they had to be first-time offenders and their parents, if they had any, were incapable of taking care of them. Depending on the age of the child, the younger ones went on to a permanent foster home once they had been loved and shown the right way to behave, and she found work and lodgings for the older ones.

Douglas died in 1931 from a blood infection. It was thought by his doctor that the infection to the wound he received in Verdun had lain dormant, flaring up again when he had a fall on the ice, with fatal consequences.

Wilby had believed when Douglas came back from the war that they'd live together to a ripe old age, and so losing him suddenly and so cruelly was another terrible blow. But as she had done after losing her baby, she wallowed in self-pity for a while, then picked herself up and looked for more children to help.

The children came and went; almost always she'd had the satisfaction of knowing she'd helped them through a difficult time in their lives, and they would go on to become well-adjusted adults. She didn't grieve for them. Knowing she'd played her part in their rehabilitation was enough.

But when Ruby came to her, from the very first day Wilby knew this girl was for her. She was the daughter she'd wanted all her life, and she hoped so much that she could keep her.

Well, she'd kept Ruby with her for years now, through thick and thin, without any regrets. With luck she would marry Luke when the war ended, and they'd have children, making Wilby a grandmother. And that would round off everything perfectly.

A ring at the doorbell made Wilby jump and look to Ruby who rolled her eyes, equally surprised, for it was a rare thing for anyone to come to the door after nine in the evening. Ruby hurriedly put the phone down on Luke.

'Do you think it could be him?' she said in a stage whisper.

'It's a bit soon since we spoke to him,' Wilby replied. 'I'd better open it and see.'

She opened the door to see a very dishevelled woman in a fur coat which had several bald patches. She wore very high heels but had bare legs, the colour of parchment.

'I'm Ruby's ma,' she said. 'Couldn't get down before, but I'm 'ere now.'

Wilby gulped, completely lost for words. She heard Ruby wheel her chair closer.

'Ma!' she exclaimed. 'What on earth are you doing here?'

Wilby had to ask her in, if for no other reason than breaking the blackout. She sensed Angie Taylor was going to be trouble, and judging by the small suitcase in her hand she was expecting to be asked to stay.

'Come into the kitchen, Mrs Taylor,' Wilby said. 'Have you just got off the train?'

'Yeah, and what a bleedin' long journey it was,' she said, pulling a packet of cigarettes from her pocket and lighting one up.

'Ma, Wilby doesn't allow smoking in this house,' Ruby said. 'Could you put that out?'

'Well, fiddle-de-dee!' Angie snapped. 'No smoking! Bet you get everyone down on their prayer bones too, an' all, bet that's why my Ruby don't want to visit 'er old ma no longer.'

'If you are going to be insulting, Ma, you'd better go,' Ruby said. 'Wilby is not a bible basher, and she only bans smoking inside because she believes it's bad for the children's young lungs. I could hardly come to visit you in a wheelchair, and even before that I didn't want to because of the way you live.'

Angie stubbed her cigarette out in the sink. 'Well I'm 'ere now and you'd best tell me 'ow you are.'

Wilby interrupted and suggested Mrs Taylor sat down and that they all had a cup of tea.

'Nice 'ouse you've got!' Angie said, looking around with a somewhat scornful look. ''Spect it costs a pretty penny to run, is your old man rich?'

Wilby felt her hackles rise. 'I am a widow,' she said. 'And the housekeeping costs are none of your business. Now I suggest you say what you've come to say, then leave.'

Angie sneered at Wilby. 'I ain't goin' nowhere tonight. I'm sure there'll be room for me in my Ruby's bed. Won't be the first time we've 'ad to bunk in together.'

'Mother!' Ruby exclaimed. Two bright red spots on her cheeks showed how angry and embarrassed she was. 'You do not speak to Wilby like that. I don't want to share a bed with you, not even a room. Look at the state of you! Get out of here, crawl back to whatever hole you came out of.'

Wilby realized that she had to be the adult here. She didn't like the look of the woman, she didn't want her in the house. But it was too late to expect her to find some-where else to stay in the blackout, and she didn't want to have it on her conscience that she'd thrown someone out to sleep rough.

'Now, Ruby, that's enough,' Wilby said. 'She is your mother and she's come a long way. She can sleep in the box room, the bed is made already.' She paused and turned to Angela. 'But you, my dear, are going to be polite and obey my house rules. So no smoking, no swearing and no unpleasantness, or I'll show you the door.'

'You didn't even tell me my girl 'ad been 'urt,' Angie spat at Wilby. 'You think she's yours, don't yer?'

'I sent you a telegram the day after Ruby was hurt,' Wilby said calmly. 'And you know this because the tele-gram boy put it in your hands, as telegram boys always do. When you didn't come or even telephone, I wrote you a letter telling you what had happened. And don't tell me you didn't get that, either. Because if you didn't get it, or the telegram, how on earth would you know she'd been hurt?'

'Yes, Ma, how would you know?' Ruby asked. 'I bet you

were drunk both times, put the telegram and the letter down and forgot. Just like you forgot about me when I had that abortion and nearly died. Just like all the times you forgot to buy any food for me and spent the money on drink. I sometimes wonder how I survived my childhood.'

Angie's face crumpled. 'Okay, you got me bang ter rights. I admit I've let you down. But I'm 'ere now, I wants to know 'ow you are, if you'll ever walk again, and all that.'

'Yes, you are here now, unfortunately.' Ruby turned her wheelchair, as if to leave the kitchen. 'All you bring with you, Mother, is bad memories. You can stay tonight, it's too late to go anywhere else now. But you leave tomorrow.'

'Just talk to me now, tell me how you are?' Angie begged.

Wilby saw how hard Ruby's face had turned, and it hurt her to think how much Ruby must have gone through with her mother.

'What is there to talk about?' Ruby sneered. 'I know you've come because you haven't got anywhere else to go. I bet you've been slung out of Rhyl Street. Did you do the business at Paddington with someone to get the train fare here?'

Wilby was shocked that Ruby could be that cruel. Yet she could see by Angie's expression that she had hit the nail right on the head.

'I'll show you to the box room,' Wilby said quickly. 'Please keep quiet, as there's two little boys up there asleep. You can have a bath if you like, the water's hot. We'll talk in the morning.'

Wilby saw Angela up to the box room and gave her a towel to use. She came back downstairs and made some cocoa to take in to Ruby.

Ruby was just sitting on her bed, leaning forward and gripping the parallel bars as if to practise walking again.

'I bet you are going to tell me off for not being nice to her,' she said.

'No, I understand too much for that.' Wilby put the cocoa down and sat on an easy chair. 'But tomorrow you will have to deal with her. You'll tell her how you are, and say she can't stay. If necessary, you'll give her the train fare back to London.'

'It's all the wrong way round with her and me,' Ruby said, and her voice was full of despair. 'I always had to be the adult. If I give her money, she'll just stay in town getting drunk. She'll get arrested, and we'll have the police at the door. Why couldn't she have been killed in the Blitz, instead of someone sweet and kind who people actually wanted in their lives?'

Wilby couldn't even bring herself to tell Ruby off for saying such a wicked thing.

'The thing is, we have to deal with her tomorrow,' Wilby said. 'And my suggestion is that I give her breakfast, you talk to her and give her a pound or two. But I'll take her to the station, buy her a ticket and put her on the train to London. That way you've done the right thing, and if she gets herself into any trouble you won't have to feel responsible.'

Ruby sipped her cocoa, looking glum. 'The worst thing is,' she said eventually, 'that I don't even know what made her go off the rails in the first place. The chances are it was something far worse than I, or even Verity, have been through. Aren't we all the sum of everything that's happened to us?'

'To a certain extent,' Wilby said. 'But we each have a mind, and we can choose whether we let the bad stuff influence us for ever or decide to rise above it. As you and Verity have.'

'But we had you, and we had each other too – well, recently, that is.'

Wilby got to her feet and gathered Ruby into her arms. 'I love you, Ruby, you've given me back far more than you'll ever know. You'll do the right thing with your mother tomorrow. I know you will. Now off to bed with you.'

Chapter Thirty-Two

Archie walked past the raddled-looking older woman pushing a wheelchair and, somewhat surprised by her appearance, looked again. Just one glance at her blotchy, flabby face was enough to know she was a heavy drinker, and judging by her very shabby clothes, she'd fallen on hard times. Yet the woman in the wheelchair was young, pretty and fresh-faced, with flame red curls.

'I can see why you likes it 'ere, Ruby,' the older woman said, her voice rough and her accent a London one. 'Maybe you and I would 'ave done better if we'd lived somewhere like this when you was a nipper.'

Archie was startled by the name Ruby. It jangled a bell in his mind.

When he first moved into Weardale Road he'd gone through all Verity's letters and other papers to find out all he could about her. He found a whole stack of letters from a girlfriend; she was called Ruby and lived in Babbacombe.

There was nothing in these letters to interest him, just the inane prattling of young girls, which was why until now he hadn't remembered the name of the other girl, and he still couldn't remember the road she lived in. He'd been walking up and down all the streets, hoping to see one with a familiar name, but he'd been out of luck.

Resigning himself to the reality that looking for Verity

would be like the proverbial needle in a haystack, he came up on to the Downs. It was a lovely spring day, and although he wasn't a nature lover he had to admit the view of the sea from there was spectacular, just as Verity had claimed.

Ruby was most definitely the name of her friend, but Verity hadn't said the girl was in a wheelchair, so that couldn't be her. Anyway, that old hag pushing her couldn't be the woman Verity's friend lived with, as she was by all accounts holier than the Pope.

Disappointment had made Archie feel weary, so he sat down on a bench. In the guest house last night he'd had a bath, scrubbed his shirt, washed his pants and socks, and although he had to put them on again this morning and they were slightly damp, it made him feel better. He'd even borrowed shoe-cleaning stuff from the landlady, and a clothes brush.

He'd walked to Exeter Station feeling fine, but when he bought the paper and opened it, there was his picture. It was an old picture – one he'd always liked, as it flattered him, wearing an evening jacket and bow tie – but he didn't like what it said about him one bit. 'Ruthless killer and con man' was how he was described. The police had joined up all the dots now, and knew it was he who had killed both Pearl and Mildred. They also knew he was in Bristol, as the barber who shaved him had called the police. He was suspicious about a man who put an eye patch on before leaving his shop, when he didn't appear to have anything wrong with his eye.

So now they knew he had a moustache and beard too.

At least he wasn't on the front page. That was taken up

with a story about people in Bethnal Green being crushed to death as they ran into the underground station they were using as an air-raid shelter. One hundred and seventy-three died, which made him killing two women seem like nothing.

Although weary, he felt strangely calm about everything. He felt he ought to be flapping and terrified; he didn't even have any kind of plan, other than finding Verity and killing her. That was the only thing that mattered to him, and maybe once it was done everything else would drop into place.

'Right, Angie, on you go,' Wilby said jovially, giving the woman a little nudge to get her on the three o'clock train. 'Sorry it wasn't a better trip for you. But at least you got a chance to speak to Ruby.'

The guard blew his whistle and Wilby sighed with relief as she slammed the train door shut. Ruby had given her mother ten pounds, but they both knew she'd spend most of that in a pub as soon as she got back to London.

Wilby walked along beside the train, waving so Angie wouldn't feel quite so rejected.

As the train gathered speed, she left the station to catch a taxi home.

'Please tell me she did actually get on the train,' Ruby called out as she heard Wilby come in through the front door.

'Yes, she did,' Wilby replied, going into the dining room to speak to Ruby. 'But you, my girl, need to learn a little compassion. I know she's embarrassing and a complete failure as a mother, and to be honest I wanted her out of here as quickly as possible, but we don't know all the reasons why she is like she is. Maybe, if we did, we'd get down on our knees and thank God for not inflicting that on us.'

'I take your point, Wilby,' Ruby grinned cheekily. 'But she didn't once ask about my injuries, and she had no real interest in hearing about Luke, or where I'll work when I'm able to again. Between thinking about her next drink and fag, she can't manage anything else.'

Wilby leaned on the doorpost and sighed. 'Well, she did leave an impressive tidemark on the bath! I doubt she'd had a bath for weeks. Anyway, she's gone now. And more to the point, how is the walking practice going?'

Ruby hauled herself out of the easy chair, braced herself, and then took two unaided steps towards the parallel bars.

'That's wonderful!' Wilby exclaimed, truly impressed. She had thought it might be weeks before Ruby found the courage to try a step without holding on to something.

'I'm even better if I do it between the bars, that way I'm not scared of falling over. I walked up and down about five times this morning. I need to hold on to turn, but I'm winning at last.'

'That deserves a celebration,' Wilby said. 'When Verity gets home, let's open that bottle of wine we've been saving. The boys can have lemonade.'

At four thirty in the afternoon Archie was almost ready to give up on the search for Verity. He'd asked several women and even more shopkeepers if they knew a Verity Wood, who had a friend called Ruby, but none of them did. He had systematically gone along every street in Babbacombe, and he was just approaching St Marychurch when he saw the little haberdashery shop. They always seemed to be run by elderly ladies, and this one was no exception. He could see the owner perched on a stool watching people passing by.

He'd always had a knack of getting older ladies to give him information, so he went into the shop asking for shirt buttons. He told her that his grandson had been evacuated down here during the London Blitz.

'My daughter wrote down the lady's name and the address when she knew I was coming here,' he said. 'She wanted me to take her some flowers or something, as a thank you. But blow me down, I've lost the bit of paper.'

'A great many people took in those children,' the old lady said. 'But most children went back to their mothers before Christmas.'

'Our boy stayed,' Archie lied. 'I seem to remember him saying there was a big girl called Ruby there too.'

'Oh, that'll be Mrs Wilberforce, she's always taken in waifs and strays,' the old lady said without any hesitation. She had a soft, very lined pink face and a broad Devon accent. 'She's had young Ruby since she were fourteen. She's got two boys with her still, and t'other young lady. Terrible shame Ruby got hurt in the bombing at the RAF Hospital, there was talk she'll never walk again.'

Archie put on his most concerned expression. 'How awful! As I recall, Ruby used to help Mrs Wilberforce a great deal with the children, our John adored her. All the more reason for me to call and offer my commiserations. What road is it?'

'Higher Downs Road, it's called Beeches and it's got a red front door.'

433

'I do hope the other young lady helps her out. Young boys can be hard work.'

'She does when she's home, but she works for the Post Office and often goes down to Plymouth or Exeter if the phone lines are down. She's a bonny girl is Verity, she was badly hurt when she first came here. I don't know if she was caught in an air raid or what, but they brought her down from London in an ambulance. She's fine now, I see her flying past on her bicycle most evenings just as I'm shutting up.'

Archie saw from the sign on the door that she shut at five thirty – half an hour from now – and with that he thanked the lady, left the shop and made straight for Higher Downs Road, which was just around the corner.

The road began at the cliff railway. He hadn't gone along here earlier today because, according to a street map he'd looked at, it was in St Marychurch. He found the house with the red front door and realized it was going to be hazardous grabbing Verity. At half past five it was still light, and possibly people would be around.

Fortunately Higher Downs Road was very much a residential street with no guest houses. The sizeable houses were not divided up into flats, and they all had five-foot stone garden walls, which would make it difficult for anyone in those houses to see what was going on in the street.

Archie had considered how he was going to kill Verity many times. He still wasn't entirely sure how he was going to do it, but he did know it wasn't going to be a quick, grab her by the throat, squeeze the life out of her, all over in seconds kind of death.

It was the thought of her terror that exhilarated him. He needed her to know that he intended to kill her because she'd ruined his life. He planned on spinning out that terror, savouring the thrill of hearing her beg for her life, taking her to the point of death several times before he actually put her out of her misery.

Earlier in the day, he'd earmarked a secluded spot to take her to, if he found her. It was the cliff footpath down to Oddicombe Beach. The cliff railway car took passengers there and back in peacetime but it had been closed in 1941, and the beach too. The cliff path was supposed to be blocked off with barbed wire too, but someone had made a gap through it. To his jubilation this path – a series of badly maintained steps, and winding paths with steep drops down through woodland – began only a couple of hundred yards from the house with the red door. He hadn't even got to drag Verity very far to get her to it.

He was still standing by the cliff railway, considering where best to wait for the girl coming home, when all at once it began to rain. It was light rain at first, but it quickly turned into a deluge. People who had been ambling along the Downs all rushed to find cover.

Archie smiled. It was just what he needed.

As Wilby began to prepare the supper, Ruby was reading the newspaper which had been lying on the kitchen table unopened since breakfast when it was delivered.

'How awful, all those people killed at Bethnal Green,' she said. 'There can't be a much worse way to die than being crushed to death.'

'Hmm,' Wilby murmured, busy with her own thoughts,

wondering if she'd done the right thing putting Angela on the train home so quickly.

The telephone rang and Ruby wheeled her chair over to answer it. 'Oh, Miller!' she exclaimed, her voice high with excited surprise. 'Where are you? Are you on your way here?'

Wilby looked round hopefully.

Ruby held the receiver away from her mouth. 'He's at Exeter changing trains,' she said, before going back to him. 'Get a taxi, Miller, at Torquay. It's Beeches, Higher Downs Road, in Babbacombe. We can't wait for you to arrive.'

She put the phone down, grinning excitedly. 'He couldn't chat, the train was due. It's going to take him per-haps an hour to get here. Verity should be here in about half an hour. How are we going to play it? Try and get her to change and dress up?'

'No, because she'll guess something is up,' Wilby said. 'We just carry on like we normally do. But there are two reasons for celebration now! I'll do more vegetables, and I'll turn the sausages into Toad in the Hole so they stretch to another person without looking meagre. It's a good job I changed the sheets in the box room after your mother left, or I'd be rushing around now like a headless chicken.'

'What can I do?' Ruby asked.

'Nothing, you can't even lay the table until he gets here or Verity will ask who the extra place is for. Thank good-ness the boys are upstairs. If they knew there was any intrigue, they'd be waiting at the front door for Verity and giving the game away.'

'They're building something vast, so Colin yelled down

earlier on,' Ruby said. 'I hope that means they are using the bricks, not the beds, wardrobes and everything else.'

She returned to reading the paper. But as she finished the front page and opened it up to the next, she gasped.

'Oh, Wilby!' she said, clamping her hand over her mouth in horror. 'Archie Wood is in here. There's a picture, and the police are hunting for him.'

Wilby dropped her potato peeler and came over to the table, reading the story over Ruby's shoulder. 'Lord save us, he's killed two women!' she gasped, her face blanching. 'That one's the murdered woman we read about in Limehouse! It says "last seen in Bristol". I do hope he isn't making his way here.'

'Why would he?' Ruby asked. 'He knows if he goes anywhere near Verity, they'll catch him.'

'A man on the run is as unpredictable as a wounded animal. He might come here thinking she'll give him shelter.'

'Fat chance of that!' Ruby snorted. 'But why haven't the police warned us he's heading this way? The ones in London promised they'd keep us abreast of everything until he was arrested.'

Wilby raised her eyes and held her hands together as if praying. 'Come home, Verity! No dawdling, stopping for a chat. Just come home.'

'She will – look, it's pouring with rain now,' Ruby said. 'She'll ride home like she's got the wind up her tail.'

Soon after Exeter the train began to run along the edge of the coast, and Miller could hardly believe his eyes. He didn't know Devon at all, and it seemed to him that this impulsive trip to see Verity was going to work because everything had gone his way so far. He'd come down on the overnight train from Glasgow to Plymouth, and although all the sleepers were taken, he got a window seat. There were no hold-ups, despite absolutely everyone warning him there would be. The train chugged on through the night, and he thought the sound of the wheels were saying, 'Soon be with Verity, soon be with Verity.'

He slept on and off, and his fellow passengers in the carriage were friendly without being intrusive. One lady insisted he share her cheese-and-pickle sandwiches and a huge slice of fruit cake. Bristol was supposed to be tricky – problems with points and signals – but there were no delays, and when he finally arrived at Exeter in the afternoon it was only ten minutes for the connection to Torquay.

Yet no one had told him that for the remainder of the journey the train would run along just yards from the water's edge, or that there would be dozens of little boats bobbing at their moorings with the sun glinting on the waves. Miller felt like a small boy again, catching his first glimpse of the sea, and he made a silent pact that if Verity still cared for him as much as he cared for her, they would marry and live here for the rest of their lives.

He knew he'd become a man whilst working for the Forestry. It wasn't just building up muscle and the physical strength needed to fell trees and haul them to timber yards. It was far more than that. He'd learned to take responsibility, not just for himself but for the younger, weaker men who had chosen to work for the Forestry, rather than joining the forces or the fire service, because they thought it a soft option. Of course, it wasn't. Felling trees when the ground was frozen, and the north wind bit through even the warmest coat and hat, was no picnic. There were no home comforts, and the food was often appalling. Then there were the accidents: a saw slipping could slice off a hand, a falling branch could knock a man unconscious or blind him, and they were miles from medical care.

Miller found all the first aid he'd learned back in London had stood him in good stead. He could sew up a gaping wound, remove an infected tooth if necessary, lance a boil, make a splint for a broken limb, and deal with a hundred other less serious medical problems. But he knew it wasn't just these practical skills that had made him a man; it was more the ability to communicate with and understand his fellow forestry workers. He'd learned to care for them, even when they behaved like savage brutes, to comfort them when they were hurt, to laugh with them at both triumphs and disasters, and to share whatever he had, be that his knowledge, his strength or his rations.

As a boy he'd been a loner, perhaps he always would be, but the difference now was that he wasn't isolated; he knew other men looked up to him, they wanted his company, and they trusted him. That felt good.

He closed his eyes for a moment as the train drew into Newton Abbot. It was raining hard now, but he was glad it hadn't begun until he'd seen the sea. His heart was pounding at the prospect of seeing Verity. He'd carried a picture of her for so long in his head, her blonde hair flowing down over her shoulders as she brushed it out before bedtime. Her slim yet shapely figure, the way she bit her lower lip when she was reading, and her lovely musical laugh.

He wondered if she'd ever known how often he'd wanted

to reach out and remove the pins from her hair and let it tumble, run his fingers through it, and kiss that lovely, long slender neck.

He only knew she'd felt the same as him when they shared that first kiss on Hither Green Station, when he was leaving for Scotland. Even then he hadn't said he loved her, only made some vague allusion to her being special. His letters were dry, passionless tomes, and he should have insisted on leave, to go and see her for a few days and make her see that she was everything to him.

What was the matter with him back then that he couldn't say what was in his heart?

His heart quickened now as the train began to slow for Torquay. He was on his feet, bag in hand, ready to leap out the moment the train stopped. He willed a taxi to be waiting.

He couldn't wait to see her.

Chapter Thirty-Three

Verity was singing 'Boogie Woogie Bugle Boy' as she raced through St Marychurch on her bicycle. She often sang while cycling and got some odd looks, but it was raining so hard the streets were deserted. She'd only passed one woman since leaving the office.

She was drenched right through to her underwear, but the thought of getting into a hot bath and dry clothes spurred her on to pedal faster.

As she turned off Hampton Road into Higher Downs Road she saw a man in a trilby and a dark overcoat, across the road from her house. He was just standing there.

Slowing right down, she hopped off her bike to wheel it in through the gate, and the bearded man crossed the road towards her. Assuming he wanted to ask her a question, she paused.

'Looking for someone?' she asked.

Suddenly, before she could move, he grabbed her arm, making her drop her bike. He twisted her arm up behind her back and stuck something sharp into the small of her back.

'If you make a sound, I'll stick this knife in you. I just want to take you down the road to talk to you.'

The moment he spoke she realized it was Archie. Fright made her almost wet herself, and although she opened her mouth to speak, no sound came out. She let him lead her away from the house towards the Downs and the cliff railway. All she could hope for was that Wilby would see her bicycle lying on the pavement and, guessing something bad had happened, would phone the police. But with a wall around the garden how would she see it?

Any other time the area by the cliff railway would have had people standing there admiring the view, but the heavy rain had sent every last person home. When she saw Archie was going to take her on to a narrow winding path that went down over the cliff to Oddicombe Bay, her fear increased tenfold. There would be no one there to appeal to for help.

The path and the beach it led to were out of bounds, blocked up since the war began. But someone had either cut or pushed the barbed wire aside. Even in good weather it was a challenging walk, but in heavy rain it was treacherous and only the foolhardy would use it.

Archie prodded her harder in the back. The blade penetrated her clothes and pricked her skin enough to know he would stab her if she resisted. She slithered on the path in her already wet shoes, but he held her arm in a vice-like grip. Even if it had been safe enough to run, he wasn't going to give her the chance.

The trees and thick undergrowth on either side of the path smelled earthy, a smell she'd always loved, but with Archie holding a knife to her back it took on the smell of an underground cellar, where death awaited her. Somehow, she knew that was what he intended; there was desperation in his movements and the few words he'd said to her. She couldn't think of anything to say that might change his plan.

'Nearly there,' he said as he forced her ahead of him down the narrow path. 'Then we can have a little chat, can't we?'

He moved the knife and held it in front of her face for a moment to scare her further. It wasn't a big knife, just one of those folding ones fishermen used, but it looked very sharp. He moved it to her throat, nicking the flesh, and at the same time twisted her arm even higher up her back.

The way he leered at her was all too familiar; he had always liked to see her terrified. It probably made him feel powerful. He'd got his wish, she was terrified, but she was damned if she'd let him see that. She was determined not to cry out.

He punched her in the stomach. 'Just a reminder not to try to be clever with me,' he warned her. 'No one will rescue you this time.'

The punch winded her, and she had a job to stand up straight. But he stuck the knife in her back again to make her move, and pushed her ahead of him down the path.

When they were halfway to the beach, and well hidden from anyone looking over the top of the cliff, he stopped. While still holding the knife to her throat, he reached into his pocket and brought out a length of cord.

'I'm going to kill you, Verity,' he said in a calm, measured voice. He held the cord in front of her, and she could see he'd already made it into a noose. With one hand he slipped it over her head, and then pulled it just tight enough so she could feel it taut around her neck. She was so scared she felt her bowels loosen.

'Please don't do this, Archie,' she begged. 'It doesn't make any sense to kill me, and you'll hang for it. If you need money, I'll get it for you. I know you aren't my real father, but I've always thought of you as my dad and loved you. You must have cared a bit for me too?'

He removed the knife from her neck and put it in his pocket. Then, just holding the noose in one hand, he grinned at her. His eyes were as cold as a dead cod on the fishmonger's slab, and the grin was maniacal, showing all his teeth, like a savage dog.

'Care for you? I never even for one moment cared for you. You were less to me than the dog shit on the pavement.'

'Even if that's true, it's no reason to kill me,' she cried out.

'I've got every reason to kill you. But before I do, I'm going to tell you exactly why.'

Miller got out of the taxi and paid the driver. Then he picked up the bicycle on the pavement, as it was blocking his way into the gate. He stood it against the wall, then walked to the front door.

It was opened by an elderly lady a second after he'd knocked. 'I'm Miller Grantham,' he said with a wide smile, holding out his hand to her. 'I'm so very pleased to meet you, Mrs Wilberforce. Verity talked about you so often.'

Wilby shook his hand and asked him in. 'Ruby and I are so glad you've come, Miller, but I'm afraid we are in a bit of a panic right now, as we've just read the paper and discovered Verity's stepfather is wanted for two murders. We won't be able to relax until she gets home.'

'How long will that be?' he asked. 'I had to wait for some time at the station to get a taxi, so I thought she was here already and that was her bike outside.'

444

'What bike?' Ruby had wheeled herself into the hall as they were speaking at the open front door.

'Yes, outside, right by the gate.' He pointed back to the garden gate. 'Dropped on the ground. I stood it up against the wall.'

Wilby almost pushed him aside, rushing to the gate. 'It's him, he's taken her!' she yelled out. 'Ruby, call the police!'

Miller dropped his bag at the front door and rushed to join Wilby at the gate. 'Which way do you think he's taken her?'

Wilby pointed towards the Downs. 'It's bound to be that way. I bet he's taken her down the cliff path by the railway.'

Miller didn't even stop to speak, just hared off down the road.

Wilby stood wringing her hands for a moment, her face contorted with anxiety, the rain running down her face unheeded.

'Have you rung the police?' she shouted back to Ruby.

She heard Ruby call back that they were on their way, and then she too ran down the road towards the cliff.

Verity looked into Archie's eyes and didn't recognize him as the man she'd once called Daddy. He was so wild and unkempt, far, far worse than he'd been that day he beat her and locked her in the Morrison shelter. Terrified as she was, convinced that at any moment he would pull on that noose around her neck and her life would be over, she somehow knew that she had to hide that terror from him, as that was what he wanted.

'So tell me why you want to kill me?' she asked, forcing

445

herself to keep her voice steady. 'Is it because my mother cheated you and pretended I was your child?'

'Do you think I care who spawned you?' he sneered, sticking his face right up to hers. 'You never meant anything to me, you were less than nothing.'

'So why kill me, then,' she asked. The path beneath her feet was slippery with mud, and she was afraid she might lose her balance and fall. That way the noose would tighten too. The rain was splattering on a big rock just above them and then running off like a waterfall. This cliff always had dozens of these little waterfalls, even at the height of summer. When she and Ruby were young girls they used to wash their face and hands in them on hot days.

'Because you put the rage inside me,' he said. 'You took everything from me.'

'How did I do that?' she asked.

'By being you. I've killed two women, strangled them like they were a couple of chickens,' he said. 'Both times I saw your face in them.'

This was shocking if it was true, but she couldn't really believe it was.

'You mean they reminded you of me?'

'I didn't say that.' He slapped her hard across the face with his free hand, but the movement tightened the noose around her neck. 'They judged me, the way you do. The way you always did, even when you were a little kid.'

'Let me go, Daddy,' she pleaded, thinking that might help her cause. 'You don't really want to kill me. You know you don't.'

She realized immediately she had said the wrong thing. His face darkened. His eyes flashed dangerously. 'Do you really think I came all the way here for anything else?' he yelled, his spit going all over her face. 'You and your bloody mother ruined my life. She was a cold-hearted bitch and you are the same.'

His hand gripped the noose, and it tightened again. Her hands came up involuntarily to loosen it, but he slapped them away, bending her over backwards, his face almost on hers. Verity couldn't see what was behind her, rocks or bushes, but she did know it was a very steep bank. If she fell back, he would surely lose his balance too and fall with her. But he might let go of the noose momentarily. She thought it was worth a try.

'Go on then, kill me!' she spat at him. 'You always were a bully, and a pervert too. Then you became a con man and a thief. You say you've killed two women, so why not go the whole hog and kill me too?'

He leaned in towards her, perhaps to slap her again. Verity kicked out at his shins, then jerked back, and just let herself go.

She felt the noose tighten as she tumbled into space. She thought she heard a shout too. But her last thought was of Ruby and how she must learn to walk again.

Miller reached the top of the cliff path, and although he couldn't see the man or Verity, he could hear a male voice that had to belong to Wood, and guessed he was perhaps thirty to forty feet below the cliff edge.

The cliff path snaked down and round, following nat-ural contours between rocks and pine trees; it was the kind of path that only someone agile and fit would use, and never in heavy rain.

But Miller was used to such terrain, and he was incensed that this man could kidnap and terrify Verity. He made his way down the path carefully and silently, only stopping to arm himself with a fist-sized rock.

Suddenly he heard Verity's voice, loud and clear. She said, 'Go on then, kill me,' and more about Archie being a con man and a thief. Then came a cracking of twigs, followed by the sound of someone falling. Miller stopped being cautious and hurled himself down the path. Just before he reached the spot where Verity must have been when he heard her voice, he saw what had happened. Verity had fallen backwards and slid downhill on her back, a distance of some twelve feet, before her slide was stopped by a rock.

Wood had clearly toppled over with her, but because he had fallen face down he could see where he was going. He'd put his hands out to stop his slide, and he was just getting on to his knees to crawl towards Verity.

He was slithering towards her, like a wild animal stalking his prey, and he certainly wasn't intending to help her.

Miller didn't stop to think but leapt down the bank without a thought for his own safety, skidding and sliding until he reached Wood, pulled him up by his collar and bashed his head with the rock. Wood slumped face down and was still.

In two strides Miller reached Verity. He saw the cord noose around her neck, and getting his fingers beneath where it was digging into her neck, he loosened it.

She had a pulse, but she had been knocked out by the fall. He moved her carefully and saw she had a head wound. He scooped her up in his arms, turned and climbed back up to the path, and then on up to the top of the cliff.

He was almost there when the police arrived.

'He's down there,' he said, nodding his head in the general direction. 'I knocked him out with a rock.'

Verity stirred in his arms, her hand went up to her head and she opened her eyes.

'Hello, sweetheart,' Miller said. 'You are quite safe and I'm taking you home.'

Chapter Thirty-Four

'I'm confused, Wilby,' Verity said. She could feel the bandage around her head; her head ached too, and her throat felt bruised. She knew that she'd been with Archie on the cliff path, but she didn't know how it had ended and how she got back to her own bed. 'I had the craziest dream that Miller was there.'

'Not a crazy dream, he really was,' Wilby laughed softly. 'It was he who saved you and carried you back here. And it was he who dressed your head wound.'

'But I don't understand.' Verity's blue eyes looked as big as half-crowns in her confusion. 'How could he be here?'

'That is a long and complicated story, and right now you need sleep, or shock will set in and make you act loopy,' Wilby said. 'Tomorrow is soon enough for explanations, but for now all you need to know is that Miller loves you.'

Verity's eyes widened again. 'Really?'

'Would I tell you something like that if it wasn't true? Now go to sleep, and let it heal you. Rest assured, if you wake, I'll be in the other bed in here. If you need me, just call out.'

Wilby tucked Verity in, left a night light burning and went back down to the kitchen where Ruby, Miller, Colin and Brian were sitting around the table drinking tea.

Ruby looked up. 'I made the boys cheese on toast,' she said. 'In all this we forgot they hadn't had their supper.'

'Is Verity better now?' Brian asked, his brown eyes

looking troubled. 'What happened to the bad man? Have the police locked him up?'

Wilby smoothed back his hair affectionately. 'Yes, lovey, Verity is much better and in a day or two she'll be right back to normal. As for the bad man, Miller was a hero and saved Verity from him. He was taken away by the police and he'll be locked up till his trial. He won't be coming back here to scare Verity.'

She paused for a moment, knowing it must have been awful for two small boys to see Verity carried in by Miller, a man they didn't even know, with blood dripping from her head. It was also very difficult at their age to grasp the idea that any man would want to hurt someone they loved. 'But I want to say how good you've both been tonight, really grown-up and sensible, and I'm proud of you. Now I want you to go to bed quietly. I'll come up later and tuck you in. We've all had enough excitement for one day.'

After they'd gone upstairs, Wilby sat down heavily, putting her head in her hands. 'Oh dear,' she sighed. 'Thank God you came, Miller. It doesn't bear thinking about what could've happened if you hadn't rushed down there and saved her.'

She couldn't possibly articulate how impressed she was by Miller. He had responded to what was a life or death situation with speed, calm and courage. He had been a real-life hero, and it was just a shame Verity hadn't been conscious to appreciate it. One of the policemen who came back to the house afterwards to take a statement had remarked that he didn't really know how Miller managed to climb back up that cliff with Verity in his arms. One slip and they both could have tumbled to their deaths.

'I don't know why everyone seems to think I saved her,' Miller said. 'From what I saw, Verity kicked Archie in the shins and then purposely fell backwards, taking Archie with her, in order to make him let go of the noose around her neck. In doing so she hoped she'd get a chance to scramble away. That took immense courage, because she must've been terrified.'

'And she'll have to relive it all again tomorrow when the police come back,' Ruby said. 'Are you sure we shouldn't have let her go to hospital?'

Miller put a reassuring hand on her arm. 'Obviously we've got to watch her closely for any sign of concussion – she was, after all, knocked out – but the reason I suggested we kept her here is because I think she'll recover more quickly amongst her family, where she feels safe. Hospitals are very impersonal, and a little frightening. But haven't you got something to tell us?'

Ruby looked blank.

'Wilby told me when we were down by the cliff railway that you couldn't come with her, because you weren't able to walk after being hurt in an air raid. Yet when we got back here, you were standing at the door with no wheelchair, and no crutches or sticks,' he said. 'I suspect you were so anxious to hear about Verity that you got up without thinking.'

Wilby gasped. 'So she did, Miller! You know I didn't even take that in, we were all focussed on Verity.'

Ruby blushed and looked embarrassed. 'You are very observant, Miller. I must have got out of my wheelchair and walked to the front door totally involuntarily, because I was wanting news of Verity so badly. When I did realize what I'd done, I couldn't bring myself to say, "Look at me!" Not under the circumstances. Besides, I nearly fell over with shock!'

Wilby beamed. 'That is so wonderful. I hope this will convince you that your spine and legs are working perfectly again?'

Ruby stood up, and took two faltering steps away from the kitchen table, then gathered herself and walked over towards the hall. She stopped and turned. 'My legs feel very odd, wobbly and achy with lack of use, but that will soon be put right if I use sticks for a bit to steady me. I can't wait to tell Luke.'

'Your sweetheart?' Miller asked.

Ruby smiled. 'Yes, he's wonderful. But you don't want me going on about him. I've got lots to tell you about Verity so you can catch up. I feel I know you, because she told us quite a lot about you, although I suppose most of that is out of date now too. But you aren't like I imagined.'

Miller laughed. 'What did you imagine? A gardener so drippy he couldn't tell a girl that he loved her? So pathetic he even got turned down by the forces?'

'I must confess, I did think you sounded a bit feeble,' she admitted. She looked at his muscular biceps which seemed to be straining the sleeves of his shirt, his resolute square chin, and a face which had a weather-beaten look. He was the kind of man who would survive on a desert island, build a house, catch his own food, make a boat out of next to nothing and sail home when he felt like it. 'How wrong could I be?'

'I was a bit of a drip when I first met Verity,' he admitted. 'Forestry work toughens you up, but then I bet neither you nor Verity are the same as you were before the war. Has anyone in England stayed the same?'

Wilby thought that Miller was quite right. The war had changed everyone to some extent. Children had to cope with so much: their fathers being away, terrifying air raids, and for those in the big cities there was often the trauma of losing their home or family members.

Women who had never needed to work before had found themselves working in factories, driving ambulances or milking cows while their husbands were away at the war. Men, many of whom had only ever done white-collar jobs, had to be turned into tough soldiers. Even those above the age of conscription who took on voluntary work as air-raid wardens or with the Civil Defence had their lives turned upside down.

Wilby didn't feel she'd had to adapt much – having evacuees was no different to the foster children she'd had before the war – but she had been challenged by food rationing. She'd always loved to cook and had been quite extravagant with ingredients and quantities. All that had to stop, because she couldn't get all those ingredients or the variety of food she was used to. She'd had to rely on the vegetables she grew, her chickens, and learn to be more creative with what she had to hand.

That evening, Wilby and Ruby took Miller into the sitting room and began to fill him in on some of the details about what Verity had gone through with Archie. They didn't tell him about the burglaries, they thought it best to keep that under their hats for now. Besides, that was for Verity to disclose if she wanted to. Then they told him about the life they had all shared since she'd come to live with them.

Ruby realized that Verity must have told him about how and why they fell out before he met her, and she felt she had to make some kind of explanation.

'I'm sure she must have told you how we came to be estranged, and how awful I was to her,' Ruby said, and pulled a vexed face. 'I bet you wondered why she ever liked me?'

'She didn't tell me any details, only that you'd said she was dead to you. I know it did play on her mind, though, and that she missed you. But in all fairness, Ruby, every one of us is guilty of something like that. We lash out when we're angry or hurt, often regretting it later, but we don't know how to put it right. But when you rescued Verity from that terrible man, you wiped out anything that went before.'

Ruby suspected he knew some of the background of how it came about, and she was touched he wasn't judgemental. 'So what now? I mean for you and Verity.'

Miller grinned sheepishly. 'I'm hoping for happy ever after. But realistically we've got a few obstacles to overcome. There's all the catching up to do for a start, and I'll have to go back to Scotland. Then there's Wood's trial. Hopefully he'll admit the murders, but if he doesn't and it comes to a trial by jury, Verity will be called as a witness and that's going to be hard on her.'

'Shame you didn't kill him,' Ruby said grimly. 'That would've saved so much effort for the police and the courts, to say nothing of the prison service.'

'I thought I had for a short while,' Miller admitted. 'He

was absolutely motionless when I climbed back up with Verity. It crossed my mind I could be in trouble too. But he was just knocked out.'

'We all read in the paper about those other two murders,' Wilby said. 'Ruby spotted today's report in the paper. We were horrified to discover he was the murderer, and worried that he was heading this way. But we didn't imagine he was already here in Babbacombe.'

'It's going to be very hard for Verity to come to terms with what he's done,' Miller said thoughtfully. 'I know he isn't her real father, but she believed he was for a long time.'

Ruby nodded in agreement. 'I know what it's like to think you've got bad blood. It doesn't help that people tell you it doesn't matter who your mother and father were, or what they did. It's like a little worm that gets inside your head and keeps on suggesting the badness is in you too.'

'Now stop this, both of you,' Wilby said firmly. 'Verity is a sensible girl, she'll rise above it. I know she will.'

The following morning Wilby woke to see Verity lying awake, staring at the ceiling.

'How are you feeling?' she asked. 'Did you sleep well?'

'I'm feeling better than I expected I would.' Verity spoke slowly, as if she was thinking about each word. 'And yes, I think I slept alright. I woke up a few times, though.'

Wilby got out of bed and went over to Verity, sitting beside her on the bed. She smoothed her hair back from her forehead, noting the angry red mark the noose had left on her throat. Apart from that, and being rather pale, she looked fine. Miller had cut some of her hair away on the

456

back of her head to see the wound properly and to clean it. He'd said it didn't need stitches, because it was just a bad graze, so he'd only put a light dressing on it.

'So what's troubling you?'

'I feel my life has just blown up in my face,' she said softly. 'I was cruising along, enjoying my job, and then suddenly this! Archie told me he always hated me, and I suppose I ought to have worked that out for myself by now, especially the last time he attacked me. But you really don't ever think the man you believed was your father would try to kill you.'

'No, of course not,' Wilby agreed. 'But thanks to Miller he didn't succeed. Archie was a wicked and dangerous man who will get the punishment he deserves. You mustn't spend another moment imagining it was somehow your fault. What you've got to do now is look to the future. Miller is here, dying to talk to you.'

'Well, that's part of it, Wilby. I don't know how I feel about him any more. I accepted he'd found someone else and, sad as I was about it, I got over it. Now that he appears to want me again, it just makes me feel second best.'

'Now listen here, madam,' Wilby said firmly, 'you don't know the full story about that.'

Wilby began to tell her the truth of the matter: how Archie had manipulated Miller into writing to say he'd found someone else. 'Ruby and I were a little suspicious, and we took the liberty recently of digging out your letters and comparing the earlier ones with that last Dear John letter. We noticed some odd things about it, which made us think Archie may have had a hand in it. Anyway, to cut a long story short, we wrote to Miller. He hadn't got anyone else, and never had, and the end result was that he came here for you. I'm so sorry that we poked into your letters.'

Verity gave a weak smile. 'That's okay, I'm very glad you found out the truth. But I'm not sure it makes any difference to how I feel now. Of course I want to see Miller, if only to thank him for rescuing me, but I don't think I can turn the clock back.'

Wilby got up from the bed and put her dressing gown on. 'Keep an open mind, Verity. He is a very impressive young man, and I think you may find him a very different one from the man you once knew. Now I'll go down and start breakfast, but I think you should have yours in bed.'

It was lunchtime before Verity and Miller came face to face. Miller had got up early, gone for a walk along the Downs, and was eating some toast when a police sergeant called to take his statement. It was quiet in the house, the boys were at school, and Ruby, Verity and Wilby were all upstairs.

Miller took the sergeant, who introduced himself as Meakin, into the kitchen and offered him a cup of tea.

'That would be very welcome,' Meakin said. He was a burly, middle-aged man with a pock-marked face which made him look rather fierce. 'Wood is in the prison hospital at Exeter. He's had a few stitches in his head, but apart from that he'll live to hang.'

Miller grinned. 'You've decided that, then?'

'Well, there isn't any doubt of Wood's guilt. By all accounts he ranted all the way to Exeter that he wanted his stepdaughter dead. One of my colleagues is at the prison now to take down his statement. We have a great deal of hard evidence against him regarding the two other dead women, and even if he refuses to confess to killing them, we can still nail him.'

Miller explained briefly his relationship with Verity, and why he'd come down from Scotland to see her. 'It was a stroke of luck that I arrived just a few minutes after Wood had grabbed her at the front gate. I didn't stop to think it through, I just went after them.'

He explained how he had heard Verity's voice further down the cliff path, even though he couldn't see her. 'I picked up a rock and crept down there but just as I got Archie in clear sight, Verity kicked him in the shins, leaned backwards and fell. I believe she did it hoping he'd let go of the noose around her neck. It worked too, he toppled down the cliff with her.'

'So you threw the rock at Wood?'

'No, I clobbered him with it. You see, he fell down but got to his hands and knees to reach Verity. I leapt down there and bashed him so he couldn't hurt her.'

'And then?'

'I picked up Verity and climbed back up the cliff with her.'

'Did you check to see if Wood was alive?'

'No, I didn't care. I thought I'd killed him, in fact. That is what he deserved.'

'Quite so, Mr Grantham. But it's just as well you didn't kill him, or you might have found yourself in trouble. It wouldn't do for members of the public to decide who can be dispensed with.'

Miller shrugged. Considering Meakin had said already

that Archie would hang, it seemed odd that he now seemed to be concerned about a man who had killed twice and would have killed again if he hadn't been stopped. 'Is that it for now?' he asked.

'Yes, but I'll have to speak to Miss Wood before I leave.'

Wilby brought Verity down, and Meakin spoke to her in the dining room where Ruby had been sleeping. Miller stayed in the sitting room alone, wishing he could hear what was being said. But with the hall between the two rooms, and both doors closed, he could hear nothing.

Then Wilby came in, bringing him a cup of tea.

'I don't like that Sergeant Meakin much,' she said, as she put the tea on the side table by his armchair. 'He's a bit too full of himself.' She sat down in another armchair, just looking at him.

Miller smiled. He liked Wilby, and he could understand now why she'd made such a big impression on Verity.

'Aren't most policemen that way?' he said. 'But how is Verity? I'm dying to see her.'

'She's fine, she slept well, no nightmares. But don't expect too much of her, Miller. I don't know if you fully realize, but it was just Ruby and I who planned getting in touch with you, Verity knew nothing about it. So I'm sure you can see what a shock it must have been for her to be rescued by you. Last night she thought she'd imagined that you were here. This morning I explained everything, but it *is* a lot to digest.'

'A bit overpowering too, I guess. Maybe it would be better if I moved into a guest house?' Miller suggested.

'That is a kind thought, but let's see how it goes after the sergeant has finished with her. How long is your leave?'

'I could take up to a week. It's not like being in the forces. I don't think they've ever shot a forester for desertion.'

She laughed, and in that moment Miller could see what a pretty woman she must have been. She might be plump and lined now, but there was such a wealth of experience in her face, and such kindness in her eyes, that it made her very attractive still.

'What do you want to do when the war ends?' she asked.

'I had planned to stay in Scotland, get a little croft and carry on working for the Forestry. But having seen Devon now, I could be tempted to settle here, even if there are no forests.'

'Once the world gets back to normal, people will want gardeners and gamekeepers again,' she said. 'In Devon and everywhere else.'

Verity told Sergeant Meakin exactly what had happened the previous day, from the moment she jumped off her bicycle at the gate to the last thing she remembered when she made herself fall backwards.

'Why didn't you call out as soon as he grabbed you? Or kick out at him?'

'He had a knife at my back. I believed he would stab me if I yelled. Besides, there was no one around because it was raining hard. Once he put the noose around my neck I was too scared to do anything. I only got a bit braver on the cliff path because I knew, if I didn't act, he'd kill me.'

'Why did he track you down to kill you?'

Verity thought that was a very odd question; it seemed Meakin was almost blaming her.

'He said it was because he'd always hated me, that I was a cold-hearted bitch like my mother. He was in such a rage, he looked wild and crazy. He said something about seeing my face in the faces of the other women he killed. But he didn't stand to gain anything by killing me, it could only make things worse for him.'

'So he told you he'd killed two other women?'

'Yes, he did, not just about seeing my face in theirs but that he strangled them like they were chickens.'

'So how did you get away from him?'

Verity shrugged. 'I kicked him and just fell backwards. I hoped he'd let go of the noose, and I suppose he must have done, or I wouldn't be here to tell you this. I don't remember anything else.'

He seemed satisfied with that, but then went on to ask a few more questions about Archie coming to live with her in Weardale Road.

'You knew he was a wanted man, yet you didn't go to the police,' he said. 'Why was that?'

'That's difficult to explain. I was absolutely horrified to see him and I did say he'd have to go, but a girl sharing my house, who didn't know what he'd done, suggested he stay the night. So I said he could stay just the one night. Anyway, he told me all the embezzlement thing was sorted out. I believed him then, because it did seem improbable he'd come to me knowing the police were still looking for him. I suppose I felt sorry for him too, because back then I thought he was my real father.' Verity paused, she knew she wasn't explaining herself very well.

'Go on,' Meakin urged her.

'I suppose I kind of wanted a family. I'd lost my mother

and my aunt very recently, war had broken out, and I was very much alone. Not a good reason to let him stay, as it turned out. But don't we all do things sometimes that we regret later?'

'Do you regret helping him burgle houses?'

Verity's head hurt, she felt a little shaky still from the ordeal the previous day, but at that question from the policeman the room seemed to swirl around her as if she was going to faint.

'Helping him burgle houses?' she said questioningly. 'Is that what he's said? I never heard anything so ridiculous.'

'That's what I thought,' Meakin said. 'But I had to ask.'

The police sergeant left then, saying he'd get the statement typed up and would bring it back for her to sign in due course.

Verity lay down on Ruby's bed. She felt sick with fright, but at least she hadn't actually denied helping Archie with burglaries. She'd only said it was ridiculous.

Was this going to come back and bite her? Archie had obviously said it thinking that, if he had to go down, he'd take her with him.

Wilby put her head round the door. She took one look at Verity lying on the bed and came right over, putting her hand on the girl's forehead. 'You are very pale. Did the sergeant upset you?'

'It was just going over it again,' Verity lied. 'And my head is sore.' She really wanted to tell Wilby everything, but it was too much, too awful. She needed time to think.

'Do you think you could talk to Miller now? He's desperate to see you.'

'Okay, but don't expect too much,' Verity replied.

Chapter Thirty-Five

'At last!' Miller said, jumping up as Verity came into the sitting room. 'I was beginning to think you'd run away to avoid me.'

'Don't be silly,' she said, and stopped short because, as Wilby had said, he was quite something to look at.

He'd been attractive before with his duck-egg-blue eyes, chiselled cheekbones and his fair, floppy hair, but he'd been thin and insubstantial. He'd filled out with muscle now; his arms, his thighs, even his neck, were all so much bigger, and his face was more rugged.

'How are you feeling now?' he asked, as solicitous as she remembered.

'My head is a bit sore, and I feel a bit shaky still, but thanks to you I'm alive. That's something to be very glad about.'

'Come and sit down,' he said, reaching out and taking her hand, leading her to an armchair, then taking the one opposite her.

Verity was glad of the space between them. She had been afraid he would start flinging his arms around her before she had a chance to find out if that was what she wanted, or not.

'Wilby and Ruby explained why they wrote to me,' he said. 'And I think they've told you exactly why I wrote that letter to you?'

Verity nodded. 'I did think it was a bit of an odd letter, not your usual style, but of course it never occurred to me Archie had instigated it. A couple of girls at work got similar letters from their boyfriends once they'd joined up, so I suppose that made me think it was all part of being in a country at war. Also, I thought I was to blame, because I ought to have made more of an effort to get up to Scotland to see you.'

'We both know what a monumental task it was to take a train anywhere in the first year of the war – well, it still can be. Overcrowded carriages full of servicemen, delays and cancellations,' he smiled at her. 'I blame myself too for not trying harder to see you. But don't let's play the blame game, Verity. It wasn't being apart that broke us up, was it? We both know now that we were duped. I find it hard to credit that a man could put a girl through so much, especially one he'd brought up from a baby. I understand it was he who told you he wasn't your real father?'

'Yes, and in the most unpleasant way too. It wasn't a total surprise, as Aunt Hazel had hinted at intrigue. I just wish she'd told me everything, and I probably wouldn't have let him through the door. Now I am so glad he isn't my real father. I think I must change my name as soon as possible. But enough of that, why don't you tell me about your life in Scotland?'

He laughed. 'You always did that,' he said. 'We'd be talking about your childhood or your mother and suddenly you wanted to stop. I'm not going to try and make you talk about those things, but maybe one day you will need to.'

'Possibly,' she agreed. 'But not today. Are you still living in a freezing Nissen hut?'

'No, I'm the boss now, so I get to live in the Head Forester's house – in the forest, of course.'

'Is it a Hansel and Gretel type cottage?' she asked. 'It sounds as if it ought to be.'

'Not really, it was once the gatehouse to the laird's estate, so it's stone built, sturdy, a bit Gothic, with two rooms, a kitchen and bathroom. The furniture came with it – that's shabby, faded grandeur – and I think it all came from the big house, or "hoose" as they say up there. But it's comfortable, very warm when I get the fire going, and I've got a little garden too. So I'm keeping my hand in, though with vegetables now, not flowers.'

'So you are the boss?' she smiled. 'That's impressive.'

'I think it's only because I'm really interested in all aspects of forestry, planting the trees, caring for them, deciding which ones are ready to be felled. And I studied up on it, whereas the other blokes just see it as a job, glad they escaped having to go to war. Most of them don't appreciate nature, the deer and other animals, yet that's all part of maintaining and protecting our forests.'

Verity had always liked that he was a thinker, a man who cared about nature. She thought it was just as well he hadn't been considered fit enough to be called up; she couldn't imagine him dealing with being expected to fire a gun at other humans.

'I can drive now too,' he said. 'I had to learn to transport the timber. It's good to be able to see other parts of Scotland too, though mostly I only drive the lorry to Glasgow and the shipyards on Tyneside. Wilby said last night how the war had changed us all. Do you think you've changed?'

'I don't know,' she said. 'Do you think so?'

'I can only see that you are prettier than ever. But Wilby and Ruby said you are far more confident than you used to be, and daring, I believe, they say you climb telegraph poles.'

Verity laughed. 'There's nothing daring about that. Except perhaps in a high wind.'

'Are you daring enough to try again with me?' Miller said.

Verity looked at him and made a 'don't know' gesture with her hands. 'I'm so very glad you came when you did, because you saved my life. But the horror of what nearly happened, coming face to face with that madman again, has made me doubt everything. It's like my mind has gone. Can you understand that? If you'd come before that happened, when my mind was clear, it would be different.'

He nodded gravely. 'I can understand all that. I think anyone would be hard pressed to even think after such a trauma, much less decide whether you need or want a man in your life right now. I think the best thing I can do is go and check into a guest house nearby. I'll come and see you each day until I have to go back. Maybe we could go for walks, go to the pictures, just as old friends. How does that sound?'

'It sounds good,' she replied, but a little voice in her head was telling her the exact opposite.

He slid off his chair and moved towards her on his knees. He took both her hands in his and looked right into her eyes. 'You look frightened of me,' he said gently. 'Have you forgotten what good friends we were? Maybe too much water has passed under the bridge for us to be sweethearts, but we ought to remain friends.'

'I'm sorry, Miller,' she said, and tears welled up in her

467

eyes. 'You've come all this way, and you saved my life, but I can't cope with anything else right now.'

'That's alright,' he said. He put his hands on either side of her head and leaned forward to kiss her forehead. 'I'll go now, but I'll ring Wilby and tell her where I'm staying. And if you find in a day or two that you want to see me, that's fine with me.'

Verity jumped out of her chair and fled. She couldn't bear her feelings of guilt at letting him down, or the fear that her time as a burglar was going to come out. She was even afraid that she wasn't normal, because of what Archie had done that Christmas when she was twelve, and again before he locked her in the Morrison shelter.

Miller remained in the sitting room for a little while after Verity had fled. He couldn't wish he'd never come – if he hadn't, she might be dead now. He knew he loved her, and he was prepared to wait, but his instinct told him that there was more to this than just yesterday's terrifying experience. He felt that something she'd tried to bury had come to the surface and it needed to be faced.

But if she wasn't even comfortable holding his hand, he wouldn't be able to get it out of her.

Wilby was in the kitchen when she heard Verity run upstairs, but she thought she'd gone to the bathroom or to collect something she wanted to show Miller. Then, a little while later, he came into the kitchen looking very sad and said he was going, but he'd be in touch.

She tried to ask him what had gone wrong, but he just said, 'The buried past, I think.'

He wouldn't stay for a cup of tea, but he said he'd

telephone the next day to see how Verity was. Then, after thanking Wilby for putting him up, he left.

Wilby flew upstairs and into Verity's room. She was lying face down on her bed crying.

'Whatever is it?' Wilby asked and sat down beside her, putting a comforting hand on the girl's back.

'I'm no good for him,' Verity sobbed out.

Wilby didn't try to get anything more out of her. She just sat, rubbing Verity's back, and waited. Over the years she'd had many damaged children sent to her to foster, and she knew from experience that it wasn't a bit of good trying to force them to open up about whatever it was that had distressed them. Even Ruby had taken some time before she stopped being suspicious that something nasty was right around the corner. The things that had bruised her came out in dribs and drabs over a long period of time. Her problem had been that she both loved and hated her mother, and she despised herself for that love.

Wilby had had children who were victims of incest or cruelty, and a couple who were so malnourished it took months to bring their health back. She remembered one poor boy who had cigarette burns on his back, the work of his father when he was drunk.

One thing Wilby did know, though, was that getting them to talk about the past was the only cure. The trick was to recognize the moment when they could be drawn out.

Verity wasn't anywhere near that stage yet. It was clear yesterday's events had brought stuff back to the surface and made her think she was worthless.

And perhaps she was afraid too. But afraid of what?

*

469

'What's going on, Wilby?' Ruby asked a little later. She had been in the dining room writing some letters while Miller had been speaking to Verity, and when she heard the front door shut, she assumed they'd gone out together.

It was only when she saw Wilby coming downstairs looking upset that she realized something was wrong.

Wilby explained as succinctly as possible.

Ruby clapped her hand over her mouth in astonishment. 'I thought it was all going to be hearts and flowers,' she said. 'Why? What is wrong with her? She's told me she still loves him so many times. How can she be like this now?'

'She's troubled by something,' Wilby said. 'I'd say it was something to do with her stepfather, it isn't about Miller. But I don't want you pestering her; she'll let us know what the problem is in her own good time.'

'Okay,' Ruby said. 'But I think I ought to move back into the room with her. I know you'd like the dining room back, and if I go slowly I can manage the stairs. We've always told each other important things after we put the light out, maybe she'll tell me about this.'

Chapter Thirty-Six

Sitting on a bench in the garden Verity read a section of Miller's letter for the third time, with tears running down her face.

I understand that you feel unable to make a commitment to me just now. But what I can't understand is why, if I so much as hold your hand or put my arm around you, you freeze up. You must know I wouldn't try to force you into anything, we were good friends for a long time before I so much as kissed you.

So, after weighing everything up, I've come to the conclusion that if I repel you that much, I just have to give up on you . . .

She didn't blame him for saying this. During the week after rescuing her from Archie, he stayed locally and called every day. They'd been to the pictures together and to the pub, and God knows she had tried so hard not to freeze on him, but it happened involuntarily.

It was early Saturday morning and a beautiful warm, April day. The letter had arrived just as she was putting the kettle on. She had intended to take Ruby and Wilby a cup of tea in bed, but once the letter plopped on to the door-mat she forgot the tea and came out here to read it.

The rest of the letter was just like all his others – newsy, warm and funny – until she got nearly to the end and came to the sad part. She thought he had probably started out writing it several days earlier, then all at once he'd seen the hopelessness of his situation. Who could blame him for saying what he felt?

Ruby came out into the garden wearing just her night-dress, carrying a cup of tea in her hand. She was walking almost normally again now, and the belief that she was going to spend the rest of her life in a wheelchair now just seemed like a bad dream.

'I looked out of the window and saw you were crying, so I guess it isn't a real love letter?' she said, holding out the cup of tea to Verity.

'No, it isn't.' Verity lifted a tear-streaked face to her friend, took the tea and tried to smile. 'He's got fed up with trying to woo me. I bet you think he was a mug for being patient that week he was here?'

'Miller is no mug,' Ruby said reprovingly, sitting down beside Verity. 'He's a kind, decent man. I wish – as does Wilby, and everyone else who met him – that it would work out between you two. But I can't help thinking he was never right for you, and perhaps you instinctively know that. I mean back when he lived in your house in Weardale Road, why didn't anything ever happen between you? Two people who are meant for each other usually can't help themselves.'

Verity said nothing. She had thought back to that period in her life so many times and although she remembered having odd little daydreams about Miller, she couldn't claim to have been, as Ruby would say, 'lusting' after him. But then she'd never lusted after anyone in her entire life, and maybe the truth of the matter was that she was frigid?

'Well?' Ruby prompted.

'Maybe I'm just frigid,' Verity said with a sigh. 'You've always been the physical kind, right from fourteen you were keen on boys. I was never like that.'

'I don't believe that. Wilby thinks that you are kind of frozen, waiting for the whole Archie thing to be resolved. Once he's hanged, you'll feel completely different,' Ruby said. 'It's only just over a week now, and then you'll never have to think about him again.'

At first when Archie was charged with the murder of the two women and the attempted murder of Verity, he denied everything vigorously. But as the weight of evidence built up against him, not just for the murders but being cashiered from the army, accused of embezzlement, and with dozens of counts of dishonesty, he folded. He knew he had no chance of being found Not Guilty in a trial by jury with Verity as the principal witness, so he made a full confession.

Summing up at his trial, just a week ago, the judge said Archibald Wood was 'a thoroughly reprehensible man who had no concept of honesty, and had preyed on women and then killed them to ensure their silence'. He sentenced him to be hanged, and this was due to take place at Exeter Prison on Tuesday the 4th of May.

Just before the trial, Verity had changed her name from Wood to Ferris, her mother's maiden name, in an attempt to cut Archie out of her life and memory. But the reality was that she didn't believe it would ever work.

'Would you like to see Bevan again?' Ruby asked. 'He and Luke are going to be stationed at Bristol soon, and I know Bevan would like to see you.'

Verity looked doubtful. Because of Archie coming for

her, and Miller turning up, Ruby had got Luke to explain the situation to Bevan. She was stuck in a difficult place; she liked him very much, but she felt she was no good to man nor beast at the present time. Bevan had sent her some flowers with a card wishing her well, but he hadn't come to Torquay with Luke since. Or telephoned her.

'I haven't got the cheek to rattle his cage again,' Verity said.

'I'm going to assume by that you'd be happy if he came and rattled yours, though,' Ruby said with a giggle.

'Do you ever think of anything but pairing people off together?' Verity asked. 'Wilby told me you thought that air-raid warden with the plummy voice would be good for her.'

'So he would. He's a couple of years older than her, a retired lawyer, and he's got beautiful blue eyes. Besides, he always asks after Wilby, so I know he likes her.'

'Everyone likes Wilby, and she likes him well enough, but that doesn't mean she wants a romance.'

'She might,' Ruby retorted. 'Everyone wants one.'

'I don't,' said Verity.

'That is a lie. You want and need one more than anyone else I know. You just won't allow yourself to admit it.'

'Haven't you got work to go to today?' Verity said pointedly. 'Who knows? You might find someone there to browbeat, and give Wilby and me a rest.'

Ruby gasped. 'Oh yes, work! I'd forgotten, better go, toodle pip.'

Verity chuckled as Ruby went back up the garden. She meant well, she wanted everyone to be as happy as she was. But for her, the day Archie tried to kill her friend was the day she found she could walk again, so she tended to see most things from a different perspective than Verity.

Ruby had a new receptionist's job in the Imperial Hotel. When this hotel had been built, it was said to be the finest outside London, and many very famous people and even royalty had stayed there. Ruby loved it, even if the work wasn't as varied as it had been in the Palace. The guests were mainly officers on leave, often with their wives, visiting military personnel, and some wounded officers who were recuperating before going back to their regiments. Verity had been astounded by how quickly Ruby had bounced back to her former self once she was walking again. Verity just wished she too could become the girl she used to be.

Last night, Ruby was showing Brian and Colin how to jitterbug. Ruby had been to a class run by an American at the Imperial to learn it, and she was finding it quite frustrating that outside her class she had no partner who could dance with her. She'd been bullying Verity to learn too, but by the time Verity got home from work she felt too tired to do energetic dances.

The war was plodding on. Verity and Ruby went every Wednesday night to the cinema without fail. Pathé News was almost as popular as the main film, although most people thought it was slanted to make it look like the Allies were winning.

Montgomery had broken through the Mareth Line in North Africa, and with the Allies pressing ahead in Tunisia, it really did look as if they had the Germans on the run. The war in the Pacific appeared to have reached a climax too, as the increasingly outnumbered Japanese had failed to dislodge the Americans from Guadalcanal in the Solomon Islands.

Luke and Bevan were involved in concentrated bombing raids on Germany's industrial heartland, something Ruby worried about a great deal. As she pointed out, everyone said how brave the pilots were, forgetting that the other men in the aeroplanes who despatched the bombs, like Luke and Bevan, or those who were wireless operators or navigators, were just as brave and every bit as likely to be killed if their plane was shot down.

Verity sat for a little longer in the garden. April was such a lovely month, all the greenery so vivid and new against the yellow of forsythia and daffodils, a reminder that winter had gone for another year and soon there would be the long, hot days of summer to look forward to. The chickens were clucking away in their pen beneath the fruit trees, and the white pear blossom was just unfolding. Her thoughts turned to Miller again, and how their last evening together had ended. He'd kissed her as they were walking back from the pub, nudging her back into a shop doorway, but it was too desperate a kiss for her to cope with. He pressed his body hard against hers, and she could feel his erection. His tongue seemed to go right down her throat, reminding her of something she wanted to forget.

To be fair to him, he'd stopped the minute she protested, but he was sulky, and she knew then that it wasn't going to work out. Her sadness now wasn't because of losing him exactly, more that she was afraid she would always feel that revulsion towards men. She also feared she was destined to spend her entire life as a spinster like Aunt Hazel.

*

'Luke and Bevan are coming down on a twenty-four-hour pass on the 27th of May,' Ruby announced a few days after Verity got the letter from Miller. 'They are going to drive down from Bristol.'

'Bevan's okay about me?' Verity asked, suddenly feeling a little anxious.

'His words were, "It'll be great to see her, I'll embarrass her with my appalling efforts at the jitterbug".'

Verity laughed. She could imagine Bevan saying that; he wasn't a great dancer, though he was an enthusiastic one. 'Did you tell Luke that Miller has broken it off with me?'

'Not exactly.' Ruby screwed up her face. 'You see I didn't want you to look like the abandoned one, so I just said it fizzled out.'

'It never fizzed in the first place,' Verity said. 'I hope you aren't going to hope for it fizzing with Bevan either?'

'All I ask is that you laugh and have a good time,' Ruby said. 'And you must help me make a gorgeous dress out of that stripy material Wilby dug out.'

On the morning of the 4th of May, Verity got up early and went for a walk. At eight, the time she knew Archie would be executed, she was in the church praying.

She didn't consider herself to be religious at all, but she and Ruby went to church most Sundays with Wilby. She couldn't bring herself to admit it to anyone, but she'd got the idea in her head that Archie wouldn't hang, in just the same way as John Lee, 'the man they couldn't hang', hadn't been executed all those years ago.

Maybe it was because Ruby used to tell her creepy stories about John Lee, about how the trapdoor failed to open three times. It was the same prison, so presumably the same trapdoor, perhaps even the same hangman. She kept getting the strange feeling that she'd open a door one day, or turn a corner, and Archie would be there.

She'd said, 'You are dead to me,' umpteen times when these thoughts came to her. She had never forgotten how powerful those five words of Ruby's had sounded to her, and she half believed that by saying them to Archie they would act as a kind of amulet against it ever happening. But today she'd decided she needed God's help, and she was here today to thank him for keeping her safe, and to pray that Archie really would die at Exeter prison.

As she came out of the church and saw the sun shining, and beautiful cherry blossom in so many of the gardens, all at once she felt lighter, as if a burden had been lifted from her shoulders. Somehow, without any confirmation, she knew Archie was dead now; she could put him, and all he'd put her through, to one side.

A new era was about to begin.

'She's so much better now she knows he's dead,' Wilby whispered to Ruby that evening as she prepared their supper. 'It's almost like she's shed a skin, there's a new lightness about her.'

Ruby glanced towards the hall. She could hear Brian and Colin playing some noisy game in the sitting room, and Verity was in there with them. 'I'm really hoping that she and Bevan will enjoy being together at the end of the month. I'm not expecting true love or anything like that, but just to see her having fun will be wonderful.'

'Well, we're all united in that hope. I have been worried

that there might be a lot of upsetting gossip about the hanging from neighbours, her work colleagues and so on. But when Verity got in from work she said people were kind, just the odd sympathetic smile, offers that if she wanted to talk they were there. But then I suppose the newspapers have printed so much about him, and what a monster he was, that most people just feel glad it's all over.'

On the Saturday night following the hanging, Ruby and Verity went to the pictures in Torquay to see *For Whom the Bell Tolls*. They came out with tear-stained faces, as the ending was so sad. At Ruby's suggestion they went on to the Imperial Hotel, as she knew all the staff there.

It was a very jolly evening. A couple of American officers insisted on plying them with drinks, they had a few dances, and by the time they made for home both girls were a little squiffy.

They walked back a little unsteadily, arm in arm, giggling about the two Americans who had been over fifty, balding and had a high opinion of themselves.

'I loved the way you kept bringing the subject back to their wives and children,' Ruby said. 'It completely stopped them trying anything on.'

'I don't think I ever want to go to Iowa now, it sounded as dull as ditchwater,' Verity sniggered. 'I wonder if all Americans are like that? Constantly bragging about their wonderful country, and pointing out England's shortcomings.'

'Most of the ones I've met have been,' Ruby said. 'But then I've only met officers, I'm sure the rank and file are a darn sight more exciting.'

Wilby had gone to bed, and the house was in darkness when they got home. Ruby made them both a cup of cocoa and put a drop of brandy in each cup.

'Like we need any more drink,' Verity said. 'My legs seem to have a mind of their own.'

Once up in their beds, with the curtains drawn, cocoa drunk and the light turned out, Verity suddenly began speaking about Archie.

'Do you think he was scared at the end?' she asked.

'I hope he was scared witless,' Ruby said. 'I think a priest sits with them till the end. I'd love to know if he said he was sorry.'

'I expect he did, in the hopes of getting the priest on his side. But really I don't think he had any kind of conscience. He just did what he wanted to do and didn't care who it hurt.'

'How old were you when he first hurt you in any way?' Ruby asked.

'About five, I think. He pulled down my pants and smacked me hard on my bottom for taking his pipe and using it to blow soapy bubbles. Mum heard me scream and she came and pulled me off his lap. She said he hit far too hard.'

'It's true, men do hit far harder than women,' Ruby said. 'I used to laugh at Ma when she hit me, it never hurt, not even when she was really mad with me. But I was hit a few times by her men and, my God, that hurt – and they always left a big bruise too.'

'Did any of her men ever try to do anything else to you?'

'You mean interfering, touching me in private places?'

'Yes. Did they?'

'Sometimes they tried, but I would get out of the way. As I got bigger I made sure I was never in when she was doing it.'

Ruby suddenly realized that Verity was trying to tell her about something. Being a bit drunk was loosening her up, and that could only be a good thing.

'Did Archie do something?' she asked gently, almost holding her breath in the darkness for fear Verity would clam up.

'Yes, it was so disgusting –' Verity stopped abruptly. 'I can't tell you.'

'You can,' Ruby whispered. 'Remember, I grew up with a mum who brought men home to our room for sex. I used to pull a blanket over my head so I didn't see, but I knew what was going on by the noises.'

Ruby heard what she thought was a sob, and her instinct was to get out of her bed and climb in with Verity to comfort her, but she was afraid that would stop her friend from continuing. 'Did he rape you?' she whispered.

Verity didn't answer for a moment but she was breathing very heavily. 'No, not that,' she said eventually.

'Did he make you take his thing in your mouth?'

She knew immediately that was exactly what had happened by the muffled sob.

'Oh, Verity, what a terrible thing to happen to you! Can I come over there and give you a hug?'

Again just a sob. But Ruby got out of her bed and got into Verity's and held her tight. 'That is a horrible picture to keep in your head,' she said gently. 'But now you've told me, it will fade.'

'It made me gag, I thought it would choke me. And the

smell of him, it was vile.' She was crying now, her whole body shaking.

'He *was* vile. But you mustn't let the thought of what he did put you off other men,' Ruby said. 'No decent man would force a woman to do that against her will.'

'I'll always be scared it will happen again. I was twelve when he did it first, and then again before he put me in that cage.'

Ruby closed her eyes, hoping for some divine enlightenment as to what to say about this.

'So all this time, this is what has stopped you having a boyfriend?' she asked. 'And it put you off Miller too?'

'I didn't consciously let it stop me, but I guess I put up some kind of shield which stopped men getting close to me,' she admitted. 'I did feel something for Miller, but then kissing someone goodbye on a station isn't a real test. The one time he came back after leaving for Scotland, Amy was there and so there was no chance of anything happening.'

'You've kissed Bevan, and he didn't make you want to run away, did he?'

'No, but I didn't feel anything else, either. If he'd so much as touched me anywhere private, I would probably have screamed and run away.'

'He's a true gentleman,' Ruby said. 'He knew Archie had hurt you – although not that, of course. Men can be very sensitive to women's needs. They aren't all brutes.'

'But imagine if I got to like a man, and even married him, and then he did that to me? I'd be a basket case.'

All at once Ruby realized that, although her friend knew what made a baby, her knowledge of what happened

482

during love-making, and how women could feel, was non-existent. Frightened badly as a young girl, she had just shut down her natural curiosity, and had probably never even explored her own body.

'Love-making is beautiful, special and very tender when you love the man,' Ruby explained, holding her friend tight and hoping she wouldn't get upset by what she was going to say. 'Sometimes people do things to each other to give extra pleasure that some would think was nasty or even perverted. But it isn't, if you both want to do it. Men kiss and fondle our breasts, and that makes us feel wonderful, they fondle us and put their fingers in down there too, and often kiss and lick us there.'

Verity stiffened.

'Stop doing that "plank" thing, you need to know this,' Ruby said sharply. 'I told you that first day we met what "up the spout" meant, same as I told you about pawnbrokers and Ma selling herself. So you can stand me telling you something you really need to know now.

'So what I was going on to say is that when a man makes us feel wonderful, we want to do stuff to him like that too. And taking his penis in our mouth comes into that.'

'No!' Verity said forcefully, remembering how Angie had said if Ruby had done that, she wouldn't have got pregnant.

'Yes,' Ruby said firmly. 'There's no law that says you must, and some women wouldn't dream of it. But I promise you that a man who loves you would never be a brute about it.'

'Have you done it?'

'Yes, I have, and I promise it isn't disgusting when you

love a man. There's lots of wonderful experiences lying in wait for us, Verity – getting married and having babies, to name just two! But for that to work and make you happy and content, you need to embrace sex. You must let yourself feel desire, and explore the wonderful feelings it gives you. God could have made us like animals, so we just mated to procreate, but he gave us love, and all this amazing sensuality in love-making to bond us tightly together in couples. He knew what he was doing! It is designed to hold us together so we bring up our children together and keep them safe.'

'I don't think my mother ever saw it like that,' Verity said doubtfully.

'I don't suppose mine did, either; to her it was just a service for which she got money. No wonder we've fallen off the rails sometimes! But let's look to Wilby, shall we? She's the way a real woman should be. Loving, devoted, and I bet she and her husband were at it like rabbits.'

'I'm not sure I like the idea of that,' Verity said. 'I won't be able to look at her tomorrow.'

'You will, and you'll see what I see. She's been the best role model either of us could ever have.'

'Yes, you are right about that. But let's go to sleep now, or we won't be able to get up in the morning,' Verity said and kissed Ruby's cheek. 'Thank you for telling me a few home truths.'

Ruby disengaged herself from her friend. 'Sleep tight in that bed I've warmed for you. Only a real pal would do that!'

Chapter Thirty-Seven

'Hey! You girls look gorgeous,' Luke exclaimed as he came out into the garden to see the girls and Wilby enjoying a gin and tonic.

Brian had opened the front door to Luke and Bevan, and in a few seconds had managed to tell them it was roast lamb for dinner tomorrow and that he could jitterbug now. Only then did he lead them to the garden.

Ruby was wearing a green and white striped dress made by Verity from some material Wilby had stashed away. With a green ribbon in her hair she really did look gorgeous.

Verity was wearing a pink dress she'd had for years, but she'd revamped it with a white lace ruffle around the neckline.

Ruby leapt to her feet to greet Luke with a kiss, and Verity smiled shyly at Bevan.

'How are things with you?' Bevan said, coming right over to her chair and crouching down in front of her. 'I've missed you.'

Verity really liked the way he had of making the person he was speaking to feel they were the most important person in the world. He looked leaner, and his face was no longer very red and shiny the way it had been when they first met.

'Very good now,' she said. 'It was all a bit nightmarish,

but that's all over now. I'm back up telegraph poles, and trying to learn to jitterbug. Ruby is brilliant at it, as are Colin and Brian, I'm sure Brian told you that! I'm lagging well behind.'

'Brian did tell me, along with the menu for tomorrow. But I'm a disaster at the jitterbug too,' he laughed. 'Give me a waltz any day.'

Wilby asked if the boys would like a gin and tonic or a beer. They plumped for beer.

'What a lovely evening it is,' Wilby said as she brought the beers out from the kitchen. 'Usually in late May it tends to be very chilly. Certainly not sitting in the garden after seven o'clock weather. Now where are you young people off to tonight?'

'We thought we'd take the girls to the town hall dance. The Star Lights are playing, a really good swing band,' Luke said.

Verity nudged Bevan. 'Look at Ruby's face. If he'd said we were going to sit on rusty barbed wire all evening, she'd be just as happy.'

Bevan smiled. 'Those two have got it bad. He talks about her all the time back at the base.'

'Ruby's the same,' Verity said. 'Anyway, to change the subject, how is Bristol?'

'We like being stationed there more than East Anglia. As far as Luke's concerned that's because it's closer to here. But it's near home too, so I get to see my folks every couple of weeks. I really hope we get to stay there.'

Half an hour later they left the house to catch the bus into Torquay. Almost every man on the bus was in uniform, and there was a lot of friendly rivalry between the different forces, which resulted in them taking the rise out of one another.

Ruby and Verity were content to be entertained by it, and it suddenly occurred to Verity that she felt really happy and glad to be out for the evening.

She had tended to blush every time she thought back to the conversation with Ruby that night after they'd got a bit drunk. She still found it hard to believe she'd actually spoken of what Archie had done to her. But she was glad she had, for it had laid a ghost, and she'd felt much easier in her mind since.

What amazed her most, though, was how much she had been looking forward to seeing Bevan again. He had taken her hand as they walked to the bus stop, and it felt good. He'd always been easy to be with, quick, funny and never intense about things. It was so good not to feel she needed to run away and hide.

As the band broke into the last number of the evening, Glenn Miller's 'That Old Black Magic', and the lights were lowered, everyone in the town hall got on to the dance floor. It had been perhaps the best night Verity ever remembered, with great music, a wonderful atmosphere and a fun partner who had made her laugh more than was good for her. When she looked over Bevan's shoulder, she saw Luke and Ruby wrapped in each other's arms, looking so sublimely happy it made her feel quite emotional.

But Bevan was holding her tightly too, his cheek against hers, and it felt right.

'Happy?' he murmured. 'It's been such a lovely evening. I don't want it to end.'

'Nor me,' Verity sighed. 'But it's a long walk home, uphill all the way. So I might be glad when that's over.'

'You seem different tonight,' he said. 'I can't quite put my finger on what the difference is, but there's something.'

She put her hand gently on his cheek. 'Things becoming resolved perhaps? Feeling I've shrugged off a burden. I don't know what's different either, but I like how I feel.'

'One day we'll sit down and talk about what you went through, because I'd like to understand fully,' he said. 'But it's not a subject for a night like this, not when I'm burning to kiss you.'

His lips touched hers as lightly as a butterfly's wing and the delicacy of it sparked something inside her. His lips were so soft and warm, playing with hers, the tip of his tongue darting into her mouth and sending little tremors down her spine.

Kissing him had never been like this before, she'd always wanted to break away, and she'd never felt that strange and wonderful tugging sensation in her belly before.

'Hmmm,' Bevan said as the big lights came on and the MC was reminding them to take care going home. 'So much for the old black magic, it kind of disappears when the lights come on.'

'I don't know about that,' she said, nuzzling her lips against his cheek. 'It still feels pretty magical to me.'

Verity woke early on Saturday morning, stretched and smiled to herself as she remembered the events of the night before. Her lips felt a little tender from all the kissing on the way home, and she was excited about Luke and Bevan coming to lunch today.

The last thing Ruby had said before they both fell asleep was that Luke had asked her to marry him, so if they were intending to tell Wilby today, it would turn into a celebration.

'This looks scrumptious,' Bevan said as Verity and Ruby carried the vegetable dishes into the dining room.

'The new potatoes and carrots are straight from the garden,' Verity said. 'But we thought you'd like some roast potatoes too, Wilby's are just the best.'

The table looked very pretty with Wilby's best glasses and the silver cutlery, two small flower arrangements with white daisies and pink rosebuds, and pale pink and white napkins.

Wilby blushed a little at the praise for her roast potatoes, although she would probably have claimed her flushed face was just the heat from the oven, and she proceeded to carve the lamb.

'I can't believe you actually got a whole leg of lamb,' Ruby said in wonder. 'How?'

'Friends in high places,' Wilby said, tapping her nose and laughing. 'Actually, he's a friend in a low place, this lamb got injured and so it had to be put down.'

'Sounds like a tall story!' Luke said. 'But even if you claimed it had flown into your garden asking to be cooked, I'd believe it, because I haven't seen that much meat since before the war.'

Wilby started to carve the meat, and Luke stood up. 'I've got an announcement to make,' he said. 'Last night I asked Ruby to marry me and she accepted. I hope that meets with your approval, Wilby?'

'Oh, Luke, how wonderful!' Wilby said, clapping her hands and pretending total surprise. 'It certainly does meet with my approval.' She beamed at him and Ruby, who was sitting next to him. 'I suggest we all raise our glasses to toast the happy couple.'

The wine was Wilby's home-made raspberry wine, which had a kick like a mule, and needed to be diluted a little. But for once even Brian and Colin were allowed a tiny amount, topped up with lemonade.

'Will the wedding be this summer?' Brian asked. 'You get extra rations to make a wedding cake, I think.'

Everyone laughed. Brian's love of cake was legendary.

'I hope it will be soon,' Wilby said. 'A summer wedding with the reception in the garden would be lovely. You could wear my wedding dress, I'm sure Verity could alter it to fit you properly.'

Ruby looked as if she could burst with happiness. 'We aren't sure when it can be. It depends on when, and if, Luke can arrange leave.'

'I'm going to speak to the CO when we get back to base tonight,' Luke said. 'And Bevan, will you be my best man?'

'I thought you'd never ask,' Bevan said.

As they ate the meal the conversation was all about the wedding: who would be invited; where Luke's parents and siblings would stay. Ruby said she wanted only one bridesmaid and that, of course, would be Verity.

Weddings in wartime meant there could be no extravagance, with so many foodstuffs unavailable or rationed. Most brides settled for a tiny cake, perched on a false one made of cardboard. But Wilby assured them she had a few items tucked away to make sure they had a good spread.

After the wonderful lunch they went for a walk along the Downs before the men had to return to Bristol.

'I wish we hadn't got to go back to base,' Bevan said to Verity.

'We can do it all again next time,' she said. 'It was the very best fun.'

'You know what was best for me?' Bevan said, taking hold of her forearms and turning her to face him.

'What?'

'Seeing you really laugh, happiness coming from inside you. It would be great if it was me that caused it. But I'm not kidding myself with that one. You've been through hell and come out the other side, that's what's done it. You'll be fine now.'

'You are a lovely man, Bevan,' she said, kissing him on the cheek.

'And you, Verity, are a delight,' he said with a wide grin. 'We've got to go now. But till the next time, keep smiling.'

Verity was indeed smiling as she waved goodbye to the men. She really did feel she might never stop.

Shortly after Wilby and Ruby had come back from morning service at church the next morning, the doorbell rang.

Wilby was just taking her coat and hat off upstairs. 'Who on earth can that be?' she called out.

Verity had stayed behind to get the lunch on, and to look after Brian and Colin. 'Can you get it, Ruby?' she shouted out. 'I'm making the gravy.'

Verity heard Ruby say she would, and then the sound of the door opening, but she took no interest, assuming it was just a neighbour.

Suddenly aware someone had come into the kitchen, Verity turned from the kitchen sink, to see Miller.

'Good God!' she exclaimed.

'No, it's only me,' he said. 'God tends to be busy on Sundays.'

Verity was astounded. She had thought she'd never see him again, and she had felt very bad about the way things had ended between them.

Ruby was standing just behind Miller, making silly faces.

'What brings you here?' Verity asked. 'Ruby, please go away.'

'Going, going,' Ruby said, walking backwards into the hall.

'Sorry about that,' Verity said. 'She can be a bit of a clown. But what does bring you here?'

'I decided I had to fight for you,' he said. 'Well, perhaps "fight" is the wrong word. Perhaps "woo" you?'

'But you said you'd given up on me,' she said, feeling a little tremor of excitement in her belly. He was wearing a very smart grey suit. She'd never seen him in anything but old tweed or corduroy jackets before. He looked very handsome.

'We all say things sometimes that we don't actually mean. I did mean it at the time of writing, but then I thought about what you'd been through with Archie, and I decided I'd come down again and see how you are now. You can tell me to go, if nothing's changed for you.'

Wilby came downstairs then and greeted Miller warmly, saying he must stay for lunch and asking him where he was staying. Ruby joined in then, as did Colin and Brian who wanted to show him a Hurricane model aeroplane they were making.

'The consensus of opinion seems to be that you are staying for lunch,' Verity said.

Miller looked at her and smiled, and she remembered how taken she had been by his lovely duck-egg-blue eyes when they first met.

Verity was quite glad that they weren't left alone together, not because she wasn't pleased to see him – she was – but just because she didn't know what she should talk to him about. Ruby was talking about Luke and how they were going to get married, Colin and Brian were pestering Miller about the model plane, and Wilby was flitting in and out of the kitchen, busy with laying the dining-room table and checking Verity had the lunch of shepherd's pie in hand.

'No roast Sunday dinner, I'm afraid,' Verity told Miller. 'We had that yesterday while Luke was here.'

'I love shepherd's pie,' he shot back, and even though they had spoken over everyone else in the room, it had the oddest feeling of intimacy.

That feeling continued throughout the final preparations for the lunch, in between Wilby passing on bits of gossip she'd heard after church, the boys telling Miller some convoluted tale about swopping cigarette cards, and Ruby asking him about a place she fancied going in Scotland for her honeymoon.

'This is looking good between you two,' Ruby whispered to Verity as Wilby asked Miller to open the dining-room window, which was sticking.

'Don't be silly, nothing's been said or done,' Verity shot back.

Lunch was a very jolly affair, as everyone seemed in the best of spirits, and Verity couldn't help but remember how much she and Miller used to laugh over meals in the old days.

Brian and Colin had to leave the table a bit early to go to Sunday School in St Mary's, in nearby St Marychurch.

'You won't be gone before we get back, will you?' Brian asked Miller. 'Cos I really do need help with the model. Verity and Ruby are useless, they put the bits anywhere.'

Everyone laughed at that, and Miller assured them he'd still be around.

Ruby and Verity had just finished the washing-up, and Wilby had taken Miller out into the garden to get his advice on the apple tree, which she felt might have some kind of blight. The plan was to have tea in the garden.

Suddenly the sky seemed full of aeroplanes. In the same instant the air-raid siren went off and they heard ack-ack guns from both Babbacombe Downs and Walls Hill, followed by machine-gun fire and the crump of bombs dropping somewhere close by.

'The cellar!' Verity shouted, as she was the one most used to air raids.

As they started to go down the cellar stairs, Wilby shouted out about Brian and Colin being in Sunday School.

'They'll be fine, the teachers and the vicar will get them into a shelter,' Ruby said. 'Go on downstairs.'

The din above seemed interminable. They sat in silence, Wilby, Verity and Ruby all thinking about the day the bombs had fallen on the RAF hospital and hoping against hope it wasn't going to be another bad raid like that one.

When the all-clear rang out, it was quite a surprise to find only ten minutes had passed.

'Another tip and run, I'm sure,' Wilby said as they went up the stairs. There had been quite a few earlier in the year, but fortunately few casualties. 'Let's hope they fell on farmland or in the sea.'

Verity reached the garden first. She looked up at a billowing plume of smoke rising up behind the garden. It was coming from somewhere up near the Council House in St Marychurch and her instinct, gained from experience in London, told her this was something bad.

'I'm going to find the boys,' she said, and without stopping for anyone else's reaction she flew like the wind through the side gate, along the road and on to Babbacombe Road.

'The church has been hit!' she heard someone shout.

As she belted up Fore Street she became aware that Miller was close behind her.

To Verity's shock St Mary's had received a direct hit and the church was in ruins, smoke and dust swirling all around the fallen stones. It was one of the worst scenes of devastation Verity had seen. She stared at it in horror, almost blinded by tears, knowing that thirty or more children and their teachers would be under that rubble. Amongst them were Brian and Colin.

The two boys had healed her with their sweetness and thoughtfulness when she first arrived back here so badly hurt. They had made her laugh, kept her company, and she'd loved them like they were her little brothers. The thought that they might be dead under the rubble, or badly injured, was too much to bear.

'We'll get them out,' Miller said, touching her shoulder to remind her he was there too, and he promptly pulled off his suit jacket and tie.

Even before the Civil Defence men and the ambulances arrived, Verity and Miller joined all the other people who had gathered to start shifting rubble and stones to search for the children.

Verity saw a little girl's leg sticking out and called for assistance. Miller and two burly men she didn't know lifted the heavy stones to reveal an upturned pew. The little girl, who was able to tell Verity her name was Susan Wright, was lifted out. She had only a bad cut on her right leg. It transpired she was one of the lucky ones.

The bomb site soon resembled an ant's nest. So many people came to help and, one by one, children were brought out. Many were miraculously unharmed but for a few scratches, but their little faces were grey with dust.

Strangely, none of the rescued children cried or screamed. Maybe it was shock but, whatever the reason, it seemed like bravery.

Older people who couldn't clear rubble brought tea and water to the rescuers. Every now and then, everyone would pause what they were doing as a small body was brought out.

Miller uncovered a girl of about eleven. Verity just happened to turn as he lifted her into his arms and carried her to the road. She wore a blue gingham dress and had long pigtails tied with red ribbons, and they dangled down past Miller's waist. Verity knew the child was dead, because Miller had tears making clear channels through the grime on his face. His white shirt was almost black with dirt, his hair grey with dust. She had never seen anything quite so moving.

With each live child brought out there was a bubble of restrained joy, yet even the parents of the saved children contained their relief and delight in deference to the sounds of parental grief and anguish close by.

But still there was no sign of Brian and Colin. As children were brought out able to stand up and speak, Verity went and asked them if they'd seen the boys.

No one had.

Wilby and Ruby arrived; they'd been delayed in getting there, as there had been other bombs over Torquay and an air-raid warden had ordered them to stay in for the time being. Wilby was distraught that the boys had not been found, wringing her hands, her face crumpled with fear.

Verity helped another uninjured girl out. She was thirteen and called Pauline. She told Verity how they had heard the plane coming in low and one of the teachers had yelled for them to get under the pews.

'I couldn't get my left leg in,' she said. 'I was afraid it was going to be cut off.'

Verity hugged her and told her she was very glad that hadn't happened. 'Now did you see Colin and Brian Waycott? Do you even know them?'

'Yes, I do know them,' she said, allowing Verity to clean the worst of the dirt from her face with a damp cloth. 'They're funny boys and they like dancing. But I don't think they were here today. They always wave to me, and usually come and sit next to me. They definitely weren't in the church when I got here.'

Verity went over to Wilby. 'I don't think they came to Sunday School,' she said.

'Of course they did,' Wilby insisted. 'They are good boys.'

Miller came over then, and hearing the tail end of the conversation, he admitted he used to duck out of Sunday School himself.

'I wouldn't mind betting they went to look at gun emplacements,' he said. 'They are like magnets to small boys, and I heard one of the teachers say just now that there were remarkably few boys at the Sunday School today. If you look around, you'll see it's nearly all girls we've got out. I think the boys might be off pretending to be soldiers.'

'Walls Hill!' Verity exclaimed. 'Brian mentioned it yesterday, I'll go there and look now.'

'I'll come with you,' Miller said. He took Wilby's hand in both of his, looking right into her tear-filled eyes. 'Hold on, Wilby. We'll come straight back if there's no joy. But my gut feeling is we're going to find them.'

It took about twenty minutes of fast walking to get to Walls Hill. This was a cliff-top area with a cricket pitch and scrubby grass beyond, and an ideal place for anti-aircraft guns, as it commanded a very wide view from Torquay to Teignmouth.

'Have you seen two small boys hanging about?' Miller asked two Home Guard men. 'Brown hair, freckled faces, grey shorts and navy-blue slipovers. Likely to ask you lots of questions.'

'Yes, we've seen them,' one of the men said. 'We shot down a plane and they were thrilled about it. But we told

498

them it wasn't safe up here, and to go home. There were more than fifteen bombers earlier, Torquay really copped it today.'

'It certainly did, St Mary's Church bought it when it was full of Sunday School children,' Miller said. 'The boys should've been in there too.'

'Oh dear Lord, no!' the old man exclaimed. 'Well, maybe it was good your boys were playing truant today. If I see them again, I'll send them home with a flea in their ears.'

'Where to now?' Miller asked Verity, looking even more troubled. 'They might have found out about the church and they're afraid to go home and face Wilby.'

'You really understand children,' Verity said appreciatively. 'I think I might know where they are. They said a week or two ago they were building a camp. It's near here, on the way down to Babbacombe Bay.'

She led the way down a track into the woods, and after about four hundred yards she heard voices. 'I think that's Brian,' she said. He and his companion were hidden from view by trees and bushes, but she called out.

'Come here, boys, it's Verity.'

There was a sudden silence which, although it only lasted for a couple of seconds, seemed longer. At last the two boys emerged looking very scared.

'Oh, thank heavens!' Verity exclaimed. 'Come on, boys, you aren't in trouble,' she called out. 'It was lucky you didn't go to the church today, it was badly bombed.'

'A man told us that, and we were scared to go home,' Brian said. 'We thought Wilby might send us back to Bristol. We were thinking of staying the night in our camp.'

Verity pulled the boys to her in a fierce hug. 'Can you

really think we'd be cross that you are safe? We all thought you were under the rubble.'

'That camp is far too near the cliff edge to be a safe place to play,' Miller said sternly. 'But you are in luck today. Ruby, Verity and Wilby were so scared you'd been killed that the worst punishment you're going to get is an overload of hugs and kisses. Now come on, quick march back home, and let's put Wilby's mind at rest.'

As they walked back, the boys in front of them, Miller took Verity's hand. Like her own it was rough with hauling stones and thick with dirt. But as her dirty hand linked with his, she felt as if nothing bad could ever happen to her again, not while Miller was with her.

Wilby and Ruby both cried to see the boys alive and well.

'I ought to be cross that you played truant,' Wilby said as she hugged the boys. 'But just this once you're safe from a scolding.'

The girls and Wilby then took Brian and Colin home, while Miller stayed up at the church to continue to help the rescue workers.

Much later that day they learned the death toll was twenty-one children, and three teachers. The vicar had cheated death because he'd slipped back home to get his glasses before starting the service, and the bomb dropped while he was gone.

'I don't know how St Marychurch will ever recover from this,' Wilby said brokenly, sitting in the kitchen with her head in her hands. 'It's such a tight-knit community, the children are in and out of each other's houses all the time, so the tragedy will hit everyone. Some of those children will be ones I've helped with their reading. I've laughed with their mothers at jumble sales and coffee mornings, and discussed their children's little problems. I don't know what I can say to comfort them.'

Ruby and Verity looked at each other helplessly. None of them could believe that such a terrible tragedy had happened so close to home, and killing innocent children. They knew Wilby was right, this wasn't something that could be brushed away and forgotten. Not for the families of those children, their neighbours, rescue workers, indeed anyone with a heart.

'You'll find the words,' Ruby said eventually. 'The people around here will do what they always do in times of trouble, which is to help one another.'

'I thank God that Colin and Brian chose to be naughty, and cheated death,' Wilby said. 'But what is the world coming to when bombs are dropped on churches and kill children?'

Ruby and Verity could do little to comfort her. This was such an appalling disaster, there were no words to soften it or give comfort.

They tucked her into bed later with a hot toddy to help her sleep, but as Verity kissed her goodnight, Wilby caught hold of her hand.

'Don't let Miller slip away this time,' she said. 'I watched him with you over lunch, and I watched him up at the church clearing rubble, and I saw someone special. And someone perfect for you.'

'I saw someone special and perfect for me too,' Verity said, kissing the older woman on the cheek. 'Now off to sleep with you, it's been a harrowing day.'

*

Miller didn't come back to the house, and they learned the next day that he was one of the many men who worked all night by the light of torches, moving stone to hunt for both survivors and little bodies.

He came to the house in Higher Downs Road at breakfast time.

'I'm filthy,' he said from the doorstep when Ruby opened the door to him. 'I wondered if Wilby's got any old clothes I could borrow. I can't go back to the guest house I booked into like this.'

Filthy didn't come close to describing how he looked. He was covered in a thick film of brick dust, plaster and mud. His once highly polished shoes were wrecked. The suit jacket he carried over his arm was nearly as bad as the trousers.

'I think we might need to hose you down in the garden first,' Ruby laughed. 'You look worse than a chimney sweep.'

'I bought the suit to come here,' Miller said, and laughed. 'It's only fit now for the dustbin.'

Wilby took over, bringing down an old dressing gown and telling him to take all his clothes off and put it on before having a bath. 'I've got a few things of my late husband's, and I know he'd like to think they were being worn by a man who worked through the night for people he doesn't even know.'

Both Ruby and Verity had to go to work, and the boys had to go to school, although Wilby said she thought the head would send everyone home out of respect for those who had lost their lives.

Miller was in the bathroom as the girls left, and they

had to shout out that he was to be back there for supper tonight.

'I don't want to go to work,' Verity said at the gate as they both wheeled out their bicycles.

'Nor me,' Ruby agreed. 'But we have to. But before we go, tell me how you feel about Miller now.'

Verity smiled. 'In the light of what happened at the church I feel guilty that I actually feel excited about him. I was touched by the way he threw himself into the rescue work, and I desperately want to see him clean again. Will that do for now?'

Ruby's eyes twinkled. 'It will. See you this evening.'

For Verity the day seemed endless, and very busy too, as the bomb at St Marychurch was one of several around Torquay, bringing down many telephone wires. Other people had been killed too, but the church was the biggest incident and the one everyone was talking about, because of the children.

It was hard reminding herself that it was wrong to feel anything but grief in the face of such a terrible tragedy; she was feeling grief for the dead and their families, yet at the same time her heart wanted to sing because Miller had said he'd come to woo her.

Finally, it was five thirty and time to go home. She had no real idea of what she was going to say to Miller, but she knew she wasn't going to tell him to go away again.

She felt she ought to be confused, as Bevan had awoken all kinds of feelings inside her too, yet she didn't feel confused at all. She liked Bevan a great deal, but Miller was in another category altogether. What she'd felt for him back on Hither Green Station at the start of the war was what she felt now. Was it too soon to call it love?

She raced home on her bike, standing up on the pedals on the hills, straining to get to him.

Wheeling her bike in through the gate, she let it drop on to the lawn and rushed round the side of the house.

He was there in the garden, sitting in a deckchair talking to Wilby. He looked round on hearing her, jumped to his feet and smiled.

'It's been a long day waiting for you to come home,' he said, holding out his hands to her.

Wilby got up and said something about getting the supper.

Just the touch of Miller's hands on Verity's made her feel they didn't need explanations, promises or anything else. Those duck-egg-blue eyes were twinkling the way they always had back in Weardale Road before the war began. His generous, soft mouth was just waiting to be kissed, and it was she who moved in first.

Nothing had ever felt so sweet or so perfect. A kiss that said the past was over and gone, taking all the hurts with it. Now they had a lifetime ahead of them to share.

She wanted him, body and soul.

'I love you, Verity,' he whispered when they came up for air. 'I think I did from the moment you gave me that apple, when we first met, because I felt faint.'

'You mean you fainted at the sight of me?' she teased.

He laughed. 'It's been a long, winding road, hasn't it? Maybe if I'd kissed you then, we could have shortened it?'

'Maybe, but I doubt I'd have been quite so certain of you then as I am now. You once said that the garden you created in Lee Park was love made visible. Seeing you digging in that church rubble yesterday, and the way you were with the boys when we found them, that was love made visible to me. I do love you, Miller, and I think I always did too.'

'But now is our time?' he asked.

She nodded. 'I think so! We've got the rest of the war to go through, no one knows how or when it will end, or what life will be like afterwards. But that won't seem half so scary, if you'll promise to be there with me.'

'Even if I can't be with you in body all the time, I promise I'll be there in spirit, and we'll plan together for a future when I'll be at your side for ever.'

Verity looked into his eyes and saw utter sincerity. It had been a long, winding road, but worth every mile of it to find true happiness and peace at last.

He just wanted a decent book to read ...

Not too much to ask, is it? It was in 1935 when Allen Lane, Managing Director of Bodley Head Publishers, stood on a platform at Exeter railway station looking for something good to read on his journey back to London. His choice was limited to popular magazines and poor-quality paperbacks – the same choice faced every day by the vast majority of readers, few of whom could afford hardbacks. Lane's disappointment and subsequent anger at the range of books generally available led him to found a company – and change the world.

'We believed in the existence in this country of a vast reading public for intelligent books at a low price, and staked everything on it'
Sir Allen Lane, 1902–1970, founder of Penguin Books

The quality paperback had arrived – and not just in bookshops. Lane was adamant that his Penguins should appear in chain stores and tobacconists, and should cost no more than a packet of cigarettes.

Reading habits (and cigarette prices) have changed since 1935, but Penguin still believes in publishing the best books for everybody to enjoy. We still believe that good design costs no more than bad design, and we still believe that quality books published passionately and responsibly make the world a better place.

So wherever you see the little bird – whether it's on a piece of prize-winning literary fiction or a celebrity autobiography, political tour de force or historical masterpiece, a serial-killer thriller, reference book, world classic or a piece of pure escapism – you can bet that it represents the very best that the genre has to offer.

Whatever you like to read – trust Penguin.